Serenade

AVERY AMES

Az
AZULINE
PUBLISHING

First Edition

ISBN-13: 978-1-7332122-4-3

Copyright © 2023 by Amy Avery
All rights reserved.

Cover illustration by D.C. McNaughton.
dcmcnaughton.com

Serenade

AVERY AMES

For Laurie,

One of my first co-conspirators in creating new worlds.

Prologue

PRINCE AIDAN SCRUBBED HIS weary face, but drowsiness still dragged at his eyelids.

Four months since his sister Cirelle went missing. If Lydia's story was to be believed, it would be eight more months until she returned. And in truth, they had little choice but to believe Lydia. The unicorn's horn she brought back with her had indeed cured both Aidan and Lady Briere, as well as ridding Palace City of the plague. Barrels upon barrels of water had been touched with the horn and sent across the kingdom, eliminating the pox entirely.

But what did Cirelle endure at the hands of the fae?

Three months ago, Aidan had awoken from his fever to find his mother at his bedside. She'd recounted Lydia's unbelievable story. The guard, he was informed, would spend Cirelle's absence in the dungeons, earning her freedom when the princess returned.

If she returned.

It was Father who came to Aidan later with his own confession. A bargain he'd also once made long before Aidan was born, and the reason it was forbidden to consort with the fae.

The king had agreed to safeguard a faerie artifact, keep it hidden, keep it secret. And as long as no member of his lineage made contact with the fae, his kingdom would prosper.

So upon his coronation, he'd declared it the highest crime to consort with the fae. Faerie artifacts and lore were confiscated and locked away in the treasury. True, there must be the odd commoner who defied the law, but it had been enough to keep his family away from them.

Until Aidan's own sister had broken their father's pact.

Aidan's fist tightened around the artifact he held, its silver filigree digging into his palm. The very item that Father promised to keep safe. With an effort, he loosened his grip. What made this thing so important? Just a padlock, lovely but innocuous, without a key.

It hummed with magic of some sort. So Aidan delved into his sister's library of contraband faerie lore, unearthed after her disappearance. The book he currently read appeared to be one she'd been working through when she left. Weeks of his own reading left him far past the page marked with the scrap of ribbon she'd been using as a bookmark. He left it where she had tucked it, this piece of lavender satin a small connection to her.

He'd visited Lydia in the dungeons, questioning her on every detail of the faerie summoning Cirelle had done. It was hard seeing his old friend—Cirelle's old friend—behind bars. Once, the three of them had played together in the palace courtyard. Now, she was a criminal. Her cell was clean, but small and sparse. And though he made sure she received adequate meals, the plain fare was no match for Cook Jana's pastries.

Lydia had told him everything she remembered; the items Cirelle offered to the sidhe, the faerie's name. The ring of toad-stools required, and the enchanted pendant Cirelle had used to locate one. Aidan had since found entries about that particular sidhe in two tomes. Ellian, a collector who would trade faerie wonders for human mementos. It was written that he knew every magical object in Faerie.

Aidan turned the page, and his breath halted. There, an illustration of a filigreed lock just like the one that lay on his desktop. Searching the lines of the artwork, Aidan chewed his lip. Yes, that whorl there, the leaf here, it was the same. Beside the drawing lay a sketch of a similarly ornate key.

The Lock and The Key: Artifacts forged by a powerful sidhe and the duergar millennia ago, when the worlds were young. They were used to open the door between the human realm and Faerie, then the two objects were separated and hidden lest they be used to close the gateway once more.

Aidan traced a fingertip along the arch of the padlock.

Closing the gates.

If those pathways were shut, humankind would be safe from the fae. No one would be abducted ever again, no human children swapped for changelings. There was even talk that the pox had been faerie in origin, too. It originated in Nycen, after all, and it was well known how tightly woven their culture was with the fae. It was even rumored that their royal family had faerie blood, generations back.

Faeries were dangerous and cruel. Perhaps their worlds would be better separated. Did this Ellian, so rumored to know the location of every object in Faerie, know where to find this Key?

If so, maybe, just maybe, he'd bargain for that information.

Tucking the Lock safely in his desk drawer, Aidan stood and made his way to the dungeons.

One

"What would you take for them?" The Scath stood on Ellian's doorstep, his voice like sand slithering through an hourglass. The shadows that made up his form slithered and writhed like smoke caught in a breeze. Agitated. All four of his eyes narrowed, glowing purple embers.

At least the creature no longer vanished from view when Cirelle tried to focus on him like he once had, one small blessing left to her after the chaos of Thieves' Night. She was still haunted by the blood she'd seen, that she'd herself shed. A life lay on her conscience, taken at her command. She hadn't known what she possessed, the knives that determined the ruler of a shadowy fae race. Now she was left with a crown she didn't fully understand, and hounded by the creature lingering on the doorstep.

The Scath growled. Once, this faerie had terrified her. Now she was his queen. Under her command, he could come no closer to Ellian's mansion than this doorstep.

She'd let the role of Shadowed Queen languish in the weeks since Thieves' Night, unsure what to do with her new subjects but unwilling to relinquish this bit of power. It was temporary, of course. She'd need to return that mantle before leaving Faerie next year.

It would be a lie to say that Cirelle hadn't entertained the thought of taking the crown in full, if only in a brief daydream. To abandon her world entirely, retiring to the kingdom of the Shadowed in the heart of Faerie, commanding the Scath and the spider-like ilthys. Wraiths and other dark fae would be at her beck and call, a queen of night.

But no. Cirelle held no illusions that such a reign would be a long one. Monarchy among the Shadowed was a title claimed through violence. A faerie couldn't harm her without permission or if she gave insult, but how long until she slipped and gave offense egregious enough?

The knives now sat firmly ensconced in Ellian's Archive, in a special spot Cirelle set aside for herself. The claimhte, two daggers of cold faerie metal that stole any warmth from the hands that grasped them.

She shook her head. "I will not give you those knives, not when you must also kill me to claim the throne."

"If they are given willingly and the correct oath is spoken— which I will teach you—there is no need for bloodshed. You may live. Just give me the crown."

Cirelle tucked a stray lock of hair behind an ear and crossed her arms. "I will give you an answer when I am ready, and no sooner."

"You have no idea what you possess, human." The Scath spat the words, his barely-contained fury leaving an ominous thrum in the air.

"Oh, but I do. You ask for sacred daggers that will make you a king. I will ensure I'm fairly compensated if I am to bargain for them. Leave," she told the Scath firmly. "And don't come back until I summon you. Or I might never trade the claimhte at all." That was a lie. Right now, Ellian's powerful wards kept her safe. The Archive that held the knives was one of the most secure places in Faerie, and the Scath knew it.

But he would find a way around it. Faeries always did.

The Scath's eyes flashed, nothing more than glowing spots of purple wrapped in light-swallowing blackness. "Yes, my queen." He bowed, and in a smooth glide, left.

Cirelle sighed as she shut the door, slumping against it.

"Again?" Shai asked from the foyer's second-floor balcony. The sidhe warrior with the ruby skin had been Cirelle's body-guard on that fateful Thieves' Night, but had since settled in as a guest at the manor. Cirelle welcomed the company, a buffer between her and her stalemate with Ellian.

"Fourth time now," Cirelle grumbled. The Scath may be her general, but he was far from a loyal subject. She'd passed a careful decree when he'd visited the day after Thieves' Night, commanding the Scath and his army of the Shadowed never to harm her, Ellian, or their allies. Neither could the faerie enter Ellian's manor.

"Why not just trade with him?"

Cirelle walked up one of the curved staircases that framed the foyer. "Because I have no idea what one claims in ransom for a kingdom."

"So ask Ellian." An old refrain already.

And again, Cirelle declined. "He'd just manipulate the situation to his own benefit."

"You two are exhausting."

Cirelle ran a hand along the banister and headed for the familiar comfort of the music room. Shai left to her own pursuits, letting Cirelle stew in her frustration. Cirelle suspected Shai would have abandoned the manor if she could, but Ellian had called in another favor and set the sidhe woman as Cirelle's warden.

Oh, he hadn't told Cirelle that, and Shai didn't admit to as much, but it was obvious. Cirelle had touched too many raw nerves, and now she was stuck with a babysitter. Shai was a lax watchdog, but still it rankled to be watched so..

So tonight Cirelle practiced her Faerie Nocturne, adding in a new, mournfully petulant stanza in the middle. She spoke to Ellian only during her required dances with him, one every fortnight according to the wager she'd lost. Part of her relished the cruelty of them, of tormenting her jailer. But she also grew tired of these faerie games. If the sniping of petty nobles had seemed exhausting in Arraven, the fae were a hundred times worse.

Especially Ellian.

The thought of him stirred a messy slurry of feelings in her, and she could never sort them all out. Anger, frustration, hurt, want. It was too much to bear, so she poured them into her music.

He'd lied to her, or as good as done so. Fae could not tell an outright lie, after all, but he'd knowingly led her astray nonetheless. All those soft smiles, that dance they'd shared at the Unseelie Palace, the laughter over drinks and games… it had all been a part of his plan. A way to dupe her into helping him get close enough to Adaleth, the Unseelie prince, and steal back the Key.

She'd never be able to unlearn what she'd seen through Ellian's magic, how she'd relived his night with Adaleth, every shudder and moan and bloody kiss. It didn't matter that Ellian hated it as much as he relished letting his darker nature loose. He'd still treated Cirelle like a stepladder to get there.

Tonight, when she was done playing her harp, she took supper in the garden, the sky clear and bright with stars. The weather was muggy, hot. The height of Faerie summer. Still,

Cirelle sat on a bench, plate in her lap, staring up at these new constellations. She was beginning to learn them now, though only through her own fanciful names and shapes. What the fae called them, or if the fair folk sought stories in the stars at all, she didn't know.

Guilt washed through her as she finished her plate of food and set it aside. How long had it been since she visited her own gods? Days, at least.

She stood and made her way to the prayer stone, the large black oval that stood as tall as a person, with tiny embedded gemstones to represent the eight constellations of the pantheon. She traced them all in order, her finger skating along the enameled lines between the stones as she recited each god's invocation.

"Divine Iska," she murmured. "I stand beneath you and ask your guidance.

"Sayolle, lend me your wisdom when others pursue folly.

"Raigen, lift me up with hope in times of despair.

"Marya, let my tongue speak in grace and courtesy.

"Irri, give me strength in the face of oppression.

"Kadriel, leave me calm in place of anger.

"Aizhiu, grant me safe travels in strange lands.

"Sharretine, make me clever.

"Lirienne, give me compassion and mercy."

Afterward, her fingertips wandered back to Irri. The Defiant. She'd always been Cirelle's favorite, standing her ground when others tried to push her down.

Tomorrow, Cirelle would dance with Ellian for the third time since Thieves' Night. She'd look up into his eyes drowning in purple desire and laugh and take her weary vengeance. She'd make him think twice about treating her—or anyone else—like a means to an end ever again.

Just as Irri would have wanted.

And yet. Cirelle flattened her palm against the stone, drifting over to Lirienne's constellation. The Merciful, presiding over the virtue of forgiveness.

Maybe Shai was right. Maybe Ellian had suffered enough for his sins. Perhaps it was time to stop tormenting him and ask for his advice on the claimhte.

But a moment later, Cirelle shook her head. No. *Give a faerie an inch, and we'll take everything.* Ellian's own words, said months ago. All he cared about was finding the Lock. And she'd not let him use her again. She needed to maintain the upper hand, and her only tool to do that was his lust for her.

Well, if Ellian used everything at his disposal for his goals, so could she.

Once more, Cirelle's fingertip followed the lines of Irri's constellation. *No. I won't let him win.*

Two

I'll drink any poison, as long as it's yours. The words still haunted Ellian, a prediction all too painfully true. Every fortnight, he swallowed down the bittersweet draught Cirelle fed him, the touch of her fingertips skimming his bared collarbone, her hips shifting against his in ways that made him ache inside. Held within his arms, but still so far away.

And always, she smelled of cinnamon and amber, the perfume she wore when she was angry with him. One that had become a constant since Thieves' Night.

She never softened, never forgave. If anything, the princess grew harder, sharper, more cruel. She became brazen with her caresses until he sang for her like her harp strings. Moans, murmured pleas, jagged breaths.

Every fortnight, she left him sick and trembling, the desire burning like flames until he could hide in his rooms and seek release.

It wasn't what he wanted.

And oh, how the princess knew it.

Tonight, she was particularly spiteful, wearing a crimson faerie gown that revealed just enough skin to tease, to lure his mind into painfully carnal thoughts. Her hands were cool in his, her fingertips a breath of icy air as they traced his jawline, feather-light.

She grinned at him, wicked, fey. Laughing at his misery.

Ellian could have made another bargain, traded away these dances for something else. But he feared if he offered, she would accept. And then he'd not see her at all, save the occasional awkward and silent run-in throughout the manor. Even when she attended his summons in the human world, Cirelle did so wordlessly, her fury a palpable heat between them.

In the interminable days between their dances, he worried he'd forget the timbre of her voice, or the way her vicious little laughs sent shivers slithering down his spine. But no. Ellian could forget nothing. Ever. His gift, his curse: perfect recall.

This night ended like all the others, his eyes tracing the teasing sway of her hips as she left him standing there, alone and drowning in a sea of his own making.

The nights were long, hollow things for Ellian. Shai remained a solace when she wasn't watching the princess, and Issen would stop by from time to time. The slim sidhe with the daffodil hair remained a confidant, consulting on their strategy to retrieve the Lock from the Lisovyk's forest revealed itself in a handful of weeks. Though Issen, too, had been one of Cirelle's protectors on Thieves' Night, it would be unseemly to assign her two watchers in his home. So Shai remained a permanent guest, with Issen only the occasional visitor to work on their plans.

"We still need something to trade for the Lock," Issen said as he sat in the antechamber, back straight, hands folded in his lap.

"I have a lead on a possible item," Ellian murmured. "That

part I can handle. But I don't know who to take with us to the Lisovyk. Not while a traitor lingers in our midst."

It hadn't escaped his notice that the intruders in his mansion on Thieves' Night had known too many details of his arrangements. Someone in his coterie had tattled, and he didn't know who. Only Shai and Issen, two of his oldest friends, would be allowed into his circle until he found the betrayer. "Shai is no good for stealth, and it's risky with just the two of us."

"Have you considered how to ferret out the traitor? If we find them, we'll know who's safe."

Ellian had a plan, but it required asking the prickly princess for aid, and he suspected she would still not give it. True to her word, her ire remained stronger and hotter than any faerie's. But it would burn itself out. Even now, he could sense her growing exhaustion in the game. He frowned. "I'm working on that, too."

With a sigh, Issen crossed one leg over the other. "I suppose that's one of your great secrets?"

"For now."

The rest of the meeting went much the same, talking in circles around the fact that they could do little until the Lisovyk's forest opened. Issen left, and Ellian was reminded he could do nothing but wait.

Ellian hated waiting. It made him restless, reckless, foolish.

Foolish enough to do something unwise about his princess problem. Right now, Shai remained a wall standing between their warring sides. Shai, however, couldn't stay forever. And as much as he told himself that the princess needed a watcher, he knew he kept the warrior around as much to hold himself in check as Cirelle.

After Issen left, Ellian wandered down the hall. The princess and Shai were in the music room, Cirelle hammering out a merry tune on a dulcimer while Shai joined in with her husky, soulful voice. For a time, he leaned against the wall outside, listening. He could picture them now, the princess's smile unguarded as she stared in rapt joy at her hands striking out the notes. Shai singing while she knitted. A cozy scene.

One that did not welcome him.

So he turned and headed to the library, to pour everything he was feeling into his journal, somewhere safe, somewhere his tongue would not tangle him in dangerous territory.

Still, the sound of the princess's song haunted him as he walked away.

Three

At night, they whispered to Cirelle, these dreams. Violent, bloody, and exhilarating. She was not a scared, helpless princess, but a warrior of smoke and shadows. Darkness came to her call, and enemies fell beneath her gleaming black blades. They dripped with blood and sang songs only she could hear.

And those nights, Cirelle would awaken restless and hungry for something she could not name. She would slip her feet into soft shoes and pad through the empty halls to the Archive, to the claimhte. Her prize.

Sometimes she'd touch them, the way one would stroke the soft fur of a kitten, or caress the skin of a lover. Icy cold, unfeeling metal. She didn't know what they were made of, save some fae material, magical and deadly.

And every once in a while, she would fancy she could hear them, a faint hiss at the edge of perception, too sibilant to make out words.

Danger. Cirelle wasn't foolish enough to overlook it. But these weapons gave her power, control, something she possessed little enough of here in Faerie.

A kingdom. Once more she wondered, what does one ask in exchange for a crown?

Perhaps one does not give it away at all.

No. She had to trade them. *But for what?*

When the weight of the question grew too heavy to bear, she called Issen, sneaking into the Archive's antechamber while Ellian was out on an errand and recruiting Shai's reluctant help.

"Just. Ask. Ellian," the sidhe muttered as she sifted through the calling coins. They were slotted into a wooden tray, but as with the library and the Archive, it seemed only Ellian knew his system of organization. So they picked them up one by one, trying to find Issen's among the hundred or so coins.

"A-ha!" Shai held one up triumphantly. An open book inside a sun's rays. Issen's heraldry.

Cirelle slotted the coin in the corner of the mirror and waited. It took several minutes before Issen appeared. Idly, Cirelle wondered if most fae possessed such mirrors, or if it were a thing Ellian gave to his allies. And how did they know when they were being called? A mystery she may never solve.

"Cirelle?" Issen's warm but worried tone broke into her reverie. "Is everything all right? Where's Ellian?"

"He's not here," she said, then quickly added, "he's fine. I just wanted to ask you something. About those knives I got on Thieves' Night."

Apprehension washed over his features, but Issen nodded.

"The Scath wants them back. But I don't know what to ask for them. As a faerie, what would you ask in exchange?"

"…And this is a question you can't pose to Ellian?"

"Exactly what I said!" Shai exclaimed from behind Cirelle, moving into frame. "But miss princess is still all huffy about the whole maiming thing."

"I lost a *finger*," Cirelle hissed. Her bare knuckle throbbed.

It was mostly healed now, thanks to faerie potions, but still it pained her when she thought of how the Unseelie queen Ayre had cut it free, a fervent gleam in her eyes. And Adaleth had watched with that cold smile. Cirelle had earned the punishment through her own impulsive actions, destroying Adaleth's poison meant to end Ellian's life, but it had been Ellian's devotion to secrecy that put her in the Palace in the first place. Ellian's secrets, held too closely to his chest, had thrown her blindly into danger.

Cirelle didn't know if Issen or Shai was aware of the other reason for her ire. That Ellian had played her just to get to Adaleth. That he'd made her a fool. Shame kept her tongue from blurting out Ellian's secret dalliance with the prince. But even without that information, wasn't her injury enough reason to be angry?

"The prince and the queen stole your finger," Issen reminded her gently. "Not Ellian. You should really speak to him about this matter. I'm not in a position to give you such advice."

"But—"

Issen interrupted, but gently. "Talk with him, Cirelle." Then the image faded, the mirror showing only her own reflection. She turned to find Shai grinning at her.

"Told you so," the sidhe said smugly.

"Ugh, I'll just leave the knives where they are."

"And Ellian thought I was stubborn."

And so life fell into a holding pattern. Shai came and went. Issen would arrive for more clandestine meetings. Cirelle was no longer welcome at such discussions, and she was all too happy to be free of faerie games.

Or at least she kept reminding herself that.

It didn't escape her notice that over the course of weeks, Shai and Issen were the only visitors from Ellian's coterie. The odd, unrelated client showed up here and there, and she attended summons when needed, but none of Ellian's compatriots from Thieves' Night showed up again.

He knew.

Ellian was aware one of his allies had betrayed him. But what he plotted, she had no idea.

Four

THE SOUND OF ELLIAN'S boots echoed down the hall, and Cirelle gritted her teeth. Shai must have seen her shoulders clench, because the faerie gave a long and emphatic sigh as she shoved her game piece across the board.

"I swear being here with you two is like living with bickering children."

Cirelle frowned and stood as Ellian's footsteps drew closer. "Am I just supposed to forget what he's done?"

Shai shrugged. "Or you could talk it out instead of sulking."

"What would we say?" Cirelle picked up her camouflage cloak—always within reach—and shrugged it on just as Ellian entered the game room.

"A summons," he said without preamble.

Scowl still firm on her face, Cirelle wordlessly held out her hand. As his servant, she was still required to bear witness to his bargains with mortals in the human realm. And though transporting themselves back and forth between the worlds meant physical contact, this tiny bit of touch was all she'd allow outside their dances.

The world misted away, and as soon as it settled, she yanked her hand from Ellian's. It was night, lit by only a sliver of crescent moon. A single moon, her world's sky, even if the constellations she could recognize were in the wrong spots.

Her gods, looking down on her.

Cirelle tore her gaze away from the stars, fighting the sudden fullness in her chest.

They stood in an alley between low buildings. There wasn't even a hint of a breeze, oppressively hot despite the evening dark. The structures were plastered in some sort of sandy grit, as if they'd been entirely coated in mortar, then painted in bright colors. The ground beneath her feet was covered in small, smooth pebbles in a myriad of colors, rather than packed dirt.

Ellian led her into the alley, and the confined space felt altogether too close for her comfort.

Cirelle pulled the loose hood of her camouflage cloak up over her head to conceal her face. The jingling sound of Ellian's silvery boots covered the crunch of her own steps on the loose gravel. Despite knowing the capabilities of the cloak, she still felt exposed as she followed a pace behind.

The short alley opened up into a wide lane, also scattered with a thick covering of the same small pebbles. It had to be impossible to drive carts through, and she wondered how the people of this city conducted their transportation. For that matter, she wondered where this town was. The buildings were capped with roofs shingled in tiles painted as colorfully as the walls. Doors were made of heavy, embroidered canvas. How did they keep out winter drafts? But the answer came to her as a beat of sweat dripped down her forehead. Winter was not a concern here.

North, then. Past her grandfather's homeland of vast, sun-baked prairies, into the desert sands of Ysaan or even further.

Behind them, buildings lined the path. Across the paved road, a low wall was built of the same colorful plaster, waist high. A veritable forest of unfamiliar vegetation abounded on the other side of the short walls. Tall trees were sparse, but there was a proliferation of flowering shrubs about Cirelle's height. Their blossoms were immense, larger than her outspread hand, and in a scattering of colors. Gold, amethyst, crimson.

Ellian walked down a path, and she discovered the shrubs were only on the outer ring. Past them lay a wide circular area, complete with pools populated by fat blue fish. A tree grew right in the center of a bubbling fountain.

The garden was empty of people, aside from a single man sitting on his heels in an alcove near the fountain. A circle of small flowering plants ringed him. No mushrooms, not here, and Cirelle felt her cheeks flush as she realized her folly. Toadstools and faerie rings could not grow in all climates, but tales of the sidhe existed in every land. Of course there had to be alternatives to faerie rings.

The summoner was handsome, broad of shoulder and dark of skin. Even at this distance, his black eyes sparkled with charm. Some sort of sleeveless robe fastened all up the front with laced ribbon. Though the clothes were faded and worn, it seemed they once been as brightly colored as everything else in this place. Wooden bangles on both forearms clacked together as he stood to greet Ellian.

"Lord Ellian of the Sidhe," the man said, lifting a hand to the opal earring she wore. His was a musical tongue, full of long resonant tones. The man ducked his head and lifted his hand out to Ellian, palm-up. The movement was unfamiliar to her, but it was impossible to mistake the meaning. "Welcome and well met. I am Jhavet Daare," he said, voice deferent. He gestured at the ground before him. "I bring you these gifts as a sign of my good will."

Even his offerings were different than Cirelle's Arravene

ones. There was a heavy necklace made of woven reeds and intricately carved wooden beads, a small ceramic box full of polished river stones in a variety of colors, a silver bell engraved with a geometric pattern, triangular cakes topped with tiny black seeds, and a bottle of some dark liquid with a brilliantly-glazed cup next to it.

Ellian knelt and investigated each in turn, slipping the necklace, the bell, and the box of stones into his pouch.

As he had with Cirelle, Ellian gracefully folded himself into a sitting position to eat the cakes and drink the proffered beverage. "I shall hear your request," he said, voice cool, and Cirelle wondered if he were casting that sparkling opalescent glamour over his eyes.

And once again, a sort of immense grandeur hung in the air, like storm clouds gathering. Cirelle had little marked its absence until it returned, but recalled what it had felt like to gaze upon the sidhe for the first time. More glamour, it seemed.

"To be frank with you, my lord," Jhavet said with a disarming smile, "I tire of poverty. I've no wish to spend a life like my father's, caring for the beasts of wealthy men, watching them flaunt their fortunes while sharing in none of it."

"Ah," Ellian said before taking a bite of one of the little triangular cakes, but he did not speak further, waiting to hear the specifics of Jhavet's request. Was that a note of disappointment in his voice?

"I seek a change of fortune," the boy said carefully. "My grandfather told a tale of a man he once knew, who bore a talisman of sidhe make. It blessed him with good fortune in any endeavor he undertook. I've read many great things of you, my lord, that you can provide anything that a person may request."

"At a price," Ellian murmured after finishing the small cake. He poured the liqueur into the ceramic cup and took a sip. With his free hand, Ellian pulled a small item from the pouch at his waist. "Perhaps you seek something like this?"

A pendant dangled on a simple leather thong from his long gray fingers. The necklace was simple, a round piece of silver much like a coin, with some design engraved on it that she could not make out from this distance. "A fortune charm, such as the one you describe. As long as the metal of this charm touches your skin, you will succeed at any undertaking. Luck will follow you."

The man's eyes widened, but his reply was cautious. "That may be what I seek, my lord. What might you request in return?"

"This charm and its fortunes may greatly enhance the quality of the mortal years that remain to you," Ellian said calmly, his head tilted as he watched the coin swinging slightly from his fingertips. He took another sip of the liqueur. "I think I shall take one of them. I ask for one of your remaining years, shortening your lifespan by one full turn of the seasons. It's a fair enough bargain," he said lightly, "considering that no mortal man knows the years he is given anyway."

Cirelle held her breath. She hadn't even known the fae could take such a thing.

Jhavet licked his lips as he considered, staring at the coin with hungry eyes. Eventually, he nodded. "Agreed."

Ellian tossed the coin at the man, who startled but still managed to catch the necklace before it fell to the pebbled ground. With one hand free, Ellian pulled a small stoppered bottle of dark blue glass from his pouch. He finished the last of the liqueur and set the cup aside. Then, standing in one smooth motion, he pulled the stopper from the empty blue glass. "First, I'll need a bit of your hair. Part of a strand will be enough," he said. The man lifted one of his thin, long braids and tugged loose a bit of hair from the end. He placed it into the bottle that Ellian held out to him.

"Now breathe into this," Ellian said as he held the bottle toward Jhavet. The man continued to look puzzled, but leaned forward and blew softly into the open neck of the bottle.

Ellian stoppered the glass quickly, dropping it back into the pouch.

"Our bargain is complete," Ellian said, then turned to leave without another word.

Cirelle stood watching Jhavet for a moment or two more as he tied the leather thong about his neck and slipped the coin under his high collar. Then she turned and followed Ellian away.

When they were well-hidden from sight, she threw back the hood of her cloak. Ellian wordlessly held out his hand. Cirelle took it and steeled herself against the unsettling sideways lurch as Ellian transported them back to the doorstep outside his manor.

She once again tugged her hand free as soon as she could. "Did you really take a year of his life?"

Ellian nodded. "That bottle now contains one year of mortal life. It will eventually be given to someone who wants more time. Perhaps someone dying of a lingering illness, or a person in their old age who wants enough time to make amends. Either way, time is always a valuable commodity."

"And will he get a fair trade on his end?"

For just a brief moment, Ellian's eyes flickered orange, before settling into a cool, pale gray. "Yes. It all balances. It must. That was a powerful charm he took."

"You seemed… disappointed, when he told you what he wanted."

Ellian snorted as he opened the door and walked into the foyer. "Most of my summons are requests for wealth. It is the most common thing humans ask for. Money, prosperity. But what you really crave is security. You all think that wealth can buy safety, can keep you free from harm, but—"

His words cut off and Cirelle stopped short as the door shut behind her. Shai stood leaning against the banister at the base of the stairs, arms crossed. Issen rested beside her on the lower steps, a strained expression on his face.

"Ok, that's it," Shai said. "We're all gonna have some social time so you two can remember what it's like to be civil and shit. Up to the garden."

Ellian grimaced and lifted his chin. "You don't command me in my own home."

"Tonight I do. Whatcha gonna do about it? C'mon, let's go."

For a moment, Cirelle stood with her hands balled into fists, her anger a hot spark in her belly. But when Shai was in a mood like this, it was easiest to play along rather than spark a tantrum. A sulking Shai was worse than anything she complained about on Cirelle's part.

Pinching the bridge of his nose, Ellian let out a soft sigh and cast Cirelle a remorseful look before replying to Shai. "Fine. But only one hour."

"That's all I need." Shai shooed the group up the stairs. In the garden, she'd set up some game on a flat patch of grass. Two wooden stakes stood about a dozen paces apart, an assortment of colorfully-painted wooden balls scattered around one. Shai collected a rosy pink one. "Pick your color."

Cirelle chose one in emerald Arravene green, hefting it. The thing was dense and heavier than she expected. Issen selected a vivid orange, and Ellian a plum purple.

Shai explained the rules, which were simple enough. One stood next to a stake and tried to roll the balls across the grass to the other stake. Whomever was closest won a point for that round, with the winner first to reach ten points.

To an extent, Shai's ploy worked. Cirelle caught herself grinning when her ball knocked Issen's out of the way for the win, and even Ellian laughed a few times. Cirelle hated the way it tightened her chest to hear that sound. To remember when his laugh had been at her jokes.

All just a ruse so she'd play into his hand like a simpering idiot. Her smiles turned to blinking away the sting of tears.

If anyone else noticed when she took a ragged breath and her grin grew brittle, they didn't say anything. But Ellian glamoured his telltale, color-shifting eyes with a plain silver mask from that point forward, his own laughter growing sharper.

Perhaps the plan had been to bring them together, but all it did was prove that the chasm between Cirelle and Ellian grew wider by the day.

The game ended with Shai the winner, and Cirelle fled without looking back.

❧

"You gotta talk to her," Shai told Ellian after Cirelle had left.

He ran a frustrated hand through his hair. "She won't listen. Not yet. She'll calm down eventually. She has to."

Shai snorted as she collected the stakes and game balls, packing them into a wooden case and clasping it. "If you say so. I gotta go put these away." Disappointment hung on the words as she turned and walked away.

Turning back to Issen, Ellian sighed. "I made a mistake. I'm not infallible."

"Have you told Cirelle that?" When Ellian didn't answer, Issen laid a hand on his shoulder. "Well, I suppose you'll have to decide which is most important to you: your pride or her forgiveness."

Five

Some distant part of Cirelle's mind knew this was another dream, but she didn't care.

Ayre, Queen of the Unseelie, knelt before Cirelle in all her cruelty, hands splayed against the white, featureless floor.

For a moment, Cirelle was overwhelmed by a similar scene, when she'd crawled inside Ellian's head through magic and had witnessed Ellian's own memories of the supplicant prince on his hands and knees.

But this was different.

Ellian was nowhere to be seen, and this was no bedroom game. The queen murmured words low and pleading, begging for mercy. Fear lit her golden eyes as she dared a glance up through her silver hair.

Cirelle's hand burned, the knuckle of her missing finger a dull ache. The one Ayre had stolen from her. She suspected it would always twinge at the sight of the Unseelie queen. Cirelle would never forget the pop of separating bone, the sharp agony it had been. Ellian had given her a glamour ring in exchange for her help, one that at least hid the injury from others, but it was illusion only. The pain and the lack was real. She was still learning how to play the harp without her pinky finger.

She lifted Ayre's chin with the point of one of her cold, black blades. The same way the woman had once done to Ellian, mere moments before she buried her knife in his shoulder.

Here, Cirelle could have done the same, but she held back. Relishing the woman's fear. Her hands were icy cold on the hilts of the claimhte, their bloodlust singing through her veins.

A thin trickle of dark blood seeped down from the spot where the knife had punctured skin, if just barely. It looked black in the hazy dream-light, but she knew it was deepest green instead. Fae blood. Inhuman.

The woman before her lacked any scrap of humanity. But still Ayre pleaded for her life in soft, aching words.

"Please," she begged, a word so rarely used by the fae. "Spare me."

"And what would you give me to do so?" Cirelle's voice was cold, a contrast to the righteous fury that roiled inside her.

"Secrets," Ayre whispered, her voice taking on a strange sibilant tone, like a chorus of whispers. "You know Ellian fears open flame, but have you asked him of other terrors? We know them all."

"Like what?"

The queen smiled. "Secrets lurk in the shadows, those hidden places where we dwell. Secrets, and hidden fears. The large looming dreads, *what if I become the thing I most hate,* and the small, many-legged squirming ones, *biting stinging skittering.*"

Cirelle shook her head. "No. I don't want secrets that may be lies. Can you restore my finger? Ellian's innocence?"

"…No."

"Then you have nothing I want."

The queen stared at her with eyes like golden topaz, the pale column of her neck stretched as she looked up.

And Cirelle slashed it open. Ayre's blood poured out in a flood, a river, an ocean.

Ah, yes. This nightmare was familiar. She relived the blood and gore of Thieves' Night over and over in nightly terrors. The human woman who had died at Cirelle's orders. An accident of sorts, but it had still been Cirelle's commands to the giant, spider-like ilthys that wrote her death sentence. Her blood drowned Cirelle in guilt-soaked fever dreams.

Except this time, it didn't feel like a nightmare. The sight of the blood filled her not with horror, but with a fierce sense of victory. Ayre's limp form fell to the floor, a spreading pool of deepest green beneath her.

The claimhte buzzed against Cirelle's palms like a purring cat, content. Satiated.

With their power, Cirelle was no longer a victim, but a warrior queen.

Six

A FEW DAYS BEFORE their dance, Ellian came to her in the music room as she strummed a bit of faerie melody from a book she'd found in the library. The glass paperweight that translated books into Arravene also deciphered any sheet music into familiar notations, opening up a realm of strange new songs for her, some of them with unusual rhythms or completely lacking a key.

Ellian cleared his throat, interrupting the song. "I need your help."

She blinked, fingers stumbling over the notes, but didn't answer.

"I… we need allies for further attempts at finding the Lock. But I need to know who to trust."

She dropped her hands into her lap. "You're flushing out the traitor."

"Yes."

"That's why you've only spoken to Shai and Issen since."

"Of course."

Cirelle bit her lip. She was still angry with him, after all, and it was dangerous to entangle herself such games. Meddling in Ellian's plots had only brought her harm.

No, that was a lie. It had also brought her the claimhte. Besides, their traitor had almost gotten her killed, too. If Ellian ferreted them out, they would be subject to faerie retribution. A bloodthirsty surge of stinging ice crackled through her, and she nodded. "What do you need?"

"You're going to give the members of my coterie a gift. But first… I owe you recompense that I have been lax in paying." He stared at the floor by her feet. "For… for Thieves' Night. For saving my life. The balance must be repaid. I owe you."

It was the first he'd acknowledged what she'd done. After Ellian was injured in his successful plan to steal the Key from Prince Adaleth, the grumpy sidhe Dirilai had brought him back home bleeding and broken. Cirelle had helped patch him up, a gruesome experience she was not eager to repeat.

If he owed her something, there was only one item in Ellian's vast magical Archive she wanted. "Briere's ring," she asked. Cirelle still simmered with quiet fury at how he'd taken both the ring and the memory of her first kiss with her lost beloved. All in exchange for a mere insult to his pride. "Give me back my memory."

Ellian hesitated, but shook his head.. "No."

"I saved your *life*," she said. "I should be able to claim whatever I want."

"That's not how faerie bargains and balances work. For a life debt, I can't merely return something previously taken. I must give something of my own." He tilted his head. "What about the harp?"

She blinked. "This one? Mine to keep, to take back home with me?"

A single nod was his only reply, those storm cloud eyes betraying nothing.

If he wouldn't give her the ring… "Agreed." Cirelle gave the smooth wood of the instrument a possessive caress.

"Now that my debt is settled, we must prepare for our next bit of subterfuge. Come with me," Ellian said, gesturing for her to follow.

He led her to the Archive's antechamber, where he handed her a small bag that had been resting on the desk. It was a lovely thing, made of soft blue velvet, its drawstring a shining garnet ribbon. Inside lay an assortment of vials, all filled with an opaque emerald-colored liquid. An elixir that had rested in a fat bottle in the Archive. She'd dusted around it often enough to recognize it.

"Luck potions," Ellian noted. "From a reclusive faerie who does not barter often. Very effective and very rare." A gleam of azure lit his eyes. "Ask me for it."

"What?"

"Ask me for the bag of potions."

"Why?"

His smile turned foxlike. "So later I can say that you requested it."

More faerie semantic trickery, dancing around words as if they were pieces on a game board. She sighed. "May I have the luck potions?"

"Good."

"You're not going to answer me?"

"Of course not. That would start a whole new bargain."

She rolled her eyes, but didn't argue.

"You will tell the group that you asked for this potion as your payment for my life debt," Ellian continued. "That you divided it up to trade them in exchange for their help on Thieves' Night. Offering them such a prize will be enough to lure them here. Then you will tell them I have allowed you to throw a party to further show your gratitude."

"Why not give them this yourself?" Cirelle asked, tugging the bag closed. "You owe them for helping you, don't you?"

"They made their bargains and oaths long beforehand. Those that asked for payment have received their items already. I can give them nothing more."

"But I can, because they helped save my current home. The manor."

He nodded. "Will you?"

Cirelle sighed. "It won't hurt them?"

An orange flame kindled in his gaze for the briefest of seconds. "Of course not. The luck potion is both genuine and indeed quite valuable."

With a nod, Cirelle clutched the bag in both hands. Ellian walked away, but she called out when he reached the door.

"What will happen to the traitor, when we find them?"

Ellian paused, one hand on the door frame. His eyes flooded the color of sapphires and soft peridots before he turned and left.

❦

Cirelle fidgeted with the vials, stirring them inside the bag with her index finger. The glass clinked together softly, a sound like wind chimes.

Her stomach flipped over at what she was about to do. To deceive a group of faeries, each of them deadly in some way.

And she would lie even to those she considered allies. Ellian had decreed that Shai and Issen were to receive the potion as well.

"I thought you trusted them," she'd protested.

"I do, but I can't exclude them without arousing some form of suspicion. And if they don't know the plan, then they have deniability. If it's needed." The last three words were said quietly. If they were abducted and questioned, he meant.

Cirelle shuddered at the thought of one of her newfound companions falling prey to Faerie's savagery. But it was a risk they'd signed on for, a path they'd willingly chosen.

So now she stood next to the desk in the antechamber, waiting.

They arrived in bits and batches over the course of half an hour. Cirelle had never been privy to faerie small talk before, isolated from much of the chatter at the palace's Unseelie meals, so unless Shai's energetic storytelling counted, this was a new experience.

Crystalline Vilitte asked Leilarie about her nephew, and there was a brief tale of toddler shenanigans as the salcha laughed, a deep sound at odds with her slim, tree-like appearance. Her mouth opened wide, revealing those shark's teeth. Cirelle still couldn't shake the memory of Leilarie's sweet, blood-soaked smile on Thieves' Night.

Vilitte also shared verbal barbs with the feline Kith. The cat's ears flattened back, his tail flicking irritably. The scene reminded Cirelle of children idly poking at a sleeping housecat just to watch it scowl and bat away their hands.

The bat-like Es sat silently, his wings wrapping him like a cloak. The flock of tiny, feather-winged Ulim perched on his shoulders, his knees, and beside him on the sofa.

Carid was complaining about something in his growling wolf's tones to the stone giant Ixikki.

Though Cirelle had been uncertain if grumpy Dirilai would accept the invitation at all, the sidhe stood silently in the corner, arms crossed and looking as if she'd just bitten into moldy cheese. Dark hair hung over her eyes, shading her dusty lavender face like a curtain.

The Scath was absent from this meeting, still forbidden from the manor. But as his queen, she owed him no favors.

Shai and Issen stood near the door. The warrior chattered away about how her favorite craftsman was making sheaths for Cirelle's daggers, even though Cirelle had specifically asked Shai to keep that request secret. A tiny spark of irritation grew as Shai complained how tricky it was to make such a thing from only measurements, without the weapon present. But Cirelle was not even going to entertain the thought of letting those knives fall into other hands.

She was distracted from her anger by Ellian walking into the room, Agdarr at his side. The squat spriggan was mid-question, asking about the garden and whether he might be able to bargain for a cutting from one of Ellian's night-blooming rose bushes.

Altogether, it was so very… human.

Cirelle had attended more tea parties and human social gatherings than she could count, and this scattering into smaller cliques, the topics of conversation, so much was the same. If she closed her eyes, she could almost imagine standing in one of the grand salons at home, surrounded by Arravene gentry.

Agdarr took a seat, flopping down cross-legged on the floor beside the sofa, and Ellian joined Cirelle at the desk.

"We're here to decide our next move," Ellian stated, glancing around the room. "But as I mentioned when I called you, Cirelle has some business she'd like to attend to first. I owed her a boon for her aid on Thieves' Night. She asked me for Sitrim's Potion of Good Fortune."

Clever faerie, Cirelle thought to herself. None of those statements were technically lies, only disparate truths strung together to make them seem like parts of a whole.

He gestured, deferring to Cirelle. She cleared her throat, clutching the bag tightly and willing her hands not to shake. "I had to think of a reward that would benefit everyone. The potion has been divided up into these vials, and I'd like each of you to have a bit of luck for aiding me on Thieves' Night. I owe you recompense for fighting alongside me and the ilthys, helping to defend my current home. I know you've received your payment from Ellian already, but I live here too, and this is my repayment of the balance."

That said, Cirelle stepped forward, circling around the room and handing out the vials. As she met the eyes of each, she asked herself, *are you the traitor?* Who had sold them out? Feral Kith, grumbling Carid, confident Vilitte, sour Dirilai?

Her hands only trembled a tiny bit as she passed the vials to their new owners. For Kith, he held up one paw. When she placed the potion on it, he made a quick motion and the vial vanished before Cirelle could see where it had gone.

They each took their share, some in puzzlement, some with the gleam of greed in their eyes, others merely pleased. None were so uncouth as to uncork and drink the potion here.

Ellian cleared his throat after Cirelle had handed out the last bottle. "That's not the only reason we asked you here. We need to plan our next move. I have received information that the Key I retrieved is a fake."

Leilarie gasped audibly, while others growled or their expressions fell.

Their work, all for nothing.

Except it was a lie. Not technically, of course. Cirelle had uttered the words at Ellian's bidding. *The Key is a fake.* Both knew it for an untruth, but it gave Ellian the wiggle room he needed for his verbal acrobatics. A necessary subterfuge.

"While I form a new plan, Cirelle has another request. Princess?"

She glanced around the room. "I'd like to throw a party for all of you, a moment to celebrate our shared victory."

The group stared at Ellian with expressions ranging from doubtful to irritable to apathetic. Cirelle's heart stuttered. They would decline, and this whole plan would be for naught. As soon as one backed out, the others would follow suit.

Cirelle stepped forward. "Please stay," she asked, letting her voice waver a little. "We fought together, but I know so little of you. Let us house you, feed you, entertain you, just for a night."

She was not as well-liked as Toben. If Ellian's former servant had asked, Cirelle had no doubt they would agree within the span of a heartbeat.

For a long, tense moment, silence held.

Vilitte led the charge, shrugging her shoulders elegantly and tossing back her short, silvery hair. "Why not?"

After the crystalline fae opened the door, the others followed. Though Kith nodded once, his stare was piercing and canny, and a sliver of dread wormed its way into Cirelle's heart.

Dirilai was the last to accept, dark hair curtaining her mousy features. "Fine."

When Cirelle turned, Ellian was watching her with hooded, colorless eyes. She turned away and left to show their guests to their rooms.

Seven

BEFORE THE PARTY, CIRELLE was pinning up her hair when a knock sounded on her parlor door.

"Yes?"

"I… can I come in?" Ellian's voice was nervous, pensive.

Cirelle swallowed. She'd expected a brownie, come to leave more of the never-ending refreshments that always sat on her parlor sideboard. She wanted to say no, but it might be something important about tonight. "Yes."

He slipped through the door, closing it firmly behind him. Nervousness practically sparked off him. Ellian had certain tells, a tension around his eyes, a twitch in his fingertips, fiddling with the edges of his sleeves. He paced the room, settling near her sideboard and tapping a hand on the wooden surface.

His anxiousness shivered its way into her own belly, her heartbeat speeding up. "What is it?" Had someone discovered their plan?

Ellian sucked in a long, shaky breath. "I've been thinking. A lot. And I know I should be finishing party preparations, but if I wait too long, I may falter."

He never rambled like this. Something was wrong.

After a long, deep breath, Ellian asked, "What if… What if I promised to keep no more secrets from you? In my plans."

For a moment, time seemed to still. "What?"

"No more deception, no half-truths between us. You ask a question and I answer. I will include you in my plans, fully, from this night forward."

Cirelle couldn't believe what she was hearing. She searched his face for the lie, the faerie trickery behind the promise. "Your word on that?"

"My oath. If you ask a question that relates to you in any way, or to my quest for the Key and Lock, you will have the answer. When I plot those schemes, I will ask your advice."

"Why?"

He took a long, shuddering breath and stepped toward her, within arm's reach. "Because you're right. Because I was wrong to do to you what I did, to keep vital information from you. And I'm sorry. I should have trusted you." He lifted a hand, but withdrew it, fingers curling away from her. "I do trust you."

For a few long moments, Cirelle stood tongue-tied. He'd apologized. Admitted she was right. Something she'd never have expected from the proud faerie.

And he'd made a promise, given his oath, a thing so sacred to the fae. Immutable. Unbreakable.

It was a shift between them, everything turned sideways, and it made her stomach clench. When she found her voice, it was hoarse. She desperately needed to lighten the tension that twisted her in knots. Managing a weak smile, she asked, "So… Does this mean I have to stop teasing you during our dances?"

A startled, relieved laugh burst from his throat, and the thickness in the air seemed to soften. "I certainly hope not."

Stars, how long since she'd heard that laugh, seen that unguarded smile from him? He stood less than an arm's length away. She flattened her palm against his chest, covered by entirely too much silk and too many buttons. "What about right now?"

His eyes bled into violet, his tongue licking gray lips. "Now is good."

The kiss wasn't gentle. Fire and heat and need consumed Cirelle, and she arched her back as Ellian's arms slid around her.

She didn't know what would have happened if they hadn't been interrupted by another knock. This time it was the brownies. Cirelle and Ellian parted with guilty blushes as the servant entered, set a small selection of bread and jam on the sideboard for later, and left. But the spell had been broken, for now at least.

Ellian cleared his throat. "Well. We've a party to go to, I suppose."

She smiled. "This isn't over, faerie."

A ghost of his old, flirtatious grin touched his lips. "I'm counting on it."

He left, and Cirelle finished her preparations with those old moths fluttering in her belly. Ellian had given in. To *her*. Admitted his mistake, and asked her forgiveness.

And stars, she'd actually given it.

But he was right. There was no time to think on this right now. There was a revel to attend.

❧

Ellian let the princess lead him in a lively dance among the rooftop garden while the brownies played an upbeat tune. Others spun around them in their own pairs, weaving among one another with laughs and grins. Cirelle looked up at him with bright, merry eyes as he twirled her in a dizzy spin. Her smile was dazzling, and it crushed his ribcage with longing.

It was, in some ways, worrying. Not again, not after Kyrinna. The memory of his former servant still squirmed guiltily in his stomach. He'd not meant her to fall so deeply for him. With Cirelle, it was not love that burned behind her eyes, but Kyrinna had started so innocently, too.

Now that he'd left his pride aside and apologized, he suspected all he had to do was utter the word and he and the princess could end this back-and-forth between them. Mutual surrender.

Surrender, and utter folly.

When the dance ended, he plucked another glass from the table, making sure to select one with a green stem. It matched his outfit for the evening, a long emerald jacket with golden embroidery. If anyone noticed his oddly consistent choice of drinkware, it could easily be written off as vanity.

Green, the safe glasses. The ones that weren't laced with a potent truth potion.

Fae couldn't lie anyway, but this particular concoction loosened lips, made them more likely to offer up their secrets rather than dance around them. He took a long sip of the safe wine and met Cirelle's flashing gray eyes, halfway through a spin in Shai's arms. The rest of their companions joined in, even dour Carid stomping to the beat. Leilarie twirled atop Ixikki's outspread hand, the stone giant's laugh a crackling rumble.

A few of the guests were absent from the dancing, meandering off into the gardens. Ellian tugged at his cravat, cursing his choice of fashion this muggy evening. Perhaps a bit of fresh air would do him some good as well. And so he found himself walking among his statuary and topiaries, taking in the night's lazy breeze, the hum of insects.

He turned a corner and froze. A sidhe stood beside the sculpture of a griffon in flight. The man was broad-shouldered

but shorter than Ellian, narrow-nosed with skin of deepest, richest aubergine and a short brush of black hair.

Alarm jolted through Ellian. "Kith."

"Ellian." The cait sidhe nodded.

Danger here. Kith never showed his true sidhe form. Few even knew his secret, Ellian among them, as much as Kith loathed him knowing.

"Why are you in your sidhe form?" As the words spilled out, Ellian winced. A bit blunt, that.

Kith held up a bite-sized cake between his fingertips and daintily devoured it. "A bit difficult to politely eat this as a cat," he admitted, his voice as much a low purr as it was in his other form. "Plus, sky and sea forbid I pass up the chance at a rare libation from your collection." He lifted his wine glass in a mock toast. Red-stemmed. A sip, then a frown. "I do fear there's something a bit odd about this vintage, though. I suppose it's possible the seal on this bottle may have cracked and left it to sour."

Ellian swallowed. The truth potion was nearly flavorless. Nearly. "I'll ask the brownies to look into it."

Kith narrowed his eyes. "I come to you in this guise for one reason. A gesture of trust. And so you can look at me in my true form as I tell you I'm not the one you seek."

"The traitor." *Vishanti take me, why would I admit that out loud?*

"Yes. The one who gave your secrets away on Thieves' Night." Kith's blue eyes retained his vertical feline pupil even in his sidhe shape. It narrowed to a slit. "Whomever betrayed us deserves what they get, but it was not me. Do not seek to poison me again." He glanced pointedly at Ellian's drink and bared his teeth in something that was only partly a smile. "You reap what you sow."

And with that final word, the sidhe set his glass on the

griffon statue's pedestal and resumed his cat's form to pad back toward the party.

Ellian picked up his own glass and held it up to the moonlight, haunted by Kith's words. His heart sank. Now he knew why he'd been so painfully blunt a moment ago. *You reap what you sow.* He licked his lips, noticing for the first time the faintest of tingles there.

Somehow, Kith had managed to poison the green-stemmed glasses with that infernal truth potion. Had the faerie bought the loyalty of one of Ellian's own brownies, or merely practiced a little sleight of hand—or more precisely, paw—at the drink table?

At the moment, there was a more pressing concern. He sat on a bench, elbows on his knees and face in his hands, rubbing his eyes and hoping for a solution to present itself. There was no antidote to this serum. It would have to run its course. Long hours during which he was likely to blurt all his secrets at any moment. So many of them stuffed inside his head. Dangerous ones.

What to do?

Of course the princess would find him there, stewing in his worry and despair. The crisp taffeta of her gown crinkled as she approached.

"You've lost your touch, princess. You're doing a poor job of spying."

Cirelle sat beside him. "I wasn't trying to sneak."

"You shouldn't be here."

"Rude," she snorted. "Why?"

"Because when I'm this close to you, I can't think about anything except kissing you."

The princess sucked in a sharp breath.

Ellian swore. "I'm sorry. I fear I've ingested one of our... special beverages."

She made a small, frustrated sound, a puff of air out of her nose. "One of these days, faerie," she hissed, "we're finally both going to have more than two minutes together alone and sober." The scent of her lavender perfume surrounded him. Not the fiery cinnamon and sultry amber of anger, not anymore.

He opened his mouth to reply, but she placed a silencing finger against his lips.

"No. Whatever you're going to tell me, save it for tomorrow, when you're not drugged. But I suppose we can't have you blabbing everything to our guests, though, can we?"

"It will look suspicious if I leave the party entirely."

A sly expression fell over her face. "Not if we both disappear." She waggled an eyebrow.

"Princess…"

"Oh hush," she waved a hand. "I won't besmirch your virtue while you're inebriated. I'll just keep you company until it passes." She held out a hand. "Whisk us both to your room and I'll leave when it's late enough to avoid arousing suspicion. Issen can keep eyes open for our traitor. And Shai, I guess. In the meantime, I can ask you all sorts of… other questions." Her grin widened.

He groaned. But it was, unfortunately, the best plan they could probably come up with. Shai had watched them dancing and laughing earlier, giving Ellian a pointed look and a raised eyebrow. It wouldn't take much for her to start making public guesses about their absence. Everyone would assume he and the princess fell victim to their own wine-soaked desires.

He took Cirelle's hand and worldwalked them both to his room. There, he sat on the corner of his bed while she took a seat at his desk chair nearby. He tried not to imagine pulling her back with him toward the mattress and kissing all that tempting golden skin.

The princess tucked her legs up under her skirt, crossing them beneath her, and chewed her lip.

Ellian sighed and began to remove his boots, waiting for the inevitable questions.

Eight

Now is my chance. Cirelle chewed her lip. Ellian sat before her massaging his temples, ready to spill any secret she asked. He removed his boots, setting them aside, then stood to unbutton the jacket. This was carefully hung in a wardrobe alongside a sea of jewel-toned silk and velvet and lace.

Cirelle couldn't help but watch, even as it felt forbidden to see Ellian in such an everyday state of disrobing. And how far would he go with her sitting here? If the shirt followed next, she wasn't sure what she'd say. Or do.

She didn't have to wonder long. Ellian loosened his cravat and nestled the gemstone brooch in a jewelry box before returning to perch on the corner of the bed, still mostly clothed.

The tiny surge of disappointment didn't leave Cirelle proud of herself, but it lingered anyway.

Ellian smiled ruefully. "You don't actually have to keep me company, you know."

"If one of our guests sees me about in the mansion, or comes to my room and finds me there with the door locked, they'll know you retired alone."

A sigh. "You're right. We shouldn't risk it."

Cirelle toyed idly with the lace cuff on her sleeve, rolling and unrolling it.

"Just ask." Weariness lingered in the words, and perhaps a bit of dread. "I can see it on your face, the questions."

"This reminds me a little too much of that question game we played once before. I don't think I really wanted to know the answers to those." When he'd confessed to falling for human servants in the past. When Cirelle had been forced to admit her own fears.

At the time, she'd been worried she'd follow in the footsteps of Ellian's previous servant, Kyrinna. The girl who'd summoned Ellian and left him so many lovelorn notes after her return to the mortal world. Cirelle had been conflicted and confused by those dances and kisses shared at the Unseelie Palace. Before she'd known it was all a part of Ellian's scheme.

And yet.

When I'm this close to you, I can't think about anything except kissing you.

But it was just lust, pure and simple. Desire on its most basic level. She felt that part strongly enough herself, staring at the small triangle of skin bared by his open shirt, somehow more tempting than all his brazen, skimpy clothing.

After all of this, when she went home months from now, would she pine and wither for him? No.

"Please ask something." This time, the request was strained. "This elixir is potent. Words fill my head, ready to break loose. If you don't ask a question… I fear I may share something worse, something you truly *don't* want to hear."

He sounded so fragile in this moment, desperate. What things were so terrible that he needed them locked away? Fae secrets. His past with Adaleth. So… "Tell me something of your life before Faerie, in the human world. What was something you loved as a child?"

"The puppet theater caravans."

Cirelle blinked. It had not been the answer she expected, but Ellian kept talking.

"They passed by the village once or twice a year, performers from Ysaan in their colorful, beribboned robes. I loved the stories, and the artistry they put into their puppets, carving and painting and clothing them. They were beautiful things, some of them even decorated with gemstones and gilding. And their tales of faraway lands seemed so big and wondrous, when I'd never left my village borders." He gave a soft, wry laugh. "I suppose it's funny now that I've crossed the breadth of Faerie, that Saedda's frozen mountains once seemed so strange and exotic."

He lay back on the bed on top of the blankets, still clothed, and crossed his arms on his stomach. Though the words kept coming, Ellian's gaze locked on the ceiling above, perhaps seeing memories painted there.

"For years, I was determined to become a traveling merchant, to cross through jungle and plains and even oceans, to see everything the world had to offer. But my family needed me to stay, to work our little shop. So I did, until—." His voice faltered. "Until it all burned away."

When a fire had killed his family. Ellian had only survived by virtue of his hardier fae nature, though the scars still covered his back.

"Don't think about that now," Cirelle said gently. "Tell me something else. A happy memory."

"Happy? I could tell you of Taoreh and Shiza. We'd grown up together, less than three years between our ages. In youthful curiosity on the cusp of adulthood, Shiza and I became lovers. Taoreh, the eldest of us, spent some time with others before joining our trio a couple of years later. We were inseparable until I left for the war. After I returned, it was like I'd never been gone. When my family died and I fled, I was too terrified and confused to even say goodbye. They likely think I died in the fire, but I hope they found comfort with each other."

"Did you love them?"

"I think I did. Though it started as something far more simple. In fact, Taoreh taught me many of the sharper bedroom pleasures that I would later use in Faerie."

Cirelle's knuckle gave a sharp pang, and she barely breathed the name. "Adaleth." The vicious faerie prince. And Ellian's submissive lover, as much as they both despised the situation.

"I hated him so much. I loathed what he represented, that he was a mirror of what I'm all too likely to become in a few centuries. And I took out that hatred on him, which was exactly what he wanted. The whole situation was rotten, and yet a part of me needed it. I'd lost everything, and it felt good to make someone else hurt as badly as I did."

His breath shuddered out of him, and he turned his face away from her. Perhaps Ellian thought that a shameful admission, but Cirelle remembered all the snide, well-placed verbal barbs she'd spat at others in her darkest moods.

She wanted to go to that bed, to touch him in reassurance, but that felt like crossing a boundary she shouldn't. Instead, she said, "I know what it's like to be so filled with poison it splatters out onto others."

"It's a sobering thing," Ellian said, "to be frightened of oneself."

The words struck a chord, reminding Cirelle of her nightmare. The one where Ayre had warned her of Ellian's fears.

The large looming dreads—what if I become the thing I most hate—and the small, many-legged squirming ones. Biting stinging skittering.

"It makes other fears seem small, doesn't it?" Cirelle asked, picking at a dried droplet of ink that had sunk into the desk's surface. "Like your fear of fire. I never liked small, enclosed spaces." She cleared her throat. "Are there others? Besides fire, or like small spaces, for you?"

Ellian was silent for a moment. Though the words still fell from his mouth freely, he yawned. "In Kishir, we have these small crawling things with hundreds of legs. Centipedes."

Cirelle held her breath.

It was true. Her dream had given her a secret. A real one.

How many more could she uncover, in that dream world?

Oblivious to Cirelle's shock and spiraling thoughts, Ellian kept talking. "A centipede bit me as a child and I had a fierce fever for a week. The wound festered and stank. If I hadn't been a sidhe—even though I didn't know it at the time—I might have lost my foot, or worse. I still can't bear the sight of the creatures."

His words softened by the end of the sentence, eyes drifting closed. Cirelle didn't wake him. Instead, she made her way out of his wing, carefully closing the door behind her, and entered the Archive.

The claimlite shone like polished glass, the delicate curve of their blades dark and inviting.

Cirelle knew the knives were the origin of her violent dreams. She was not quite that foolish. But now she also realized they held knowledge.

Shadows hold secrets, her dream had claimed. And it had given her one of Ellian's. Her fingertip slid along the flat of a blade, so cold it made her shudder. But there, she could almost hear a voice, a distant call, a song. Not unlike the forest near her home in Arraven, full of slinking, sibilant whispers.

Danger.

But also power.

And power was something that, here in Faerie, she needed most.

Nine

SHAI VISITED LESS IN the following days, now that Cirelle and Ellian weren't sniping at one another at every turn. They hadn't touched each other again, not yet. Cirelle suspected they both feared what might happen once they tumbled over that precipice.

No, they teased, and made idle flirtations, but no more.

A stalemate. Each waiting for the other to cross the line first.

Once, Ellian entered the music room while she strummed the forlorn melody she'd composed here in Faerie. It still wasn't quite finished, even after months of refining. There was still a piece missing, though she couldn't determine what. Not yet.

Ellian's boots jingled as he took a seat in a nearby chair. A common enough occurrence. He'd enter, take a seat, and listen to her play in silence, his fingers lightly tapping the rhythm on the armrest while he closed his eyes.

This time, he spoke. "What is that piece? You play it so often."

Cirelle shrugged. "I wrote it after coming here." She finished strumming the last notes and let them fade into silence. "I call it my Faerie Nocturne."

Ellian was silent, and when she glanced up to meet his eyes, they shone deep sapphire blue.

Uneasy, Cirelle stared back down at the strings of her instrument and wordlessly plucked out an old Gilbran ballad, letting the moment pass.

Over those long days, all too often Cirelle would slink into the Archive and peer at her blades, caressing them with the longing of a lover.

"Tell me more," she asked them. For here in Faerie, secrets were weapons, and she could sorely use some of those.

But when the next vision came, it was something other than hidden information.

As always, she was aware this was a dream. The claimhte were cold in her grasp, her hands heavy with the chill. Though fog shrouded all but a few feet around her, she'd know these filigreed panels and pale stone anywhere. One of Ellian's manor hallways.

There. A door, cracked open. A narrow stairwell led upward beyond it.

Ah. The garden.

Her footsteps made little sound as she ascended, the cool stone against her bare feet mimicking the ice of the knives in her grasp.

Sunlight bathed the garden, and Cirelle blinked at the brightness. When her vision cleared, dark splatters on the stone path pulled her forward. Faerie blood, a trail of it. At night, such blood had always seemed nearly black, but the sunbeams revealed its true dark greenish hue.

Heart in her throat, Cirelle followed the gruesome trail. Drips and splashes, leading deeper and deeper into the heart of the garden. Here and there, she'd pass a snow-white flower that had been smeared with the ichor.

She knew what she would find, though Cirelle couldn't have said how. Dream logic.

Ellian lay in the center of his garden, birds chirping and sun shining overhead. Blood puddled beneath him, and his eyes stared glassily at the sky.

And one of the claimhte lay buried in his chest.

Cirelle glanced down to find one missing from her grasp. Perhaps it had never been there at all, or it may merely have been the fickle nature of such a dream.

Time wavered, her memories hazy. Had she done this? She should feel something. Regret, grief, sorrow. But all Cirelle could do as she approached was stare at the drying blood, her bare feet sinking into the sticky stuff.

You could be free.

The voice, both hers and not hers, jolted her awake.

Cirelle gasped, tossing the blankets aside and sitting up to suck in lungfuls of air. Her hands trembled, and she clutched the sheets tightly.

Stars, had she just dreamed of Ellian's murder at her own hands? Awake, the thought left her sick, shame and guilt and disgust swallowing her.

She curled back up in bed, but sleep was a futile effort. The vision of Ellian's garden soaked in his blood wouldn't abandon her. She needed to prove it a lie, to reassure herself. Then she could return to sleep once more. Just a quick trip up the stairs. Cirelle slid out of bed and padded toward the garden in her nightdress.

She'd long since grown used to the darkness of the manor, the way the sconces of faerie lights would flicker on and off as she passed. Tonight, however, she was reminded of the unease she'd felt in her first nights here, when Ellian had been an imposing and mysterious figure, and the realm of Faerie seemed full of unseen danger.

When she stepped out of the stairwell into the garden, she startled at the sight of Ellian at a nearby balcony, leaning on the railing and staring out at the landscape. Without turning, he said, "It's nearly dawn. You should be going to sleep."

He was alive, the dream indeed a mere nightmare. Cirelle's heart raced, though relief flooded her like a gulp of hot cider. She swallowed and stepped up beside him, the stone railing cool beneath her fingers. "So should you." A splash of indigo colored the horizon, the first precursor to the sunrise. She'd not slumbered long.

Stars, how long had it been since she'd seen the sun? Since her return from Adaleth's palace, weeks ago? Cirelle leaned her weight on the railing, her forearms flat against it. "I...I'm sorry. For taking advantage of the truth potion. I should have just left. If you want to use a memory jar and take away what I learned..."

Ellian drew a long, ragged breath. They were quiet for long minutes, watching the sky lighten, a smudge of orange painting over the indigo and fading the sky to pale blue above.

"No." The word came quietly. "No one else knows some of those things. I've never even spoken some of them aloud. But... I like it, that you know."

A sudden pressure choked Cirelle, a lump in her throat. She swallowed it down. Instead, she asked, "So why are you up?"

He seemed to welcome the change of subject. "On this day, it's tradition to watch the sun rise, to witness its full journey, and watch it set. A ritual."

"Oh."

The warmth of the sun washed over them as it crested the horizon. It was larger than her own, a brilliant orange rather than pure golden white. It crept over the edge of the mountains, bathing the hills of Ellian's estate in an amber glow.

They stood in silence until the golden sky turned blue and the lands below were lush and green. Cirelle blinked at the brightness. In the sunlight, Ellian's hair shone like the richest sapphires, and it made his gray skin warmer somehow, like dust rather than cold slate.

"Come, let's sit," Ellian said, taking a nearby tray of refreshments, likely left by a brownie, and guiding her through the garden. A small blanket rested on a flat patch of grass, only large enough for one person. After all, he hadn't expected company.

For a moment, Ellian wavered, glancing from Cirelle to the blanket with something approaching dismay.

"Oh, you big baby." Cirelle swept the hem of her nightdress aside and sat on the soft grass near the blanket with her feet tucked beside her.

Ellian looked a bit sheepish as he settled on the blanket and set the tray between them. On it lay a scattering of small plates with various light foods. Bread, cheese, jam, grapes, and thin slices of cured meat. A crystal glass and a bottle.

Noting Cirelle's grimace at the bottle, Ellian laughed. "Not wine," he noted. "Just juice made from faerie fruits."

"It won't impair me in any way?"

His eyes danced, now the color of pure ocean waters. "If something like this leaves you tipsy, I wasted some perfectly good Summerwine testing your tolerance that first night."

Cirelle caught her mouth hanging open and shut it with a sharp clack. This wasn't Ellian's usual superior smugness or the heat of their attempts at seduction. The jibe had been something else, a casual jest of the sort shared between friends. A new ease settled over him, a smile that was wide and without affectation or sorrow.

Returning the grin, Cirelle took a glass and held it up with a shrug. "Bottoms up, I suppose." It was, indeed, just unfermented juice, crisp and sharp on her tongue. Something a bit like apple, with a floral note beneath the fruity tang.

The sun had crept higher. Summer's warmth still lingered, though the promise of autumn's chill hung in the air, a waiting presence. Already, some of the blossoms had begun to turn, the roses withering, their petals turning brown at the edges and falling to litter the ground.

Cirelle glanced upward, shielding her eyes from the brightness as she stared up into the cloudless blue sky. "So this is it, then? Just staying awake and watching the sun?"

"Yes." Ellian took a breath as if to say more, paused, and fell silent.

"What?" Cirelle turned to find his eyes a deep midnight blue.

"Traditionally, the sun ceremony is spent with one's family." He sighed and leaned back on his arms, face tilted up toward the rising sun. She followed suit, lying back and pillowing her head on her crossed arms. The sun beat against her skin, a golden warmth she hadn't felt in a long time. The grass was still damp with morning dew, but slowly warming. Ellian's voice was soft as he added, "I have no family left to watch with me."

"I'm sorry," she whispered. "Am I intruding? I didn't mean to bring you sadness."

When his eyes slid to her, they swirled pink and blue, rose petals against a summer sky. "You don't. And you aren't."

Those moths in her ribcage returned, beating their wings against the insides of her chest. As the sun rose higher, her eyes traced the lines of his face, his jaw, those lips. The last time she'd seen Ellian in the sunlight, it had been at the Unseelie Court's Hunt, with larger problems at hand.

Ellian said, "You're welcome to stay. You're a member of

my household, so I suppose that makes you the closest thing to family I have."

"Did your other servants watch with you?"

A faint smile. "Sometimes. Toben did, after the first year. Before that… it's been a long time."

"You miss him, don't you?"

"He was a good man. A good friend."

Cirelle smiled back at Ellian. "Yes, he was." She wondered if Toben thought of them at all, now that he was reunited with his family. Silence fell once again, but this time it was a comfortable one. Absently, Cirelle sat up, plucked a grape off the tray and tossed it high in the air, catching it in her mouth. She bit down, the flavor green and ripe and bursting with tartness.

Ellian laughed and shook his head. "I'll admit, that's not something I expected to see from a princess," he said. "Though I shouldn't be surprised at this point."

Cirelle blushed. "Yes, well, I was never a very good princess."

"Perhaps not," Ellian cocked his head at her, his smile growing sly. "But you'll make a formidable queen."

Her cheeks burned even hotter. "I won't be. Queen, that is." The bitterness in her own voice startled her.

"I thought your suitors were both princes."

"Neither one is set to inherit, and even if they were, Gilbras and Asheir leave the ruling to men. A queen is merely a title there. I would be expected to sit idly by."

"But you wouldn't," Ellian grinned. "I think within a month you'd have anyone dancing to your tune, king or no."

Cirelle was embarrassed by the tears that sprang to her eyes, and turned her face back up to the sun. "It's still a cage."

"More so than being trapped in Faerie, in this house?"

She didn't even have to think about it. "Yes." She blinked away the tears, a tickle as they trailed down her cheeks. Sometimes, she was so homesick it was like a physical illness. She longed to run through the streets of Palace City again, disguised as a serving girl and eating herb dumplings from a market stall. Or to sit across from her brother at the gaming tables and savor the look on his face when she won a third game in a row. To dance her familiar Arravene gallanads in her own palace. To see humans, to taste her favorite lemon custard tarts hot from the oven.

But then she thought about what awaited her and wondered if she'd hide here forever, given the chance. Cirelle would be whisked away from Arraven so soon after she returned. And now… it almost seemed a more pleasant option to remain here in Faerie than be dragged off to Gilbras or Asheir. Even Rhine's charms faded in her memory compared to what she'd experienced here in Ellian's home. And Beddig was worse, obsequious and smitten and clingy. Cirelle closed her eyes as her throat started to close up.

She was shocked from her maudlin thoughts when something small flew past her face. Her head whipped around to stare at Ellian, incredulous. A grape bounced away from her, coming to a stop in a clump of grass. "Hey!" She cried indignantly as she sat up. In retaliation, she plucked another grape from the tray and tossed it at him. "You're in a strange mood today."

Ellian plucked it from the air, threw it upward, and caught it in his mouth as it fell. "Perhaps I'm just enjoying the company." Cerulean eyes again, a teasing smile.

Cirelle rolled her eyes against the tightness in her chest and flopped back down on the ground to watch the sun climb slowly higher. For a while she lay on the grass, enjoying the warmth of the sun on her skin. She caught herself starting to drowse, and sat up to rub her eyes.

"You don't need to stay, you know." Ellian watched her pour

some juice as he picked up a slice of bread, topping it with a piece of cheese. "You can go to bed."

"I'm not a quitter," she scoffed, taking a long gulp of juice, somehow still pleasantly cold.

He returned her comment with a knowing smile, head cocked slightly.

"What?"

Ellian shook his head, then indicated the still-rising sun. "There are hours left yet, princess."

"You think I can't do it? Watch me."

With a shrug, Ellian took a bite of his bread. "Suit yourself."

Cirelle ate another grape as the sun crept higher in the sky. "So what is this holiday? Honoring some faerie hero or prophet?"

Ellian didn't respond, and Cirelle turned her head to see if he'd even heard her. He stared off into the distance.

Realization crept up on her. "This isn't a faerie holiday, is it?"

"No."

It was from his human life, before.

"It's all right," he said. "I've long since reconciled the two halves of my life. I changed so much about myself when I came to Faerie. My schedule, my name, my very personality. After… when I left, I realized I couldn't run from my human past for-ever." Ellian held up his half-eaten piece of bread on one finger, nudging it this way and that until it perched in balance. "So I found the midpoint between the two."

Cirelle nodded, but a single word in his admission had piqued her interest. "You know, I *thought* Ellian sounded more like a sidhe name than a Kishi one," she said slyly.

"It is. No one knows my true name anymore. Names have power among the fae. We all use false names."

"Really? So Shai and Issen and Dirilai, none of those names are real?"

He shrugged. "They're as real as any other nickname would be. But their true names, the ones that encompass their entire being, those remain hidden."

Cirelle took another long gulp of her juice. "What sort of power? If one were to know a name, what could be done with it?"

"Any number of things. The worst? Crawling into that faerie's head and turning them into a puppet."

"So if we could learn the prince's true name…" she said cautiously.

Ellian let the heavy pause hang in the air for a moment before responding just as carefully. "The thought has occurred to us, yes. But it's easier to change the course of a river than to find out a faerie's true name. The only other living faerie who knows it would likely be his mother."

"Oh."

Another silence fell, and a cold shiver ran up and down Cirelle's skin despite the sun's heat. Should she be proud or concerned that her thoughts had led her down the same dark path as faerie logic?

She turned her head up to the sky, closing her eyes. Fae-touched, indeed.

Ten

When the princess's eyes drifted lazily shut, Ellian didn't wake her. Instead, he enjoyed the soft sound of her breathing as he watched the sun skate across the sky. The brownies brought another meal at midday, this time providing two glasses and heartier fare. They crept in on silent feet and away again without so much as a twitch from Cirelle.

He stared up at the clouds and reveled in a weight lifted.

In truth, he hadn't realized how insidiously the princess's anger had been slowly eating him alive. But she'd accepted his apology, his oath. And he would keep it. It was terrifying to know this woman had access to all of his ploys, did she dare but ask. She hadn't yet, in the days since their truce, but someday she would.

And he would answer.

Ellian's stare followed the arc of the sun, lulled by the sound of songbirds and late summer insects and Cirelle's gentle snores, until dusk began to settle. So what if he occasionally drifted into watching her sleep instead of the sun, marking the hair tangling across her face, or the way her fingers curled gently in a lax fist, wondering what dream thoughts made that soft smile tug at her lips?

Purple stained the sky, then indigo. As stars emerged, he sat up and stretched. He called to Cirelle once, twice. No response. Her head was pillowed on one arm, mouth slack, deep in slumber.

"Princess!" Louder this time. Finally, she stirred, a lazy yawn and stretch without opening her eyes. She mumbled something incoherent and settled back into the crook of her elbow.

Ellian sighed and moved closer, calling a fourth time, unable to touch her without permission. This time he spoke her name, feeling terribly intimate on his lips. So rare, the number of times he'd addressed her this casually. "Cirelle."

This time she blinked and opened bleary eyes the hue of thunderclouds. She smiled sleepily. "Ellian." The princess propped herself on an elbow and lifted her free hand to his cheek, her face unbearably open. Unguarded. Her voice was low, hoarse with sleep. "I dreamt of you."

A small shiver rippled through him. He licked his lips. "Oh?"

Cirelle's dreamy expression turned wicked, her hand sliding around to the back of his neck, urging him downward, closer.

He didn't resist.

The kiss was a soft, tentative thing. Not the spark and flame of their last one, but something sweeter than that. Deep, slow, dizzying.

He should stop this. But the words caught in his throat when the bold princess pushed him gently back onto the grass. Suddenly, he didn't care that he lay on the bare ground, not when she settled atop him, hands against his chest, kissing him like this. Her hair tickled his cheek. She smelled like some floral perfume, heady and sweet. Her skin was pleasantly cool, a mortal's touch.

And stone and sea and sky, the way she pinned him was maddening. When his hands settled at her sides, she made a small sound and rolled her hips against him.

He sucked in a sharp breath. This couldn't really be happening. Any moment now she'd come to her senses and stand to leave.

But he knew the lie in that.

Before Thieves' Night and their rift, Ellian had always been the one to stop, not the princess. The first time, when she'd wanted to use him as a salve against loneliness in her parlor. The second, at the Unseelie Palace, when they were both too intoxicated. In this very garden mere days ago, when he'd been dosed with truth potion.

But nothing stood between them now.

Still, as her hands slid his shirt loose from his trousers, Ellian paused. Kyrinna's face swam in his mind, the folly it had been to bed her. But Cirelle would never be a heartsick fool. It wasn't love that made her questing hands dip lower, trailing a line along the top of his waistband, beneath his shirt.

And yet. Ellian slid his hands to her shoulders, urging her gently away.

Frustrated anger sparked in her eyes. And hurt. "What is it this time?" she hissed, already scrambling backward, ready to flee.

It felt like a knife to the gut, her pain. Ellian stopped her by sliding his grip down to her wrists and holding her hands to his chest. His voice was a hoarse croak. "I… this isn't refusal." He dropped his glamour, let her see whatever his eyes would reveal. Violet, surely, but she must know that much already from the hard length under his trousers, pressed between their bodies. Would they also show that traitorous pink, too? And if they did, had she puzzled out what it meant yet?

Cirelle hesitated, going very still. Her expression grew cautious. "Then what?"

"I just… I need you to assure me you really want to do this."

She laughed, a sudden bark of a sound. "Oh, you stupid, chivalrous faerie." She ground her hips teasingly against him, trailing a hand up his collarbone, along his jaw, tracing the edge of his lip until he closed his eyes and shuddered. Her second laugh was softer, a wicked little thing. "Yes." She leaned in close, her lips hovering just over his. "Is that what you needed to hear?"

He nodded, unable to form words. This time when she kissed him, her hands found the lacings of his trousers, but not before she stroked a slow, hard line against his length through the fabric that made him gasp and buck his hips.

After those dances in the ballroom, Ellian had expected her to tease, to torment him for an eternity, but it seemed her spring was coiled as tightly as his. A part of him hardly dared believe this was really happening. Maybe he'd fallen asleep, too, and all this was just a dream. He drank in the sight of her, knees on either side of him as she straddled him and smiled, hair still mussed in an auburn tangle. He couldn't touch enough of her, his hands sliding over her hips, or under her nightdress to caress her stomach.

Heart in his throat, his fingertips trailed back down, down, down, slipping beneath her undergarments. She groaned. *Vishanti take me,* he thought as he found the dampness between her legs. Was there any feeling quite as intoxicating as knowing someone wanted you?

Moonlight limned her silhouette as she threw her head back and let out the most satisfying little moan. Ellian activated one of his rings, the one on his middle finger that warmed whatever it touched.

"Stars," she gasped, then laughed as her head dropped and her eyes met his. "I should have known that thing was for more than just tea." Her grin was wide, unaffected, and it almost hurt to look at it.

"Oh," he smiled back. "I'm full of surprises."

The princess leaned over him, the length of their whole bodies touching, and kissed him again. "Show me."

Cirelle ignored all of the warning bells in her head that told her this was a horrendously bad idea. Ellian's tongue slid into her mouth, his hand was between her legs, and she was well past the point of wanting this, needing this.

And stars, Ellian knew what he was doing with those oh-so-warm fingers, a slow and steady rhythm that built a tingling pressure at the base of her spine. She should slow down and savor this moment, but she couldn't, her hips moving in time as she moaned into his mouth. Too long. She'd been starving for months and her body had taken over.

Ellian, it seemed, had at least a scrap of self-control. His hand withdrew, and she made a small pleading sound that elicited a low laugh from him. "Not yet, Princess. You've been teasing me for weeks upon weeks. I'm not about to let it end in minutes." He urged her to sit up, tugging her nightdress upward.

Cirelle needed little prompting. She slipped the whole thing over her head, watching him as she tossed it aside. Burning violet, his eyes, like sunlit amethysts. A pale ring of rose pink lined their edges.

With a wicked smile, she rolled her hips against him again. His groan was the most satisfying sound, and suddenly she couldn't bear the layers of fabric between them any more. She made short work of her underthings, though she had to move off him to do so.

Ellian took the chance to sit up and swap their positions, urging her onto the ground now, the faerie grass velvety-soft against her bare back. His shirt was untucked and loose, his hair a sapphire tangle in the moonlight, and he'd never looked more tempting or more beautiful.

His gaze roamed over her, too, his mouth a smile that seemed almost awestruck as his fingertips trailed teasing lines between her breasts, down her belly, along her arms. Cirelle pressed trembling hands against his chest, under his shirt, sliding it off his shoulders to fall to the ground.

Kneeling between her parted legs, shirtless, trousers half-undone, Ellian was like some feverish dream come to life, all slim angles and trim muscle. Her hands wandered over his skin, so warm. Once, she'd wondered if he burned so hotly everywhere, and now she had her answer. Her fingers drew a line over the planes of his stomach, past his bellybutton, then even lower. He sucked in a breath and went deathly still as her hands tugged his trouser laces fully loose. He shivered beneath her touch, and a spike of tingling heat sparked in her chest. This ethereal, immortal creature, trembling at her caress.

It was a giddy feeling, such power.

He watched her with that lavender stare as she pushed his trousers down over his hips, freeing him. Hard and ready and eager. Ellian licked his lips and cleared his throat, but it seemed words failed. Instead his hands spoke for him while they explored her skin, and the silent stroke of his tongue as he bent over her and kissed her throat.

They didn't need to speak, not any more. She barely noticed as he kicked off his boots and trousers completely, so lost was she in the feel of his lips on her neck, her collarbone, her breast.

Cirelle couldn't have said how long they spent just savoring the touch of one another's skin, their hands and lips and tongues exploring every inch of each other. It was a languid sort of pleasure, and the fire in her belly grew hotter and sharper with every minute.

When she felt she could bear it no longer, Ellian poised himself above her, his tip brushing the spot between her legs. He held himself steady and his pensive expression asked a silent question.

Cirelle breathed in deep, and let out the word in a sigh. "Yes."

He was gentle, though she could feel him holding back. A slow slide in, until they locked together. When had her legs wrapped around him? She swore softly, then whispered another breathless, "yes."

They stayed like that for a few long heartbeats, entwined, unmoving, just reveling in the rightness of it. Why had they waited so long for this? Ellian was as much a part of her as her own limbs in this moment. They existed almost outside time, in a space entirely their own. The starlight haloed his hair, glinting off the silver hoops in his ears. She drowned in his stare, in the soft pink that washed over the violet.

Cirelle suspected she knew what that rosy hue meant, and closed her eyes against it. Instead, she rocked her hips, urging Ellian into movement, and he obeyed. Out, in one long, smooth motion, then back in. She sucked in a sharp breath and grasped his hips, pleading. Faster. More.

He obliged, finding a pace that left her uttering breathless curses in between his name and the names of her gods, the words sighed into his lips as he kissed her deeply. Then that damnably warm hand slipped between their bodies as he moved inside her, finding that small sensitive knot and circling gently in time with his thrusts.

"Void take me," she hissed, back arching.

His only reply was a soft, satisfied murmur. He leaned back, watching her, one hand cradling her cheek while the other did such devilish things between her legs and his length filled her.

She couldn't look away as the pressure ratcheted higher and higher.

Then she shattered into a thousand glittering pieces, and for a brief moment, she wasn't herself anymore. She was pure, shimmering light, a million stars. Distantly, she heard herself crying out.

When she came to herself again, Ellian lay beside her, stroking her hair. She let out a long, shaky sigh and curled up against him.

As consciousness slowly returned, one uncomfortable thought swam to the surface. "I… did you…?" She found herself unable to state the words, suddenly awkward.

He caressed her cheek. "Yes, but not… it's in the grass. I wouldn't… not without permission."

She laughed, still giddy. "Such faerie sensibilities. Though… thank you. I don't think it would be the best idea to return to Arraven with child by a sidhe." She draped a leg over his, head on his chest, listening to the rise and fall of his breathing.

"You can't." His response was gentle. "Humans can't bear sidhe children. Nor do we carry mortal diseases."

"Oh." Cirelle planted a small kiss on his throat, letting a wicked little purr enter her voice. "Then next time… you have permission."

He was silent a long moment, and she felt him swallow. "So… there will be a next time?"

Cirelle laughed and nipped his neck. "Oh, yes."

Eleven

THE NIGHT AFTER THE Sun Ceremony was scheduled for their regular dance, and Cirelle spent the evening preparing. She donned one of those diaphanous faerie gowns that bared her leg nearly to the waist, and the matching flimsy sidhe underthings.

No lip stain, though she did smudge a bit of dark kohl over her eyes. Hair loose, so Ellian's hands could tangle in it.

Dance they would, but she knew the night would not end there.

And it didn't. Their hour of dance was barely up before she pulled him against the wall in a breathless kiss. His hands sought the edges of her faerie undergarments, sliding them down, down. Then the world misted around them, and they stood beside a bed in one of the guest rooms. Cirelle knocked the decorative pillows to the floor and lay upon it, kicking off the insubstantial underthings as Ellian joined her there. Feverish, desperate, they spent themselves in each other, reveling in what they'd denied themselves for so long.

The days blurred together, her long hours in the Archive spent daydreaming about what would come after, losing herself in the honey-salt taste of Ellian's kisses and the sound of his sighs. Shai visited less often, and when she did, she would leave the music room with a laugh and a simple, "have fun" when Ellian entered and fixed Cirelle with a hungry violet stare.

It seemed like this would last forever, but reality came crashing back down upon them one night. They lay on Cirelle's bed, shivering and sweat-soaked in the afterglow.

"So," Ellian said, drawing patterns on her stomach with a fingertip. "I promised to share my plans with you... In nine days, I go to see the Mosul."

"Who is that?"

"One of the gentler fae. He has an item I need."

"I want to go with you." The words spilled from her before she could stop them.

Ellian was silent for a long moment. Then, "no."

"You said he's gentler. Is he dangerous?"

His response was grudging. "Not terribly, no."

"Then let me out." She turned to face him. "You told me I could be included, and I don't want to be sitting here, waiting, wondering if you're all right. I hate feeling helpless, trapped here like a bird in a cage. My wings ache."

Ellian took her hand gently, placing the softest of kisses on her knuckle, where her missing finger should be. The glamour ring made her hand look whole, but his lips were warm against the smooth scar tissue there. "After what happened at the Unseelie Palace... I won't let you be hurt like that again for the sake of my mission."

"I can bring my knives."

A grimace. "I'd prefer you didn't. You shouldn't touch those."

"Why?"

"Because they're more than just metal. Those blades are dangerous, and you should trade them back."

"I've been meaning to ask you about that... What does one ask from a shadow faerie in exchange for a throne?"

"If I were a human in Faerie, I'd ask for protection from the Shadowed as long as I lived. But whatever you ask, I'd prefer you do it soon. I don't like having those things under my roof."

It hadn't occurred to her that she could keep the protection of the ilthys and the Scath while forfeiting the throne that came with it. But a sudden, unexpected wave of possessiveness washed over her. The knives still whispered their forbidden knowledge to her in shadowed dreams, the fears and weaknesses of her enemies. Because of those knives, she knew that Queen Ayre was terrified of high spaces. When she'd asked for more of the Unseelie queen's secrets, they'd whispered a word that felt like a name, *Rivila,* but refused to tell her more. Was it a person? A place?

She could ask Ellian, but he'd want to know where she got such information. His expression right now showed how deeply he'd disapprove.

"Well they're not your knives," Cirelle snapped. "They're mine. And I don't think I'd trust the Scath's word or protection, not without the daggers to command him. While I hold them, I'm safe."

Ellian snorted. "There's no such thing, not here. Not anywhere. Not even in your comfortable human palace."

"I was safer there than I ever was in Faerie." Her knuckle's scar ached again.

"That much is true." Ellian rolled onto his back and sighed. "And that's exactly why I fear for you outside these walls."

"Then bring Shai with us. She can help."

"I can't rely on Shai all the time."

"Please."

A shaky breath. "I'll ask Shai. If I can secure protection, you can come."

Cirelle grinned. "Deal."

Twelve

CIRELLE WOULDN'T EVEN HAVE known of the next summons if Shai hadn't been at her side when Ellian came to find her. They were in the garden, and the warrior was idly knitting a scarf. Cirelle had gaped the first time the sidhe brought out a roll of yarn and needles, but a challenging look from Shai had made the princess bite her tongue.

A small harp rested in Cirelle's lap, and she played a gentle melody, an Asheiran lullaby. The tiny florafae gathered cautiously around, bobbing their heads and fluttering their glimmering wings to the beat.

It was a peaceful scene, until the chime of Ellian's ridiculous boots broke into the gentle reverie.

"Shai." His voice was low, soft.

The sidhe barely looked up from her current stitch. "Hm?"

"I need you to attend me on a summons."

Cirelle's head snapped up, her fingers freezing in place and the melody halting. The florafae scattered. Something was wrong. Ellian always took Cirelle on his summons, never Shai.

The warrior blinked. "I, er, what?"

"A summons," Ellian repeated. "I need you to come with

me. Cirelle will be safe here." There, just for a moment, his voice cracked ever so slightly.

Shai shrugged, tucking her needles into place and setting her knitting aside. "Whatever." She took Ellian's hand and they were gone.

Cirelle's old, familiar sorrow plucked at her once more, scraping with ragged claws. This had to be her failing, somehow. Stars, it had been weeks since this despair came clutching at her. *Your fault, his disdain. A failure.*

What had she done to displease him so?

Her will for music withering, she returned the harp to the music room, also taking Shai's bag of knitting and placing it on a table just inside the sidhe's chamber. Best not to leave it to the mercies of the mischievous florafae. She busied herself in mundane tasks, retreating to the small office inside the Archive to tidy the latest paperwork.

The claimhte sang at her from their shelf, a gleaming temptation. She couldn't resist tracing a fingertip down the side of a blade as always, savoring its chill.

She comes.

Cirelle blinked and yanked her hand away. This voice from her dreams, the one that urged her to kill and offered her secrets, had never spoken to her during waking hours.

Swallowing, Cirelle reached out again, pressing a cautious fingertip to the metal. "Who?" she whispered.

Do not trust her.

Cirelle asked for more answers, but the knives went silent.

She comes, they'd said. Who?

While Cirelle sorted paperwork, she stole glances toward the magical shelf where the offerings would appear. When Ellian went on summons and placed objects in his magical belt pouch, they arrived on this very shelf, to be sorted by Cirelle into the Archive. His treasures, taken in exchange for whatever the recipient asked of the faerie.

It didn't take long before the items appeared.

A wooden teacup, dyed scarlet and carved in runes Cirelle now recognized as sidhe writing. A tiny golden music box. A half-empty glass bottle of dark liquid.

And last, a trinket that made Cirelle's breath catch.

It didn't look like much. A simple knotted bracelet of colorful string, the kind children made and exchanged.

But she knew this one. Green and brown and gold in a repeating pattern. She'd woven it herself, a decade ago.

No.

A shake of her head, as if that would stop this. Now Cirelle knew why Ellian hadn't asked her on the summons.

As Cirelle clutched the bracelet, she heard the front door open and close, then her name called. Ellian, cool and indifferent. Cirelle reluctantly dropped the bracelet and stepped into the foyer to confront him, to ask him what her oldest friend had bargained for.

Ellian and Shai didn't stand there alone. A familiar figure stood before them, wan and thin.

Lydia.

Thirteen

This wasn't at all what Lydia had expected of a fae lord's lands. When she'd made her bargain with Ellian, she'd braced herself for any number of possibilities here. A moldering dungeon, the faerie laughing at her folly as he threw her into the cell next to Cirelle's. The princess locked away in a gilded tower with Lydia left to wait outside the door.

It had taken precious weeks for Aidan to secure Lydia's release from the dungeons for this quest. Even a prince had to defer to his King and Queen. He'd sent her off with two simple commands. *Bring her home safely. Seek the Key from this sidhe who knows so much of magical items.*

Once she'd left Palace Arraven for the eerie, fae-touched woodland nearby, three more days passed before she could find a faerie ring of toadstools in the forest. When Cirelle had summoned the faerie, she'd used a magic amulet that sought out such a ring. Lydia had no such help. Those nights spent in the whispering woods were ones she'd not want to experience ever again, haunted by nightmares and taunting dreams that tried to lure her off the paths.

When Lydia managed to summon Ellian, she'd made her request. "I want Princess Cirelle back."

"Your princess swore an oath to stay in Faerie for an allotted time. She will return to your realm when that bargain is fulfilled, and no sooner."

Lydia's heart sank. There was no room for argument in this sidhe's cool tones. She chewed her lip. "Then take me to her. Let me stay with her." If only she could see Cirelle again, Lydia could keep her safe, at least.

Ellian had looked her over then, head to toe. Possibly taking in her ready stance, the worn but well-tended armor of the palace guard. The daggers at her hips. She'd at least been wise enough not to draw steel this time.

Some unknown realization dawned on his face, his fingertip tapping his chin. "Yes… You will remain in Faerie until Princess Cirelle no longer resides in my home, at which point you return here to Arraven. In exchange, you will be your princess's attendant and bodyguard during your stay."

A lump formed in Lydia's throat. *Yes.* He was giving her exactly what she wanted, and phrasing it as if it was his own request. She couldn't ask for better luck.

And once she was in Faerie, once she knew Cirelle was safe, Lydia would question him on the Key.

Now, after a short journey through parts of Faerie, she stood in the lavish foyer of Ellian's dark and beautiful fae mansion. Cirelle greeted her in trousers and a loose linen shirt, clean but common. She looked healthy enough, practically glowing with an energy she hadn't possessed in Arraven. Not for years.

The princess hurled herself at Lydia, her arms wrapping tightly. "What are you doing here?"

"I asked to come. For you."

"Oh, Lydia… you made it safely. And the pox? Aidan—Briere—"

"Both cured. Both safe. The horn worked. Arraven purged the plague from our streets, throughout the whole kingdom. We even sent barrels of the healing water down the river to soothe your disgruntled suitors."

At the mention of her suitors, the princess's eyes darted guiltily to the faerie, then back to Lydia. Cirelle's cheeks flushed. Ellian's lips thinned into a frown and something dark flashed across his features.

Oh no.

No.

Surely not.

Lydia opened her mouth to say something, but Cirelle cut her off. "Are the suitors… handling my disappearance well?"

"From what Aidan told me, both kingdoms have agreed to postpone the treaty, but they'll want to sign and complete it the moment you return."

The princess's shoulders slumped.

Ellian cleared his throat. His tone was brusque. "I'm certain you both have plenty of catching up to do. Cirelle, help her find a room—your choice—and prepare her for her three-day guest period. She and I will dine together tonight."

Something dark and challenging flared in Cirelle's expression. "You can't—"

"I'll see you tomorrow in the Archive," the faerie interrupted her. They shared a long, tense stare, communicating something Lydia couldn't decipher before he turned to ascend the steps and slip through a door.

Cirelle watched him go, cheeks aflame, fists clenched at her sides.

"Er…" Lydia asked. "What was that about?"

The princess opened her mouth, only to gasp like a fish for a few seconds, turn a brilliant shade of red, then heave out a sigh and shake her head. "Nothing."

"Are you all right? What's going on?"

"Just faerie bullshit," Cirelle muttered.

Lydia blinked in shock, but the princess shook her head with a huff. "It'll be ok. I'll deal with him later. Just come with me. I'll get you settled and you can take a bath before supper."

Cirelle led her through halls dim and dark, but clean, not a cobweb in sight. The lights flickered on and off as they passed through, like they were being followed by a ghost. "You seem… well," she ventured quietly as they walked.

"Well enough," the princess said. "My tasks aren't terribly onerous, and will be even less so with your assistance. For your first three days, though, you're just a visitor, not a servant."

Lydia grimaced. "I'm not certain I wish to be a friendly guest of the creature that abducted you, Your Highness."

Cirelle waved a hand. "He's not so bad." Again, that pretty little blush, and she turned away. "He's still a faerie though, so watch your words tonight. There's—" A choked little sound slipped from her, then another painful silence before she puffed out a frustrated breath. "Just be careful."

"You say he's not terrible, then warn me to be cautious in the same breath, Your Highness. Which is it?"

Cirelle laughed. "You never have been afraid to call me out, have you? Truly, you're in no danger of real harm, not with Ellian, no matter how he puffs himself up and acts all aloof and mysterious. But he's still a sidhe, and he can't help that nature cropping up now and then. Especially when you're both taking each other's measure. Oh! And don't say 'thank you' if he passes you the salt or something. If you thank a faerie, it leaves you in their debt. Ah, here we are." She arrived at a door and cracked it open. A lush parlor lay on the other side, in shades of sea foam and teal. Cirelle smiled. "Mine's next door. Your bedroom is across the hall too, right beside mine."

This wasn't a room for a guard. This was a chamber appointed for a visiting duchess. "I… I can't take this, Your Highness."

"Nonsense. It's not being used otherwise, and wouldn't you rather stay near me?" Cirelle's smile was sly.

Lydia groaned. The princess was right. Best to stay close, in this haunted manor of silence and shadows. "Fine."

"Besides, this wardrobe is mostly trousers and shirts, not gowns. I've stolen a few, but there's plenty more, and most of them will fit you better anyway." Cirelle showed her the bathing room and the enchanted spout that poured water into the tub, along with the closet and the sidebar that always held water and the makings for tea, or treats left by the brownies. "That's who maintains the place," Cirelle explained, "a crew of these small fae, paid in bowls of cream and plenty of sweets. Gentle, but not terribly chatty. They prefer to do their tasks and otherwise keep to themselves in their wing past the dining rooms."

She left Lydia to bathe, with the admonition that Lydia could dress down later, but should show well tonight or it might be seen as an insult. Then the princess went across the hall to prepare the bedchamber. She waved aside all of Lydia's protests that such a thing was improper.

After a bath, Lydia took Cirelle's advice and donned some of the nicer clothing in the wardrobe, black trousers and a jacket of mauve velvet over a cream-colored shirt. The jacket was a little loose in the shoulders, but otherwise fit passably well. She braided her long blonde hair in a simple tail and tugged on a gleaming pair of boots. If this wasn't fancy enough for the faerie, too bad. She already felt out of place, and wasn't about to toss

on some gown. Lydia had never in her life worn velvet before. It felt stifling, too hot, too ostentatious.

Dinner alone with Ellian. Should she ask about the Key, what he might want in exchange for any information he had on its whereabouts? Or was it too soon to strike another pact?

Worse, her gut twisted at the way he and Cirelle had shared that look before he left, how the princess had blushed when she spoke of him…

No. Lydia shook her head. Surely her imagination was getting away from her. Still, a dark, poisonous feeling bloomed in her chest. It wouldn't be the first time Lydia had needed to save the princess from herself. When they were children, she'd always been the one to deflate Cirelle's schemes before they exploded in her face.

Except for that mess with Briere… but the princess still didn't know Lydia was aware of that. A chance moment atop the west wall, hearing muffled giggles, only to look below and see the princess and the countess climbing out a window and down a tree. She'd followed, heartsick at the reckless risk Cirelle took with such wild antics, or with those stolen kisses she and Briere shared.

Lydia had watched over the princess ever since, a silent shadow, a guardian spirit. But then she'd failed when it mattered most and let Cirelle be stolen away to Faerie, into the clutches of a sly sidhe. Lydia had seen firsthand what a pretty smile could do to the princess. What poison had this creature filled Cirelle's head with?

No, he couldn't be trusted. Lydia wouldn't ask him about the Key just yet. She would treat this like a soldier. Take the lay of the land, survey the battlefield, learn of her opponent's strengths. And hopefully his weaknesses.

She stared longingly at her blades, lying in their sheaths on a side table, but suspected carrying a weapon to supper was a faux pas the faerie would not permit. She was surprised he'd even slipped up enough to allow steel into his home. Iron was deadly poison to faeries after all, and steel along with it.

With a last deep breath, she crossed the hall to the bedchamber. Cirelle stood by the bed, fluffing one of too many pillows.

"Lydia!" She chirped cheerfully. "You look lovely! That color suits you."

"I… thank you, Your Highness." Heat crept into Lydia's cheeks. Damn, she'd missed that smile.

Cirelle didn't seem to notice. "Well, it's nearly suppertime. The bells should ring any minute." Her bright expression fell, the shimmer leaving her voice. "I'll lead you to the dining room."

Heart in her throat, Lydia followed.

Fourteen

Ellian swept into the dining chamber to find the guard already seated. She'd dressed well, and he detected Cirelle's hand in that.

The soldier certainly seemed genuine enough. The softness in her smile when she looked upon the princess was a dead giveaway. Perfect. He couldn't keep relying on Shai to guard her when he could not.

From time to time, Ellian and Cirelle had shared anecdotes or amusing stories of their pasts, and this woman's name cropped up in more than a few of those tales. Cirelle spoke of her as a loyal friend, perhaps a bit too serious for her own good, but honorable.

Certainly that much was true, if this woman was willing to come to Faerie just to protect her liege.

But Ellian hadn't survived this long by trusting appearances or taking things at face value. After showing Lydia her cloak of camouflage and giving her the earring to translate faerie languages—the same tools loaned to all of his assistants during their service—the food arrived.

Like her princess, Lydia poked at the food warily until Ellian assured her it was safe, free from magic or poisons. Even then, she seemed reluctant, but took a cautious bite.

"You should try the wine," he urged. The usual routine. The food was not enspelled, but the enchanted summerwine was another matter. This was a similar concoction to the one he'd dosed his coterie with, the one that Kith had slipped Ellian instead. Imbibing it unlocked hidden desires and motives. With Cirelle, there had been the surprising effect of her rather brazen affections. Declined at the time, of course, not while she was under the sway of that wine.

But right now, he desperately needed to know if this woman was as straightforward as she seemed, if she was to live under his roof while they continued their search for the Lock.

Lydia lifted the glass, watching the way the faerie spirits shimmered in the light. She frowned, then set it aside. "No, tha—I'd prefer not to."

So. Lydia had been warned about thanking faeries. A pity. He could have used that.

He also gritted his teeth at her refusal. She was not the first to decline the wine, and he suspected she would not be the last. But his plans for the Lisovyk mission were gaining momentum, and he didn't have time to play a second card in this game, or the third, and certainly not the fourth.

Lydia's blatant dislike of him wafted off her like a perfume. He had to know why. Mere distrust of the fae? Protectiveness over her princess? Or something more sinister?

Four years ago, he'd invited a human woman here as a servant. Paloma. She'd drunk deeply of the summerwine and overplayed her hand by trying to slide a sharpened iron hairpin between his ribs. The woman had wanted his hoard of treasures for her own. Sloppy with drink, her attempt had been avoidable, though the mistake left him with a small scar on his collarbone.

Paloma had spent the rest of her months of service locked

in a set of rooms in his manor, food slipped through a slot in the door. It was a luxurious prison, but a jail cell nonetheless.

He didn't want to do that to someone Cirelle loved, but neither could he trust someone with malice in their eyes, no matter how much she tried to hide it.

So he provided no other beverage. She would drink the wine or she would go thirsty for now. Water and tea awaited her in her parlor, in accordance with hospitality. The woman would not die of it.

"Cirelle has mentioned you," he said smoothly. He caught one agitated fingertip tapping on the tabletop and forced it to still.

"Her *Highness*—" Lydia emphasized the title, "—and I have been friends since we were young."

She offered no more, her shoulders stiff.

"Is it odd, in Arraven, for a princess and a mere soldier to be close?"

There, a twitch in her cheek.

Lydia finished a bite of stew and reached for the wine instinctively, then pulled her hand away from the glass before lifting it. "It's not common, but not unheard of."

Frustration washed over Ellian, and he made sure to lock that silver glamour over his eyes. He'd get nowhere with idle pleasantries. Time to increase the heat. "It's quite courageous," he said, "to follow your princess into the unknown. Not every guard would be so brave."

Lydia gave him a terse smile, but her pale cheeks flushed crimson. "I'm not every guard."

He cocked his head. "Does she know how you feel about her?"

"I don't know what you mean. I'm pledged to the crown, so I came." And yet she seemed altogether too focused on her plate,.

A faint tingle on his pinky from the ring that detected lies. Not a full untruth, that, but not the whole truth either.

Had Cirelle noticed the depth of Lydia's relief upon seeing her well and safe, or truly realized what those joyful tears meant? Or was the princess oblivious to the signs that seemed so clear to him? When Lydia had begged him to come here, to be with Cirelle, there'd been a strained desperation in the plea.

This feinting had gone on long enough. He needed her off-balance if he was to get anything from her. Truth had a way of slipping out in moments of anger. So he watched her closely as he said, "You love her."

The woman's head snapped up, her eyes meeting his own with a fire blazing in their depths. She set her fork down with a clatter. After a long, heavy silence, she said, "As much as anyone loves a friend."

"Friend." Ellian sharpened the word like a knife. He'd never had a problem sharing lovers before, but the woman's distaste for him set him on edge. Honorable, Cirelle had called her. And what would an oh-so-protective, honor-bound soldier do, should she find that Ellian had welcomed Cirelle into his bed? That he'd cuckolded Cirelle's suitors?

"Friend. No more and no less," Lydia said stiffly, pushing her plate away. "And what are you, to her?" Sparks flew with the words. Anger, disdain, suspicion. "Don't think I didn't see that look you shared."

Of course. Cirelle had never been coy with him when it came to mentioning her past lovers or her appetites. If this woman was truly close with the princess, she'd know that.

Would admitting his relationship with Cirelle be enough to push Lydia to violence? Uncertain. He didn't know this woman well enough to predict her reaction, but he didn't like the fanatical gleam in her eyes right now.

It was possible he'd welcomed a disaster into his home.

And yet… he needed Lydia. The visit to the Mosul was a few days away, and he wouldn't take the princess out of the manor without protection. Shai was unavailable, and Cirelle had huffed and moped and pined over it.

He hated how much it stung to see her miserable.

But this woman was relentless. "What lies have you fed her?"

"Fae cannot lie," he said. "There's little need for anger. In this moment, we both want the same thing. Cirelle kept safe and sound. And that's what I ask of you in your time here. Will you protect her with your life, if it comes to it?"

The reply was instantaneous, certain. "Yes." A pause. "Even if it's from you."

Nothing from his ring. Truth.

Danger, but truth.

"Good. Because I have a task for you. Soon I will make a trek out into Faerie. I wish to bring Cirelle with me, but I want someone who will watch over her."

"Leave her here."

"I've given her my oath that she can attend, if I secure protection."

"Then I refuse protection."

"There are others I can ask. I do this as a courtesy to you. If you refuse, you will stay here." None of that was technically a lie. He could ask Shai, even though he knew the warrior was unavailable at that time. Not on the anniversary of Hiea's death. And if Lydia refused, both she and Cirelle would have to remain at the manor, no matter how it crushed the princess's spirit to do so.

The guard hissed in a breath, her shoulders bunching and fists clenching. "You endanger her."

"That's what you're for. Wouldn't you rather be the one at her side, to watch over her?"

She closed her eyes and nodded. "Fine. I'll go. But this meal is over." She pushed her chair back from the table.

Ellian set down his own fork. "I'll show you the way to your room." Though she looked ready to protest, he added, "I insist." He walked her back in tense silence. The brownies had informed him that Cirelle selected the room next to hers. Of course.

The guard slammed her door shut without so much as a good-night.

Ellian turned to walk back, but Cirelle's door was cracked ever-so-slightly. Listening for the jingle of his silvery boots, perhaps? Cirelle wouldn't know Lydia had refused the wine. Was she waiting to see if he seduced Lydia into a kiss?

He stopped just outside the barely-open door, keeping his voice low. "Expecting a show, princess?"

She opened the crack wider, affixing him with one of her most potent glares. "You didn't—"

"Let me in," he interrupted, "and we can talk." Where he didn't risk the guard opening her own door and overhearing. The walls were thick enough he didn't worry about noise traveling with the doors closed.

The princess scowled, but stepped back and gestured him inside, shutting the door behind him. "I can't believe you cursed me!" She spat. "I tried to tell her about the wine, but I couldn't. Just like Toben. How did you even do that, without my permission?"

Ellian stepped into the center of the room, away from her ire. "The enchantment is on the earring."

"I—You—" she turned a rather alarming shade of scarlet, her fists clenched and heaving in angry breaths.

"She didn't drink the wine."

The princess grinned. "Ha!"

"She's… rather formidable," he admitted. "But I came here to ask for a promise. You can't tell her about… about *us*."

Cirelle affixed him with a look he couldn't quite interpret. "Ashamed of me, faerie?"

"She seems… protective."

A soft rasp of a laugh. "Well, that's a fair assessment."

"I don't want to risk her doing something rash."

"Like what?"

"For one? Stabbing me in my sleep with the steel blades I allowed her to bring into my home, on the intent that she use them to protect you rather than murder me."

"Lydia wouldn't do that."

"Are you so certain of it, if she feels it's her duty to save you from the scheming faerie that seduced you?"

"First off, I did my own share of the seducing," she said before her grin faded into a grimace. "But I see your point. Lydia is a bit, er, enthusiastic about my virtue. When I was eleven, she broke a boy's nose for trying to kiss me as part of a game."

Ellian stepped forward, lifting a hand close to her cheek, hesitating just before touching her skin. "Please. Until I know more of her, I need you to keep this secret."

Cirelle sighed and leaned into his touch, taking his other hand in her own. "I hate lying to her. But I won't tell her." She chewed her lip. "I promise."

He wanted to thank her for it, a human instinct he'd never quite squashed completely. But a faerie thanked no one. Instead he tugged her into his arms. She came willingly, smelling of lilacs and burying her face in his shoulder.

He stroked her hair and sighed, and wondered what sort of new tangle he'd gotten himself into.

Fifteen

To Cirelle's relief, the rest of Lydia's three-day guest period was uneventful. The memory of Cirelle's first tumultuous days seemed so distant now, like a half-remembered dream. She'd had her first taste of fae brutality when Orwe's lifeless body had been left on Ellian's doorstep, and in return for her spitefulness and insults, Ellian had stolen Cirelle's memory of her first kiss with her first love, Briere.

Ellian and Lydia took meals together, while Cirelle ate in the garden or her rooms, but in the hours after her Archive duties, Cirelle would spend the time catching up with her old friend.

It had been years since they'd been able to sit at any length in idle chat. It seemed a strange luxury, free time to spend in one another's company. Sometimes, like tonight, Cirelle would strum a tune in the music parlor while they both reminisced about days long past.

"Remember the time you shoved the cook's boy into the creek?" Cirelle laughed. "What was his name?"

"Niaf," Lydia's lip quirked in a small smirk. She shrugged. "He accused us of cheating at Kingsring."

Cirelle flushed. "Um, I *was* cheating."

Lydia blinked, then snorted a laugh. "Well, he was an ass anyway."

"That he was. I missed that, you know. Your honesty. The noble ladies are all too scared to tell me no, save my mother. I've missed my voice of reason."

Lydia picked at a loose thread on her sleeve. "No insult meant, but you didn't often listen, Your Highness. I wager here in Faerie it may be much the same. Voice of reason I may be, but you still make your choices."

Guilt swallowed Cirelle for the secret of her dalliances with Ellian. It was all too easy to picture the look of strained horror that would fall over the guard's face if she knew. So Cirelle kept her promise to Ellian and held her tongue.

At the end of Lydia's three days as a guest, the guardswoman was surprised to learn her duties would be a clerk's tasks. "But… Your Highness," Lydia reluctantly said as she stared down at the tight ledger lines written in Trade, "I only have my basic Arravene letters, and I cannot read or write Trade." A small, bitter spark flickered in Lydia's eyes, and her cheeks flared brilliant pink.

Cirelle winced. She'd forgotten that guards could learn letters, but only if they wanted to. Lydia had preferred to spend the hours on swordplay instead. "Well," Cirelle pointed out, "We've an entire library and hours' worth of free time a day. What better time to learn? I'll help you."

"That is unseemly, Your Highness."

"What? A princess tutoring? Just like a princess dusting shelves for hours on end?" Cirelle waved a hand. "What about a trade? If I teach you to read and write, will you show me how to use these?" She lifted one of the claimhte from their shelf. Shai had dropped off the sheaths a few days before Lydia's arrival, in exchange for a musical performance.

She drew the blade and tilted it, admiring the way the light gleamed off the polished metal. It tingled and chilled her finger-tips as always, and she almost fancied she could hear the whisper of a midnight breeze in her ears.

Lydia stepped forward, holding out her hand toward the dagger, but Cirelle sheathed it quickly and set it back on the shelf. Some possessive urge snarled at the idea of anyone—even Lydia—handling the knives.

The guard looked wary. "What are those?"

"They're mine," Cirelle admitted. "I… found them, more or less."

"But you don't know how to use them. You don't need to."

"I might, here. Teach me."

"Your Highness…"

"Please, Lydia." Cirelle lifted her chin. "Don't make me turn it into a decree. Right now, I'm asking as your friend."

Lydia stood stiffly but sighed. "Yes, Your Highness."

"Good. We'll start both lessons tomorrow after our duties."

The next day in the library, Cirelle pinched the bridge of her nose as a headache threatened. When it came to reading and writing, Lydia was a determined learner, but her pace was frus-tratingly slow for Cirelle's limited patience. They commandeered a corner of the library for their lessons, pulling books written in Trade and piling up sheets upon sheets of Lydia's practice writing. When they'd spent two hours repeating the basic Trade letters and the guardswoman seemed ready to set fire to all of it, they switched to swordplay in the garden. Cirelle dug up some wooden practice daggers from a dusty room of storage and Lydia showed her a few stances and basic defense moves.

"You're holding back," Cirelle accused after Lydia landed a light blow on her shoulder.

"Of course I am, Your Highness. I'm not going to bruise my princess."

"I'll bet Captain Timisen gave you a fair number of bruises."

That got a sharp laugh from the guard as she came in for the attack again. Cirelle lifted her practice blade, but it was too slow, too sloppy. Lydia's dull weapon prodded her gently on the shoulder. The soldier frowned. "Do it again. I'm not trying to rough you up. We're just working on building up your reflexes until the defensive moves become instinct. But it's no good. It takes too long. You *might* master a few of the defensive stances and maneuvers by the time we leave, but that would be all."

"Who knows?" Cirelle managed to nick Lydia's blade with her own, knocking it far enough off-course to avoid mock injury. "Maybe I'll be a prodigy. I could surprise you."

"It wouldn't be the first time," Lydia admitted, then nodded down at Cirelle's practice sword. "Again. Is your arm getting tired yet?"

The princess's blade wobbled with her shaking muscles, but she bared her teeth. "Not even a little. Keep going."

"Are you really sure this is necessary?" Cirelle grumbled as she pulled her booted foot out of ankle-deep muck for the umpteenth time. A disgusting slurry of mud, stagnant water, and algae coated her lower legs. Unable to extract herself from the sludge, she sighed and held out her hand for assistance. "A little help?"

"It is," Ellian assured her, pulling Cirelle out of the sucking sinkhole. "Necessary, that is." His arm wrapped around her waist, lifted her out of the puddle with a horrible slurping sound, and set her atop a fallen tree.

Behind her, Lydia avoided the puddle as she kept a wary eye out for any danger, one hand hovering at the hilt of a dagger. She kept her silence at Cirelle and Ellian's good-natured bickering, but her lips were stuck in a perpetual half-grimace.

Cirelle futilely tried to wipe mud off her boot using the bark of the fallen log. She was certain the stench of the swamp had seeped into every fiber of her clothes, every strand of her hair by now. "When we get home, I'm telling the brownies to toss this outfit in the midden heap."

Ellian chuckled, leading the way again. With a huff of protest, Cirelle stepped off the log and followed.

"I'd have thought," he said with dry amusement, "that you were used to dirt after dusting the Archive twice a week."

"Dust and mud are two very different things."

"Noted. I will remind you that I encouraged you to stay at the manor several times, but you absolutely insisted you had to come along."

"You promised." Once Lydia had agreed to come, Ellian was bound. He'd given Cirelle his word: if he secured protection for the princess, she could tag along.

The claimhte, however, still lay in the Archive, at both Ellian and Lydia's insistence. It was a rare sight to see them a united front; even in parlor games when they were sorted into a team, the two could never seem to work in tandem. But in this, they both shook their heads. "You don't know enough of swordplay yet," the guard protested, and Ellian agreed. So Cirelle had huffed, but left the knives behind.

It didn't stop the faint keening in her head, like a dog's distant whine to be let out of its kennel and hunt. To distract herself, she asked, "How much farther until we reach this Mosul, anyway?"

"Not much longer."

Cirelle barely sidestepped another puddle of sludge, half-hidden underneath algae and moss. "And he's the only one who can give you what you need?"

While he'd been in the throes of planning his Thieves' Night heist, Ellian had passed off the plotting of the next phase to Issen. Ellian had confessed that is attempts to track down the Lock's location ended in the same place. The Lisovyk was the last recorded creature to possess the Lock. In less than a fortnight, when the moons and stars aligned just so, the Lisovyk's hidden forest would be open to anyone from sunset until dawn.

But first, they had to acquire something they could trade.

Hence their trek through this godsforsaken swamp. Cirelle sighed as she brushed by a sticky plant, its slime smearing along the back of her hand. "There isn't anyone who lives in a nice, dry grassland or on some lovely rolling hills who owns something the Lisovyk wants?"

Ellian cast a wary glance at Lydia, but Cirelle didn't care. She had promised not to tell Lydia what she and Ellian did between the sheets after the guard went to sleep, but she wouldn't let him keep her friend in the dark about everything.

He frowned. "If the seeds were plentiful, the Lisovyk wouldn't need one so badly. There." He pointed up ahead.

And in the middle of this miserable sludge stood a house on stilts, algae crawling halfway up the stone posts. The house itself was a cozy little cottage, made of red brick and topped with a ceramic roof. Nothing that would rot in the hot damp of this awful place.

When they knocked on the door, the faerie who answered was surprisingly nonthreatening. To all appearances, the Mosul seemed little more than a wizened old man. The hair on his scalp all seemed to have migrated to his chin in a long beard of yellowish-gray. Liver spots dotted his wrinkled skin, but his eyes shone clear. Once, it seemed he'd been a tall man, but his back now stooped with the years he'd borne. Only his softly pointed ears gave him away for a faerie.

"Ellian!" The man greeted them with a wide smile and a cackling laugh. His eyes landed on Cirelle and Lydia, and he sketched a bow. "And two lovely young maidens, as well."

Half-covered in stinking muck and wearing her drab work clothes, Cirelle had not expected herself or Lydia to be called 'lovely maidens'. Cirelle returned the man's smile. "Pleased to meet you."

"Likewise," the man replied, gesturing them to sit. The cottage was small but comfortable. The furniture had a well-worn, patched look to it that spoke of much use over decades, maybe centuries. A shelf of books lined one wall, and a hearth of banked embers burned in the fireplace.

Cirelle couldn't help but notice that Ellian skirted wide around the hearth, taking the farthest seat. Lydia took a spot on a sofa at Cirelle's side.

"Tea?" The old man asked, filling a copper kettle from a pitcher and setting it on a rack over the coals before poking them to life. Ellian flinched when the fire sparked and flared, but Mosul didn't seem to notice.

While the old man fussed with the fireplace, Ellian caught Cirelle's eye, then shook his head in a tiny gesture.

Cirelle replied, "Um, I'm fine. No tea for me or for Lydia." She had to forcibly shut her mouth to stop from adding 'thank you'.

"I'll have some," Ellian added smoothly. After a few more niceties had been exchanged, they got to business.

"So why have you come here?" Mosul asked.

Ellian said simply, "We need the Lhyrria seed."

Cirelle was glad she hadn't accepted the tea. She'd have choked on it. "The what?" The Lhyrria, the ancient trees that anchored the magic of Faerie. Ellian had mentioned a seed, but she hadn't known it belonged to one of this realm's most sacred trees.

The sidhe shot her a warning glare and looked back at the Mosul. "I'm willing to trade." He withdrew a small velvet bag from his pouch, tugging it open to spill its contents onto his palm. Flat gray runestones, such as were used in Saedda for fortune telling.

"These belonged to Urisk," Ellian said, stirring them in his hand. "And before him, the Gray Lady."

Mosul's eyes widened, his lips parting. He closed his mouth with an audible click and swallowed. "Done." He stood and crossed to a shelf in the corner, plucking a rectangular wooden box from it. Like a carnival showman, he flipped the lid open and gestured to what lay within. A winged seed longer than Cirelle's hand, with a sparkling, silvery sheen. "A seed from the eldest Lhyrria."

Ellian nodded. "The rune stones for the seed. Agreed." The air shuddered, acknowledging the bargain, and just like that, the meeting was over. Mosul handed the seed's box to Ellian, where it disappeared back into the pouch.

The old faerie took the bag of rune stones and placed it on the new empty space on his shelf. "Safe travels."

"Until we meet again," Ellian nodded, then stepped out the door with Cirelle and Lydia on his heels.

Once they'd descended to the swampy ground, Cirelle asked. "So can you whoosh us back yet? I'm dying for a bath."

"Yes, please," Lydia added, still watching the trees warily. "I don't like the feel of this place."

Ellian shook his head. "Mosul keeps up a barrier. No world-walking within a mile of his cottage. We've got to walk out first."

"Oh, joy," Cirelle grumbled as she picked her way through the marsh.

Ellian reminded her, "we walked a mile in. You can wait a little longer for that bath." That teasing smile was back, accompanied by eyes so startlingly blue in this swamp of browns and mossy greens.

Cirelle wanted to ask him if he'd help her wash up, but she couldn't, not while Lydia glowered behind her. Instead she sighed and narrowly avoided another puddle covered in tiny, round leaves. Cat's tails scraped against her knees, leaving bits of their fuzz all over her damp trousers.

Definitely throwing these clothes in the trash heap when we're done here.

"What about you?" she asked, pointing at his own damp and grubby clothing and recalling the way he'd always grimace at even a bit of sauce on a fingertip. "You can't possibly enjoy this. You hate getting dirty."

"I can also acknowledge when it's truly necessary. It's not my first time suffering the outdoors. The jungles of Kishir may not be the same as marshland, but crawling through thick vegetation will leave one just as filthy."

"Is that what you did?" Cirelle tried not to sound too intrigued, collecting bits of his history in scraps and pieces.

"Yes," he replied, forging ahead. "I was a scout in the army."

"You were a soldier?" Lydia asked cautiously from the rear of the party.

"Technically. I had little skill with a blade, but I was observant and had a good memory, so they set me to reconnaissance instead."

A good memory. An understatement, given Ellian's ability to recall anything with perfect clarity.

He'd mentioned the war before, but Cirelle hadn't prodded at the time. Now, she did. "You were in the Emperor's Army?"

Ellian stopped so suddenly that Cirelle almost walked into him. When he began moving again, his reply was quieter. "Not the Emperor's."

Past history lessons clicked into place. Kishir, Ellian's homeland, had suffered an uprising around the time he'd have been just reaching adulthood. She knew that already, but hadn't put the pieces together until now.

"You were part of the rebellion."

"More accurately, my brother and sister were part of the rebellion, and I tagged along to keep them safe." He made a small sound like he would have said more, but shook his head and fell silent. The same brother and sister who later perished in the fire that left Ellian with permanent scars.

"I'm sorry," Cirelle murmured, and they walked in silence for a while.

Eventually, Ellian broke the heavy mood by remarking, "I will admit it *is* worth getting my own hands dirty to see a princess covered head-to-toe in swamp muck. It's going to take you an hour just to get the smell out of your hair."

"Hey!" Cirelle reached forward to smack him indignantly on the shoulder. "I swear when we get back I'm spending two hours in the bath and drinking an entire pitcher of ice-cold water. I have sweat in places you wouldn't believe."

Behind her, Lydia made a strangled sound at the impropriety of the statement, but Cirelle ignored it to watch Ellian grimace.

"What?" she asked. "Faeries sweat too, I've seen it. And you're telling me it's not—" Cirelle's words cut off with a yelp as something clutched at her ankle. She fell, windmilling her arms while the thing dragged her over the fallen log and closer to the edge of a murky pool.

Cirelle managed a single word as her foot was dragged into the warm, algae-covered pond. "Help!"

She scrabbled for something to hold onto, but the damp bark of the log crumbled under her fingers. For a terrified blink of an instant, Cirelle's eyes met Ellian's. He'd whirled at her outcry, eyes solid black as he called her name and lunged toward her. Behind her, Lydia shouted. The guard darted forward just in time to grasp Cirelle's hand, but it slipped loose, their hands wet from the muggy swamp air.

In less than a heartbeat, she was under the water. She struggled to find the surface, to gasp in a breath of air. But it was all reeds and muck.

Her lungs starting to burn, Cirelle clawed at the thing that held her ankle, nails sinking into something soft and putrid. Its grasp didn't loosen, and sharp teeth bit down hard on her hand. It seared and stung like fire. Cirelle screamed.

A fatal mistake. After her breath burst from her, Cirelle took an instinctive gasp. Brackish water flooded her mouth, green and rotten. It filled her lungs. Her whole body shrieked in pain, burning with the need for air, and the darkness claimed her.

ॐ

Time skipped. Cirelle awoke coughing, her throat scraped raw and her chest aflame. Strong hands rolled her onto her side, mud squishing beneath her. Algae-green swamp water exploded out of Cirelle's lungs and stomach in a bout of retching that left her limbs trembling.

"Stay with me, Your Highness." Lydia, her voice strained. She stood over Cirelle, dark ichor dripping from her bared blade.

Cirelle's hand was burning. It felt like the flesh had melted away, red-hot and filled with foulness. A circular row of bleeding tooth marks glared an angry red and purple, ringed in putrescent green.

Ellian swore in Kishi, lifting her hand in his own. Perhaps he tried to be gentle, but the faintest touch felt like a blade shearing off her skin, and she shrieked in pain.

Lydia hissed, "You're hurting her!"

Without another word, Ellian scooped her up in his arms, cradling Cirelle against his chest as he lurched through the woods, scrambling over fallen limbs and skirting puddles as quickly as possible. The crash and slosh of water behind him must be Lydia, keeping up.

Cirelle's arm was on fire now, too, and she welcomed un-consciousness when it came again.

Another jump in time. Cirelle awoke on a bed of cool grass. Not swamp moss, but clean, well-tended garden grass. Her entire arm was tingling to the shoulder, the burning settling into a throbbing, stinging sensation. Voices argued nearby, but Cirelle barely heeded them as she lifted her head to stare at her hand. Someone had cut her sleeve up to the shoulder, baring an arm that had blackened around the bite, blending to an angry red as it neared her shoulder.

"I don't 'have to' do anything," a sharp woman's voice bit off the words. "Not for her." It seemed familiar, but Cirelle couldn't tear her eyes from the arm that no longer seemed her own. It was a dead weight attached to her body, pulsing with pain but unmoving. She couldn't even wiggle her fingers.

"Name your price." Ellian, in a tight, agonized voice.

"Ellian." Cirelle croaked the name, throat scratchy and sore, turning her head the other way to look at him.

As she did, she realized where they were. That wolf statue nearby was all too familiar, surrounded by shrubs and night-blooming flowers. Ellian's garden, the moons shining high above. It seemed too pretty a place for the pain that wracked her, the scent of his roses too cloying.

Ellian loomed over Dirilai, who stood with her arms crossed. At Cirelle's hoarse rasp, he turned, rushing to kneel beside her. His glamour had vanished, those eyes burning like emeralds in the sunlight, ringed in deepest onyx. A faint, thin line of pink traced their center.

He was covered head-to-toe in swamp sludge, his hair hanging in limp, wet tangles around his face. Tiny bits of leaves clung to him all over. He watched Cirelle with a gaze so intense it tightened something in her chest, even through the pain that pulsed up and down her limp arm.

Ellian extended a hand to brush wet hair from her face, but stopped, curling his fingers and pulling them away.

Despite the pain, one thought flickered to mind. Ellian was here, and Dirilai, but… "Where's Lydia?"

A pause. "Safe. Under a brief sleep spell. She was… distraught." His hand lifted to touch his cheek, and for the first time Cirelle saw it was split, bleeding from a small cut and starting to swell. She followed his gaze to a bench where the soldier lay, eyes closed, chest rising and falling in slumber.

"Cirelle…" Ellian spoke again, his voice cracking. He turned to Dirilai again and repeated, "What do you want in exchange?"

Dirilai watched them both with cold eyes, emotionless as flakes of black stone. She cocked her head. "The Key."

"What?"

"The Key," she repeated, voice flat. "Will you give it to me, if it means her life?" Dirilai knelt to peer more closely at Cirelle's arm. "The venom spreads. She has perhaps another half hour." She stood, brushing off her knees. "So I suggest you either give me the Key or say your goodbyes."

Ellian's eyes met Cirelle's, sapphire blue and faded green and that pale pink spreading through both, before they darted back up to Dirilai. "I can't. Pick something else."

Dirilai shook her head, pitiless.

His voice was raw when he asked, "What would you do with the Key?"

"I won't tell you that. It's possible that I've gotten an amazing offer and I'll sell it away for my own ends. I could use it as a carrot to make the prince my pawn. Or perhaps I've found the Lock and want to see them both destroyed personally." She shook her head. "It doesn't matter, for the purposes of the bargain." Her eyes narrowed. "Will you give it up to spare her life?"

Cirelle knew the answer the moment Ellian looked down at her again, knew it before he uttered the words. Anguish haunted his eyes, sapphires and obsidian and spring carnations. He was silent for several long seconds.

Finally, he spoke. "I'm sorry." It was barely a whisper.

Agony blazed up Cirelle's arm, but she lacked the strength to do more than whimper. Ellian's words had pierced her worse.

He'll let me die, she thought, closing her eyes as tears down the sides of her temples. Her breath was fire in her lungs. To keep the Key safe, he'd do anything, sacrifice everything. He'd risked his own life for it, had lain his own dignity upon that altar, had let other members of his rebellion die for the cause. Now she would join Orwe and whomever came before him, forgotten soldiers in a war few knew even waged.

"Cirelle." Her name was a ragged gasp from his lips, a plea, a goodbye. It was difficult to breathe. She opened her eyes and saw his hand hovering above her good one. It would take only the slightest movement to brush his fingertips with her own.

She flinched away from it and turned aside as the panic shrieked through her.

I don't want to die.

But she would. And Ellian would watch it happen while Dirilai stood beside them, merciless.

Cirelle tilted her head up to the sunlit sky and imagined her Arravene stars there. She painted them in her memory, tracing their lines in her head.

"Divine Iska," she began the rite, hoping they were listening. There would be no priest to utter the words for her, so she spoke them herself. "Please guide my way and lead me to my home among your stars." Suddenly, another fear took hold of her. "Ellian," she said urgently. "You have to burn me, after. In my own world. I know you don't like fire, but it's the only way I can go home. Let Lydia take me back. She'll make sure the rites are followed." She had to rise as sparks, fly up to the heavens so her soul could find its place up there.

Wordlessly, Ellian nodded. His lips parted, and he took a long breath. Then something else washed over his face. "I…" he rasped the word softly, then paused.

Cirelle stared into those eyes and watched them flood with soft pink, the color of the dawn sky. Resolve washed over his expression, and peace. He gave her the slightest of nods and swallowed.

No.

He was going to do it.

Stars, Ellian was about to sacrifice the Key.

For her.

He sucked in a ragged breath, giving her a grim smile before he opened his mouth to speak.

"Oh for goodness' sake," Dirilai interrupted from behind him, unable to see Ellian's expression. "Move over." She nudged him with one bare foot.

"What?" Ellian snapped.

"I can't heal her if your shadow breaks the moonlight, idiot. Go stand over there."

Cirelle's heart skipped a beat, and she wasn't sure if it were the poison or Dirilai's words that did it.

In shocked silence, Ellian stood and strode over to the edge of the clearing. Cirelle kept her eyes on him as Dirilai said over her shoulder, "The Endless Rose, that's what I want for it."

Ellian's response was instantaneous. "Yes." The air shivered.

Dirilai leaned over Cirelle, still scowling. "Do I have your permission to heal you, girl?"

"Yes," Cirelle rasped as relief flooded her. She locked gazes with Ellian even as Dirilai began to dance around her.

Stricken, that was the word for the look on Ellian's face. She'd never seen him like this. Not after he'd seen and buried Orwe's body, not when the prince had shown up at his home.

His eyes flickered through every color. Black and cobalt and emerald, pink and pale green. Ellian kept his arms wrapped around himself, as if they held him in place. His mouth was a tight, tense line, his brows drawn together.

And Dirilai danced, weaving threads of light into a pattern that followed her every motion. From within the circle, it was a dizzying sensation, those silvery strands criss-crossing over Cirelle like a spider's web.

Then it was over. Dirilai knelt and pressed her hands lightly against Cirelle's skin. A stinging burn jolted through her, there and gone in a flash. Sensation returned to her arm, and Cirelle yanked it up to her chest, probing it with her other hand only to find it hale and whole. No sign of the poison.

Dirilai stood and scrambled out of the way as Ellian once more rushed to Cirelle's side. Later, Cirelle would wonder if he'd have taken her in his arms if he could. But at that moment, all she felt was a giddy, near-intoxicating joy at being alive.

And she was haunted by the awestruck, gentle look on Ellian's face as he stared at her with rosy eyes.

He'd been ready to do it.

All his planning, the sacrifices he'd made, gone in a blink to save her.

He reached toward her now, her name almost a whisper. "Cirelle."

"No." She shook her head. She couldn't face this, not right now. "I… I need to be alone for a while."

Hurt spread over his features, but Ellian withdrew, leaving her to find her way to her room.

Seventeen

CIRELLE AWOKE AS DUSK FELL. She lay staring at the ceiling while her stomach turned in queasy knots at the thought of Ellian's rosy, pained gaze upon her, ready to utter the words that would doom years of planning.

But then again, maybe she was mistaken. In her first days at the manor, Cirelle had witnessed the brutal consequences of Ellian's mission. His enemies at the Unseelie Court had left him a gruesome gift, the beaten and bruised corpse of one of his allies.

By inviting her into his confidence and his plots, Ellian offered her a double-edged sword of risk, too. He'd been open about how much this mission meant to him. Keeping the gates between Faerie and the mortal realm open was more important than any single life. Even hers.

She must have been imagining things. There was no way Ellian would let the Key fall into other hands, not for anything. Not for her, certainly. And yet she couldn't even take comfort in avoiding him. Tonight was their usual hour of dance.

She wasn't sure how she'd explain that to Lydia.

Oh stars, *Lydia*. That cut and bruise on Ellian's cheek had to have come from the soldier, though he hadn't said so in as many words. What punishment would Ellian take from the woman for daring to strike him, even if it was in a panic?

That thought was enough to urge Cirelle out of bed and into the hall. She found Lydia sitting against the wall between their doors, asleep.

"Lydia!"

The guard startled, then scrambled to stand, pulling Cirelle into a hurried embrace. "Thank Raigen," she said. "Ellian wouldn't let me in the room. Put a spell on the door and everything, said you needed rest."

"I… are you all right? After you hit him, did he…?"

Lydia grimaced. "I'm forbidden from studying my letters for a fortnight, and I'm on bread and water rations for as long. Not even tea."

"That… that's it?" It was a feeble sentence for assaulting a faerie. This would mark the second time he'd let Lydia off the hook, considering she'd drawn steel on him at their very first meeting.

The guard shrugged. "Certainly worth it."

They took breakfast in Cirelle's parlor, Lydia eating her bread and noting that at least it was fresh, though a dollop of butter wouldn't have hurt. Cirelle felt guilty eating her sliced fruit and flaky pastry, but Lydia assured her it was fine.

Cirelle, for her part, was all too willing to avoid Ellian until they danced. What would she say to him? Could she ask him whether he'd been ready to destroy all his plans for her? Though it stung to think he'd let her die, the alternative was a more terrifying prospect.

If he'd been willing to sacrifice all of his plans for her, that meant there was far more than she'd thought to these dances, to their bedroom games.

As she and Lydia finished sweeping the Archive, Cirelle was

forced to confess the truth of the dances to Lydia. "I… er… I won't be able to spend time with you tonight," she said, feeling her cheeks warm. "Weeks ago, I lost a wager to Ellian. A card game. And now every fortnight, we have to dance together in the ballroom for an hour."

Lydia's expression grew ever more sour with each word. "Your Highness…"

"I know. It was stupid. But a bargain is a bargain. Especially with a faerie." Cirelle tucked the broom away in a closet and made her escape. "I'll see you tomorrow." She fled Lydia's disapproval before the guard could say another word.

Standing in the center of her large closet, Cirelle debated what to wear. Something bold and powerful? Another of those sultry fae numbers, burying her doubts between the sheets? In the end, she settled on a demure Arravene gown that required a brownie to help her into it. One that would not be easy to remove. Until she'd sorted through her own doubts, there would be no flirtation, no kisses. She pinned her hair up, to avoid tempting Ellian into caressing it, and smeared a dark, berry-colored stain on her lips.

In the ballroom, Ellian waited for her as always, the enchanted astralir playing a solemn vespane. He stood straight, shoulders back and chin up. A gray glamour over his eyes masked his emotions.

That invisible wall around him sent a shiver down her spine. It meant he, too, had something to hide. But was it his guilt at nearly letting her die, or something else entirely?

The second the doors shut, the words burst from her. "Would you have done it?"

Ellian's throat bobbed as he swallowed. Silence held as a war waged behind his eyes.

"You promised me truth, if I asked a question about me

or the Key." She cleared her throat and repeated the question. "Would you have given her the Key?"

He didn't flinch, didn't look away, but pain left his face taut. "Yes."

"Wh—"

"Be certain you want that knowledge. If you ask, I cannot refuse it."

She already knew. The anguish in his expression gave it all away. Still, a terrible compulsion forced her to ask. She'd tumbled off this cliff and couldn't stop falling. "Why?"

His voice cracked on the words, a sharp-edged, bitter laugh bursting from him. His hands clenched into fists. "Because damn me for it, but I think I'm falling in love with you."

Cirelle couldn't breathe, couldn't think. The edges of her vision went black. No. This couldn't be happening. This wasn't what she'd wanted. Kisses and teasing and sex, that was one thing. She'd never agreed to this. It had only been half a year, for stars' sake!

Too terrifying, the thought of a faerie's affection, that word on his lips. *Love.*

It was too much.

The pity and regret and sorrow in Ellian's voice was overwhelming. "I'm sorry. I know you don't…" His voice caught.

Cirelle tried to suck in breaths and failed, rasping, "I can't do this."

"I know. But you asked, and I must answer truthfully."

No. Cirelle shook her head. *I wish I didn't know this. I shouldn't have pushed.*

Then a dark, painful idea came to her. "Take it away. The memory. Take away Dirilai asking for the Key, and this whole conversation. Use one of those memory jars."

"I… I can't."

Her chest a painful roil of anger and hurt and fear, Cirelle strode forward, and shoved him hard, forcing him back a step. She bared her teeth and did it again. "Now can you? Have I earned punishment enough?"

His glamour fell, his eyes a shocked shade of canary, then gleaming angry orange. "No."

She lifted her hand to strike him, but he caught her wrist. "Cirelle…"

Her name, whispered so softly, so gently, so painfully, it broke her. She wept, even as she clutched at his shirt and buried her face in it. "I can't. I can't know this. You *have* to take it away. Please."

Ellian held her in his arms, chin resting atop her head. "All right."

A few minutes later, they sat in a parlor, a memory jar between them. A scrap of her shirt from last night lay in the jar, still coated with swamp muck.

She blinked away ragged tears as Ellian sat across from her, tucking something into the pouch at his side. Wait. Where was she? She recalled shoving him. She'd been upset over… something. But what? For dragging her through the swamp last night? For nearly getting her killed? But it had all turned out fine. He'd traded some artifact to Dirilai. The Something Rose.

"I'm sorry," she apologized, feeling raw and stretched thin as she wiped dampness from her cheek. "What were we doing?"

"We were about to dance," he said, holding out his hand. "Though I'll make it an easy evening. No Durlish reels tonight. Last night was hard on you."

There. A flicker of something behind his flat glamour.

She did feel a bit dizzy. Still recovering from the poisoning? Maybe Dirilai's healing hadn't quite restored her to full health after all.

She nodded. "All right then, it's a deal."

Ellian didn't have the heart to take Cirelle to bed after their dance, though she tried her best to convince him.

"You were just healed," he told her. "Take it easy for a night or two."

She'd rolled her eyes and grinned. "Fine, but I expect you to make up for it later."

He'd watched her walk away, then made his way to a study in his private wing, tucking the memory jar in the corner of a shelf lined with mementos of his human life. He didn't dare place it in the Archive or mark the jar in his ledger.

Then, with a heavy heart, he made his way to a cold, empty bed.

He told himself it was for the best, in the days following. He hadn't planned this. Had tried his best to avoid it, in fact. But through all of her flaws, despite his best efforts, something about this woman had burrowed beneath his skin. Saying it out loud last night had been like a knife to the gut, the words making it seem so much more real. That was his burden to bear, though, not hers. It would only wound her, the knowing. For a brief moment, his heart had been laid bare before Cirelle, and she'd fled as fast and far as she could go.

That knowledge was like a constant splinter buried under his skin, but it was one he could endure. He'd felt worse grief.

And yet he couldn't refuse Cirelle's advances forever. If he rebuffed her for too long, she'd only ask more questions. Worse, she might turn those doubts inward and punish herself for it. He'd seen the bleak moods that gripped her sometimes. The first night she'd kissed him, Cirelle had been in the depths of one of those spells, her self-hatred burning hot and deep.

He wouldn't be the cause of one of those bouts of despair.

After a few nights, when Cirelle insisted she was well and healed, his will crumbled at her touch. In truth, it was no different than before. Burying those feelings deep, squashing them down, all while drinking in the sound of her giddy laugh as he brushed a ticklish spot on her arm.

It mattered little that this meant something different to her. It still brought her joy, and that was enough.

Or at least he told himself.

When the tenure of Lydia's punishment was over, she resumed her reading lessons with the princess and the three of them returned to taking meals together. Though admittedly, suppers had become less flirtatious and heated after the soldier arrived. Even so, the woman watched them both with a hawk's gaze, and he wondered how much she suspected. She'd hinted as much, that first night.

Well, he'd not give Lydia the fuel to confirm such worries. In her presence, he and Cirelle were allies and nothing more.

Meanwhile, the mission to the Lisovyk's woodland approached, Issen's plan coming together. Lydia was not allowed in Ellian's meetings, and though he'd asked Cirelle not to reveal his plans, her loose tongue on the Mosul visit left him concerned. Lydia was here for one thing and one thing only, to protect Cirelle. He'd not have another wrinkle added to his plans or his missions, not now.

Yet there was little to do until the day of the Lisovyk mission arrived only mere days from now. It would be risky with only Issen accompanying him, but Shai would be an ill fit for stealth and he still didn't trust the rest of his coterie. The truth potion had been a disaster, and no other good opportunity had presented itself for ferreting out the traitor. So until he could sort it out, he must assume they were all compromised.

It should be a simple enough task. Creeping into the forest, making the exchange with the Lisovyk, and slipping back out again.

He just hoped the Lhyrria seed would be enough.

Eighteen

Cirelle squinted at the faded text of the giant tome Ellian held open, each of them standing on opposite sides of the desk in the Archive's antechamber. No illustrations graced the pages, just a scant paragraph of information on the Lisovyk, the creature whose normally-hidden woodland would reveal itself in scant days. Cirelle was not allowed on this mission, and she had to admit relief at that. Issen and Ellian would venture into the woods alone. Stealth was tantamount, so Shai would remain at the manor with Cirelle and Lydia, waiting.

"The Lisovyk is a recluse and despises visitors," Ellian explained, "But he'll take the seed, I think. I hope."

"The seed seems like a dangerous thing to give away," Cirelle warned.

Ellian shook his head. "It won't grow another Lhyrria, but it will produce a tree that helps ward his woodland against ill-meaning visitors."

Cirelle bit her lip, staring down at the page as if her glower could force the words to reveal more.

The doorbell rang. Cirelle rushed to answer it, heart in her throat as her thoughts flickered to Orwe. The first time she'd heard Ellian's bell ring without warning, a corpse had been left on his steps.

Lydia emerged from the west wing, reaching the front door before Cirelle and hauling it open. Dirilai spilled through in a cloud of her scent, sage and dried herbs and wood shavings. Her eyes were furious and her chest heaved. "We have a problem."

Cirelle ushered Dirilai into the antechamber, Lydia on her heels. At the sight of the two, Ellian slammed the book on the Lisovyk shut, circling the desk to block it from view.

"He's coming," Dirilai hissed through gritted teeth.

"Who?" Cirelle asked.

The sidhe woman's eyes narrowed as her head whipped around to stare at Cirelle, dark eyes lit with a fierce fire. Her angular features gave her the appearance of a phantom, a gaunt ghost with dusty lavender skin and sleek hair like wet black silk. "Who do you think?" Fear, that's what lay in her eyes. "The prince. He knows Ellian brought a human into his palace."

Cirelle's mouth went dry.

"How?" Ellian's voice was low, a warning.

Dirilai closed her eyes. "I told them." When Ellian took a step forward, she stood her ground, tilting up her head and opening her eyes to meet his furious ember-orange gaze. "He asked me a direct question, Ellian. No loophole to talk around. Somehow, he suspected already. He knows I can see through glamours, and asked me if I'd seen anything behind the sylvan at the masquerade. He wanted to know what I saw." Her dark eyes narrowed. "Don't think I won't suffer for not telling him immediately."

"I don't understand—" Lydia began, but Cirelle placed a gentle hand on her arm to silence her.

Ellian swore under his breath in Kishi and whirled to pace the room. "Cirelle, Lydia, go to your rooms."

Despite the panic that snaked through her, Cirelle balled her hands into fists and stood her ground. "Why? He already knows I'm here."

"And I can't be," Dirilai muttered. "I've given you all the warning I can. I didn't tell him about the—" She glanced at Lydia. "about Thieves' Night. I don't think he knows that much." She shook her head and misted away without another word.

Ellian was still swearing, an unending litany of profanity under his breath as he paced, a mix of sidhe and Kishi curses. If Cirelle hadn't been so frozen with terror, she might have found the sight amusing.

Prince Adaleth had once threatened her in his palace. *I'd take great pleasure in putting stripes on your back.* Would he follow through on those words now? Could he do worse than severing her finger? Her thumb rubbed the empty knuckle, the smooth scar tissue. She still hadn't told Lydia about that, and the glamour ring Ellian had given her hid the damage.

"Your Highness," Lydia said. "If someone is coming, I think we should hide."

Cirelle swallowed, turning to Ellian. "What do we do?" She was proud that her voice didn't tremble as much as her insides did.

"Nothing," Ellian spat out the word like bitter poison. "There's nothing I can do. He's my prince, whether I want him to be or not."

"So we just wait and take whatever punishment he metes out?" Cirelle's fear burned, forging into anger. "All your plots, all your plans, and your only answer is just 'let's wait'?"

Ellian's pacing stopped, and his back slumped against the door to the Archive. His eyes met hers, solid black pools. "I don't have any plans for this."

The doorbell rang, a single clang that trailed off into silence.

The quiet that followed was heavier than any cacophony would have been.

"What if we just don't answer the door?" Cirelle offered weakly. Her knees had turned to jelly. She could feel the prince's presence even here in the antechamber, the heavy weight of his magic.

Ellian wiped his face with one hand, his laugh a bitter, humorless thing. "I can't avoid him forever, and the longer we wait, the graver the insult. Besides, he can break enchantments. Including my wards."

Stars. Issen had told her once that Prince Adaleth possessed powerful magic, but the ability to shatter wards and break spells? It meant nowhere was safe from that icy prince.

"Cirelle…" Ellian started to lift a hand, clenched it into a fist, then dropped it to his side as he pushed away from the door. Without another word, he stalked out of the room, straightening his shoulders.

Cirelle followed with her heart in her throat, a wary Lydia beside her. She'd expected guards, some show of force. But instead, the prince stood alone on the doorstep. Shorter than Ellian but taller than Cirelle, he was even more sharp-edged than she remembered. He grinned indolently, showing small, even teeth.

The prince did not come garbed for a fight. He wore Unseelie finery, a fitted white coat that flared out behind him, adorned in ebony trim. Lace spilled from his throat and the cuffs of his jacket, a silvery hue that shimmered in the light. His skin was as pale as she remembered, the wan blue of a cloudy sky, his hair like glimmering snow. Winter given flesh.

He didn't ask permission, but strode into the foyer as if he owned the manor, his polished black boots clacking sharply against the tile mosaic. The wards didn't even make him pause.

No, instead Cirelle *felt* them crumble, like a bubble popping inside her chest.

Stiff and reluctant, Ellian knelt, his head bowed though his shoulders trembled with rage or fear. Or both.

"Oh, Ellian," Adaleth said. "Do stand."

Obeying, Ellian stared down at the prince with an expression that hid neither his fury nor his terror.

The prince's smile vanished. "Someone has made a grave mistake, hasn't he?"

Ellian remained silent, though his shoulders tensed, his hands fisted at his sides.

Lydia nudged Cirelle into position behind her, against the antechamber door. The guard's hand grasped the empty space at her hip where her blade should be, and she muttered a curse. She spread her arms out, shielding Cirelle with her body. Cirelle half wished she'd obeyed Ellian's wishes and hidden in her room. The other half of her didn't dare leave Ellian alone to face this viper.

The prince's lambent green eyes caught Cirelle's over Lydia's shoulder. They lit with a sharper awareness as he cocked his head. "Ah, there you are. So *that's* what you look like under the glamour?" His mouth curled into an expression of distaste.

It only took Adaleth three strides to reach them. Lydia settled into a fighter's stance, hands clenched into fists before her like a brawler, but the prince made a small gesture and the guard was knocked to the floor as if a giant hand batted her aside. Her head hit the tile with a sickening sound and she didn't rise again.

Cirelle screamed. "Lydia!"

Before she could rush to Lydia's prone form, the prince gripped her wrists and pinned them to the door. *Wait, how—?* This near, the sense of his magic was a physical weight, like walking against the wind. His scent enveloped her, sodden foliage and frost.

He leaned in. "You know, months ago, you gave me permission to do to you whatever Ellian did," the prince murmured, his grip tightening. "So very stupid. And just what, little human, have you let him do to you?" There was a revulsion in the words now, a disdain pure and unadulterated. Before she could respond, the prince pushed away from her and approached Ellian once more.

Cirelle darted to kneel by Lydia, hands probing the guard's head. Blood matted Lydia's golden hair, and she flopped limply in Cirelle's grasp. But she breathed.

The prince ignored the humans. "Really, Ellian," he said coolly. "I'll never understand this fascination with such beasts."

"I was one of those beasts, once."

"No," the prince corrected him, walking around Ellian in a slow, appraising circle. "You were never one of them. But you're not one of us, either, are you? Poor soul. You could still take a place in my court, you know."

"As a servant, a slave."

Adaleth stepped close and whispered the words so low Cirelle barely heard them. "During the day. But at night…" he turned his head aside, a half-smile slipping onto his lips. "Well, that's another story."

"What do you want, Adaleth?" Ellian snapped.

The prince's eyes flashed. His hand shot upward in a backhand so hard it whipped Ellian's head to the side. His voice was the sound of the Void, empty and cold. "You don't have permission to call me so familiarly."

"Not here, you mean." Blood beaded on Ellian's lower lip, but his response was defiant, punctuated by a harsh laugh.

For a moment, Adaleth merely glared with angry, glowing eyes. Then he grinned, a slow spreading smile that made Cirelle's blood run cold as he strode toward her. The prince's burning grasp yanked her upward by the arm. Baring his teeth, he grabbed a fistful of Cirelle's hair. She yelped, but he ignored it and spoke to Ellian. "Remember this, Ellian. She gave me permission to do anything to her that you have." Adaleth's shark's smile widened, his voice a low purr. "Have you fucked her yet? I could find out."

Cirelle's knees turned to water. With anyone else, she'd have spat in his face, snapped at him. But Adaleth triggered a gut-deep fear that went beyond reason.

Ellian snarled. "You couldn't bring yourself to touch a human so," he said. "And we both know it."

The prince's eyes narrowed. "Perhaps under the circumstances I may make an exception. Such a foolish, foolish mortal, to grant me such freedom." While a blind, screaming panic built within Cirelle, the prince's eyes glinted with a dark humor. "So, Ellian, do I have your attention now? What do you call me?"

Ellian's face was a portrait of agony, those eyes a swirl of colors. Midnight blue, deepest black, palest rose. He bowed his head. "Your Highness."

"Good." Adaleth dropped Cirelle's arm, wiping his hand on his jacket as if he'd touched something grimy. "Now," he began, taking slow strides toward Ellian. "You insulted me by bringing forbidden filth into my palace. You did so knowingly. Worse, you used a *human* against me in a deliberate provocation." He placed one pale fingertip against his chin, a mockery of deep thought. "What punishment would suffice?" Idly, he waved a hand in the air, and fire flickered in its wake.

Ellian flinched, eyes locked on to the fading flames.

Adaleth glanced at Cirelle again. "Perhaps I could take the price of payment out on your human."

"No, you can't." Ellian's response was firm. When Adaleth's head snapped back around, Ellian gritted out, "Your Highness." His hands clenched and unclenched at his sides. "The laws don't allow for my punishment to be transmuted to another, and we both know it. So what sentence have I earned?"

"A week," Adaleth stated crisply. "Seven days in the palace, at my personal beck and call." He lifted a hand and traced Ellian's cheek with a fingertip that flickered with flames. Ellian closed his eyes and stiffened, chest rising and falling in rapid breaths. The prince smiled. "For *whatever* I choose, at any hour."

"No!" The word burst from Cirelle's lips before she could stop it. She clapped her hands over her mouth as if to shove the protest back in.

"Two weeks," Adaleth amended, turning to watch Cirelle coolly, his flame-drenched hand hovering near Ellian's face. "Since your pet doesn't seem to know her place."

Cirelle stared mutely at Ellian. *I'm so sorry. Don't do this.*

His gaze spoke more clearly than words. *I have to.* Sidhe laws, faerie rules. He'd committed an offense, and now Adaleth took his recompense.

But the prince had left little doubt as to what he'd demand, and it made Cirelle's stomach wrench into knots. She'd lived Thieves' Night with Ellian, had been there for every moan and caress, for the disgust so deep it drowned him.

"Starting now." The prince's words sounded like a death knell.

Ellian dodged out of the prince's grasp to dart over to Cirelle. "Cirelle…" The way he said her name, as if it cut him to say it, left her stomach roiling uncomfortably. Ellian's eyes were deepest blue, richest green, and a thin thread of pink around the center.

He surprised her when he leaned in closer, pressing his lips lightly against her own. A chaste kiss, nothing like their usual heat. Softer than a sigh, he breathed her name into her mouth before the prince reached them, clutched Ellian's wrist, and then they both were gone.

With no one here to see, Cirelle fell to her knees beside Lydia once more, sobbing out her frustration into the echoing, empty halls.

Nineteen

THANK ALL THE GODS that Lydia still breathed, though blood matted her cornsilk hair. Cirelle stole the last of Ellian's purple healing potion from the Archive, damning whatever consequences she'd reap when he returned.

If he returned.

No. He had to.

She dabbed the potion onto the back of Lydia's head and dribbled the final drops into Lydia's mouth, mumbling prayers to Lirienne, god of medicine and mercy.

The guard stirred in a bleary daze, trying to scramble off the floor until Cirelle insisted they were safe. She helped Lydia up and to her room, explaining what happened while they walked.

Guiltily, Cirelle admitted she'd been to Adaleth's palace once before in disguise, and that ploy was the cause of Ellian's abduction.

"Why?" Lydia croaked. "Why would you do something like that?"

Cirelle chewed on her lip. "Ellian needed me."

Lydia groaned as she sank into her bed and tugged the

blankets up to her chest. "Your Highness. You can't trust him. Faerie is… not right."

"He's not what you think."

"Fae aren't mortal, Your Highness. They don't have our morals, no matter how well they mimic them. And I'm concerned about how much you've sunk into this world. Wearing faerie fashions, playing their instruments, laughing with Ellian like he's an old companion. It worries me that you seem to have made this place as much a home as Arraven already."

Cirelle snorted. "I'm not sure about that."

Lydia shook her head. Hazel eyes met Cirelle's, moss and honey intertwined. She touched a fingertip to the space between her brows. "Here, on your face, there's a tiny little crease, a line that never quite goes away. You're not quite twenty, Your Highness. Worry lines should be far in your future." Her hand slid away. "But back home, that little wrinkle was always there, even when you smiled. It showed up when you started your royal studies."

Cirelle swallowed, her throat dry, and Lydia continued.

"The girl I knew when we were little, she didn't bear that weight. The fearless child who bossed us about and talked us into messes of trouble."

Cirelle cleared her throat. "I seem to recall you trying to talk me out of most of those schemes." A faint smile crossed her lips.

Lydia returned the wistful grin. "Trying. But more often than not, we'd still all find ourselves climbing a garden trellis in a game of spider-queen despite the gardener's warnings." The soldier sighed. "Even when you were angry or upset, when we were children, you were *alive*. Until you were taken from us and turned into a princess, a doll with an ever-present wrinkle between haunted eyes."

Cirelle swallowed, her tongue sticking to the roof of her

mouth. When she summoned the words, her voice cracked on them. "I hated it."

"I know. It was obvious to anyone who truly knew you. But here in Faerie, in our game of sailor's runes last week, I noticed that crease between your brows was gone. I heard you laugh louder than I had in years. In this world, you're… more *you*. I haven't seen you like this." She hesitated, then added, "at least not since Countess Briere left."

Cirelle stared down at her fingers as they picked at the hem of a sleeve. "It was hard to lose her. She was a good friend." A lie. Well, not entirely. But *friend* was such a feeble, inadequate word for what she and Briere had shared.

Lydia's voice was not far from her usual solemn tone, but there was a faint note in it that may have been sarcasm. "Friend?"

"Yes." Cirelle's flush deepened.

"You don't have to lie to me, Your Highness."

"I don't know what you mean."

Lydia's reply was soft. "You and Lady Briere weren't quite as secretive as you tried to be, Your Highness."

Cirelle's heart leapt into her throat as the soldier's words sank in. It took a few moments before she could speak. "How… how many people knew?" Her face burned, and her hand had stilled where it plucked at a loose bit of thread.

"Only a few guards and maids, I think. I doubt any of them told your family or the rest of the gentry. But it's hard to hide things from servants, Your Highness."

Cirelle sighed. "And you told no one yourself?"

"Of course not. It was… you were happy again, after you'd seemed to wither."

Lydia had known Cirelle's deepest secret and kept it. "Thank you."

Memories of Briere ached. Four years since Briere had married, and that part of Cirelle still bore bruises.

Lydia swallowed. "Here in Faerie, you have that spark back. And it worries me. What does that mean when we go back home? What will you have become by then? I'll stand aside, helpless, and let that worry line in your brow deepen while the life you hate slowly kills you." She shook her head. "Until they whisk you away to fade in some foreign kingdom, that is."

"Lydia…" Cirelle couldn't find any words for the sudden swelling pain inside her ribcage. "Why did you even come here?"

The soldier barked a bitter laugh. "I—" she stopped. Shook her head. "I didn't want you to be alone. But you're not alone at all, are you?"

Cirelle didn't answer.

The guard rolled over in bed. "I need to rest. Tomorrow, we'll keep going and wait for Ellian's return."

After a long moment's hesitation and a soft good night, Cirelle left Lydia. But rather than seeking her own bed, she made her way to the antechamber and called Issen. He answered with a yawn, wearing a robe in a pale cream hue. "Yes?"

"I need your help. Ellian is gone for two weeks. The wards are down. And we have eight days until the Lisovyk's woodland opens."

Issen blinked, then his usually soft expression went stern. "I'll be there in a moment."

Twenty

CIRELLE ROLLED OVER WITH a yawn, only to fall off the sofa. The impact with the floor made her yelp.

Then she remembered everything about the night before.

Issen and Shai had arrived at the manor while Lydia still slept off her injury. Issen took stock of the situation with a frown. "We can't replace the wards on the house," he admitted. "I've nothing Tallia would accept in exchange for it. You or Lydia could bargain on his behalf as members of his household, but only if Ellian informed you of his intent to do so beforehand."

Cirelle bit her lip. She had one bargaining chip of her own. The knives, the claimhte. She opened her mouth, then shut it. No. She wouldn't give such power to Tallia, a member of Adaleth's inner court. "So we just sit here, vulnerable?"

Shai kicked at the door frame lightly, as if prodding the nonexistent shields. "You can both stay with us. We don't have Ellian's wards, but we'd be there to protect you."

"What about the Archive?"

Issen cleared his throat. "I can cast a trap on the door. It's not as effective as one of Tallia's wards, but would be… quite unpleasant for anyone who tried to enter the Archive."

Cirelle sighed. "Then do it." But as they entered the antechamber, she held up a hand. "Wait!" She slipped into the Archive and found the small box she was looking for, clutching it tightly. On her way out, she passed the claimhte. They hissed in her mind, and she grabbed them, too.

"All right," she said as she re-entered the antechamber. "Now you can do it."

"What's that?" Shai nodded toward the box.

"The seed Ellian was going to use to bargain with the Lisovyk. You said if he told me of his intent to make a bargain, I can do it on his behalf, right? As his servant?"

Issen frowned. "We'll discuss the ridiculousness of that idea after you're safely at our home, and after you've had some rest."

Cirelle gripped the box tighter. Ellian was gone, and the thought of what he might be doing with the cold, cruel prince even now left worms wriggling in her belly. Her knuckle stung again.

Issen cast his spell, leaving a faint golden glow around the door. Then they roused Lydia enough to explain what was going on. Cirelle and Lydia packed small bags with a few necessities before Shai and Issen worldwalked them to their home.

It was not a mansion, but a cottage, a large main room with a single hallway. White-painted wooden beams held up tall ceilings, and a large hearth opposite the door held a swinging hook for a kettle or pot. One wall bore a weapons rack, another was made entirely of bookshelves, and the final wall beside the front door contained small cubbies full of brightly-colored yarn.

And they were very, very pink walls. Someone had painted them the color of strawberry cream, with girlish swirls of white flourishes. The furniture matched, pinks and purples and whites in patterns of roses and tulips.

"Sorry," Shai said as she took Cirelle's bag and set it on the scuffed dining table. "We only have one guest bed, and it's not big enough for two. One of you will have to take the sofa."

Issen coughed politely and gave a conspicuous nod toward the hearth.

"Shit!" Shai swore. "Yeah, guests. Um, tea? Coffee?" She darted off to a cupboard for supplies, then swung a steaming kettle out of the fire.

"Coffee?" A beverage imported from lands across the sea, Cirelle had never had it. It was more of an Ysaan delicacy, while Arraven preferred tea. She allowed herself to be ushered into a small divan, Lydia beside her. Issen sat in an opposite armchair, a thoughtful frown on his face and his salmon-colored eyes distant.

"Not coffee," Issen told Shai, "not this late. Tea."

"We don't really need tea," Lydia said, rubbing her temples, but Shai returned holding a steaming mug and pressed it into her hands. She fetched a second for Cirelle.

The scent of lavender and bergamot filled Cirelle's nose. She lifted it for a sip, but Lydia reached out and placed gentle fingers on Cirelle's wrist to stop her.

"It's safe," Shai huffed indignantly as she plopped onto the sofa.

"To be precise," Issen added, "By taking you in, we are shouldering Ellian's care of you until his return. Any rules that hold within his home also apply here for that time. That includes entitlement to your food and drink, and your board."

Lydia still wasn't mollified. "It's not poisoned or enchanted?"

Shai snorted. "Of course not. You're our guests."

Cirelle gave a rueful grin. "Ellian did give me bewitched wine on my first night as a guest." She stared into her cup, ignoring Lydia's spluttering at that revelation.

"Well, that's Ellian. This is just plain old mortal tea, taken from your kingdom even."

Still, Lydia set aside her tea without drinking. Cirelle sipped hers with the hope the familiar flavor would soothe her ruffled thoughts. However, when Lydia yawned widely, Cirelle set the drink down and shooed her friend into the guest room despite protests. Shai and Issen, too, retreated to their own rooms for the evening.

Cirelle left Lydia on the small guest bed, claiming the sofa for herself. "You can argue with me about sleeping arrangements tomorrow," she'd told the weary soldier, "after we've both slept. But for now, consider it an order from your princess."

Lydia grumbled, but fell asleep almost immediately. It didn't take Cirelle much longer, curling up inside a soft knitted blanket and wondering if it was Shai's handiwork.

Tomorrow, Cirelle would present her plan to the three of them. She just hoped her meager diplomacy skills and a lot of sheer stubbornness would be enough.

Twenty-One

ADALETH TOSSED AND TURNED in his bed. Such a delicious, excruciating torment, knowing Ellian remained bound in the dungeons, so close and yet still so obstinate.

After long, restless minutes, the prince heaved a sigh and rolled out of bed. He threw on a dressing gown, but no more. If this plan went accordingly, he wouldn't need to be garbed. He plucked a bottle from a shelf in his room, not bothering with drinkware. Ellian would be grateful enough for the reprieve, with or without a glass.

On bare feet, Adaleth padded through stark white and empty halls.

No one should have been up at this hour, but of course Meivre was awake. Still clinging to the old ways as ever, including a nocturnal cycle. Most of yesterday's party guests had long since gone home, but her clear, soft laugh echoed out of the music room along with a gentle violin melody. Ah. Adaleth didn't know who she'd tangled in her web now, and didn't particularly care.

However, the music room's door lay wide open, and there wasn't another path he could take. Hoping Meivre was fully enraptured by her latest conquest, he slipped past.

No luck.

"Your Highness?" Meivre's voice dripped sweetness as always. Adaleth kept walking, but the woman poked her head out into the hall a moment later. He ignored her and kept walking until she added in a low voice. "I know who that bottle is for."

Adaleth paused, turning slowly.

"A little bird may have told me we have a new guest. Downstairs, that is." The music had not stopped, her companion still playing in the parlor as Meivre leaned against the door frame. "Strange, however, to offer a dog wintersweet." The implication hung in the air.

She knows. "Are you threatening your prince?"

"Just a friendly warning. It may be a secret from most, but I won't have been the only one who heard of his arrival. I'd be careful just who sees you with that, is all. My prince." With a nod, she stepped back into the music room and the private recital.

Kill her. She's a threat.

No, that's what his mother would have done. If Meivre stepped out of line, measures would be taken. But for now, he would watch her. Tonight, though, he had more important matters. He continued on his way and crept down to the dungeons. The blinding paleness gave way to plain gray stone, filthy with years of use.

And here, Ellian lay chained. Stretched out on cold cobblestone, sleeping.

The prince thunked the bottle down hard by Ellian's head, loud enough that the man startled awake. He jolted up, though he could not stand, not with the shackles that bound his wrists to the floor on a short chain. The best he could do was settle into a kneeling position, the bottle before him. The dark glass gleamed in the sliver of moonlight that seeped through the tiny slit of the high window. Ellian didn't ask what was in it; easy enough to guess. It wouldn't be the first time he turned to such substances to make sidhe depravity more tolerable to his mortal sensibilities. The night before the Hunt, Ellian had drowned himself in wintersweet.

Ellian dragged his gaze up from the bottle. Stone and sea and sky, the hatred there was dizzying. Crimson eyes, burning with a fire Adaleth had missed so dearly.

"What do you want?" Ellian's voice was husky with sleep.

Adaleth knelt on the stone, only the thin fabric of his dressing gown between him and the grimy floor. So foul, so deliciously repugnant. He shuddered. "Drink it. Take my bargain. You'll spend the rest of your sentence in luxury, eating hot meals in my room, wearing only the finest clothing. When you wear clothing at all, that is." His smile turned salacious. He bowed low, his hair falling into the dirty floor. "And…" he licked his lips, "doing to me as you please. You hate me even more, don't you, for what I did to her? Take the price from my flesh." Just the sound of the words spilling from his throat left Adaleth aroused, the sheer subservience of them.

He could picture it now. Ellian downing the wintersweet in long gulps, throat bobbing. The way his expression would glaze over, eyes swirling scarlet and purple. Maybe he wouldn't even wait to be unchained, ordering Adaleth to service him here and now, in this filthy dungeon. The prince swallowed, licking his lips, still on his hands and knees.

Ellian cleared his throat. "No."

A curse burst from Adaleth's lips as he stood. "Eventually, Ellian, you'll realize you are sidhe. Not mortal. And until then, I can wait. Your choice. Your days can be painful ones or pleasant. I'll return tomorrow night, after Niridi is through with you." His best torturer, Niridi. Adaleth would tell her only to make

Ellian suffer, not why. And tomorrow, he'd once more make this offer in secret.

He leaned forward to take the bottle back, but Ellian's hand shot out and grabbed Adaleth's wrist. Hard. The jolt of lust that spiked through Adaleth left him breathless.

"Someday," Ellian hissed, voice low with threat, "you will reap what you have sown with all your misery and suffering. And I'll be there, watching." He released Adaleth, hand falling back to his side. "Now go. My prince." The last was added bitterly, with just a hint of defiance.

Adaleth nearly struck him for that. But nothing he could do would be the equal of Niridi's upcoming mercies.

"Sleep well, Ellian," Adaleth said as he reached the cell door. "You'll need it for tomorrow."

Twenty-Two

"Absolutely not," Issen said. "Aside from the obvious drawbacks of your own well-being, are you aware of the repercussions I'd face from Ellian if harm came to you?" The four stood around the small dining table in one corner of Shai and Issen's cottage, the Lhyrria seed's box between them.

Cirelle snorted. "No worse than what's happened to me under his care."

"Exactly," Lydia said, expression dark. "You were poisoned, Your Highness. I won't see something like that happen again."

The guard didn't even know about Cirelle's missing finger. Cirelle still wore the glamour ring bestowed upon her by Ellian in exchange for taking the wound on his behalf. It created the illusion of a functional finger, though there was nothing truly there. It also quite conveniently masked the thin white scars she'd gotten on her forearms on Thieves' Night.

"You said it yourself," Cirelle insisted. "Ellian told me he intended to trade the Lisovyk the seed. I can bargain on his behalf. How long until the Lisovyk's woodland is accessible again?"

Issen grimaced, plucking at a loose thread on his sleeve. "A little more than three hundred years before the stars and moons align correctly."

"See? We have to. With the four of us, we could do it."

With a glance at Shai, Issen shook his head. "No offense, Shai, but this mission requires silence. Not your strength."

The sidhe woman huffed, crossing her arms, but she didn't argue.

"Then the three of us," Cirelle said.

Issen shook his head. "I'm certain you're capable enough with a blade, Lydia, but I'm the only one who knows what we might face in those woods, should this go sideways. We need at least one other faerie before I'd even consider it."

"Your Highness…" Lydia's voice was tight. "You can't seriously be considering this. Whatever Ellian wants from this Lisovyk, it's not worth your life. Or mine, or even his." She gestured to Issen.

Except it was. Cirelle still bit her tongue at telling Lydia about the Lock. Ellian had warned her to keep her secrets close, and the more clueless Lydia was, the less danger she was in from their enemies.

Like Ellian's coterie, if he ever spoke to them again.

Wait. The coterie.

"What about Ellian's group from Thieves' Night?" She said quietly. "We could get one of them to help."

"We still don't know—" Issen began, but she cut him off.

"I know. But we don't have a lot of options."

For a long time, Issen was quiet, eyes locked on the wooden box. "Most of them wouldn't do it. Not without Ellian. But… Kith is in debt, indentured to Vilitte. He needs to gather wealth to regain his freedom."

"Wait, *that's* why he helped us?"

A nod. "He'd do it, for a price. And as long as we're cautious with our words, we can wring an oath from him to tell no one else."

"Then we call him. Back to the manor."

"I still haven't agreed," Issen warned.

"Please. I'll compensate you, whatever is needed. When I return to Arraven, I can convince my brother to relinquish something from the treasury."

"Promises I've made to Ellian would already cover that." He sighed. "And you're right. We can't miss the opportunity. Don't make me regret this."

Cirelle grinned. "Lydia, you're in, right?"

"If I can't convince you to stay here, I'm not leaving your side." Lydia's face was pinched, her hand gripping the back of a chair.

"Let's go see if I can bribe Kith into helping, then."

In Ellian's antechamber, Issen and Shai helped her find Kith's coin and call him. The cat answered with a glare, ears back. "What?"

Cirelle cleared her throat. "I need your help."

"No. Where's Ellian?"

"He had to leave temporarily. But we need your help for a mission. I'm prepared to pay."

Kith cocked his head, ears pricking up. "I'm listening."

"First, I need your oath that you will tell no one of what is said in this conversation. Not a single soul other than Ellian or myself."

The cat's eyes narrowed. "Fine. You have my oath I'll not tell anyone save Ellian of what I hear from you today."

Cirelle rolled his words around her head and nodded. "We enter the Lisovyk's forest in a week. We need backup in case things go poorly."

A pause. "And what would you be prepared to give in exchange?"

"What would you demand?" *Please don't say the claimhte.*

Kith pondered for a moment. "The glamour ring you wear."

"Glamour?" Lydia hissed in a whisper, but Cirelle made a silencing motion. She hadn't known that Kith could identify the ring's purpose just by looking at it, but that little mattered.

"Done," Cirelle said, "After we leave the Lisovyk's forest safely, you can have the ring. Meet us here at Ellian's mansion at dusk in seven days."

"I will." The mirror went dark.

Twenty-Three

CIRELLE SLEPT POORLY the next six nights.

Every time she closed her eyes, visions of Ellian's broken and bloodied corpse haunted her. In the worst nightmares, she was the culprit, her hands slick with his blood. In other dreams, she took violent vengeance for his death, slicing the sidhe prince from navel to throat with her claimhte, laughing all the while.

She'd wake up in a cold sweat, then pace the room fretfully. After that first night, Lydia had swapped rooms so the guard slept on the living room sofa, while Cirelle did her best to wear a rut into the floor of the guest room.

By the third night, Shai brewed Cirelle valerian tea just to help her sleep at all, but the nightmares still haunted her and left her weary each morning. Her temper frayed, and she grew prone to snap angrily or burst into sudden tears at the slightest provocation. She and Lydia sparked against each other, until even her friend kept a distance.

Issen was a calm, still pond among the tension. He sometimes kept her silent company, seeming to detect when she preferred to be alone. Once, she tried gaming with him while Shai and Lydia sat nearby and argued about the merits of a heavy broadsword versus lighter daggers, but cards were an insufficient distraction.

Would Ellian's cruel side emerge again, the one he hated? Was he bedding Adaleth even now?

Her knuckle hurt, and she swallowed back bile.

The days passed in a hazy, agitated blur, until it was time.

"Are you certain you still wish to do this?" Issen asked as they waited outside Ellian's empty manor. It was late afternoon, the sun dipping toward the horizon. His only weapons were the small knives strapped to his calves, but Cirelle had seen how effective they were on Thieves' Night. And this time, he'd also have his magic.

Lydia stood silently nearby, hand on the hilt of a blade.

The Lhyrria seed's box rested at the bottom of Cirelle's knapsack, and the claimhte were a heavy weight against her back, the sheaths strapped beneath the bag. She'd tied her hair into a tail, but the hilts tickled the hairs at the base of her neck, a prickling sensation.

It was the first time she'd truly worn the knives like this. Shai's craftsman had done a fine job, the leather of the straps and sheaths durable, and as comfortable as she expected they could be.

Cirelle tested them now, reaching behind herself to slide the weapons out a few inches in the motion she and Lydia had practiced, then pushing them back in with a click. For this mission, Lydia had reluctantly agreed to let her bring them. Knowing that the ilthys could protect her, Lydia had decided it was better than letting her go in unarmed.

"I'm ready." She straightened her shoulders as she answered Issen's question. "We have to do this." If she didn't, they may lose their only chance at the Lock, at preventing anyone from ever slamming the door between their worlds.

Silence fell, until Kith appeared at the gate. Worldwalking in between one breath and the next. No greeting, ears flattened back, tail swishing. "Let's go."

Issen took the women's hands and worldwalked them to the edge of a vast forest, Kith behind them. There was no scattering of vegetation around this woodland; the grassy plain abruptly ended at a wall of trees, trunks shooting straight up into the sky and spreading into a thick canopy.

"Once we're in the forest," Issen reminded her, "no talking until we meet the Lisovyk."

"I know," Cirelle replied. She quoted from Ellian's book. "The Lisovyk will bear no disturbance in his forest. A snapped twig or rustled leaf he will let pass, but the unnatural sound of speech or whistling outside his central clearing is sure to bring his ire. I remember."

Issen led the way. Lydia took up a position behind Cirelle, with Kith in the rear, padding along without a single sound. Issen moved like a swirling breeze on bare feet, light and liquid, his steps soundless. The soft creak of Lydia's leather armor gave her away, but that small disturbance wasn't enough to draw the attention of the forest's master. Cirelle, too, tried to move as quietly as possible, carefully stepping on soft loam or mossy stones when she could, rather than cracking twigs beneath her feet.

There was no true path in these woods, but still all roads led to the Lisovyk. If they walked anywhere in this forest, they moved closer to its master. The woods grew ever darker as they walked. The forest closed in behind them, the underbrush growing thicker in their wake. The canopy clustered tightly overhead, blocking out the sun's dying rays in a permanent gray twilight, the air strange and ghostly. Their way was lit with glowing fungus and vines of flowers that flickered with an eerie inner light.

Here, there was no noise, the lack of it oppressive and thick.

No chatter of birds or insects, no rustle of movement through the underbrush. Still, Cirelle felt the gaze of hidden, predatory eyes boring into her back as they ventured further in. Shadows swam at the edges of her vision, and she stumbled more than once.

How many hours they spent in that forest, Cirelle couldn't have said. Surely it should be full dark by now, but the hazy gray light lingered.

Then, an opening. A clearing. The canopy of branches laced together high above, but a wide circle stood bare of trunks save a single, enormous rotted stump in the center.

"Why have you entered my woodland?" A raspy voice croaked. The stump shifted, and unfolded into the shape of a man. He stretched and stood, looming twice Cirelle's height. Old tree bark flaked away in place of skin. A beard of moss hung from his chin, and his eyes were black as an empty night sky. His back curled into a slouch, his long limbs dangling.

Issen stood just behind Cirelle, but she must be the one to strike this bargain. Lydia's tense worry pressed at her back. Kith may as well have been absent, a ghost, for all she heard or sensed him.

She cleared her throat and bowed. "Great Lisovyk, I come seeking a bargain."

"I bargain not with humans," the creature grumbled. "If you leave now, I will open the way and let you free, as you have not disturbed my forest. But hasten." He began to curl back in on himself, turning once more into the husk of a dead tree.

"I bring a seed of the Lhyrria," Cirelle blurted, digging into her pack for the box.

The creature stopped, its head poking up from the formless mass he'd become. "Truly? Do not lie to me, mortal." There was a warning in those words. She found the small box and pulled it out, opening the lid to show the seed. It shone a pale, shimmering silver in the fuzzy gray light.

"Truly."

The Lisovyk unfolded again, leaning over to peer at the seed. "Where did you get this?"

"I serve a member of the sidhe. He acquired it fairly in a bargain."

The creature's eyes narrowed, darting to Issen. "That sidhe?"

"No." Cirelle shook her head. "My master is currently indisposed. I bargain on his behalf."

The Lisovyk sat back on his heels, long arms resting atop his knees. "And what would you ask for such a treasure?"

Now or never. Cirelle took a deep breath. "An artifact known as the Lock."

Behind her, Lydia made a small strangled sound, but Cirelle couldn't afford to take her eyes off the Lisovyk. A strange noise came from the creature, and it took Cirelle a moment to realize it was a laugh. Bitter, harsh. "Then I fear you'll take that seed back from whence it came, human. I no longer have the Lock. It was stolen from me many years ago."

Cirelle's heart sank. "Do you know who took it?"

The Lisovyk shook his head. "No. But I can give you something to help, in exchange for that seed."

Wariness tingled along Cirelle's skin. "What do you offer?"

In reply, the Lisovyk stood, taking heavy strides to the opposite side of the clearing. His limbs creaked and groaned. Sticking one enormous finger into a bole of a tree, he returned to her. On the tip of that finger was a silver necklace, curved and shaped like a single long feather on a dainty, broken chain. When worn, the feather would wrap around one's throat.

Cirelle frowned. "What is this?"

"The thief dropped it when they stole the Lock," he replied.

"I will not leave my forest, but you may be able to use this to find them."

It was a tenuous link, but it was the only clue they had left.

She glanced at Issen, who merely gave her a knowing, weighted gaze. This was her choice alone.

Cirelle took a long, shaking breath. "For the necklace, and also safe passage out of your forest for myself and my escorts, I offer this seed from one of the Lhyrria."

"Agreed." The Lisovyk dropped the jewelry into Cirelle's outstretched hand, plucking the seed's box from her. "The forest will guide you out. I suggest you don't return."

With those ominous words, the Lisovyk curled around the small silver box, once again nothing more than a large tree stump.

Heart pounding, Cirelle slipped the necklace into an inside pocket of her pack, making sure it was securely buttoned. Slinging it back over one shoulder and rearranging it over the sheaths, they made their escape from the lair of the Lisovyk. Lydia met her gaze with a tortured expression, but held her silence.

Twenty-Four

THE TREES ONCE MORE closed ranks behind them and opened ahead. The strange gray twilight faded to black as they neared the forest's edge, draining all color from the world.

The uncanny stillness of this wood—and the sensation of being watched—left Cirelle with her heart in her throat.

A rustle in the bushes caught her attention just as a dark shape hurtled out of the underbrush.

Kill it. A hiss in her mind, like boots on broken glass. Before she realized what she was doing, the knives were bared in her hand, just as a rabbit darted past her, black-furred and golden-eyed unlike any she'd ever seen in the mortal realm.

Cirelle hauled in a steadying breath, biting her lip and sheathing the blades. Lydia did the same beside her.

Well, at least some of the training is paying off, she thought. The motion to draw them had been smooth, instinctive.

Issen silently turned and led the way again. Finally, there. Just ahead, a broad patch of grass lay outside the tree line, bathed in moonlight. A dozen steps and they'd be free.

As they drew close, dark smoke swirled at their feet, blocking their path and coalescing into a familiar shape.

The Scath's four violet eyes flickered at Cirelle. Anger. She could *feel* his cold fury thrumming in her chest.

Issen took a step to stand in front of her, dropping into a fighting position and drawing those small knives of his. He stood lightly on the balls of his feet, his stance wide. A pale light flickered to life before him, as if he stood before a miniature moon. Light. Issen had once told Cirelle his gifts were considered meager among the sidhe, the ability to manipulate light, water, and earth.

Lydia moved beside Issen, drawing her own blade. The Scath stared. He had no visible mouth, but Cirelle could *sense* him smile. This time, when she drew her knives, it was slow, deliberate, heart in her throat.

She held her daggers awkwardly before her, wishing she'd had longer to train. One in front, defensive, one up and back for offense. The stance she and Lydia had practiced. But stars go black, these daggers were so much heavier than those wooden practice blades.

If only she could speak, Cirelle could banish the Scath. The general had already been commanded not to harm her or any of Ellian's allies, nor to let any of his Shadowed army do so. But his eerie stare right now left her queasy anyway. He was planning something.

She was right.

Three fae emerged from the woods on either side. Not Shadowed.

The creatures were a head taller than Cirelle and Issen, lanky and with a moldy gray complexion. Tight caps topped their heads, deep crimson and glistening wetly. Their nails were yellow, grown into ragged claws.

She'd met a member of their species on the night of the Midsummer revel, an eerie creature who'd leered at her with bloodied fangs.

Redcaps.

The first lunged at Issen, who slipped aside, slicing at the back of the redcap's knee as he dodged past.

The second redcap slashed at Lydia's face, her dagger glancing off a worn, heavy bracer at his wrist. The guard managed to avoid the claws, ducking and stepping into the redcap's reach. As she lunged forward, the creature caught her second blade between its bare hands, grinning as blood dripped between long, knobby fingers.

As he danced around his redcap, Issen pointed one of his knives at the Scath. A flash of light burst forth, making Cirelle blink. The Scath's shriek wasn't an audible sound. It tore through her head, vibrated along her arms from her grip on the claimhte.

She backed up against a tree, still holding her knives in the position she and Lydia had practiced, her arms starting to burn and ache. Fierce hope bloomed in Cirelle's chest. She'd brought sunlight to a battle with shadows. Issen's light.

As she blinked away the spark of stars in her vision, the scene came to her in flashes.

Issen in a deadly-fast dance around his opponent, a flurry of claws and silvery metal.

Lydia, teeth gritted, struggling to twist her blade free of her beast's grip.

A third redcap clawed at a clump of mud that slid over her face like a living thing, filling her eyes and her nostrils. Kith pounced at her back, claws out. The redcap reached behind her and grasped his tail. Without warning, the cat was gone. In his place, a sidhe with plum-colored skin and inky black clothing.

Not a cat after all. Cirelle cursed herself. She should have known.

Having yanked his tail free, Kith shifted back into cat form and lunged again, teeth sinking into the redcap's calf.

Cirelle expected a bellow of rage, but the redcap merely snarled without sound.

So they, too, knew to make no outcry.

The scuffle of feet on forest loam, cracked twigs, and the wet sound of blades slicing redcap flesh were a grotesque enough symphony of their own.

Lydia bared her teeth, the redcap pushing her blade away, unnaturally-calloused hands still whole despite the slick blood that dripped to the forest floor.

Issen dodged a swipe of claws, his tiny knife burying itself to the hilt in the creature's thigh, but he lost his grip on it. The creature knocked Issen aside and lunged for Cirelle.

Fast. So fast for such large beasts. Before she could think, those yellow claws were slashing toward her. She pressed her back harder against the tree as she yelped and slashed with one of her knives. Not as steady or as smooth as it had been with her practice blades, the motion was a wild flail that only nicked its forearm.

But that wasn't the worst of her worries.

Her small yip had been an instinctive sound, but it was still a voice in this sacred forest. The trees rustled ominously, as if stirred by a phantom wind.

Tiny tendrils of shadow swirled into one, the Scath coalescing from the mist behind the redcap and gloating.

Oh dear, it mocked in that hissing, sighing voice. But the words echoed in her head, up her arm, as if spoken through the blades in her grip. *It seems you've pricked the Lisovyk's ire. He'll be here soon.* The redcap caught her wrist as she stabbed toward him. He smiled.

A shudder ran through the bark at her back, the ground vibrating with an enormous thump. Then another. Footsteps.

The Lisovyk was coming.

Her companions each fought their own battles, all while the Scath stood by and waited, a scavenger lusting for the knives in her hands.

Wait. *The claimhte.* She could speak now, they'd already angered the Lisovyk anyway. "Ilthys! Come to me!" The air filled with the chittering, clacking sound of the ilthys, her spider-like protectors. They slipped from the darkness, forming from the pools of shadow.

The redcap holding her wrist craned to look up as one of the spiders formed over Cirelle's head, clinging to the tree.

Her voice was flat, hollow. "Ilthys. Kill the redcaps." The blades in her grip sang their approval at the bloodshed.

It took only moments for her spider-like protectors to leap upon the redcaps, their teeth crunching into flesh and bone with a nauseating, wet splotch of sound. Hers lost his grasp on her arm when a sharp leg pierced his shoulder.

This time, Cirelle didn't vomit.

Issen sat up from where he'd been tossed aside, scrambling to his feet. Lydia stood with mouth open in a silent cry of horror. Kith sat with his tail around his paws, watching the slaughter calmly.

The Scath tossed back his head and laughed.

Cirelle didn't even have time to ask why. The thumping of the Lisovyk's footsteps grew unbearably loud as he burst out onto the group with a roar of sound. He batted the ilthys aside like wadded-up paper.

"You dare?" He growled. "You dare defile my woodland with not only sound, but with blood?" His immense form loomed over Cirelle, the face that had once looked so wise now contorted with rage. One giant hand lifted, his arm swinging down to swat at her.

The ground opened up beneath him, dropping the Lisovyk

three feet into a hole that had just formed. Off-balance, his swipe barely missed Cirelle.

Issen. Light, and water, he'd said… and *earth*.

"Run!" Issen gasped. Lydia darted toward Cirelle and grabbed her upper arm to urge her toward the edge of the trees and safety.

Kith fell in behind them, snarling at the Lisovyk. Guarding their retreat. Keeping his word.

Shaking off Lydia's grip and managing to shove one of the claimhte back into its sheath, Cirelle ran. The ilthys swept in between her group and the Lisovyk, even as the creature regained his footing and clambered out of the hole. The spiders swarmed him like ants, but he tossed them aside and kept coming.

They fled.

The tree line was right there, just ahead.

And then the Scath appeared in their path.

Cirelle swiped her blade at him and kept running. As Issen passed, the Scath's hand darted out and wrapped around Issen's wrist. The sidhe cried out, a harsh caw of pain. Cirelle grabbed his other arm with her one free hand, and he was caught in a deadly tug-of-war between Cirelle and the Scath.

"Let him go," Cirelle commanded.

"As you wish, my queen." The Scath bowed his head and faded into shadow. Behind him, the Lisovyk barreled toward them.

Cirelle and Lydia hauled Issen the final steps out of the woodland, Kith on their heels. The bellow of the Lisovyk followed them, the creature halting at the edge of the tree line as if held behind a fence. Full dark had fallen, his shape a hulking black mass silhouetted against tree limbs.

"Curse you all!" The faerie roared, then retreated.

Cirelle panted, but had no time to recover. The Scath reformed before her, standing just outside reach. Behind Cirelle,

Issen once more collapsed to the ground, but she didn't dare spare a look at him.

"Stay still!" She commanded the Scath, and his shadowy form froze. "How dare you?" She drew her second blade once again. Blood trickled down her forearm, making her grasp on one of the blades a slippery thing. When had she gotten hurt? Now that she noticed it, a long scratch on her forearm dripped and stung.

Still, she gripped the knife tighter, welcoming the sensation of cold that trickled up from the hilts and numbed the pain.

"You only commanded me not to harm you myself, or with any of my army." His voice, raspy as ever, dripped with satisfaction. "The redcaps were mercenaries."

Her chest heaved in heavy, angry breaths. "You dare attack your queen?"

"If my queen cannot defend herself, she is unworthy of the crown." Cirelle could *hear* the shrug in his tone. "We are faeries, my queen. I have been patient, but I *will* find a way to claim those daggers. I give you one last chance to bargain. Name your price. Perhaps knowledge? The shadows see much. What secrets do you wish to know, my queen?"

The same promise her blades had made, in her dreams.

Sudden as a flicker of lightning, Cirelle had it. The solution to two of her problems at once.

"The traitor," she said.

"What?"

"Thieves' Night," Cirelle clarified. "Someone among our company told an enemy our plans. Find out who shared that information, and you will have your daggers."

The Scath laughed, an awful sound like teeth scraping bone.

"Very well. I accept your bargain." The response was laden

with both humor and condescension. The air shivered. Gracefully, the Scath bowed. "I already have your answer, my queen. It was I."

No.

His own people had been the ones betrayed.

The Scath moved closer. "I gave that mortal what she needed to kill my former queen and steal the claimhte. I was oath-bound not to attack her directly, as I am with you. The daggers should have come to me." His eyes flared. "Until you ruined everything."

Cirelle's vision blurred. *The Scath.* He'd betrayed not only Ellian, but his own people, his own queen.

His greed had nearly gotten them all killed. If Cirelle hadn't picked up these knives, she and her allies might be dead.

Ellian wouldn't have survived Thieves' Night.

Kill him. An icy whisper in her head.

Her arms moved almost on their own.

The Scath spat a startled hiss, then a small gurgle. Cirelle withdrew the knives from his stomach and stepped back. He reached for her, shadowy arms clutching the air. Cirelle sliced at them, severing his misty fingers as he screeched. Now her lessons returned, a movement Lydia had drilled into her coming smooth, thoughtless.

The cold metal met the Scath's neck, biting through solid flesh. The knives scraped against something hard. Bone. Not mist and shadow after all. Or perhaps that was merely the magic of the claimhte.

The Scath crumpled to the ground, and she followed. The rage that flowed through her did not burn, but froze. This *thing* had almost murdered them all, twice over.

The violet glow in the Scath's eyes dimmed. The shadows vanished, leaving behind a dry husk like scorched charcoal.

Cirelle's vision swam. A dull roar rang in her ears as she stared down at what she'd done.

One sound pierced the fog. Lydia, shouting her name. The soldier stepped forward, using her daggers to knock Cirelle's blades out of her grasp.

"Your Highness!" Lydia said as Cirelle scrambled for the claimhte and shoved them into her sheaths, ashamed to meet her friend's eyes.

The knives sent an icy jolt up Cirelle's arm. Her voice was distant and cold when she spoke. "A bargain made and kept," she said. "I told him he would have the daggers. And he did."

Lydia sheathed her own blade and gripped Cirelle's shoulder. "Issen needs help."

Cirelle turned to meet Issen's blush-tinted eyes, tight with pain and sorrow. He lifted a hand toward her, and her stomach turned.

A chunk of Issen's arm was just… gone.

Where the Scath had grasped him, Issen's pale yellow skin had turned inky black like soot, and a large piece of flesh was just *missing*.

Worse, the shadows spread as she watched.

"Issen!" She rushed to his side.

"I know," he said, standing without her aid, the pain on his face. His voice was raspy, a thin thread, and he wobbled on his feet. "Both of you. Take my hand. Quickly. Kith?"

"My bargain is done," the sidhe hissed, still in his cat's form.

"Take the stupid ring then and go," Cirelle spat, yanking it off and hurling it at him. He plucked it up from the grass on a single long claw and vanished.

Cirelle grasped Issen's unblemished hand while Lydia's fingers wrapped around her other wrist, and the world misted around them.

They reappeared in the front yard of a small cottage. Not Shai's. Moonlight illuminated a garden of herbs and flowers in front. Polished planks of rich wood formed the slats that covered the house, the door pale oak.

Issen's eyes rolled back in his head and he tumbled to the ground, limp and boneless. Stars, the black blight on his arm was spreading so quickly. His whole hand was consumed, and it crept upward toward his shoulder. Lydia knelt at his side, sorrow in her eyes.

Cirelle dared a glance at the cottage door. Was it safe?

It had to be. Issen had brought them here. She ran toward the cottage and pounded on the door. "Hello?" She called. "Please. Somebody!"

She shouldn't have been surprised at the grumpy face that peered through when the door opened. "You."

"Dirilai," Cirelle breathed. "We need your help."

"What now, human?" The response was snappish.

"It's Issen. He's hurt. Badly."

Dirilai peered over Cirelle's shoulder, at where Issen lay down the path, Lydia beside him. "And you need me to heal him."

"Please."

"What would you give, princess?"

Cirelle faltered. She had nothing of her own left here in Faerie.

Save one thing.

"These." She unclasped her belt and thrust the sheathed claimhte at the sidhe. "Save Issen's life and they're yours."

Dirilai's eyes sparked. "The title of a queen."

"Yes."

The faerie pursed her lips and shook her head. "No. That's a mess I'd rather not take upon my shoulders."

Tears skimmed Cirelle's cheeks. "I have nothing else."

Dirilai smiled. "You do. A promise. That you will do anything—everything—in your power to ensure the Key and the

Lock do not fall into the hands of Queen Ayre or Prince Adaleth. Up to and including giving your own life, and I will save Issen's."

It was not a promise to make lightly. Cirelle swallowed. "Agreed."

The world thrummed.

Dirilai threw the door open, shoved past Cirelle, and stalked down the path to lean over Issen. She urged Lydia to move and the guard came to Cirelle's side, her hand finding Cirelle's.

Then Dirilai began dancing.

Cirelle knew something was wrong when the faerie pressed the light into Issen's body, only for the dark stain to recede a few inches and begin creeping up again.

It was a long battle, and by the end of it Dirilai was dripping in sweat, panting as if she'd just run up a dozen flights of stairs.

Afterward, Cirelle knelt by Issen's unconscious form. "You said you'd heal him."

"No, the agreement was that I save his life. He breathes."

He did, slow and shallow. But his left arm withered below the elbow, the flesh melted away to a skeletal thing of blackened skin stretched tight over bone.

This happened because of me. "Why? Why didn't you heal him completely?"

Dirilai pursed her lips, as if the admission pained her to say it. "I heal by moonlight. His wound is shadow." She shook her head. "I did my part. Now you keep your end of the bargain."

Before Cirelle could say more, a bell rang from within the cottage, a single heavy peal. Dirilai spat a curse. "I'm needed at the palace. And I don't want you lurking in my garden." She knelt to grasp Issen's good hand and held her other out to Cirelle and Lydia. "I'll take you all back, but quickly."

Cirelle hesitated. "Take us back to Issen's home, not Ellian's." The faerie nodded but didn't ask more. Cirelle and Lydia placed their hands in Dirilai's. The world faded, and they stood on the walkway to Shai and Issen's cottage.

Lydia carried the unconscious faerie while Cirelle knocked and prepared to give Shai the bad news.

When Shai answered, she swore over Issen's prone form and carried him to his room. "Later, you'll tell me everything," she'd said before closing the door.

Cirelle's own scratches and scrapes burned. She held her arm close and insisted on washing and wrapping them herself, over Lydia's protests.

She couldn't tell the soldier she wasn't ready to reveal her missing finger just yet, now that the glamour ring was gone. Or the old thin scars beneath the new scrapes.

But neither was as grievous as Issen's injury.

My fault.

❧

"You damn idiots," Shai muttered the next morning at the table. Her usual bluster had vanished. She prodded at Issen's arm. He winced now and then, but claimed it didn't hurt when Shai wasn't poking it. Lydia watched the proceedings in silence.

Shai ceased her examination and leaned back in the sofa. "I've never seen anything like this," she admitted. "I'm not a healer, but I've been in a lot of fights. This is new."

"Is there anyone who can help?" Cirelle asked.

"No." Issen's response was certain. "The damage is already done. It's healed over." He shook his head. "There are… options, but my arm as it was is gone." There was a floaty, disconnected quality to his voice, and his peach-tinted eyes had gone glassy. "The sooner I get used to that, the better."

He'll never play his stringed faerie instrument again. Cirelle had robbed her friend of music.

"You should have let me go," Shai growled at the both of them. "If you'd given the Scath those knives weeks ago, this wouldn't have happened."

She was right.

Cirelle glanced at the nearby shelf where the knives lay. She longed to shove them back into the Archive, but even that wasn't completely safe at the moment. Who would come to claim them next?

"I know," she replied miserably.

Twenty-Five

Lydia paced back and forth in Shai's living room while she played that moment over and over in her head, that enormous tree monster watching as Cirelle named the item she sought. *An artifact known as the Lock.*

The princess now stood in the center of the room, wringing her hands. "Lydia…"

"No." This wasn't happening. Her eyes latched on the princess's maimed hand again. A whole finger, just… gone. After the chaos with Issen had settled, Lydia couldn't help but notice it. She'd held her princess's hand and hissed a litany of profanity, cursing Ellian's name for doing this to Cirelle. But of course Cirelle had defended the faerie, under his spell as she was. It hadn't been Ellian, she explained, but the same faerie prince who now held Ellian captive.

Even so, all Lydia could see was her own failure to protect her princess. Lydia had let Ellian whisk Cirelle here, to this land of claws and teeth. Her mistake had let all this happen. Not just the missing finger, but the pale tracery of scars on Cirelle's forearms, the way Ellian had slipped into her head, her heart.

All Lydia's fault.

She'd even failed at the one task she'd been sent here to do; find the Key. Lydia too well recalled Cirelle's earlier words. "Adaleth wants to close the gates between worlds." And Ellian wanted to keep them open. Which meant he sought the Key and the Lock. Whether he intended to destroy them or just hide them away, the end result was the same.

Prince Aidan had sent Lydia here to find the Key. Her liege, her future king. But she could no longer merely ask Ellian about it. No. She'd need to be sneakier than that, trying to glean more information from Cirelle or the faerie.

I can't do this.

"Please," she begged her princess. "Leave me be."

And Cirelle did, retreating back to the guest room.

Damn it all. Her stomach twisted at the thought of deceiving her princess. But Ellian had crawled into Cirelle's head. She'd been so passionate when she spoke about leaving the door between the worlds open. The princess would never agree to aid Lydia or Aidan's quest.

Which meant lying to Cirelle.

Lydia swore again under her breath just as Shai walked in. After one look, Shai grunted. "All right." She walked to the weapons rack and selected two swords, both wooden, blunted. Practice weapons. She tossed one to Lydia and jerked her head at the door. "Outside."

Lydia caught the sword easily, her brow furrowed.

"You're pissed off as shit, or scared, or whatever," Shai said. "So let's go work it out." She grinned. "If you can land a blow, that is."

Pride flared. Lydia's hand clenched the hilt of the practice sword tightly. Oh, how she longed to land a few hits on Ellian for getting Cirelle into this whole mess, but perhaps Shai would do.

"You're on."

A flat area of packed dirt rested beside Shai's house, with open, moonlight plains stretching beyond as far as the eye could see.

They saluted one another and launched into battle. The tall, broad-shouldered sidhe didn't even break a sweat as she swatted aside Lydia's blows. She moved in a strange, sinuous way Lydia had never seen before, and it was impossible to predict her moves.

Lydia could feel her attacks getting sloppy, but rage blinded her. She railed at the faerie with a wild flurry of angry strikes, only a few of which landed. She swung and stabbed and parried until her muscles screamed at her and the sky began to lighten.

Lydia panted as she leaned on the sword. "I yield," she muttered through gritted teeth.

The sidhe grinned. "Good. Tomorrow, I show you why I won." She rolled her shoulders and took the sword from Lydia's hands. "But now, let's go eat breakfast."

Twenty-Six

CIRELLE FOUND HERSELF sitting in Shai's tiny guest room once more, staring at the necklace the Lisovyk had traded them. It was beautiful. Exquisitely crafted, each ridge of the feather was perfectly replicated in a gleaming silver-blue metal.

Would Ellian be able to trace it back to its source? It was the only crumb of good that might come from this mess.

Cirelle turned away and left the necklace behind. Maybe some of the tea Shai constantly kept at the ready would help.

Still her guilt clung to her. How would Issen cope after losing his music? Was this scrap of a clue worth the price he had paid?

She ghosted around Shai and Issen's home, aimlessly drifting from one idle pastime to another even though none gave her peace. Issen offered to let her borrow his strange instrument, but she couldn't bear to play within his earshot. She did take him up on the offer to read his books. A handful were in Trade, and she practiced letters and writing with Lydia, between the soldier's sparring matches with Shai.

When she wasn't fretting over Issen, Cirelle tried not to think about what Ellian was going through. It made her sick to imagine him in Adaleth's bed once again, of the cruelty the prince brought out in him.

She wondered if after days of it, Ellian would begin to enjoy it.

Did Shai or Issen know Ellian's dark past? From time to time, Issen would cast a sympathetic look her way, and she wondered.

And then the two weeks were over.

That evening, Cirelle's nearly wore a path in the tile of Ellian's foyer as she walked in fretful circles. Shai sat on the stairs, Lydia standing nearby. Issen remained at the cottage, still recovering.

When the doorbell rang, Cirelle rushed to open it.

For one eternal moment, time stood still. Ellian sprawled bonelessly on the stoop. A myriad of bruises and cuts covered his skin. The shirt he'd worn the night he was stolen had been wadded up and tossed beside him on the doorstep. Even worse than the lacerations were the swollen blisters covering one arm. Burns.

He didn't move. His eyes were closed, one blackened and swollen shut.

Orwe's blank, unseeing stare filled Cirelle's vision, and she couldn't remember how to breathe. A strange buzzing sound rang in her ears and a cold numbness washed over her. Almost in a daze, Cirelle knelt to nudge Ellian's limp shoulder.

He can't be dead, not like Orwe.

She didn't realize she was crying until one tear dripped from her nose and splattered on his chest.

A sound echoed to her, muffled as if very distant. It was her own voice, calling Ellian's name in breathless rasps.

Then something cut through the roar in her ears. "Cirelle!"

She turned to see Lydia kneeling beside her.

"Your Highness… He's alive," the soldier said. "He breathes."

Cirelle blinked, letting words to sink in. But Lydia was right. Ellian's chest rose and fell softly, wheezing in near-silent rasps.

Relief stole the strength from Cirelle, and her shoulders sagged. "We have to help him."

Shai carried Ellian into the antechamber, while Cirelle futilely and frantically searched the Archive for more of that purple elixir, even though she knew she'd used the last bits of it on Lydia's head injury.

After a few hopeless moments, Cirelle had to admit there was nothing here to help and returned to do what she could. Shai was examining Ellian in a clinical way, lifting his arms and prodding for broken ribs. Lydia stood nearby, shifting her weight from foot to foot.

A cluster of brownies entered, their arms full of bandages, vials, and small earthenware pots. After dropping their supplies on the low table by the sofa, most of the brownies scattered, but one remained, her wide copper eyes sympathetic.

"We've gathered what we could, my lady," the brownie said. "Not magic, just herbs, but they'll help. I can't give them to him, by faerie law. No gifts." She looked up at Cirelle. "But you can."

Cirelle knelt by the table, her eyes stinging with tears. And she couldn't even say thank you. "But aren't you giving them to me?"

"I don't know what you mean, my lady." The faerie's cheeks dimpled with a small smile. "I just set them here and left the room for a few moments."

Her meaning was clear.

"This one's for the bruises," the brownie pointed to a small tub containing a green paste. "That one's for cuts, and the third one is for burns." She lifted a small vial of yellowish liquid. "This is to drink for the pain, but you'd best see if you can get him up to his room before that one. He'll sleep for half a day."

Cirelle just nodded. The brownie gave Cirelle a soft smile, then cast a single sorrowful glance at Ellian before she left.

The brownies had also brought a small pitcher and basin of water, along with some clean rags. Remembering Dirilai's admonishment on Thieves' Night, Cirelle rinsed her hands. Everything now was a strange echo of that night. Ellian lying on his own sofa, battered, while Cirelle knelt on the floor and washed his wounds. There were a handful of cuts, but the burns gave her pause. In small circles, they scattered his arm like a gruesome constellation.

Shai helped, handing Cirelle the pots or jars as she asked for them, and murmured suggestions when Cirelle missed a spot. Lydia kept her silence, standing beside them and chewing her lip.

Halfway through the burns, Ellian's good eye flickered open and he jolted up. Cirelle rocked back on her heels as he sucked in great, gasping breaths of air. His visible eye was solid black, his teeth curled in a snarl.

His gaze paused at Shai and Lydia before it locked onto Cirelle and color filtered into his iris. Canary yellow, then a rare pale brown before it bled back into gray.

"Cirelle." He slumped back against the arm of the sofa. "I'm home." He shifted and winced.

"Yes." What had he gone through, that he'd awoken in such terror? "And you're injured. Now sit still." She dabbed her fingers into the salve for burns and reached for his arm.

Ellian flinched away, his good eye blinking wearily. "I can tend myself."

Shai snorted. "Oh? And you'll bandage your own shoulder how?"

His lips set in a line.

Cirelle stared at that prideful face so bruised, his swollen eye. "Stop being stubborn and let me do this."

His lip twitched, and Ellian held out his arm with a dramatic sigh. Even that small motion made him hiss in pain. As gently as possible, Cirelle lifted his arm and lightly dabbed unguent onto the burns with light touches. He still winced, but did not pull away.

"What happened?" she asked, almost a whisper. She began winding gauze around his burned forearm.

Ellian glanced away and closed his eyes. "I don't want to talk about it."

"Ellian…"

"No," he said, staring hard at her. Cirelle wondered if he deliberately avoided looking at Shai and Lydia. The word was a murmur, strained and thin.

Cirelle didn't press the matter. She tied off the bandage in a tidy bow. Ellian stared at it for a long moment, then smiled faintly.

Those moths in her belly rattled their wings, a warning.

She pushed her sleeves up out of the way and picked up the bottle for bruises. What had happened at that Unseelie palace of sugar-coated horrors? She'd seen what Adaleth asked of Ellian. Cirelle had even lived those sweat-soaked moments in Ellian's memory. But she'd also seen what happened to Orwe, to those who displeased the prince. Had felt it herself. Her knuckle throbbed.

Ellian groaned and turned to plant his feet on the floor. When he stood, the glamour covered the old burn scars on his back once more. Vain even when he swayed on his feet. And yet he did nothing to cover his blackened eye or the other wounds.

He stumbled when he tried to take a step, and Cirelle darted forward to steady him. "I'm at least helping you to your room."

She cast a guilty glance at Shai. "Would you be willing to stay in a guest room for a bit? At least until we get the wards back up?"

The soldier stretched. "Sure. Come on Lydia, let's go get some sleep. Cirelle can handle him."

Lydia's expression was dark, pensive, but she gave a sharp nod and followed Shai out of the room.

Maybe it was a mark of how injured he really was, but Ellian remained silent through this exchange. Cirelle pocketed the small pot of liniment and the yellow vial, then guided him out of the antechamber and slowly, painfully up the stairs to his wing.

In his room, Ellian fell onto the bed and sank his head into the pillows with a long sigh.

"Here," Cirelle held out the vial. "If you won't let me do any more, at least this will help with the pain."

He groaned softly and sat up, taking the tiny bottle from her grasp. His fingertips shook. It was a measure of how weary and wounded he was, that he tossed the concoction back without question.

When he lay back down, he yawned and his good eye already drooped with grogginess. Fast-acting, whatever that potion was.

After his eyes had closed and his breathing had slowed, Cirelle pulled the liniment for bruising from her pocket. As lightly as possible, she patted it around his injured eye, the skin dark purple and inflamed.

He didn't stir at all, and Cirelle squashed down her worry. It was just the medicine making him sleep soundly, that's all. His breathing was steady and deep.

She set the pot of salve on the side table so he'd find it when he awoke and turned to go. The latch clicked as she opened the door, and somehow that did make him stir. He gasped in a breath and rolled toward her.

His voice was pitifully small. "Don't go."

"What?"

"Please." That rare word. "I…" he paused, taking a long breath and lifting a hand toward her. "Stay with me." The words were thick, drowsy.

Heart aching, Cirelle swallowed and nodded. "All right."

Ellian's eyelid flickered shut. His breathing slowed again. Cirelle turned to head to the bed, but froze when her gaze skated past his desk. There, sitting on the corner next to that journal of his, lay a golden scale the size of her thumbnail. A piece of her dress, the night they'd first danced together at the Unseelie palace. Tentatively, Cirelle stepped forward and picked it up. The metal was cool and smooth in her fingertips, and she turned it over in her hand.

Darting a glance backward to find Ellian slumbering deeply, Cirelle set the token down and reached for the journal. She flipped it open with her pulse racing.

Tiny, aimless doodles decorated the margins of the pages, leaves and feathers and meaningless swirls. Of course the text was written in Kishi, the looping vertical lines completely unintelligible to her. She flipped through it to find the last dozen or so pages crossed out. Page after page of handwriting, all scratched through and scribbled over.

Feeling suddenly uneasy, Cirelle closed the book gently.

What secrets had Ellian written in those pages?

And why did he wipe them out?

With a shiver, she slipped into the bed. Ellian stirred, wrapping a sleepy arm around her middle. Unease flickered through her.

They'd never slept in the same bed. Always after their trysts, each would return to their own room. This… this was something different. Something that filled her belly with warmth and made her breath catch, like her lungs were full of broken glass.

She didn't know if she loved it or hated it.

დ

Ellian was still fast asleep when the doorbell rang again.

Cirelle's heart leapt into a sprint. She should let the brownies get it. But what if it were the prince at the door, come to gloat? Would she lunge at him with tooth and nail? Slap him? Cower and cringe?

Cirelle gently extricated herself from Ellian's slumbering embrace and left to answer the doorbell. He didn't wake.

It wasn't the prince on the doorstep.

"Dirilai." Cirelle started to close the door.

The faerie snapped, "do you want him to be healed?"

Cirelle halted with the door halfway shut. "In exchange for what?"

The faerie woman shook her head. Her lips were caught in a grimace, as if it pained her to utter the next words. "I need no payment from you."

Cirelle stared her down. "Then from whom? Nothing is free, faerie."

The sidhe's mouth thinned and her eyes darkened. "I will heal him because of a bargain made in the past," she said. "No new payments will be required."

For a few heartbeats, they both stood their ground.

"You're too late, Dirilai." Despite the offer, Cirelle didn't trust the faerie. "His injuries are already tended to."

The sidhe grimaced.

"What happened to him, at the palace?"

Dirilai sighed, shaking her head. "We should talk."

Something in her tone gave Cirelle pause. She opened the door the rest of the way, gesturing Dirilai inside. "The antechamber."

As soon as the antechamber door clicked shut, Cirelle whirled on the sidhe. "What happened to him?"

Dirilai leaned against the door. "Every day of his stay, Ellian was given a choice. And every day, he chose the dungeons." Those pitch-black eyes bored into Cirelle's with a long, weighted look. An icy shiver dripped down Cirelle's spine. Dirilai knew Ellian and the prince's secret.

Ellian had chosen torture over the prince's bed.

"How?" Cirelle murmured. "How do you know?"

The faerie snorted. "I'm the court healer, fool. Do you know how many times I've had to patch up the prince? Eventually, I figured out who was doing that to him, and it didn't take a genius to piece together what was going on."

For a moment, Cirelle leaned on the desk for support. Did Ellian know that Dirilai was privy to his darkest secret?

"I also know Ellian left decades ago and didn't look back," Dirilai said. "On Thieves' Night, he returned that viper's den, yet now he refuses Prince Adaleth these past two weeks?" Her canny eyes narrowed and pierced Cirelle's. "Why?"

Cirelle swallowed hard. "Last time… it was for the Key," she explained to herself as much as Dirilai. "He didn't truly want to go back. For his mission, he'd do it. But not when there's no purpose."

"Ah," Dirilai pointed out, "but there is. The prince now knows Ellian would rather refuse him. How long will it take him to wonder if there was another reason Ellian came to his door on Thieves' Night? From there, it's not a far leap to figure out Ellian came for the Key. It's a risk." She crossed her arms. "I healed him several times over the past two weeks. After each instance, he chose to go back. Once he would have sacrificed everything to keep the Key safe, including his own pride. So again I ponder, why would he choose the agony of the dungeons when the other torment would have better served his cause?"

A cold lump formed in Cirelle's stomach.

Dirilai's voice lowered. She turned her head, and her dark, canny eyes once again met Cirelle's. "I have to wonder if it's you."

Cirelle didn't answer. Her tongue seemed to stick to the roof of her mouth, the words caught in her throat. She coughed, loosening her tongue. "It's not," she said.

Dirilai scoffed. "I saw the two of you at the palace, girl, when you were disguised as a sylvan."

Her cheeks aflame, Cirelle shook her head. "That was an act." It choked her to say the words, and shame consumed her.

"Was it?" the faerie snapped, pointing a finger at Cirelle. "This mission has been brewing for years, and I won't have a single upstart human compromising him now. Not when we're so close."

Anger sparked. "I think you should leave now."

Dirilai's expression was half-sneer, half scowl. "You made me an oath. Don't forget it."

"Go."

She did.

When Cirelle returned to Ellian's room, he stirred. "Cirelle..." he said weakly. "I have to tell you..."

A tiny thread of fear tangled around her. "Shh. You should sleep."

For one long moment, his gaze met hers, swirling half a dozen colors before the drug claimed him and he lost consciousness once again.

This time, Cirelle took the chair at the desk, Dirilai's words rattling in her head.

I have to wonder if it's you.

Twenty-Seven

AFTER ELLIAN AWOKE, Cirelle awkwardly took her leave. He seemed to have little memory of the night before. Relief and regret mingled within her, but she said nothing of how he'd asked her to stay, his arms around her while he slept.

Cirelle sent the brownies to his chamber to make sure he had whatever he might need when he awoke. Tea and food, herbal remedies for pain.

He didn't emerge at all that evening, leaving Cirelle pacing and fretful.

Still, she didn't need her valerian tea that night, and her horrific nightmares had abandoned her. Her sleep was blissfully dreamless and deep. When she awoke, she no longer felt like a walking corpse.

Ellian remained in his wing for three full days, only leaving briefly on the first day to summon Tallia and trade for a replacement of his wards.

The second day, the brownies took Ellian food, scurrying into the wing and out again. Irritation took the place of Cirelle's worry. She grew short with Lydia in their lessons. For her part, Lydia grew sullen as well, quiet and terse. Too often, her eyes lingered on Cirelle's missing finger, on the faint white traces of scars that snaked up her forearms.

By the third evening, Cirelle was well and truly angry. He'd been through an ordeal she couldn't comprehend, and Cirelle tried to be patient, but she felt frayed like a worn rope. *Two weeks of worrying about him. I bargained with Lisovyk in his stead, fought redcaps and the Scath. Issen got hurt. And he won't even talk to me.*

After breakfast on the fourth day, Cirelle's temper snapped. She had few duties left in the Archive, since Ellian refused to come out of his rooms and take her on summons. Still, Cirelle was growing accustomed to her working clothes and had donned them this morning anyway, pulling her hair back into a simple tail.

Cirelle barged through the doors of his wing. "Ellian!" The name echoed down the hall before her, punctuated by the heels of her boots on the stone. "It's time to stop sulking, or hiding, or whatever it is you're doing." She poked her head into open doors, all empty, before reaching his bedchamber.

She knocked loudly, calling his name again.

"What?" He stepped out of a room across the hall, shutting the door firmly behind him before Cirelle could glimpse what lay beyond. At least he was dressed normally, in shades of rich blue and black. He bore no jewelry save his rings and a single silver hoop at the tip of each ear, but he wasn't lying morose in his bed.

"Are you going to hide in here forever?" Cirelle snapped.

"Who says I'm hiding?"

"I do." She took one tentative step toward him.

"Perhaps I just need more time to recover from my wounds."

Cirelle snorted. "That's awfully feeble, for you. That's all you can come up with?"

That earned her a flicker of a smile, a flash of aqua blue in his eyes, there and gone before the scowl returned. "You're not supposed to be in here uninvited."

"I know," she waved a hand, taking another step closer. "Faerie rules, punishment and all that. Do whatever you must. Banish me from the music room, steal all my desserts for a week. But I'm dragging you out of this wing whether you want to go or not. We need to talk." Her voice cracked a little. "About what happened with the Lisovyk."

"You—what?" Ellian's eyes flared pale yellow, and this time he took a step toward Cirelle. "You went to the Lisovyk?"

"Yes. Not alone. With Issen and Lydia… and Kith." She stared up at him, challenging him to chastise her for it.

Silver slammed back down over that gaze before Ellian closed his eyes. "Mad, reckless princess," he muttered, leaning against the wall. A small laugh bubbled out of him. "Why would you do that?"

"Because it was important." Cirelle took another step, within arm's reach now. "Because it was our only chance at the Lock, and I wasn't going to let it slip by. But… he didn't have it. Still, he gave us a clue. A necklace dropped by the one who stole it."

Ellian kept his unreadably gray eyes cast up at the ceiling as he spoke. "I counted the days," he said quietly. "And I knew when our chance at the Lisovyk had passed. I never thought…" he let the words trail off. "And you took Kith? You know we can trust no one."

"We needed more backup. I'll explain everything if you come out to the antechamber with me." Her stomach curdled at the thought of telling Ellian about Issen's injury. About how she'd killed the Scath. "I'll show you the necklace." She lifted a hand to touch his arm, but Ellian flinched away from her. It stung.

"Ellian," she said, meeting that inscrutable gaze. "Those two weeks…" but the question died on her lips. *Why did you choose the dungeons?*

"Go back to the antechamber. I'll meet you there to discuss this necklace."

That small, sharp pain beneath her ribs made Cirelle snappish. "And what punishment have I earned for trespassing without invitation?" She hissed the words at his back as he walked away, her fists clenched at her sides. The hot burn of tears welled up in her eyes and she blinked them away in fury.

He spoke without looking back, his voice cold and stilted. "You faced down the Lisovyk for my sake. I think that earns you a pass. This time."

He met her in the Archive antechamber almost half an hour later, and she wondered what he had done in those long minutes. Had Ellian needed to let his own anger cool, upset with her for going to see the Lisovyk? Or for bringing up what had happened to him over those two weeks he was gone?

How much torment had he endured, all because he refused to crawl into the prince's bed?

And why? He hated Adaleth, yes, but was it really worse than the torture he'd suffered in the dungeons? Dirilai had healed Ellian multiple times, only for him to be thrown back into a cell to be burned and beaten.

It made Cirelle's stomach tumble and wring itself into knots.

Dirilai had seemed so very certain of why. *I have to wonder if it's you.*

No. It was his hatred of the prince. What she and Ellian did together... it was just pleasure, nothing more. Certainly not worth enduring torture. Her chest ached, her ribs too small for her lungs. She was pacing the room when Ellian finally arrived, nearly bumping into him as he strode through the door. Cirelle scrambled back.

Ellian's eyes flashed a dark color before he glamoured them

again. His face was impassive as a statue's, his cautious mask back in full. "The necklace?"

Cirelle sat on the sofa, pointing at the nearby chair with a shaky hand. Steeling her courage, she picked at a worn spot in the velvet. Could she admit to him what she'd done? How she'd dragged Issen on the mission that ruined his arm? Or how she'd stabbed the Scath and felt only a cold nothingness afterward?

She met Ellian's eyes, took another deep breath, and told him everything.

When the last words had spilled from her, Cirelle felt raw and hollow. She curled up on the sofa, arms wrapped around her knees.

Ellian wouldn't even look at her. He stared across the room, expressionless.

Silence held.

"Are you going to speak?" she asked.

Ellian rested his elbows on his knees and sank his head into his hands. "What do you want me to say?"

There, irritation. A familiar sting. "Anything."

He sighed. "What's done is done." There was no inflection in his response whatsoever. "The traitor has been both found and dealt with. I'll speak to Issen tomorrow. Now we move on." He stood.

"What about the potion I stole to heal Lydia's head injury? The purple one?"

He shook his head. "There were only a few drops left. A day forbidden from the library for that one." The declaration was weary, strained. "Now show me the necklace."

It was a cold sort of dismissal. Her cheeks burning, she got up.

She led him to the shelf where it rested, catalogued with the rest of his artifacts. Her throat felt dry, scratchy like it had been scraped with nettles. A cold numbness settled into her. "The Lock was stolen from the Lisovyk years—maybe decades or even centuries—ago, but this was dropped by the thief." The necklace looked innocuous enough. The chain had snapped, leaving the two ends dangling from a long, curved feather, cleverly crafted. Not even a speck of tarnish marred it.

Suddenly, it seemed a pitiful prize, a bit of junk traded for a treasure at too high a cost. "I'm sorry," she apologized.

Ellian shook his head, lifting the necklace in one hand. "No." His hand wrapped around the feather. "This is our only clue, and I may be able to hunt down its former owner. It's obviously duergar make, and they keep meticulous records. We have a lead, thanks to your reckless courage." Still, his reply lacked teeth.

"My foolishness, you mean."

"You got the only clue to the Lock, to saving our worlds."

"At the cost of Issen's arm."

"He knew the risks. As do we all. You included."

Like Orwe did.

"So I'm truly one of you now?" She asked quietly. "Now that I've bargained for you, killed for your cause?" Her stomach tightened at uttering the words again, at admitting what she'd done. Thieves' Night had been the heat of battle, desperate self-defense. The Scath had been murder. There was no other word for what she had done.

And yet, the thought did not break her. A numbness filled her where shame should have been. She felt guilt for Issen, but only cold vindictiveness for what she'd done to the Scath.

Ellian's eyes went dark again before he blinked the color away. He turned aside to replace the necklace on the shelf. "I think," Ellian replied carefully, his gaze avoiding hers, "that you've been one of us longer than we'd either care to admit."

I knew it.

Lydia stared at the entry in the Archive's ledger, written in Cirelle's looping handwriting. The sloppy edges of the letters were unmistakable.

Key. And a date, some weeks ago, after Cirelle's arrival.

Taking note of the location listed, Lydia turned the book's page to the current entry before leaving it. She made her way through the shelves.

There. A small, pale wooden box with brass corners. It looked plain enough, but thrummed with energy. She could almost hear it buzzing like a beehive, feel it tingling against her skin. The small chip slotted in front of it was a bright crimson. *Do not touch, danger.*

Was it truly a risk though, or merely a way to keep her prying eyes off of it? The entry only said "Key". There was no way of knowing whether this was *The* Key. But there was also no way of knowing whether there truly were deadly wards on that box. No. For now, she'd bide her time until she could think of something.

Damn it all. There was a reason she was still just a guard, not a captain by now. Lydia followed other people's orders, never creating her own. But now she was adrift in this deadly, toxic place with no anchor, no one to turn to for guidance, and a princess who needed her.

With one last look at the box, Lydia turned and made her way back to her room to plan.

Twenty-Eight

DESPITE CIRELLE'S VICTORY with the Lisovyk, a listlessness seemed to settle over Ellian. He grew pensive, withdrawn. When Cirelle touched him, he flinched and drew away. Her flirtations went unanswered, deflected, and he certainly didn't share her bed.

Stars, what had he endured in Adaleth's dungeons?

Or what if that wasn't it at all? It *was* her fault his friend had lost the use of his arm. It was *her* mission that had gone sideways, with only this necklace to show for it.

Did Ellian hate her now, for her failure? It ate at her. Guilt. Shame. Sorrow. Old companions. It had been some time since she felt this creeping despair, but it hounded her steps once more.

Lydia did her best to cheer Cirelle, but could not banish her doubts or the certainty that Ellian's new reticence was her own doing.

The date of their next dance drew near. When she awoke that evening, queasy nerves left Cirelle jittery. She ate her breakfast in her parlor alone. During idle hours after Archive duties, a summer storm confined them all indoors. Lydia practiced her letters in the library while Cirelle sat nearby and picked at the strings of a strange faerie instrument she'd found lying in the back of a cabinet in Ellian's music room. She twisted the knobs to tune it, and plucked at it with a clawed ring.

Ellian poked his head into the room. A sharpness surrounded him, his expression itching for a fight. "Finished with updating the paperwork already?"

Something in his tone made Cirelle bristle. The music stopped and she gave him a flat stare. "Yes, we did."

His brows drew together. He whirled on a heel and left without another word.

Through this exchange, Lydia had barely looked up from her pen and parchment. She cleared her throat, but said nothing.

"I'll be back," Cirelle said, setting the instrument aside. Things couldn't go on like this. "Wait," she called out after Ellian in the hallway, and his steps faltered.

He turned, but did not speak.

"What's wrong?" she demanded, glaring up into that icy expression.

"Many things are wrong in this world. You'll have to be more specific."

"You promised to answer my questions. So tell me. What has your bloomers all in a twist? Did I… did I do something?"

His eyes flickered dark blue before he covered them with silver. "That's not… if you really must know, today would be my nameday. In the human world, in my human life."

"Oh." That wasn't at all what she'd expected. And it certainly didn't explain why he'd drawn away from her days ago, but it at least gave a reason for today's sourness.

"So tell me about it, then. What do they do to celebrate in Kishir?"

His gaze skittered away from her. "On the middlemost day of each month, everyone in the village born during that month is celebrated. The honorees get a crown of woven leaves and a garland of flowers to wear, and they have to give a blossom to every person who requests one." Ellian leaned back against the wall, crossing his arms. "It's a game throughout the day, to see who can collect the most flowers. And if anyone manages to snatch the crown of leaves from the celebrant's head, they earn a kiss for their cleverness. At sunset there's a feast which ends with desaru, a special sort of dish prepared only for nameday celebrations. It's a thin pie made of chopped nuts and fruits. Then the entire village joins in a dance out in the central square."

Cirelle swallowed and replied. "It sounds very festive." She resisted the urge to reach out for him, a habit that once felt so natural. Now unwanted, now awkward. Instead, she continued. "Namedays in Arraven are much more staid affairs, at least among the nobility. A great tea is held in the afternoon, and the celebrant wears his or her best clothing, usually made especially for the day. Sometimes there's a formal ball. It's a far stuffier sort of celebration."

Ellian uncrossed his arms with a sigh. Another break in the wall around him, a wistfulness lingering in his gaze as he stared past her. "Foolish, I know, to mourn a tradition I haven't truly celebrated in decades. I've even stopped counting how many namedays I've had."

"It's not silly," Cirelle said, suddenly homesick for even the uptight nameday celebrations of her home. She'd at least looked forward to the ball every year, the music and dancing. Her own nameday would pass just as winter turned to spring. What would she do to celebrate, here in Faerie?

Ellian shook his head, his coolness settling back over him like a fog. Cirelle mourned as the shield went back up, the coolness settling into his eyes. "I have a client coming in a few minutes."

Cirelle sighed. "I know, I booked it."

He didn't bother replying, shaking his head again and slipping out into the foyer.

As soon as he was through the doors, Cirelle dashed back to the ballroom, bursting through the doors with a wide grin.

"Lydia, I have an idea."

❧

"Are you sure about this?" The guardswoman asked as they slowly recalled how to weave the leaves and flowers into garlands, an old trick they'd learned as children. So many of these Faerie flowers and plants were unfamiliar, and it took some trial and error to find ones with stems pliable enough to use. The best turned out to be her favorites, the tiny star-shaped flowers that faded from pale blue at the tips to deep pink at the center. Cirelle plucked off vines, pinching them free with her fingernails, then began attaching them together. She twined other flowers in as she went, a wild array of blossoms in her favorite hues, from rich purple to ocean blue, and rosy pinks for variety. The whole thing was woven through with thin strands of ribbon Cirelle had found in one of the abandoned rooms, among a set of dusty old embroidery supplies.

Lydia had been set to plaiting the leafy crown. She was making faster progress than Cirelle, her movements simple and efficient.

"Yes, I'm sure." Cirelle's fingers were starting to remember the motions, weaving the flowers more deftly as she went. Still, Lydia finished before Cirelle did, testing the crown on her own head.

Cirelle smiled to see the serious warrior woman wearing a

crown of leaves. Even Lydia gave a ghost of a grin, though her words were dubious. "It's a bit silly, isn't it?"

Cirelle nodded. "That's the point," she laughed as she tied off her garland. "Something broke in Ellian over those two weeks. And if a bit of absurdity can help him heal, so be it." *And if it helps him forgive me.*

To that, Lydia didn't respond.

"Come on, he should be done with his client meeting by now." Cirelle took the crown from Lydia's grasp and looped both over an arm, standing and sweeping off her trousers with the other hand. "Let's go."

Hiding the items behind her back, she stood on the second floor of the main entry, leaning against the railing to wait for Ellian's client to exit. When the faerie left and closed the door, Ellian stared up at her from the foyer, his eyes narrowed and suspicious. Lydia sighed softly, resigned, but it only made Cirelle's smile widen. A fey giddiness had taken over her, and she danced down the stairs with light steps.

"Should I ask why you're smiling like the cat that ate the canary?" Ellian sighed as he approached. "Or would I rather not know?"

Instead of answering, Cirelle darted up and tossed the garland about his neck, then crookedly placed the crown of leaves on his head.

"Now give me a flower," she demanded with a grin.

Ellian stood there, completely motionless and staring for a moment, before straightening the crown and narrowing his eyes at Cirelle. He lifted the flower garland between two gray fingers. "Did you put this together? Or did you make Lydia do it?"

Cirelle huffed at him indignantly. "I did the garland, but she did the crown."

"I'll have you know," Lydia said sourly as she descended the steps, "It was entirely her idea."

"Well," Ellian sighed dramatically, his eyes glimmering sky blue for the first time in weeks, "there was little doubt of that. You're far too practical for such frivolity." Cirelle wasn't sure if that was a compliment or insult.

"Hey!" Cirelle called. "Frivolity is good every once in a while. Stars know a little fun won't kill either of you."

And finally Ellian smiled. A little. It thawed the ice in Cirelle's chest a bit further, a tiny thread of her old feelings leaking through. Those moths in her belly shook their wings, if not bursting out into flight.

"All right, then," Ellian said. "Let's go see if the brownies know how to make desaru."

❧

An hour after dinner, Cirelle paced in the ballroom, heart hammering in her chest. She'd donned one of those scandalous fae gowns in emerald green tonight, shimmering and iridescent like a peacock's feather. Intricate lace details in gleaming gold scattered around her throat and along the sleeves. Her hair was long and loose, the red completely faded by now.

Stars, had it really been months since she'd arrived in Faerie?

She stood in the center of the floor, waiting. Determined. The dances had always been their way of speaking without words. And she was certain once Ellian had her in his arms again, he'd kiss her once more. After that, things would go back to the way they'd been before.

When Ellian entered, the garland of flowers rested about his neck, minus a few blossoms, and the crown of leaves still sat atop his head.

His gaze was cool steel, his face that calm mask she was coming to know all too well lately.

Cirelle's heart sank, and her plan died half-formed. She stepped into the position of a baliterre with resignation. Whatever had happened with Adaleth, it seemed recovery was long distant, if ever.

What if it's not Adaleth? Her traitorous mind plucked once more at that fear. *You've disappointed him. A failure.*

Ellian went through the motions with a lackluster reluctance, as if he didn't even want to touch her.

I'm a fool, she thought, *to think a necklace of flowers would change anything.*

Several times, Ellian opened his mouth or cleared his throat, but did not speak. After three stiff dances, she cracked. "What? Whatever you have to say, spill it."

"I know what you expect… at the end of the evening." He shook his head. "But I will not take you to bed," Ellian said flatly.

It was like a slap. "Because… because of what happened with Adaleth?"

"No."

Silence held.

He was only an arm's length away, but Ellian might as well have stood on the opposite ridge of a canyon. Those eyes gave away nothing, mouth set in a hard line. But his breathing was shallow and rapid, and his nostrils flared.

Cirelle found her words. "You can't… you can't turn me aside like that without even giving me a reason, and still ask me to dance with you every fortnight."

"Very well then," he said quietly, voice hollow. "No more dances."

Her heart skipped a beat.

"Can—" her voice was a croak. Cirelle cleared her throat and continued. "Can you do that?" A faerie bargain was inescapable, wasn't it?

Ellian's smile was grim, but still he stared at the wall rather than at Cirelle. "We made a pact. I can't remove it, but I can transmute it. Give me…" he paused, thinking. "Promise me a boon. A future favor, called in when I choose, and you're free of the dances."

He was taking everything away. She'd truly failed. Oh, how deeply he must loathe her now, to do this.

His next words were said softly, but still hurt. "You've one chance at this, Cirelle. I suggest you take it."

The simpering gentleness did it. Her temper snapped. Cirelle stepped forward and snatched the leafy garland from his head. *If anyone manages to snatch the crown of leaves, they earn a kiss for their cleverness.*

Ellian glared, a glimmer of color finally entering his eyes. Orange as burning coals, as a sunrise, more brilliant than autumn leaves. Anger.

It was better than the flat nothing of the past days. She stared up into that furious gaze, traitorous tears welling up in her own eyes. She blinked them away.

There, so quick she almost might have missed it, a flicker of deepest blue before that silver curtain slammed down. Ellian turned aside from her again, squeezing his eyes shut. His arms uncrossed and he turned to leave the ballroom, his footsteps unbearably loud in the echoing space, even as the enchanted astralir in the corner continued to play a sweeping tune.

"I haven't agreed to your offer yet." Cirelle's command came out sharp, an imperious declaration.

At the door, he turned his head to regard her coolly. "You'd rather do this every fortnight? You were the one who said you didn't want to dance if I didn't bed you. I gave you a way out."

Cirelle bared her teeth. "Yes, we'll do this over and over again, both of us miserable over it, if you're too cowardly to kiss me," she taunted, holding up the leafy crown. "Isn't that what I earned by taking this?"

Another flicker of orange in those eyes. Then he moved. Too fast. Cirelle had only a moment to brace herself as he strode toward her.

Then his hands were in her hair, his mouth on hers. It wasn't gentle. She could feel the rage in his trembling fingertips, in the pressure of his lips crushing her own.

It didn't matter. She'd won.

Cirelle laughed, pulling him closer, not caring that his rough kiss stole her breath.

Ellian shuddered, a small sound caught in the back of his throat. And then he was gone, her arms empty. His hands clenched and unclenched into fists at his sides, and his eyes stayed firmly closed for three long seconds before he opened them. Colorless and gray, but he panted softly, chest rising and falling with rapid, labored breaths.

Cirelle asked the question again. "Ellian… why?" *Why did you brush me aside, why do you hide from me?*

"Because…" his voice rasped on the words. "Because I don't want to do this anymore."

Invisible, venomous claws tore Cirelle open, and she couldn't breathe.

Faeries couldn't lie.

She closed her eyes, the tears finally spilling free. The crown of leaves fell from her hand. *Run away, escape,* a tiny voice inside her urged, and she listened. Staring at the floor, Cirelle darted past him before Ellian could see her cry.

"You'll have your boon," she choked out as she reached the

door. "I give my oath." The air shuddered, acknowledging the pact.

"Cirelle." There was a weight to her name when Ellian said it, but it could have been anything. Guilt, anger, regret.

It didn't matter. Pretending she hadn't heard, Cirelle opened the doors and fled.

Twenty-Nine

OVER THE NEXT TWO WEEKS, they settled into an uncertain holding pattern. Cool, but Cirelle was proud she at least managed to remain civil. Summons came and went, the two of them traveling together as Ellian collected odd bits of human paraphernalia in exchange for pieces of his treasure trove.

Cirelle recovered slowly. The wound of Ellian's dismissal was a raw one, but the pain grew familiar. Even the guilt over Issen couldn't plague her so sharply forever. Music returned, though it often slipped into forlorn melodies. She maintained the Archive and spent her free time composing, teaching Lydia's reading lessons, or browsing the gardens. Lydia's mood brightened as Cirelle spent less time with Ellian, and even the swordplay lessons with the claimhte took on a bit of cheer.

In the library, Cirelle found some books on Faerie history, but they were all ancient, telling of things that happened half a millennium ago or more. There were mentions of a ruling Seelie Court, the Summer Court.

And what happened to them? Cirelle had to wonder. *Why are the sidhe now ruled by the cold and heartless Unseelie?*

She wanted to ask Ellian but feared mentioning Queen Ayre

or Prince Adaleth to him at all. Never again did either of them mention Adaleth's abduction of Ellian.

Nor did they discuss Cirelle's trip to the Lisovyk.

Shai visited more often again, and Cirelle didn't know if Ellian had asked her to, or if it were merely the budding friendship between the sidhe and Lydia. Cirelle also wondered if Lydia even realized she were softening toward one faerie, at least.

Today, though, Cirelle pushed a game piece toward Shai and narrowed her eyes. Lydia sat in the third place at the triangular game table, chewing her lip and staring at the board. Strategizing.

But something was wrong with Shai. The faerie was uncharacteristically fidgety, tapping the table impatiently between moves, scratching her nose, shifting in her seat. Since yesterday, the warrior had been increasingly restless.

"What is it?" Cirelle finally asked, bumping one of Shai's pieces off the board and moving it to her side of the table. Lydia's hand hovered over her corner of the triangular game board, chewing her lip.

Shai blinked. "What is what?"

"The thing that has you all antsy."

Lydia snorted. "Yeah. Your foot's been tapping this whole game."

Cirelle narrowed her eyes. "Is it Ellian?"

"No."

After a brief glance at Lydia, Cirelle murmured, "Adaleth?"

Shai shook her head. She chewed on her lip, then blew out a breath. "It's… I went to the human world a week ago. I, uh, I wanted to check on your kingdom. Where you lived."

Lydia let out a huff of air, dropping the piece she held. "Arraven? Why?"

A shrug. "Curiosity. But there was gossip…"

Cirelle asked, "about what?"

"You. And the neighboring kingdom. The betrothal."

"My suitors? Have my parents chosen one of them?"

"I heard the name Rinn, I think?"

Lydia's voice was pained as she muttered, "Rhine."

Stars, Cirelle's betrothed seemed like a long-forgotten dream. A few stolen kisses, the memories of a woman who no longer existed. A frivolous girl, ignorant of how cruel the world could be. Did her intended pine for her while she cavorted with a faerie and forgot what Rhine's voice sounded like?

Shai added, "from what I overheard, the other kingdoms signed a treaty. Peace until you return. When you come back, you'll marry Prince Rhine."

Which would forge an alliance with Asheir, pulling the teeth of Gilbras, no longer a threat at their backs.

Cirelle's stomach churned. That had been the purpose of her betrothal in the first place. An alliance with one of the coastal kingdoms would shift the balance of power too far in its favor for the other to challenge. "That's not new."

"If you don't marry Rhine within a fortnight of your return, there's no treaty. No alliance. The people I overheard worried it would mean war."

And it would. She was trapped. Cirelle's entire life, given as the cost to prevent that conflict. A piece in a game once more. But after everything Ellian had done for his people, could she do less for hers? "I have to send my family a message," she whispered. "Can you take a letter back for me?"

Lydia's hand clutched the game piece tightly, her knuckles going white.

Shai hesitated. "I guess? How... how will they let me in?"

"You can glamour yourself, right? It's nearly Aidan's nameday, there'll be all sorts of bustle. You can just glamour yourself to wear the green and gold of the palace's livery and act like you belong. They'll let you through. Take the letter to Aidan. You can tell him who you truly are, and he'll get the note to my parents."

Cirelle didn't even know why she hadn't thought of this yet. Shai was familiar with her world, and could be a go-between. It was so startlingly obvious, now that she thought of it.

She crossed to the corner of the room where a stack of paper rested on a desk, alongside a pen and inkpot.

"Cirelle…" Lydia said, but whatever she intended to say died on her lips.

On the top piece of paper, Cirelle scratched out her the words with trembling hands.

Aidan. Please pass this on to Mother and Father.

I'm sorry. I've been sentenced to six more months in Faerie, but I will marry Prince Rhine on the very day I return if you deem it must be so.

She skipped a line, then added:

So you know this is really from me: I'm still angry about the bluebird.

Signed, Cirelle.

'The bluebird' had been her favorite childhood toy, a clever wind-up contraption that flapped its wings and played a tinny little song. Aidan had stolen it when she refused to let him play with it, and he'd accidentally broken off a wing. Such a small, inconsequential thing, but memorable enough he'd know the letter was not a forgery.

It was a brief note, but it contained all she had to say. Heavy chains wrapped her heart. Only months of freedom left. And she couldn't even lean on Ellian. Not anymore.

Cirelle signed the message, her lifelong prison sentence, and dusted it to dry. Her knees failed her, and she slumped into a nearby divan, blinking the tears from her eyes. Her familiar sorrow washed over her, a crashing wave.

"I'm sorry," Shai said, standing awkwardly by the table.

"It's not your fault."

Silence fell until Shai broke it suddenly. "Do you want me to leave?"

Cirelle nodded. The faerie took the note, folded it, and left. Cirelle hugged her knees to her chest and wept. Lydia came to sit beside her, taking Cirelle's hand in hers.

They stayed like that for a long time.

ೞ

The return letter was curt.

Cirelle,

Rhine was sorely ruffled by the insistence he wait six more months. We acceded some trade benefits to mollify him, but you will wed within three days of your return.

Her father's signature stared back at her from the bottom of the page.

Shai shifted from foot to foot in the library as Cirelle stared at the words, clearly uncertain whether to stay or go. "Uh... so should I take another letter back to your parents?"

"No—"

Cirelle's reply was cut off by Ellian walking into the room, his expression dark. "Did I just overhear that correctly?" His withering glare pinned Shai down. "Are you ferrying letters back and forth to Arraven?"

Shai chewed on her lip. "Just the one."

Ellian shook his head. "No more."

"What?" The word exploded from Cirelle's lips. "Why? You never forbade I communicate with my family."

"I am now." He shook his head. "Our enemies have spies in both realms, maybe doubly so now that your residence here is known. You endanger your family by doing this."

"You don't trust me not to commit your secrets to paper?"

"That's not the point. It is an unnecessary risk, and I forbid it."

Cirelle snarled silently. Shai grimaced. "I, er, I think I'm gonna just go." She left, and neither Ellian nor Cirelle stopped her.

"You are a jealous coward, Ellian," Cirelle hissed. "You push me aside, but then you won't even share me with my own family."

"It's not—"

But Cirelle didn't bother to listen. Without even a retort, she stormed out.

Thirty

The Key haunted Lydia's thoughts. She couldn't be certain it was *that* Key, but if Ellian hunted the Lock, it was all too likely. If he got both pieces and destroyed them, the faerie and human realms would remain forever woven together.

And Cirelle would never be free of his clutches.

Lydia knew why the princess had fallen apart at her agreement to marry Rhine, and it wasn't homesickness for Arraven. It was that damnable faerie and the claws he'd sunk into Cirelle.

And Lydia was going to do something about it.

32-18B.

Lydia repeated the number to herself as she crept through the Archive. Cirelle's lessons had paid off. Now that Lydia could read passably well, Ellian and the princess had left the bookkeeping to the soldier over the past week while they plotted their schemes.

She passed the shelf Cirelle had set aside for her knives. The princess hadn't told her the full story of those. Or at least not a true one. Cirelle was a passable enough liar, but Lydia had grown up with her and knew every tell. No, there was something about those eerie blades that Cirelle did not want Lydia to know, and that worried the soldier.

But today she would do something about that. Cirelle was busy reading in the garden, and Ellian rarely came into the Archive proper. This was her chance.

32-18B.

She reached the set of shelves marked 32 and settled the rolling ladder into place. Shelf 18 would be tall enough that she'd need it, no matter how much her heart leapt into her throat at even that tiny elevation.

It's easier than patrolling the walls at the palace, she reminded herself, and began her ascent.

Shelf 18, slot B.

There it lay, looking so innocuous. A crimson length of string, perhaps three feet of it, neatly coiled.

Lydia had stumbled across its entry in the books by sheer luck, and a plan had taken root. Seeing Cirelle poisoned still haunted the soldier's memories. Then the redcaps. The princess had been both maimed and scarred in the service of that bastard.

It curdled her gut. And what dangers still awaited her princess while Ellian tangled her further in his schemes? Her mind seethed at the way he and Cirelle stared at each other when they thought Lydia wasn't looking. The sly little glances, the blushes. Those had cooled since his abduction, but how long until that flame sparked to life again?

Though Lydia lacked a personal interest in sexual exploits, that didn't mean she was oblivious.

It was time to take a drastic measure. One she would never have considered, if her princess's safety wasn't at risk.

Lydia's fingertips hesitated as she reached for the string on the shelf. Chewing on her lip, she took a breath and grabbed it, shoving the coil into her pocket. She quickly descended the ladder, rolled it back into place at the end of the row, and left the Archive with her stolen bit of magic.

Two days later, Lydia's hands tingled as she fiddled with the string in her pocket. It never tangled, no matter how much she twisted it in her fingers. It buzzed with magic, ready and waiting.

But the opportunity had not presented itself. Not yet.

It had been too long already. How long until Ellian realized his Archive was missing an item? It would be just her luck that he'd need it for a client, and then her ruse would be discovered.

She had to act soon.

So she watched and waited. After lunch, Cirelle left for the music room. Lydia tagged along with the princess as usual, but watched Ellian as he walked the hallway ahead of them.

He took the turn toward the gardens, and Lydia seized her chance.

"I think I'll head up to the garden to drill a bit," she told Cirelle, settling her hand on the hilt of the blade she now always wore at her belt, even inside the manor. After the incident with Ellian's kidnapping, she didn't trust the barriers Ellian had rebuilt. And there were enemies within these walls, too, even if Cirelle refused to see it.

The princess gave a smile and a wave as she stepped into the music room. "Have fun."

Lydia kept walking, trying to steady the tremor that had overtaken her.

I can do this.

Deception was not a skill she'd ever possessed. But the memory of Cirelle's pained, poisoned cries spurred her onward. She found Ellian on a bench, a purple journal resting on his lap. He tapped at it thoughtfully with the tip of a pen. He'd held neither item on his way out to the garden. Lydia's eyes flicked toward that bag at his waist, more faerie magic he flaunted so brazenly.

He glanced up as she approached and startled.

"Expecting someone else?" Her fist clenched around the knot of string inside her pocket.

Ellian folded the book, setting the pen atop it. "This is the first time you've ever sought me out. So yes, I'll admit I'm surprised."

Lydia withdrew her hand from her pocket, the string carefully tucked between her curled fingers. Stiffly, she sat on the bench an arm's length away from him.

"I've come to bargain," she said.

"Again?"

Lydia's cheeks warmed. She'd been desperate when she sought him out before, when she made the deal that landed her here.

She was even more so now.

"Leave her alone," Lydia demanded, her fingers aching as she kept her fist tightly clenched on her knee. "Set her aside. Don't wrap her in any more of your schemes. Send her home."

"Ah," he said, settling back into the bench, resting one arm along the back of it. Close. So easy.

But first she would try to bargain. "What would you take from me to send her back?"

The faerie shook his head. "I can't. A year of her life spent in Faerie. That was her oath. And then an extra six months added after."

"Then for that time, leave her out of your plans, away from whatever web you're spinning."

"A spider now, am I?"

Lydia's lips pressed together in a scowl. "If the shoe fits."

"I can't give you what you want," he said. "I promised her she would get a say in my plans. An oath I cannot break." His steely-gray eyes managed a passable mimicry of sorrow. Something Cirelle ignored, but Lydia could not.

Ellian shook his head. "If that's all you wanted, then I suppose our business is done."

"No, it's not." Lydia moved with a warrior's reflexes. She grasped his arm with her left hand, shaking loose the string as she wrapped the red cord around his wrist. One, two, three loops and it snagged tight.

"I bind you to me, faerie," Lydia hissed, then leapt off the bench.

Ellian yanked his hand back, holding it before him. He scratched at the red lines of the string that had embedded themselves into his skin like a gruesome tattoo.

He tried to stand, but Lydia interrupted him. "Stay seated!"

The faerie's motions were cut off abruptly and his body slammed back down onto the bench.

But when the surprise flickered away from his face, it was not replaced by anger. Resignation took its place.

"You," he said quietly, hands fisted in his lap. He gave a small cough of a laugh. "Not her."

It took a moment for the words to sink in.

"You knew it was missing," Lydia muttered. "But you thought Cirelle took it."

Ellian nodded.

"Then why didn't you say anything?"

The insufferable faerie had the gall to grin at her as he ticked points on his fingers. "One, I was curious. I wanted to watch her play out her hand. Two, there are situations in which it might not be entirely unpleasant to be your princess's thrall." His smile turned into something almost a leer.

"Ugh," Lydia snorted. "That's the first thing that will stop."

"Oh? And what do you intend to do with me, my new master?" There was a vicious, mocking tone in Ellian's reply. His posture was carefully casual, but she watched his hands tremble with anger and a brief flicker of orange peeked through the gray of his eyes. "Will you leave me here on this bench for eternity?"

"No. I'm going to keep her safe. You're going to avoid Cirelle as much as you are able, and if she asks why, you will not tell her I am the cause. There will be no more of those secret little looks you share, and you will keep her far from any other faeries."

"You want me to make her a prisoner, lock her away in a tower. All alone."

"She'll have me."

A wickedness bloomed in Ellian's smile. "About that." He lifted the hand that held the binding mark. "Did you even bother to read how to break this binding?"

"*Until the owner of Hasker's Cord sheds a single tear,*" Lydia recited.

His eyes darkened. "And that doesn't worry you?"

"I'm not much of a crier."

"Truly?" He beckoned her closer and tipped his head forward as if to tell her a secret. Lydia caught herself leaning in and forced herself to stop.

"I can't lie," he reminded her.

Lydia just gave him a flat stare.

His words dipped low, midnight given voice. Venom dripped from his tongue as he said simply, "She'll never be yours."

It would have hurt less if he'd struck her. Lydia's breath caught in her throat, and her eyes burned. She blinked. Panicking, she tried to stop it, but still a tear fell, sliding down her cheek and dripping from her chin.

Ellian stood, the bond broken, uncurling the string from his wrist and tucking it into that bag at his hip.

Only ice lay in his command as he said, "Follow me."

Lydia stood with one hand on her blade's hilt, her body tensed for battle. "And if I don't?"

He held up a hand, wiggling his fingers to display their assortment of rings. "It's your choice whether you come willingly." That first time they'd met, he'd used one of those rings to send her away. She didn't know what else they could do, but did she dare to find out?

"And what am I following you to?" She asked, cautiously easing her stance. When his back was turned, could she manage to pierce his heart with steel before he reacted? Would his death free Cirelle from her oath, or leave the princess defenseless in a strange and dangerous realm for months yet?

Ellian stared, his stony gaze unreadable, voice flinty. "Your punishment."

"Which is?"

"For the sake of your princess, more lenient than I'd otherwise be inclined to make it."

Lydia swallowed. So not death, then.

"I lose patience. Will you walk, or must I force you?"

Her hand dropped from her dagger's handle. "I'll walk." Still, she held her head high and glared at him the whole way to the antechamber.

They passed the music room, and Cirelle's strumming stopped abruptly. Her head poked into the hall behind them. "What's going on?" She demanded in her typical strident tone.

"A matter of justice," Ellian said coolly as he kept walking.

"Wait!" Cirelle commanded as she scurried to block his path. He circled around her and continued with long strides. When the princess physically grabbed his arm, the sidhe stopped.

"Follow if you must," he told her quietly, "but this business remains between myself and your guard alone."

Cirelle's face flickered with uncertainty, and she dropped her hand to fall in step as she searched Lydia's expression for answers. "Lydia, what did you do?"

The faerie answered for her. "She tried to bind me. And failed. Now the debt must be paid."

Cirelle's eyes grew stormier than usual, her fingers brushing Lydia's, wrapping around her hand. Still Ellian kept walking, and they followed as Cirelle whispered, "You didn't. You couldn't." She shook her head, a loose tendril of her hair falling across her forehead, faded back to brown. An insistent note prodded the words, as if she could make it true through her will alone.

Lydia didn't respond. There was nothing to say. Ellian could only speak truth, after all.

When they entered the antechamber, Ellian opened a drawer in the corner and plucked out one of those calling coins. He peered at its inscription for a moment, then strode to the mirror on the wall and slotted it into the corner.

A tense silence held until Cirelle broke it. "What are you going to do?"

Ellian didn't look away from the mirror. "I'm sending Lydia away."

Lydia's heart seized in her chest. "No." She couldn't leave Cirelle alone with this monster.

The faerie continued. "I suspect the prospect thrills you about as much as becoming your thrall appealed to me."

She bit her tongue, fists clenched. Balance. She'd known her plan might fail, but had thought she'd be the only one paying the price. Now Cirelle would be at the mercy of this viper, the two of them alone while he whispered sweet poison in her ear.

The reflection in the mirror flickered, another scene replacing it. Shai peered back. Gray leather pauldrons rested on her shoulders, more decorative than functional, but the neckline of the clothing that showed between them was trimmed in rich purple lace.

"Ell!" The woman smiled, a wide and contagious grin. "What's up?"

"Shai," Ellian nodded at the woman. "I have a task for you."

"Oh good. I need a break. Issen's been droning on about some old treaty for hours."

A weary tenor voice floated from behind her. "You asked me for history lessons. It's my *job* to lecture."

Shai waved a dismissive hand. "What do you need me to do?"

"Lydia needs to stay away from my manor for a time. Would you keep her for a fortnight?"

Lydia stopped breathing. *Two weeks.* What was it with faeries and fourteen days? And how many terrible things could happen to Cirelle in that time?

"Ooh, sure!" Shai's response was effusive. "Things have been a bit dull lately, anyway."

"Could you be ready in one hour?"

Shai nodded, despite a muttered protest in the background from Issen.

"Very well," Ellian replied, still emotionless. "We'll arrange payment when you arrive."

"Sounds good. See you in an hour!" Shai gave a brief wave and the image vanished, replaced by Ellian's reflection again.

He turned to Lydia. "You have an hour to pack and say your goodbyes." Without another word, he left.

Swallowing a hard lump of fear, Lydia turned to her princess. Cirelle stood silent, but a shimmer of tears gleamed in her eyes.

"Lydia…" Cirelle flung her arms around Lydia, her face pressed against Lydia's neck.

Would the princess's affection ever stop sparking a bittersweet ache?

She'll never belong to you.

Lydia sucked in a sharp breath and returned the embrace.

"Be careful," she told Cirelle. "Don't trust him. I'll be back before you know it."

☙❧

An hour passed too quickly. Lydia scrambled to pack. Ellian had informed her she was allowed to borrow clothing and other items from her chambers, as long as they returned to the manor with her when her time was up.

Cirelle insisted on helping, though she mostly stood aside looking fretful and angry by turns.

"Why?" The princess asked as she folded the same shirt for the third time, finally giving up and laying it inside the bag. "Why would you do something so reckless?"

"So much like you, you mean?" The guard's gaze lingered on Cirelle's missing finger, the thin white lines of scars on her forearms. "Because he's dangerous," Lydia said, knowing the princess would not believe her.

"Dangerous enough to risk something like this? Or worse?"

Lydia ran a weary hand over her face as she tossed in a pair of trousers, barely-folded. "Yes."

Then the doorbell rang. Lydia swore softly and fastened the knapsack. Whatever she had, it would need to be enough.

As she walked through the darkened halls, Cirelle at her side, Lydia's stomach twisted itself into tangles.

Shai awaited them in the foyer, standing beside Ellian. Layers of violet and gold ruffles cascaded to her knees to reveal tall gray boots, with matching leather pauldrons and greaves.

Lydia met the woman's smiling eyes, a vibrant yellow-orange.

"Ready?" Shai chirped with a short wave.

"No." Lydia tried to keep her voice flat, but the dread and irritation and fear all spilled out in the one word. Shai had never been anything but friendly, but Lydia couldn't help resenting her right now.

Shai's grin faltered briefly, but she held out her hand anyway.

Ellian cleared his throat.

Lydia cast him a glare but reluctantly lifted her hand and placed it in Shai's. The woman's strong fingers curled around Lydia's and the world shimmered away.

Thirty-One

Ellian couldn't reconcile all of this.

Cirelle cared for the guardswoman, but Lydia was a dangerous threat. If she was willing to try to bind him, would she slide a knife between his ribs next? He called Tallia and traded another valuable artifact to strengthen the wards on his wing to let only Cirelle through. Even that was a bit of foolishness, considering he'd cut things off between them.

Still, the princess pined for her friend. She grew sullen, and snappish, and more than once he caught the glimmer of unshed tears in her eyes before she turned aside or blinked them away.

It was like a disease, a sickness that ate him from the inside out.

Perhaps it was inevitable that it couldn't last forever.

∽

One night, Cirelle reluctantly took up Ellian on an offer for a game of Nightswheel. She still simmered with anger and hurt, but it would only fester worse if she were left alone with her thoughts.

She was ashamed that the game and accompanying idle chatter actually worked. Her fury over his punishment of Lydia softened, briefly forgotten. Ellian could have done far worse in retaliation, Cirelle was certain. Trying to bind him was surely a grievous crime. Shai and Issen would care well for Lydia. She was safe.

So tonight Cirelle played this game, and she laughed. Ellian had fetched a bottle of human brandy for them to share, and she could almost imagine this like old times. It felt as if Toben would poke his head through the door at any moment and asked to be dealt in.

The conversation had turned toward childhood antics, each trying to best the other with some story of ridiculous mischief.

Ellian told of the time he and his siblings broke his family's cart and tried to repair it with increasingly ridiculous and desperate materials before blaming it on the family dog.

Cirelle burst into a fit of laughter.

"The dog?" Cirelle set down her cards and wiped her watering eyes to grin at him.

His own smile that heartbreakingly rare one, wide and unfeigned, his cerulean eyes swirling with sunrise pink. "I was five. It was the best we could come up with."

"And what happened?"

"Our long-suffering parents gravely accepted our explanation and let us off the hook. I think they felt sorry for us after seeing the wheel wrapped in leaves and twine."

"Gracious of them."

His smile faltered as he rolled a game token back and forth. He opened his mouth, shut it, opened it again. "Tomorrow, there's another faerie revel," he said cautiously. "In a forest, among various fae. I had not intended to attend… but I think I've changed my mind. I would like you to accompany me, if you are willing."

A tiny tremor of dread crawled along Cirelle's skin. "A sidhe party? Or like the Midsummer Festival?"

"Neither." He shook his head, his eyes flickering back to silver as he spoke. "Though some sidhe may attend, there will also be other faeries present. It will be smaller than the Midsummer party, and perhaps a few other humans may attend as well."

"Other humans?"

"I'm not the only one to keep company with mortals."

Cirelle snorted. "Not from the way the other sidhe spoke at the palace." She recalled all too well the looks of derision she'd suffered.

"That was the queen's influence, and the prince's." His good cheer faltered at their mention, but he took a deep breath and continued. "A few other sidhe like to keep humans in their home, despite their outward attitudes. And among the other species, there are the fae-stolen, those swapped for changelings."

"So what would I do at this party?"

Ellian grinned, eyes flashing blue again. "Enjoy yourself."

"No, I mean, what's the mission?"

"There isn't one. It's a revel, and I'd like you to be my guest."

A cold lump formed in the back of her throat. "Ellian… you ended it."

He stared down at his hands, tracing an aimless pattern on the surface of the table. "I know. This is a request, not a command. If you refuse… I understand. But I'm asking nonetheless."

She chewed her lip. This was folly. She should say no. But the word that fell from her lips was, "Yes."

Cirelle donned her best garb once more, a form-fitting sidhe gown made in layers upon layers of cream lace edged in gold. A tiara dotted with brilliant yellow topaz gems adorned her head, with matching jewelry at her wrists and throat.

Ellian waited for her in the garden, wearing one of his ostentatious ensembles in a deep crimson and black, finished off with those peculiar boots.

His smile was soft as he held out a hand. "Ready?"

She touched her fingertips to his palm and nodded. The world faded away and reformed around them. They stood in a forest, the tree towering over them covered in spiky leaves twice as large as her outstretched hand, in a vivid sunshine yellow. The musty, woodsy scent of autumn wafted through the air on a chill breeze.

Moonlight slanted through a sparse canopy in every color of flame. Her feet crunched on a thick bed of fallen leaves. Only a smattering of red and gold foliage still remained on the branches, and tiny orange lights bobbed in the air, like flickering fireflies.

"Where are we?"

"The woodland of the eldest Lhyrria, the one whose seasons match your world's own. Tonight, we celebrate autumn's last days before winter settles upon us." He offered his arm.

Cirelle sighed and rested her hand on his elbow. She would have walked by herself, but the footing was uneven. The ground gave away beneath her now and then, the leaves covering a sunken dip in the ground or a gnarled tree root that threatened to trip her. She almost lost a shoe once on a fallen branch, but her flailing hand caught Ellian's shoulder and he helped her regain her balance.

After a minute or so of walking, Cirelle heard voices and song. A strange faerie tune, vague and airy like the wind whistling through leaves, but with an unmistakable musical rhythm.

They emerged onto a clearing. The leaves had been swept aside, leaving a soft meadow of old, dry grass the color of cornsilk. The trees arched overhead at the edges, shadowing the unusual fae that had gathered in this clearing.

And what folk they were, as varied and wondrous as those she had danced among in that cave months ago. One woman wore a loose gown of silk belted tightly at her waist, draping over one shoulder and leaving her other breast bare. A ghostly-pale faerie bore a full ballgown with so many layers of delicate pink gauze that it rippled like water with every movement. One man wore a sleek bodysuit that looked like sparkling silver fish scales, while another was garbed in little more than boots and a black loincloth.

Cirelle even recognized two sylvans among their number, and felt her cheeks redden at the memory of the disguise she'd once donned, at what she'd done while wearing it. There were other humans too, notable for their round ears and mortal flaws. Still, they dressed as strangely as the fae and danced alongside them.

A small group of faeries stood off to one side, playing otherworldly instruments.

And the strange folk were all swirling, swaying and moving together in time with the eerie song. Unlike the feverish nature of that wild summer festival, there was a grace here, a gentleness.

"Shall we dance?" Ellian said softly at her side, and she startled.

Her pulse skipped a beat. "I thought we were done with dancing," she told him, her voice thick.

"Of the obligation," he corrected her. "This is an invitation."

"And if I refuse?"

He shrugged, but his eyes flickered dark for a brief moment. "Then we don't dance."

Maybe it was the music, maybe it was the lights flitting among the treetops above, or the glow of the twin moons and the night sky so full of sparkling stars. Perhaps it was all of those combined that made this feel more like a dream than reality. But whatever the reason, Cirelle nodded.

They moved together easily by now, falling back into step as if none of the trauma and tragedy had befallen them, as if they were back in his ballroom that first time. Before everything between them had become complicated, full of memories of sweat-soaked skin and tangled limbs, of regrets and things left unsaid.

Ellian's hand supported her hip as she dipped gracefully under his outstretched arm, hands fluttering together and apart like fickle butterflies. Cirelle let the music lead her, moving without thought or worry, trusting that Ellian would catch her when he needed to.

For a time, she tried to forget the honey taste of his kisses, the gentleness with which his hands had explored her body. How it had felt to work together for something bigger than the two of them, a shimmering, ephemeral connection. Or his nameday, when he'd ended it all. Instead, Cirelle breathed in his wood-smoke and cedar scent, and danced. After a spin that left her dizzy, Cirelle grinned at Ellian and shivered as the sunrise-pink hue spread wider through his eyes.

When a particularly fast-paced dervish of a dance had ended, Cirelle's legs cramped and she panted for air. "I need a rest."

Ellian led her to the edge of the clearing. Other fae mingled there, standing beneath the boughs of autumn leaves.

No sooner had she leaned against a large tree than someone called Ellian's name. It was another faerie, a spriggan, approaching them with an amiable grin. "Ellian," he said, "I have to introduce you to Pogren. He's looking for something I think you possess?"

Ellian's lips pressed into a firm line as he glanced back and forth between Cirelle and the newcomer. He leaned in to whisper in Cirelle's ear, his breath warm against her skin. "I won't be gone long. Be careful around them." She already knew that well enough, but there was an urgency to his voice that she didn't quite understand, and it sent a shiver of apprehension down her back.

He turned to the newcomer with a smile, his voice startingly jovial after his warning. "Migdo, well met," he said, making a little bow. "Where is this Pogren?"

"Follow me," the other faerie said, and they left Cirelle behind. She rested against the tree for support, her calves still aching though her breathing was settling.

Without Ellian, the night suddenly seemed more eerie than magical. She was alone, surrounded by strange and likely dangerous faeries. She'd done the same at Midsummer, but Ellian had been watching her. Now he was gone and she was truly on her own. The only protections she had were the rules that bound the fae. If she agreed to nothing, by word or motion, then they could not do more than speak to her.

Cirelle put some steel in her spine. Mingling with these creatures couldn't possibly be worse than navigating the Unseelie Court, or the creature that had nearly drowned her, or fighting redcaps.

Only few moments after she lost sight of Ellian behind a small group of fae, a woman approached from behind the tree.

Cirelle knew her. Petite, a handsbreadth shorter than Cirelle and slender, with small breasts and narrow hips. She wore a flowing, sleeveless gown that faded from deepest indigo at the shoulders down to pale dusty lavender at the hem. Skin the color of strawberry cream and hair made of amethyst threads. The eyes, in particular, were entirely fae, sparkling a bright magenta hue that Cirelle had never seen on a mortal.

Meivre.

The woman who'd once tried to seduce Cirelle in her sylvan disguise, just to wound Ellian's pride. And a member of Adaleth's Inner Court.

As the woman looked Cirelle up and down, her lips curved into a sardonic smile. "So you're his latest plaything," the woman muttered disdainfully. Of course. This was the first time she met Cirelle, as far as she knew. Doubtless Adaleth would have kept secret the humiliating fact that Ellian had snuck a human into the palace.

Cirelle bared her teeth. "You'll find easier prey elsewhere, sidhe."

"Oh," the woman murmured, a predatory gleam entering her eyes. "So sharp-tongued." She tilted her head speculatively. "Poor little human, dancing among wolves with her ink-stained fingertips." Cirelle remained firmly against the tree, hoping the woman wouldn't hear her heart pounding. She deliberately avoided looking at her fingers, which were indeed stained with ink from this morning's work in the Archive.

"You intrigue me, you see," Meivre admitted, reaching out one long-nailed hand to trace a line down the tree bark just a few inches from Cirelle's face. *She can't touch me unless I let her,* Cirelle reminded herself, but it was hard to believe that when the woman leaned in close. "Ellian was careless tonight," she said. "It's not the first time he's brought one of his toys to a celebration, nor is he the only one to do so. But he failed to guard those telltale eyes of his. Do you know what it means when they turn pink like that? I do." Her head turned. Cirelle followed her gaze to see Ellian returning with long, quick strides, eyes now blazing the color of flames.

The fae woman didn't look too concerned. Instead, she

smiled, a wicked feline grin. "Think on what I've said, little human."

Cirelle couldn't help herself. "Perhaps I would, if you'd actually done more than dancing around words, like you faeries always do."

The woman's grin widened. "Hm. Why ever did he choose you?" She shook her head and slipped away.

When Ellian approached, his voice was low, as if he feared to be overheard.

"Meivre," he murmured, "What did she say to you?"

"Nothing," Cirelle said. "Just more fae posturing."

"Did she threaten you?"

"No," she shook her head. "Only vague insults. Why? Were you expecting threats?"

He sighed, the orange flicker in his eyes fading and his stance relaxing a little. "I'm not sure. I don't know what her game is." He turned his head to look out at the crowd, which had begun to disperse. "And there's always a game."

The music had gone silent, and Cirelle hadn't even noticed when it faded. The revelers were now drifting into the woods, in pairs or small groups.

Disappointment surprised her. "The celebration is over?"

Ellian's expression softened even further, his lips curling into a knowing smile. "Not all of it," he murmured. "But the rest is enjoyed in much smaller, more… intimate groups."

A moment later, she understood his meaning, and her heart started racing again. Did he…? No. He'd ended it.

"Come with me?" he asked her, holding out his hand.

It took Cirelle a moment to recover her voice. "Ellian…" she began, taking a step back. They'd left this behind them, hadn't they? Ellian himself had slammed that door.

His lips smiled, but his eyes didn't, pale and colorless. "That's not what I ask of you. Not tonight. Only that I have one more thing to show you while we are here."

Reluctantly, she let him lead her through the forest, the crunch of dry leaves accompanied by the silvery sound of his boots. Ellian picked out a path she could not discern, weaving through trees and stepping over fallen logs. As before, he helped guide her over the uneven terrain.

At one point, they crossed a small stream. A miniature waterfall spilled over stones that glimmered and shone in a rainbow of colors, from cool icy blue to rich violet and soft pink. Cirelle marveled at things Ellian walked past as if they were common; trees covered in luminescent blue vines of ivy, dangling flowers that chimed like bells in the breeze, a graceful deer-like creature with three sets of antlers that startled and leapt away.

Ellian eventually led Cirelle to a small cave in the side of a hill, a doorway lined in an arch of carved rock. Faerie lights lined the tunnel, which angled steadily downward with shallow steps. A chill breeze wafted toward them from deep within the mountain, and Cirelle shivered in her lacy dress.

The scent of stone lingered as their footsteps echoed along the tunnel. No more words were spoken until they turned a sudden, sharp corner and emerged into a brilliant cavern.

Cirelle couldn't help her sudden intake of breath. Every wall glimmered with veins of sparkling stone. Faerie lights glowed like miniature moons, held aloft by some unseen magic as they bobbed slowly far above.

But the greatest wonders hung between the lights, dangling strands of glass in every shape and color imaginable, ringing against one another in an idle breeze that swirled about the cavern. The wind emerged from another tunnel on the opposite side, danced through the room, then exited behind Cirelle and

Ellian. Among the chimes lay bells of gleaming silver in various sizes, adding their clear voices to the glassy chorus.

It was almost a melody, but not quite. The faint whoosh of the wind, the tinkling of the bells, the soft clinking of the glass. Amongst the glittering walls, surrounded by the enchantment of this nearly-music, Cirelle lost herself. She closed her eyes, tilted her face into the breeze, and listened.

Ellian remained silent beside Cirelle until she turned to him. "It's beautiful."

"It's called Arandaral," he said. In the shifting, shimmering light, it was difficult to see exactly what color his pale eyes bore.

"The Singing Mountain," Cirelle murmured, her earring providing the translation. She took a few cautious steps to stand directly underneath the dangling chimes. Some hung so low she could nearly touch them, if she reached high overhead and jumped. "Who built it?"

"A clan of duergar that exists no longer."

"What is it for?"

This time, Cirelle read his eyes clearly, aquamarines sparkling. "What is music ever for? Or any art? It's here to be enjoyed." He tilted his head and met her gaze with a small smile. "I thought you would like it."

Cirelle stared up at the bits of glass, throwing their own shards of light all over so she stood in a kaleidoscope of reflected colors. "I do." She closed her eyes for a moment and twirled slowly beneath them, listening to their song shifting as she turned.

When she opened them, Elllian stepped closer, that sad smile painted on his face.

A tiny thread of anxiety poisoned the moment, a nagging worry in something Meivre had said, something Cirelle didn't want to confront. Something she had never admitted to herself, no matter how much she'd suspected somewhere deep down. The knot of dread in her belly grew. Cirelle cleared her suddenly dry throat. "Maybe we should head back."

"Soon," Ellian said. "Not yet." He stepped into the center of the cavern, holding out a hand in the unmistakable invitation to dance once again.

Cirelle's mouth felt like sandpaper. "Months ago, you said you didn't want to dance anymore." She took a cautious step backward. "Why tonight? Why now?"

He stared at her, those eyes painted deep blue and black and rose. "Because as autumn dies and winter claims the land, we faeries mourn the losses and celebrate the joys that the past year has brought us." He cast her a smile that was still somehow very sad. "And this year brought me you." A frightening intensity lingered in his gaze.

Cirelle's breath burned in her lungs, and the hot sting of tears pricked her eyes. "Don't mock me. You were the one who pushed me away, shut me out. Now this?" She squeezed her eyes shut. "I only have a human's patience. I can't endure more games, Ellian."

"Nor can I," he said, the words so faint they were nearly drowned in the music of the cavern.

Cirelle's eyes fluttered open to discover he'd stepped closer still. "What is that supposed to mean?"

No teasing in his expression now, only infinite sadness. "Dance with me and find out."

Cirelle should have said no. She should have demanded they return to his manor and leave this foolishness behind them for good. But her hand settled into his with a worrisome familiarity instead. An ache grew as he pulled her close.

Just one more time, she told herself. *One more dance.* Then she would be done with these fickle games.

The chimes had no true rhythm, and this dance was not a whirling reel, a stately gallanad, nor a sultry faerie one. Instead, they found their own steps, a gentle sway as they rested in one another's arms. Her cheek lay against the lapel of Ellian's jacket, his chin resting atop her head. He seemed heedless of the fact that her tears soaked into the fine silk of his coat.

His scent wrapped them both, and it tightened the ache in Cirelle's chest. Why couldn't Ellian ever just make sense? He'd uttered the words himself. *I don't want to do this anymore.*

He came close, then pushed her away. Again and again.

Now he held her in his arms and his chest shuddered beneath her cheek. Breaths rasped in and out in a ragged rhythm.

She shouldn't be doing this. Cirelle had sworn never to become one of Ellian's lovesick fawns, yet here she was, dancing beneath faerie bells with her heart too crowded in her ribcage.

As they swayed, Cirelle's frustration and self-pity and self-loathing grew until she could stand it no more.

"No," she croaked the word, only barely keeping it from a sob. She tugged free of his arms. "I want to go back." She blinked, and those traitorous tears continued to fall down her cheeks. Did the sparkling lights paint them in pretty patterns like trails of starlight?

"Cirelle…" Ellian's eyes swam with a rainbow of color, like fiery opals, before settling into a deep blue.

"No," she shook her head. "I told you, I'm done with these games. I have borne a lot in Faerie. I looked into the face of Adaleth' anger. I ran at the head of an army of shadow spiders. I hunted down the Lisovyk. I felt faerie venom gnawing its way through my veins." She spat out the last words, halting and harsh. "I lost a finger and became a *murderer*. But of all the things I've endured, I can't bear this. Not anymore." Her voice only shook a little, and Cirelle was proud.

"Neither can I." Ellian's response was quiet, serious, no teasing or mockery. He met her eyes squarely and stepped closer.

Deep carnation pink bled into the center of all that sapphire blue, and Cirelle's heart stopped.

Meivre had warned her. *Do you know what it means when his eyes turn pink like that? I do.*

The sidhe woman had not specified, and faeries were so very tricky. But Cirelle knew. She'd just never allowed herself to think the words, as if that would keep it from being real.

Ellian lifted a hand, his thumb reaching to brush the tears from a cheek, then pausing a hair's breadth away.

A precipice, a moment of decision.

Cirelle leaned her cheek into his hand, and he wiped the tear tracks from her face with gentle strokes. He leaned closer, hesitating.

With a long, shuddering breath, Cirelle tilted her head upward and kissed him, tasting her own tears as she did. It was not one of their fiery kisses, as much battle as release. No, this one was a surrender.

He broke away first, pulling away just far enough to rest his forehead against hers and breathe her name. "Cirelle." With a long sigh, he stepped back. Dropping a hand into his pouch, he lifted something out and held it up between them.

A memory jar. Not Briere's. One that held a scrap of dirty fabric.

Cirelle's heart leapt into her throat. "What is that?"

He held it out to her. "I want you to have this back," he said, a strange thickness in his voice.

A cold drop of fear slid down Cirelle's spine, and she took a step back. "You took another memory?" She didn't even recall him stealing it.

"You begged me to. I stole that moment from you, too."

Cirelle swallowed. The jar seemed to taunt her, tempting.

What had she wanted to forget so badly? Curiosity swallowed her whole. But…

"Faeries don't give gifts," she said.

"Consider it payment for tonight. For agreeing to come with me. For the dances."

It would be wiser to say no. Whatever she'd wanted to forget was probably left better buried.

But she must know.

Cirelle took the jar from him. "How does it work?"

"The memory will be restored when it is opened."

The glass was cold and heavy in her palm, the lid twisting open with a soft scrape. For a brief, crystalline moment, the world stopped. Then she remembered everything. The look on his face that night as poison filled her, his lips parting to give away the Key. For her. And his answer the night after, in the ballroom.

Love.

He'd actually uttered the word, and Cirelle had fled from it.

The jar slipped from her fingers, shattering on the stone. Weeks ago, Ellian had confessed this. Had been living with it ever since. No wonder he'd run so hot and cold.

Ellian didn't even glance at the broken glass at their feet. "Don't go back. We can make another bargain. You can stay here with me, as long as you choose. Another year, two years." He hesitated. "Forever."

Cirelle felt dizzy. The colored lights swam before her, and the room was suddenly suffocatingly hot. She stumbled over to an outcropping of rock to sit. It took her several long, shaky breaths to find her voice. "What?"

Ellian followed her, kneeling on the stone floor so his eyes were at a level with hers. They were black as a moonless midnight, terrified. "I mean it."

A mad, awful laugh burst from Cirelle's throat, and she

squeezed her eyes shut as more tears spilled loose. She felt like a washcloth that had been wrung out, twisted and drained. "No. This isn't happening. Are you asking me to *marry* you?"

"Sidhe do not wed as mortals do."

"But you want me to stay here?" A shrill note had entered her voice. "Forever? And leave my world behind?"

His gaze met hers. "Is it so awful a fate? You'd avoid the cage your suitors made for you. And I..." he coughed, glancing aside. There was a pause, a shaky indrawn breath. "I'd be here."

Cirelle barked that laugh again, hysteria threatening. "I don't even know what this is, Ellian," she gestured between them. "You were the one who pushed me away. '*I don't want to do this anymore.*' Your words. You didn't want me. But now you do?"

He still wouldn't look at her, sitting and leaning his back against the stone she sat upon. "I never said I didn't want you."

"Yes, you did."

"No, my exact words were 'I don't want to do this'. And I didn't. I didn't want half of you. To hold you and know that you'd chosen to run from me. From the truth."

Cirelle's heart skipped and stuttered. "It's too fast. You cant... I haven't even been in Faerie a full year." *This can't be happening.*

"How long did it take you to realize you were in love with your countess?" he asked hoarsely.

Cirelle chewed her lip. She'd known she loved Briere within a few months of meeting her.

But this... this was something completely different. Something she wasn't ready to face.

Her voice trembled. "Why? Why me?" *Why, after all the other mortals? You let the others go home.*

"No one else has faced down faerie creatures for my sake, armed with nothing more than her sharp wits and sharper tongue," he said, and Cirelle could hear the weary smile in his voice even as a bitterness laced the words. "None of the others stole a crown to protect me. You're the first of my servants to have saved my life. And no one has insulted me so, or teased me so mercilessly, or written a song about me."

"The song isn't about you," she protested.

"Isn't it?"

She answered with silence, the shame of that knowledge washing over her in a guilty wave.

His voice was strained and hoarse. "You drive me to distraction, and I never want you to stop."

Cirelle's mad laughter died in her throat.

"Stay," he implored again. "Would you remain here, with me?"

For a few brief, wild moments Cirelle really, truly considered it. To stay here forever? She could help Ellian hunt down the Lock, could spend her free nights playing the exquisite instruments in his music room or reading the multitude of books in that library.

And she would have Ellian, truly *have* him, completely hers. It was a dizzying thought and a terrifying one. But she didn't love him. She couldn't. To bed him was one thing, but to give away her heart? No. He was a sidhe, immortal and capricious.

And what would happen as she grew older? What if Ellian awoke one day, months from now, years from now, and had grown bored of her? He said she'd be free to go when she chose, but where? She couldn't return home then.

Oh, stars.

Arraven.

She'd given her word to return on time. To prevent a war.

"I can't." She choked out the words, and they were tasteless on her tongue. "I can't stay here. I promised to go back. Rhine will declare war if I don't." The tears still flowed, and now her nose had begun to run as well. "I'm sorry, Ellian."

He was silent a long time.

The pause grew so deep that Cirelle tore her gaze from the chimes to look at him, though it wrenched something inside her to do it. Ellian's eyes met her own, swimming the color of cobalt glass. "Etishen," he said softly. "My real name is Etishen Ral Ves." He turned and stood, that old mask falling back into place, those eyes fading to gray.

Cirelle's heart stopped, then lurched back to life with a painful jolt. Words eluded her, fluttering in her mind like wayward sparrows she couldn't catch. Did anyone else alive know his name?

"I give you that freely," he said. "One of the few gifts we are allowed to bestow without recompense."

Her lungs didn't seem to work properly any longer. "Why are you telling me that?"

"Because I wish to. Because I trust you. Because..." he paused. "Because I can." The last was blurted, feeble, and she got the impression it wasn't what he'd intended to say.

But he wouldn't utter that word to her ever again.

"Ellian..."

"I said I couldn't play these games any longer, and I meant it. I've asked once already. If the answer is truly no, then this game ends. So I ask a second time. Will you stay with me, here in Faerie?"

She closed her eyes, squeezing out more tears. "No."

Silence fell again.

"I'm calling in the favor you owe, in return for ending the dances. Give me one night."

"What?"

"One night without walls, without letting your fear take the reins. A single night spent with me, and your favor is repaid."

Her tongue felt dry, but Cirelle made it work. "And what will I have to do, on that night?" She didn't think she could return to his bed. Not now, not with what she knew.

"Only what you wish to. All I ask is that you leave doubt behind you, no thoughts of the future or of other obligations. A single evening where you surrender to your whims and wants without forcing them aside." He turned to pierce her with conflicted eyes, swirling shades of sapphire and rose. "Tomorrow night, from sunset to sunrise. Afterward, I will ask my question a third and final time. If your answer is still no, then this will be over and done. No more of these games, no more dances. No flirting, no touches. None of it, ever again. But first I will have tomorrow."

Cirelle took a deep breath, her heart doing somersaults in her breast. A handful of hours in which she could set worries aside, to live only in the present. "Yes."

Over the singing chimes, she felt the shiver in the air even as she unraveled inside.

For one brief moment, Cirelle wondered what would happen if she took it all back, if she fell into his arms right now?

No, that could not happen. "Can we just go home now?" she croaked.

When she looked up at Ellian, Cirelle was baffled by the triumphant gleam in his eyes as he held out his hand to transport her back. It was only when they'd returned and she fled for her chambers that she realized why. She'd called his manor 'home'.

Thirty-Two

THIS IS UNBELIEVABLY FOOLISH, Cirelle thought to herself as she clasped the necklace about her throat, a filigreed collar in gold dotted with gemstones the color of ripe plums. She'd tried on perhaps a dozen gowns before settling on fluttering layers of chiffon and lace in every shade of violet. The sleeves were short and draped, the neckline low.

Lydia would be livid.

But Lydia was still at Shai's. Dark kohl lined Cirelle's eyes, leaving them looking like pale grey storm clouds. She'd brushed her cheeks with a translucent powder that possessed a golden sheen, bringing out the warm hues of her bronzed skin.

Cirelle had foregone the lip stain after a long internal debate.

An evening without doubts or walls, Ellian had asked of her. One night lived solely in the present, following her whims and desires.

Can I do this?

This agreement had seemed a thrilling proposition last night, enchanted by that Singing Mountain and stricken by the naked emotion in Ellian's eyes. But now, jitters consumed her as she made her way to breakfast.

Ellian had not held back either, garbed in fabric that looked like brushed silver, embroidered with tiny jet beads all along the collar. Not one of his bold, skin-baring ensembles, but a tailored jacket and midnight black shirt beneath it, a large sapphire brooch at his throat. His boots sang a soft, silvery melody as he shifted his weight in the doorway of the dining chamber.

Stars, is he as scared as I am?

Of course he was. Ellian had bared his soul to her last night. His eyes skated up and down the length of her, taking in the dress, the cosmetics, the jewelry. But his gaze lingered on her face the longest.

His eyes gleamed like two silver coins.

"No," Cirelle lifted her chin and stared him down. "You asked for me without walls, and I demand no less. Today, we can both follow our whims and do what we want, but I demand honesty while you do."

Ellian blinked. "If you wish." They bled through with a sea of pink and lavender, startlingly pale against his slate-gray skin.

Cirelle's cheeks burned beneath their coating of shimmery, translucent powder. "So," she said awkwardly, a nervous cough interrupting her words. She let the sentence die there.

A faint ring of azure blue blossomed around Ellian's pupil, and that small, knowing smirk touched the edge of his lips again.

How long had it been since Cirelle had seen that teasing grin? The one that spoke not just of mockery, but of a sly, arrogant certainty as well? She'd thought her pulse couldn't beat faster, but she was wrong.

"So," he said. "Perhaps we should start with breakfast?"

Unable to speak, Cirelle nodded and followed him into the room.

The table was set the same as always, a steady bit of familiarity to cling to. Cirelle heaped pastries and fruit upon her plate,

trying not to let her hands tremble. She failed, but Ellian didn't remark on it.

"So how does this go?" she managed to ask haltingly after a few bites of strawberries and cream.

"How do you want it to go?"

"I'll settle for food and conversation."

"Easy enough," he replied, slowly and conspicuously tracing the edge of his teacup with a fingertip. Her eyes darted toward the motion, and Ellian's grin widened.

Cirelle narrowed her eyes at him. *So we're back to this.* "Ellian," she sighed. "It's only breakfast."

"I have twelve hours," he replied with his eyes glinting cerulean. "And I intend to enjoy each one of them."

Heaving another long sigh, she poured herself more tea. "This is going to be a very long day, isn't it?"

"And you'll love every minute of it," he purred. "If you let yourself. Which," he lifted a finger to point at her, "you swore to do."

She wanted to huff at him, to scowl, but a slow smile crept onto her face instead. "Then game on, faerie."

He laughed, a sound that wrapped around her and slid down her spine. "That's the spirit."

After that, it was easy to fall into old patterns. Gentle mockery, playful teasing, insults hurled without malice.

She didn't realize how much she'd missed it.

It lightened a burden Cirelle hadn't known she carried. A day without worries, without regret. As breakfast ended, Ellian suggested a board game in the parlor, and Cirelle lifted one brow. "It's a bit early for Raven's Gambit, don't you think?"

He laughed. "I was thinking perhaps fox-and-hounds. It's been a while."

The words left a twinge of something dark in Cirelle's chest. "It has."

An awkward silence fell until they set out the game pieces. This game had been one of the first things she and Ellian had done together. Back then he'd still put up his walls, his show, playing the part of the arrogant fae lord.

So much had happened between them, and there was never any going back, not truly. Too much had been said, too many feelings, too many nights spent in one another's arms.

Worse, they were both haunted by a myriad of ghosts. Kyrinna, Briere. Ellian's still-unnamed beloved, the human he'd fallen for long before her. Cirelle had not forgotten that admission, the night they'd played their game of truths with Toben. It felt like a century ago.

She opened her mouth, then hesitated.

"No walls," Ellian reminded her as he moved his first piece into play.

Still, Cirelle shut her eyes as she asked the question. "Tell me about them. The human—humans?—you loved before."

He sucked in a long breath through his nose, let it out.

"There were two, before you. The last was Gineon, fourteen years ago. The first was Lina, ten years before that. She… she helped me find myself again, after the second time at the Unseelie Court. Patient and kind, but strong. She was what I needed, a gentle river to cool the fire that ate at me from inside. But her time ended and I sent her back. I didn't even think to ask her to stay. We'd made a bargain, and I was still new to faerie rules. I didn't know she could choose to remain of her own free will."

Cirelle's tongue felt too large for her mouth, thick and sluggish. Still she managed a few words as she nudged her fox pawn across the board. "And the other?"

"Gineon was a bit like you, I think. Impulsive, and playful, and an incorrigible flirt. But he didn't have your temper, or your cutting tongue. By the time he arrived, I had learned to reconcile the two halves of my life, the human and the sidhe. But an emptiness gnawed at me, and he brought humor into my life. He didn't reciprocate my feelings, though he was happy to warm my bed for a time. So he left, too." Ellian shrugged, pushing one of his hound pieces into a new spot. The words bit into Cirelle, a well-placed dagger. But Ellian continued. "They were each what I needed most at that time, the thing that most brought me peace."

Cirelle snorted a bitter laugh. "If there's anything I haven't brought you, it's peace."

His eyes shone cerulean and rose. "Exactly. Before you arrived, I'd grown melancholy, exhausted and tasked with too many duties as we planned for Thieves' Night. Leadership was a heavy burden, one I never expected. Then you came along, fierce and independent and temperamental. You didn't need my protection or guidance. You challenged me." That smirk curled his lips as a wash of lavender fell over his eyes. He pushed another piece into play. "And you're an absolutely insufferable temptress, which was a nice bonus."

Cirelle blushed. "That was a good thing?"

"Of course. Don't tell me you didn't enjoy it, too."

She had to laugh at that. "Well, you did make it rather easy," she remarked playfully as she hopped her fox pawn over a hound and slipped it into the free space. "I win."

"Best two out of three?" Ellian asked.

"You're on."

☙❧

It seemed Ellian had made additional plans for lunch. Rather than their usual repast, a covered basket sat on the dining chamber table when they entered. Looping the handle over one arm, Ellian gave her a blue-eyed grin and gestured for her to follow. "Come, let's go to the roof."

Curious, Cirelle followed. She hadn't thought to don a cloak, and she shivered in the late autumn chill. It was a damp day, cool mist settling on her skin.

Ellian held out a hand in a familiar gesture.

Cirelle cocked her head, puzzled. "Where are we going?"

"It's a surprise."

With a sigh, Cirelle placed her hand in his. The world misted away. When it cleared, the first thing she noticed was the heat. Warm and humid, with a wet, green smell.

They stood on smooth gray stone above a vast canopy of green.

It's a building, Cirelle realized. They perched atop a towering monument. The trees clustered close, growing right up to the edges. And such trees. They were immense, with wide, glossy leaves as large as carriage wheels. Cirelle stood at the edge of the rooftop, no ledge to stop her from tumbling off this immense structure.

The sky had that purplish tinge just before sunrise.

A sky with a single moon, and stars she recognized. Though they were in the wrong place, she picked out four of her gods' constellations, fading as the sky brightened.

"We're in my world," she said softly. It would be night in Arraven, but here it was dawn. With a sudden certainty, she turned to Ellian and asked, "This is Kishir, isn't it?"

He nodded, staring out over the jungle below. "The village where I grew up once stood that way," he pointed.

"Once?"

When Ellian replied, he turned to her with sapphire eyes.

"The war took its toll on this region. All of the villages near here are gone now. There used to be a city around this temple, but the vines and trees have claimed the smaller structures, the dirt-packed roads… all but this building."

Cirelle was silent. The better part of a century since he'd lived here as a human. What would it be like to revisit and find that everything you once knew had been washed away by time? Cirelle imagined watching Palace Arraven crumble over the course of a century, and blinked back the threat of tears.

Her hand twitched, but she let it drop back to her side.

No. No walls, no doubts. Cirelle lifted that hand again and found Ellian's, twining their fingers together.

The sky had grown lighter, the edge of the familiar white sun cresting over the trees so very far away. Nothing but jungle for miles to the east, while the west rose upward in jagged mountains.

Without words, they watched the sun rise. Cirelle's sun, her world. Home. Her chest felt full and heavy.

When the sun had fully risen, Ellian tugged lightly on her hand, still holding the basket in the other. "Come." He led her to a gap she hadn't seen in the wall behind them, covered in crawling vines.

Cirelle suddenly knew why Ellian's manor garden was on the rooftop. A wild array of overgrown plants lay scattered about the plaza atop this temple. Once, it must have been beautifully tended, long since left to go wild. Still, the paths were wide enough that some few cobblestones remained. The walkway was impassable in places, covered in thick vines with enormous flowers, but they picked their way through to a wide central plaza. The stones lay in a mosaic of white, gray, and rust, forming circular geometric patterns. It was here, in the center of this untamed garden, that Ellian slipped his hand from hers, knelt on the ground and set out the items from the basket. First, a blanket of soft blue cotton, then a small meal of simple fare.

He settled cross-legged on the blanket and grinned up at her.

"A picnic?" Cirelle teased as she sat across from him. "You have hours remaining, and you chose a picnic?"

With a sly smirk, Ellian tossed a berry to her. She caught it and popped it in her mouth. A burst of flavor on her tongue, tart and bright.

"Why here?" She asked, picking up a small sandwich. "Why not in your own garden?"

He shrugged. "I wanted you to see it. Where I came from." His eyes flickered dark for a moment. "Or at least what's left of it."

Again, Cirelle reached for him, squeezing his hand. She glanced around at the strange and amazing plants that surrounded them, at the sky that had dawned a clear blue. "It must have been beautiful."

"It was." A wistfulness clung to the words, and a wave of pity washed over Cirelle. There was nothing she could say that would fix this, that would bring back the world he'd left behind or the people that had populated it. The sandwich held less savor now, but Cirelle chewed resolutely, washing it down with water from one of those self-filling flasks.

"Why come back?" She asked softly.

"Because it's a piece of who I was, and it reminds me that the man I used to be is not the same one I've become. But I can't forget him. I carry a piece of that human inside, no matter what Faerie has made of me."

Cirelle was silent a few moments, glancing down at her food, at her hands. "I'm starting to wonder what it's making of me, too," she admitted.

"You might just be finding the 'you' that was hidden there all along," he said.

"What if I don't entirely like what it reveals?"

It was Ellian's turn to reach for her, fingertips hovering above her arm. She shifted so their skin touched, his warmth a welcome comfort.

"Then you adapt, learn to live with it," he said, eyes shifting to a pale brown. "I know what it's like to turn into something abhorrent. At least you don't have that to worry about."

"I don't?" She'd been viciously cruel and vindictive at that Unseelie palace. Had used the ilthys to kill. The memory of her Thieves' Night murder left her cold and shivering, the phantom of that faerie's blood coating her hands. She wiped them self-consciously on her skirts.

"No," Ellian shook his head. "Fierce you may be, but never heartless." His smile turned soft, and a ring of pink spread from his pupils to flood his eyes.

It wrenched something inside Cirelle to see that, now knowing what it meant. When had she first seen that color there?

The answer came to her in a sudden flash. At the Unseelie Court after their dance, Ellian had looked upon her with rose-tinted eyes.

"Tell me about it," she asked. "Your human life. Your family. You've shared a few stories, but I want to know everything."

So he did. For an hour, Ellian told her about his siblings, his parents. The cozy life they'd had before the rebellion. And how his elder brother and sister joined while he tagged along despite his reservations. And after the war, the fire the loyalists had set upon their home. His voice cracked on that one, and Cirelle squeezed his hand.

Ellian cleared his throat. He sat up, reaching for one of the tiny sandwiches. "Come, let's eat. I have something else to show you and time is a factor."

The smile on his face was a bit forced, but Cirelle met it with her own wan grin. He was right. Today was not a day for revisiting tragedies.

"You just love keeping me in the dark," she muttered.

"Maybe. Perhaps it's nice for me to keep you on your toes for once, instead of the other way around." His grin warmed.

"Like you don't enjoy it."

"Never said that." He tossed another berry at her, and she wasn't fast enough to dodge.

It hit her right between the eyebrows. "Hey!" She scowled. "How can you even do that, without my permission?"

"But you gave me permission. 'Today we can both follow our whims and do what we want.' You should know better than to say that to a faerie." Finishing his small sandwich, Ellian lifted an eyebrow, a gesture of challenge. She'd missed that air of mischief about him, and a fullness swelled in her chest. A sudden impulse gripped her. Normally, she'd have shoved it aside, but that was not the bargain she'd made for this evening. Cirelle gave in to her whim. She leaned over the tray, grasping Ellian's shirt in one hand to pull him closer.

His eyes widened, flashing pale yellow for the barest instant before their lips met.

It was a brief kiss, positively chaste compared to some of their previous ones. Cirelle released him, grinning as she pulled away.

"What was that?" Ellian asked, incredulous.

Cirelle shrugged, still smiling. "You said to do what I want."

"If that's the response I get for throwing a berry, I should have flung fruit at you more often." The yellow had washed away, drowned in a sea of summery blue.

"Faerie courtship customs are stranger than I thought."

"Well, be that as it may," he said with a laugh, "our time here is up, and I think you'll find this next custom much more familiar." He stood, pulling one more thing from the basket. A length of heavy fabric in a deep blue. No, a cloak. "You'll want to put this on,"

"Why?"

"Because where we're going next, it's quite cold." He extended a hand as she draped the cloak about her shoulders and clasped it. She curled her fingers around his, and the world faded once again.

Thirty-Three

WHEN THE MIST CLEARED, Cirelle's breath frosted the air. They stood in a small, moonlit garden behind an inn or some such, the architecture style all too recognizable. Cirelle knew the pattern in the cobblestones, the smell of this place.

Tears pricked her eyes. "Palace City." The sounds of merriment drifted toward her, though the darkness of night encompassed the streets. Cirelle counted the days. "Stars," she swore. "It's the Festival of Raigen." The god of hope among the Iska. His festival was celebrated at the end of autumn, when winter came close and hope was most needed. It was also when his constellation was most visible in the sky. For five days, the festivities continued from midday to midnight.

Home.

Palace City.

"But I can't be seen here. Maybe before, when people weren't looking for a lost princess, but now that I'm gone?"

Ellian casually arched one eyebrow. As he did, his charcoal skin slipped into a human shade of light brown, his hair an inky black. His fine clothing shifted into plain homespun with a woolen jacket, and the tips of his ears rounded.

Glamour.

Cirelle glanced down at her own hands, which had paled to a creamy white, her fancy dress also now simple cotton.

"I tweaked your features, too. No one will recognize you. Now we're just two human commoners out to enjoy the festival." His grin was wide, and though his eyes remained gray, she knew they glimmered azure underneath.

She couldn't say thank you, so Cirelle threw her arms around him instead. Her home, her people, her festival.

Ellian stiffened in her embrace for a moment, then relaxed and returned it. "Let's go. We've only a few hours left until midnight here."

A giddiness had taken Cirelle, and she found herself laughing as she tugged on his arm, leading him to the central plaza.

It was a riotous affair, with dancers in a large roped-off circle, fortune-tellers plying their trade in tents, vendors selling food and drink from market stalls, and other merchants selling wares ranging from scarves to luck charms. The aroma of a dozen foods assaulted Cirelle's nose. Trilling flutes played a lively reel, and the chatter of conversation rose across the plaza.

At one booth, Cirelle paused, her mouth watering at the sight of a favorite festival food. Little spheres of fried bread sat on a wooden platter, dotted with chopped onions and savory herbs.

Ellian stepped forward and passed the merchant a few coppers, then took two skewers of the dumplings.

Blinking, Cirelle took hers warily. "No gifts," she said.

"No," he agreed. "But this is all part of the original bargain. We agreed to follow our whims tonight, and this is my wish."

"More tricky faerie semantics?" Cirelle asked before taking a bite of dumpling. It nearly scorched her tongue, but the flavor was like an old friend come to visit.

"So," she had to ask, "Was that real money you gave him, or glamoured pebbles?"

He chuckled. "This time, they were real Arravene coppers from my Archive."

It was odd, watching him handle coin money. As far as Cirelle could tell, faeries operated solely on barter.

They ate as they wandered, the plaza lit by dozens of colorful lanterns hung just for this evening. Ellian gave even those tiny flames a wide berth, but said nothing of them.

Just hearing the familiar chatter of her own language left Cirelle strangely overwhelmed. It was so familiar, but now also alien. She'd spent half a year in Faerie, and already her mortal home felt like an old jacket that was comforting to own but no longer fit quite right.

Still, after several faerie revels it was relaxing to attend a simple human festival. No games, no dangers. A tension loosened within her. It left her in high spirits, tugging Ellian behind her to show him the sights of Raigen's celebration. There was a sculptor who worked in warm sugar, creating fantastical candied lollipops for children as they watched. In a large tent, a troupe of acrobats performed graceful and athletic feats.

It was only a matter of time until their steps led them toward the area set aside for dance. Lively songs, no passionate faerie dances here. She pulled Ellian out into the circle, and he willingly followed with a merry glint in his eyes. As always, he matched her steps easily. Cirelle danced with abandon, her cheeks aching from laughter.

Ellian grinned too, guileless. He watched her closely, taking in every breathless laugh, every grin. A softness in his eyes spoke of his own walls left behind. It tugged on something inside Cirelle, and for tonight, she let it.

One night, he'd asked of her. A night in which she left her worries of the future behind and lived in the moment. Well, right now she focused on the feel of Ellian's hands against her own, the smoky scent that wreathed them both, the way he brushed her hair out of her face after a fast-paced dervish of a reel.

The dances didn't let up, a whirlwind of footsteps. When Cirelle's calves began to burn, she led Ellian out of the ring.

What was it about dancing that always made Cirelle leave common sense behind? Or perhaps it was the opposite. Maybe dance cleared her head and banished the tiny, gnawing worries that pestered her like pebbles in a shoe.

Her world had narrowed to a single point, the faerie who followed her with light steps and a smile. Cirelle guided him away from the party, into a narrow alley cast in darkness. She had no fear of cutpurses or the other unsavory folk that slunk around the edges of such festivals, not with a faerie at her side.

In the shadow of that alley, she twined the fingertips of both hands through his and pulled him close, her back against the brick wall.

For several long moments, she merely grinned up at him, their bodies very nearly touching.

No barriers, not for either of them. Not tonight.

He leaned closer, and Cirelle tilted her chin upward to meet him. His head angled to the side, his cheek nearly brushing hers as he bent to whisper in her ear. Warm breath stirred her hair and caressed her earlobe as he spoke. "I think I very much want to kiss you now, princess."

Still asking permission, even though she'd already given it. "I think I very much want you to, faerie."

Kisses have a language — angry, teasing, anxious, tender. This one was acceptance, an acknowledgment of what they both knew. The words Ellian had left hanging between them, the ones she'd begged him to steal away. Now returned, and right now she didn't care. Cirelle's breath left her in a shudder and Ellian's hand cupped the back of her neck. She traced her tongue lightly along the edge of his upper lip and felt him sigh into her.

"Hey!"

Startled, they broke the kiss and turned, flinching, toward an approaching torch. As the wielder came closer, Cirelle could make out his uniform. One of the city guard.

Cirelle groaned, reluctantly pushing Ellian away as the guard approached.

"You two, break it up and find a room," the guard said. Cirelle recognized his accent, the inflection of an Asheiran. Rhine's kingdom. Her future husband.

Reality crashed down on her. No matter what she did tonight, she'd live out the rest of her days in Rhine's coastal kingdom, far from here, or Faerie. Or Ellian.

Her voice was hoarse as she grasped Ellian's hand and pleaded, "Let's go."

He didn't hesitate. The world faded away, replaced by the alley near the inn where they'd first appeared. A dozen hurried steps led them to the garden, and another sideways shift left them in Ellian's familiar rooftop garden once more.

Once there, Cirelle dropped Ellian's hand.

One night. She was supposed to have one single night without these worries nipping at her heels. Tomorrow, she and Ellian would be done. That thought felt like she'd swallowed knives, but tonight had been her one chance to live the *what if*, to see what it could have been like.

Until that guard showed up and reminded her of her duties.

The burning heat of tears pressed against the back of Cirelle's eyes. Tears of fury, of bitter regret and pain. She squeezed her eyes shut.

Ellian's fragrance wrapped around her a moment before his

arms did. Cirelle could have pulled away, could have run again. But not tonight. Tonight was for letting go, for admitting just to herself what she truly wanted. So she let him hold her while her fury crested and burned away, let him stroke her hair until she'd wept herself hollow.

When she finally pulled free, Ellian's glamour had dropped, his eyes a familiar mix of cobalt and carnation. Something inside Cirelle twisted at the thought that his feelings for her caused him as much pain as anything else. Cirelle wished she could wipe away that blue as easily as he brushed the tears from her cheeks.

Following her sudden impulse, Cirelle took his face in her hands and kissed him gently. Not on the lips, but on the cheek. A thank-you, the only one she was allowed.

"I'm sorry," he said.

"For what?"

"For… everything." The pink vanished, overwhelmed by sapphire blue, and it felt like a slap.

Cirelle had thought herself emptied of tears, but apparently not. As they brimmed once again, Ellian led her to one of the garden's many benches, this one carved of stone with an arched back to it.

Silence held for several long moments while Cirelle decided whether to ask the question. But she'd agreed to honesty, for this night, to follow her whims. And right now, that included asking him, "If you had it to do all over again, knowing that tomorrow this ends, would you?"

He stared up at the sky, an arm's length away, but also more. "I don't know." A pause. He shook his head with a bitter laugh. "Yes."

Cirelle's stomach wrenched itself into a knot. "How many hours do we have left?"

"Six." He turned to look at her, eyes an unreadable swirl of colors.

Cirelle scooted closer, tilted her head to lean it against his shoulder. "Eight hours." So little time. His arm slid around her waist, between her back and the bench, and he didn't reply.

Despite the hourglass running out, they sat like that for a time, watching the stars move slowly across the sky.

It was a gentle silence, heavy with their own thoughts, with Cirelle settled in the crook of Ellian's arm.

They'd both agreed. No walls, no worries, but it was impossible to banish them entirely. At the end of the evening, Cirelle would say the word that ended this forever. Ellian's cool mask of casual civility would return. No more teasing smiles or innuendos.

The thought wound about her, binding like a rope.

How long did they have left now? Perhaps five more hours to feel the warmth of his skin against hers, to linger in such closeness. It would be unbearably cold afterward, kept at a distance with only Lydia for solace.

She shivered and sighed, blinking away the tears again.

Ellian heard. His arm about her tightened, and she huddled closer. "Let's do something else," she said quietly, unsure she could bear this silent closeness any longer.

"I chose the activities so far," he said. "What do you want to do?"

She thought for a moment. "The Singing Mountain," she told him. "There must be other places in Faerie just as wondrous. Show them to me."

"With pleasure." He stood, holding out a hand to help her up. Cirelle took it, and the world misted away as she rose.

They spent hours exploring Ellian's favorite sights in Faerie. There was a mountainside overlooking endless ocean, where the sky danced with a curtain of brilliant, colorful lights. A river made of flowing, flickering violet flame. An immense public garden that put all others to shame, browsed by an astonishing variety of fairies. Sparkling silver waterfalls that cascaded over vast cliffs to crash in shimmering rivers below.

And cities. There were faerie cities of such wonder Cirelle could never have dreamed them up. Glass spires rising high into the sky, bricks of pure gold lining the streets, and everywhere bustling crowds even at midnight. Another city lay high among a tree canopy, made of ropes and elegantly carved wood, a forest network completely hidden from view below.

When Cirelle felt there were no other wonders Faerie could possibly hold, Ellian gave her a sly smile. "One more." Cirelle grinned and took his hand.

Thirty-Four

THEY EMERGED IN A HEDGE MAZE of rose bushes, their thorny vines an arm's length from snagging Cirelle's airy dress.

"Quickly now," Ellian whispered as he tugged her quickly down the path.

"Why?"

"Because these are not public gardens."

Cirelle bit her lip to keep back a laugh. Trespassing seemed such a minor crime after everything they'd done together, but she held her tongue as they wove their way through a garden gone half-wild.

They slipped through a wooden gate and out into woodland as awe-inspiring as every other faerie forest Cirelle had seen. Half the world of Faerie seemed to be blanketed in trees, each stranger than the last. These bore leaves of blue, of lavender, of plum purple. The moss and grass at her feet shimmered in iridescent shades, and a sweet fragrance hung in the air. Here it was twilight, and Cirelle wondered if they'd traveled far enough to visit another piece of this day, like they had when they went to Kishi, or if this forest was always bathed in purple-tinted half-light. The chatter of birdsong accompanied them, an oddly familiar sound in this eerie wood.

There was no true path, but the trees were sparse enough to weave through them, Ellian leading, fingers entwined with Cirelle's. A butterfly flitted past them, aglow with a faint light, each wing larger than the span of Cirelle's outstretched hand.

After a time, the woods thinned suddenly, and Cirelle sucked in a gasp.

The tree was larger than she'd ever have imagined, immense in a way that her mind could barely comprehend. The trunk stood twice as wide as Palace Arraven's largest tower, and stretched so far above that mist shrouded its uppermost leaves. The ones that had fallen by Cirelle's feet were as large as the surface of a writing desk, in brilliant shades of violet and crimson.

And the magic in the air was so strong it pressed on all her senses, a buzzing in her ears, a smell of ozone and cloying scent of sweetness on the mild breeze. The air shimmered, sparkling with a faint light that she caught only out of the corner of her eye.

It could only be one thing.

"Lhyrria," she breathed.

"Yes."

This was one of the most important spots in Faerie, one of the anchors that held magic in place. Standing here, Cirelle believed it.

She kept moving forward, Ellian trailing behind her with his hand still in her own. As she approached the trunk, the sense of magic grew stronger. It called to her, like a shiny bauble that begged to be held. The siren song of the tree was too much, a rope pulling her closer. She lifted a hand.

Ellian's protest and tug on her other arm was too late.

For half a moment, it felt just like any other tree. Cool, papery bark against her skin.

Then it struck.

With a nauseating wrench, Cirelle left her body behind. She blinked, seeing herself collapse to the ground from above. Ellian called her name and gathered her in his arms.

The world shifted sideways. Fog caressed her skin with its damp, icy breath. Cirelle glanced down to find herself garbed in one of the Unseelie's gauzy dresses in a deep indigo blue. Beneath her bare feet lay a path of tiny, pebbled stones.

A dream. It must be. The shining walkway of smooth gravel extended before her, fading into fog. With the oddly calm certainty of this dream-state, Cirelle knew she must follow the trail to the end.

The world outside the path was a misty haze of white, a vast nothingness that muffled even the crunch of stone beneath her feet.

Until one sound emerged in the silence. Music. One of her own songs played with excruciating beauty on a harp even clearer than the one in Ellian's manor. Strangest of all, it was an old one, a piece she'd written for Briere and hadn't played in years.

The song grew louder as she drew ever closer.

Of all the things she expected to find at the end of the path, a mirror image of herself was possibly the last. A perfect replica of Cirelle sat at the harp, eyes closed. The false Cirelle was identical in every way save the Arravene gown she wore, corseted and full-skirted in her kingdom's heraldry colors, green and gold. Her instrument was Cirelle's gilded harp from home.

Cirelle sighed. "Of course. I think I've read this story."

Her shadow self glanced up from playing, gave a fierce grin, and let the notes die. "Have you?" Mirror Cirelle's eyes gleamed.

"Here is where I confront my fears and have some revelation, isn't it? It's an old tale."

Mirror Cirelle laughed. "You can, if you wish. Or we can just play." A second harp and stool appeared.

"Play what?"

Her other self gave a sly grin. "Ah, that's the question, isn't it?"

True Cirelle swallowed, a nervousness finally settling into her bones. "It matters, doesn't it? What I choose?"

A nod. "Perhaps."

Well, this was Cirelle's dream, and there was little to do but follow the steps of the dance. She took a seat on the stool, only to realize the harp before her was the one from Ellian's music room, the one she'd come to know so well. The one that now belonged to her. She strummed a few cascading sets of notes, testing it.

Almost without thinking, her fingers danced over the strings, playing the first few measures of her Faerie Nocturne.

With a mysterious smile, the Mirror Cirelle joined in, playing the counterpoint Cirelle had written.

Over the music, her twin asked, "you wish to return to your body, do you not?"

"Of course."

"Then there is but one price to pay." The other Cirelle's stare pierced her. "Tell me why you chose this song."

Cirelle swallowed. "Habit. I've been playing it so often."

"That is a lie."

Without ceasing the song, Cirelle closed her eyes. The Faerie Nocturne had become more than familiar. Ellian had pointed it out last night. This was his song, whether she had intended it or not. Its earliest skeleton had been born of her nervousness when she'd first met him. And though she'd meant the rest of the piece to encompass her experience in Faerie, Cirelle was forced to admit one thing to herself. Ellian *was* Faerie, to her. Even Cirelle's first moments here, staring in awe at the forest they'd walked when she left her world, had been spent with her fingers twined in his.

Bits and pieces of faerie melodies were interspersed throughout the song, little repeated measures that mimicked the music played at the Unseelie palace when she and Ellian had danced together the first time, or frenetic cascades of notes from one of the revels he'd taken her to. Phrases she'd subconsciously woven into the piece, only now seeing them for what they were.

Whenever Ellian had pushed her away, Cirelle had sought refuge in the notes of her harp. She used the song to quell those moths in her stomach by giving them voice, the final verse full of sharp, painful longing. Perhaps the first time she'd played it, those notes had been laced with homesickness, but they'd since come to represent something else entirely.

Even now, strumming the chords, Cirelle's chest grew tight.

This wasn't a Faerie Nocturne. It was Ellian's song, every little frustrated, discordant twang she'd worked into the melody, every trilling shower of notes that left her light-spirited and giddy. Cirelle sighed as the final, questioning notes spilled from her fingers.

The song ended with uncertainty, with a choice left to be made.

But I made that decision last night. Cirelle's eyes stung with unshed tears, and her heart beat unevenly.

Her shadow self interrupted. "So tell me now, why did you choose this song?"

All these months, Cirelle had been writing Ellian's song. And her own, interwoven into the notes alongside his.

"Stars," she swore as the tears finally spilled free. "I think I'm in love with him."

The jolt of awakening was a painful one, sucking in a gasping breath as Cirelle sat up in a bed. She reached up to wipe her eyes clear, and her hands came away damp.

The tears from her dream had followed her here, it seemed.

"Cirelle." When she turned her head to find Ellian, he leaned forward in a chair beside the bed. His smoky fragrance suffused the air.

Seeing those familiar features staring at her with tenderness, his eyes pink and fawn-colored brown, undid her. Cirelle unraveled like a poorly-knitted sweater, the revelation from her dream leaving her bleeding and raw on the inside.

Stars go black, she cursed herself hopelessly, staring at that rosy hue in his eyes. And now the Lhyrria had forced her to see the reflection of those feelings in herself.

What do we do now?

"You're all right," Ellian breathed the words as he bent toward her, a sigh of relief. His hand was outstretched as if to touch her, to remind himself that it was true.

Like Thieves' Night, when he'd been wounded and Cirelle couldn't stop brushing his hair aside or resting her fingertips on his shoulder, all to reassure herself he would be okay.

She flinched away, heart still fluttering like a startled hare's. *I can't love him. I promised myself. I swore I wouldn't do that, wouldn't be like the others.*

An oath she had apparently broken.

Ellian's hand dropped to the coverlet, a question written in eyes now sapphire blue.

What could she say? "I... I'm sorry." Inadequate words, but they were all she had. She stared down at the blanket that covered her. Silk so fine it looked like bronze. A coverlet she recognized.

I'm in his bed. A quick glance around the room confirmed her suspicions.

Beneath the blankets, she still wore her fine gown, even the cloak and her slippers. *He wouldn't even remove the shoes without permission.*

"Cirelle," he said. "What happened?"

She debated how much to tell him.

No walls tonight.

"I had a vision," she admitted. "A dream." She wiped her face with one hand.

Ellian started to speak, then stopped. He pushed away from the bed to slump in the chair. "And should I dare to ask what it was about?"

The question tore something loose, something Cirelle had been holding onto tightly. The tears started again as she rasped a sharp laugh. "A mirror of myself. My harp, my songs." She turned a broken gaze to meet his colorless eyes. "And… it was about you."

That unreadable mask fell over his face like a curtain closing. "Oh." He shook his head slightly, his gaze skittering away. "I see."

Except he didn't, not at all.

She couldn't bear it any more. Sliding out of the warm blankets, her slippers sank into the plush warmth of the rug. She glanced at the door, at her escape.

"Wait," he said, though regret lingered in the word. "We have three hours yet," he said.

Cirelle held her arms about herself, an inch away from breaking apart completely.

"I'm sorry," he said quietly, the words holding a sorrow that plucked painfully at her. "But a bargain was made, and even I can't change that."

Reluctantly, she sat on the edge of the bed, facing away from him. Uncomfortable hours left to stew in this new revelation, to live with the stinging ache of sitting so close, of breathing in his scent.

They both sat unmoving and silent for minutes. The tension grew, every breath tightening Cirelle's ribcage further until the sobs broke free with sudden and embarrassing violence.

Humiliated and angry with herself, Cirelle slipped under the blanket and huddled into a ball, tugging the coverlet up over her ears. It may be Ellian's bed, but the blanket still felt like a shield.

"Stone and sea and sky," Ellian swore under his breath. The chair creaked as he stood. "Oath be damned," he muttered, striding over to the door. "I'll leave you be."

The thought of him leaving was suddenly more painful than his presence. "Wait."

His hand paused on the knob.

"What happens if one of us breaks the bargain?"

"There are… repercussions." He shook his head. His voice was flat, emotionless. "I'll pay them. But to do so, I have to be the one to break it, to leave. You may stay here this evening. I'll sleep in a guest room."

The knob turned, and he yanked the door open stiffly.

"No." The word startled even Cirelle. But the wave of self-pity had passed as suddenly as it drowned her, and her familiar stubborn anger now filled that space.

His eyes, when he turned, were pensive.

"Stay," Cirelle said, her voice far more confident than she'd have expected.

Ellian shook his head, but still paused in the doorway. "You don't have to endure my presence just to fulfill the bargain."

The words kindled an old, familiar fire in Cirelle. She tossed back the blanket and propped herself up on one arm to better meet his stare. "Who said it was just to fulfill the bargain? I speak for myself."

A faint glimmer in his gaze, there and then gone. A hint of his usual spark.

"We're to follow our whims and wants tonight, correct?" She didn't wait for a response. "Well, I want you to stay. Do you want to leave?"

His reply was cautious. "No."

Cirelle flopped back down on the bed. "Good. Now get back here, faerie. This bed is way too comfortable for me to leave just yet."

That earned her a laugh, a real one. "And where should I sit, princess?"

And just like that, their banter was back, a familiar patter. It left Cirelle both dizzyingly happy and intensely nervous, those moths back at it again.

She gathered all her courage. No worries for tomorrow. Tonight was all she had. After tonight, Ellian would slip through her fingers. A few scant hours left before it all walked away.

"Well, it is an awfully large bed."

For a moment, he was silent, staring at her with something akin to wonder. "Wait. Are you…?" He let the sentence trail off.

Honesty. Worms slithered in Cirelle's belly, partners to the moths. "I don't know." Could she do this once more, with the knowledge she still held? No longer for mere pleasure, this would be something else. Something infinitely more painful, when it was over.

Their eyes met, his flooding with a mix of rose and black and lavender. He didn't speak a word, but let the door close. Circling the bed, he slid under the blankets, keeping a careful arm's length away. Cirelle unclasped the cloak and wriggled out of it, shoving it out of the bed to puddle on the floor. Her slippers followed with a soft thump.

Perhaps Ellian tried for his usual blithe charm, but his question was tense as he spoke to her back. "Now what, princess?"

Cirelle closed her eyes, fighting back the urge that overwhelmed her with his presence so close. But that was not what she had agreed to do this evening. To follow her heart, however foolish, despite the grief tomorrow would bring.

Under the coverlet, she turned, the motion twisting her dress and tangling it in her legs. She ignored it. For a few moments, she closed her eyes, taking long, deep breaths. When she opened them, Ellian's were so unbearably near, rose blossoms and violets. With one hand, she brushed his hair back from his face, then lifted her chin and placed a single gentle kiss on his lips.

There was a painful release in the gesture, a perplexing and muddled mess of emotions spilling out of her in one giant rush. Then in the aftermath, a calm.

She had let go, given in, and there was a peace in that.

Her breath slipped out in a sigh against Ellian's lips.

"Cirelle…" The whisper was so quiet she'd never have heard it were she not so close. A weight hung on her name, need and want and agonizing indecision.

"No more barriers," she reminded him. "I swore an oath." She moved closer, pressing her body along the length of his, though her skirt still ensnared her legs. Another kiss as her hands threaded into his hair. When she pulled away, she let her eyes speak for her. All the feelings she'd been fighting and denying for months, Cirelle set them free.

Tasting the syllables on her tongue, she spoke his true name for the first time. "Etishen."

It broke something inside him. Ellian shuddered, his breath hitching. His eyes flickered through several colors before he closed them. Keeping them squeezed shut, he whispered, "say it again."

Cirelle's smile was somehow both soft and sly at the same time as she breathed his name once more. "Etishen."

He kissed her, long and slow and with a startling intensity. She felt her name murmured against her lips, full of longing and things neither of them would say.

Except… could she be brave, say what lay in her heart, just this night? Even if she knew it would all be gone tomorrow? In far too little time, all of this would disappear like morning fog.

Cirelle let the words die on her lips. Instead, she let Ellian kiss her. Hands tangled in his hair, she pulled him closer, never close enough.

With a tearing sound, Cirelle's frustrated movements ripped the seam of the delicate skirt entangling her legs. There was no time for Ellian to react, though. The moment she was free, Cirelle hooked her leg over his, pressing his body into hers.

His warmth filled the space beneath the blanket, stiflingly hot. Cirelle tossed the coverlet off their bodies and pushed the kiss further, deeper, her tongue sliding across his lip, coaxing his mouth open.

And his hands, those gentle scholar's hands, stroked lines of fire along her skin. One traced a teasing caress up her arm while the other cupped the back of her neck. Everywhere his skin touched hers, she burned. This was nothing like before, not anymore. Not when her own emotions threatened to strangle her.

Her hands moved lower, one pressing a palm against his chest while the other slid down his side, beneath the jacket, to hook a finger inside the waist of his trousers.

Ellian growled, a low rumble of a sound, and one of those gentle hands wandered to her hip, slipping lower until he caught the torn edge of her dress. Tantalizingly slow, he traced light circles up the outside of her thigh, sliding the skirt up higher on her hips.

His mouth left hers to scatter a line of kisses along her jaw, down her throat. Cirelle tossed her head back to let him, gasping when he nipped her lightly.

He laughed, a soft rasp that brushed against her skin, kindled a heat both in her belly and lower.

She managed one short, breathless sentence. "Who's the tease now, faerie?"

The second laugh was one of pure, simple amusement, and he pulled away just enough to look into her eyes. Azure and lavender wove a tapestry in his eyes. She smiled, and both colors washed away in a tide of pink.

It left Cirelle's breaths too short, her lungs and heart too full to speak.

One chance to admit it, to say the words, to give him the truth.

"Ellian… Etishen… I …" She paused, taking a long steadying breath and staring into those eyes of startling rose.

"No," his gaze darkened, flickering black. "Don't say it."

Irritation flared to life, and she drew back. "What?"

Such a striking color, threads of palest pink against an inky black sky. "If you say it… I won't be able to bear it when you leave."

She closed her eyes. "It's a bit late for that, isn't it?"

He sighed, one hand brushing through her hair as he pushed himself away from her. His laugh was a dark, brittle sound. "Far too late." He shook his head. After a long moment, he rolled away from her. "But I fear I've little heart to face tomorrow with those words hanging between us. Best leave them unspoken."

It hurt, cutting her like a jagged-edged blade. "But you'd go for a tumble anyway?" The words burned her tongue like poison, harsh and angry.

He sighed. "No, I won't." He slid out of the bed, standing.

Cirelle sat up, pointing one accusatory finger at him. "No walls, Ellian. You said that."

"I asked you to leave *yours* behind." A weariness clung to the statement. "I said nothing about mine."

Her anger burned white-hot now. "You damnable, fucking *faerie*," she spat the curse through the tears that stung her eyes.

Ellian's expressionless mask fell over his face as he slumped into a chair opposite the bed. "I am. And I am not. I won't do this again, Cirelle."

The sound of her name scorched and seared.

"Won't do what?"

He shook his head. "You made your choice. I asked you twice. We know what happens at dawn, and I won't leave you with those memories to cut you open later."

The words fell from her lips before she could stop them. "Like Kyrinna?"

He refused to look at her.

Fury consumed her. "You're a coward."

No reply.

Cirelle tossed the blankets aside. Her toes sank into the lush carpet as she stood. "I don't care what you're afraid to hear. You don't command my tongue." She took a step toward him, but Ellian continued to stare at the back of his hand, clutching the edge of the armrest tightly. Cirelle took a deep breath, steadied her courage, and admitted her newfound revelation out loud. "I love you."

His head snapped up and his breath hissed sharply. A dizzying swirl of colors in those wide eyes. Pale yellow surprise swirled with sapphire sorrow and rose-colored adoration. They closed as Cirelle stepped closer, and Ellian shook his head softly as if he could force the words back.

"It's too late to pretend I don't." Cirelle stepped closer yet. "And you're letting your fear destroy the one night we have."

His head tilted back to meet her gaze, Ellian's eyes flooded with black and blue as he breathed. "And when the sun rises? Will your answer remain the same?"

It was Cirelle's turn to close her eyes. "Yes." She clutched the fabric of her skirt in both hands to keep herself from reaching for him. "I made an oath to return, to marry. It is my duty." The words tasted like poison on her lips.

"You did everything in your power to slip that snare before." Ellian's response was strained. "And yet you'll run toward it now."

Cirelle's nails dug into her palms even through the fabric of her skirt. "You once asked me if giving myself to a loveless marriage was any worse than the sacrifices my subjects make. And now I face that fate to save my people. But we have right now. You asked for tonight, and you have it. You have *me*."

He watched her wordlessly.

Her heart hammered a staccato, arrhythmic beat. "We can end this night with a fight, or we can end it with a better memory. Something to cherish when I am trapped in a castle by the sea." She croaked out the next words. "When you find another human to love."

So blue, those eyes. The color of the night sky just before indigo fades to black.

"Just give me tonight," she said. "No walls."

Anguish washed over his face. His hair fell in a wild disarray, a stray lock of it nearly falling into one eye. He looked so young, so vulnerable. So *human*.

Cirelle lifted a cautious hand to brush that bit of hair aside, tucking it behind one pointed ear then cupping his cheek softly.

Ellian's eyes closed, his breath held. A moment later, it shuddered out of him in a long sigh. His shoulders slumped. His hand left the armrest to take hers from his cheek and lift it to his lips. A kiss pressed gently against her palm. Lightning raced from Cirelle's hand to her core, down to her toes. She gasped, a soft whisper of sound.

Ellian kissed her fingertips, one by one, slowly. An ache formed low in her stomach.

When he spoke, Cirelle almost had to strain to hear the words.

"You win."

A slow, tentative smile blossomed on her face. "I always do, don't I?"

The faintest thread of azure crept into his eyes. "You do." The brilliant blue grew, and his voice took on that velvety quality, that deep rumble that felt like a caress. "But the game isn't over yet, princess." He dropped her hand to grasp her hips and pull her closer, even as he slid forward in the chair so she stood between his knees. Cirelle's breath quickened, and her hands tangled in his hair as she closed her eyes and leaned down for a kiss.

His grip loosened on her hips, hands sliding down the outside of her thighs. One of his hands found the torn seam in her dress and fingertips touched bare skin. It felt like fire, like lightning. He pressed his palm flat against her thigh. So painfully slowly, it slid up the front of her leg, lifting her dress with it. His other hand echoed the motion on the opposite side, and Cirelle thought her knees might buckle.

So warm, those palms, those fingertips. Such long, clever fingers that walked their way ever further upward. His thumbs traced small patterns on the inside of her thighs.

Ellian broke the kiss, leaning away. Cirelle opened her eyes to meet blazing purple ones, a knowing smile on his lips.

She couldn't speak, couldn't form words while his fingers so gently and earnestly explored her skin. They'd done this so many times before, but this was so much *more*. Cirelle's hands had somehow slid to his shoulders, and she gripped them tightly, trembling.

His fingertips brushed the lower edge of her undergarments, the strange and flimsy faerie things she'd become so accustomed to. They slid under the hem and Cirelle couldn't stop the small moan that slipped from her lips. Her eyes closed again unbidden.

Then, abruptly, his hands were gone, her skirts falling to drape her legs once more. Cirelle's eyes snapped open. Ellian took both of her wrists and lifted her hands from his shoulders.

He said one word, and it made Cirelle's heart stutter. "Bed." His voice was hoarse, his eyes nearly glowing violet and pink.

They fell together onto the rumpled silken coverlet. Cirelle's dress tore further as she shifted toward the center of the bed, and she didn't care. Ellian was kissing her, his hands in her hair, at her shoulders, her hips. He unclasped her heavy necklace and tossed it casually beside the bed. His lips left a trail along her cheek, her neck, her chest. Cirelle's hands fumbled at the buttons of his jacket. His tongue traced a small line along the upper edge of her dress's neckline, and Cirelle made a very undignified noise. Ellian only laughed, a small rumble of sound.

Somehow, she managed the buttons. Ellian paused long enough to slide off the jacket, and it, too, was unceremoniously thrown onto the floor. It didn't take long for the shirt to follow. Cirelle's palms slid along the planes of his stomach to grasp his hips and pull him closer, eagerly, fiercely.

"Wait," he murmured against her ear, his breath warm. It made her shudder. For one terrifying moment, Cirelle thought he'd push her aside again, but when she turned to meet his gaze, no worry lingered in his eyes. A smile danced at the edge of his lips. His skin was flushed in the cheeks, a rosy hue tinting the gray.

"What?"

"If I'm to have a chance in this battle," he said, a wicked note hanging on the words, "I deserve a fair fight. We must set the rules of this duel." He lifted an eyebrow as his fingertips danced along the upper edge of her dress's neckline, slipping just under the fabric and making her shiver.

"Oh?" Cirelle breathed, playing along. "And what rules might those be?" Her hand drew a teasing line down the center of his stomach, and she felt him shudder. Stars, she'd missed that. And now, there was another ache, another need beneath the simmering desire. Something deeper, warm and strong and tender all at the same time.

"First," he said, mischief in his gaze, "a slower pace. To-night… this isn't a reel, to be over and done so quickly, my princess."

The '*my*' made Cirelle's throat go dry. She swallowed. "What do you suggest instead?"

"A different dance." His hand slid under the torn seam of her skirt once again, teasing, caressing the inside of her thigh. Cirelle sucked in a breath, her back arching and legs parting. Ellian's eyes blazed violet, and Cirelle's fingertips dug into his skin where she grasped his hips.

Just as Ellian's fingers toyed with the edge of her underthings once more, he paused, a darkness settling into his gaze. "You're certain of this?" he asked gently. Cautious as ever.

For answer, Cirelle clutched his hair and pulled him in for a fierce kiss. "Don't you dare stop now."

His promise was murmured against her skin, soft as a sigh. "I won't." No, instead his fingers hooked the edge of her undergarments, sliding them down. She kicked them off as Ellian too, moved lower. When his tongue brushed between her legs, she let out a soft sound, back arching. He laughed softly, the rumble of it sending ripples through her body as that oh-so-warm tongue began doing things that banished any rational thought from her mind. The world was swallowed in that heat, the molten shiver settling low in her belly, a pleasant pressure like starlight filling her entire body.

Her hips rose to meet him, and Ellian made a small, satisfied sound. She replied with her own urging, barely forming words, just his name and *yes* and *please*, over and over in a rising crescendo.

Just when the waves threatened to crash down on her, he stopped. "Oh no," he said softly, moving up and loosening the laces of her dress. "Not yet."

Cirelle sat up, helping him remove what remained of her dress and tossing it aside. "Cruel faerie," she muttered as he pulled her close, his lips finding that sensitive spot just beneath her ear and making her gasp.

"I promise you'll disagree with that sentiment by the time the night is over," he purred.

And he was right.

She lost herself in him, in the now of it, the heat of it, the wanting and the thrill of his touch. He was so unbearably gentle, it was maddening. Kisses scattered on skin, and hands caressing everywhere, as if he wanted to memorize every curve of her. He took his vengeance for all those dances she'd teased him so mercilessly. Thrice more he brought her nearly to the edge, then backed away from it, until she breathed curses at him and he laughed softly against her throat.

Then, finally, after an eternity of a need so all-consuming she could barely think, he slid into her. She shuddered and moaned and murmured his true name between urgent kisses as he moved inside her, until stars burst behind her eyes and she crashed over the cliff in gasping waves. Her fingers grasped his hips so tightly the knuckles went white.

As her breathing steadied and her eyes opened, he made to move away, but she held him in place. "No. You, too."

"But—"

"I'm not letting you win this game entirely," she laughed, lifting her hips to draw him deeper. The sense of fullness was even more intense, after her bright, brief burst of pleasure. "We can call it a tie?"

His chest rose and fell once, twice, and he nodded. He moved inside her only three more times, and then cried out, back arching.

A single, hoarse laugh slipped from him as he rolled to the side, panting. "A draw, then."

After they'd both caught their breath, Cirelle lay curled against him, tracing idle patterns on his dust-colored skin with a fingertip. She felt truly at peace for the first time since she'd arrived in Faerie.

Tiny, invisible daggers twisted themselves into her heart at the knowledge of what would come all too soon. It was almost a cruelty to know now how deeply Ellian loved her. They lay in silence, tangled in each other's arms until the spell had to be broken.

"Time is nearly up," Ellian said reluctantly, extracting himself from her embrace and sitting up.

Cirelle's stomach lurched, a sensation of falling. Words thick and clumsy on her tongue, she slipped out of the bed and threw her gown back over her head. The poor thing was bedraggled now, the skirt hopelessly torn along the seam and the bodice unlaced.

Still, it was something, a scrap of armor against what was about to happen.

Behind her, Ellian had put on trousers. With his hair a tangled mess, he almost looked more tempting, and a cold lump of sorrow formed in Cirelle's chest.

His eyes met hers, black and rose.

"I ask a final time," Ellian said, his voice carefully toneless, though even he couldn't keep a faint tremor from it. "Will you stay with me?"

Cirelle's eyes burned, and she closed them, unable to look him in the eye when she said it. "No."

Silence held, and Cirelle dared to open her eyes, though she still couldn't breathe.

He blinked, then stared down at the coverlet where they'd lain only minutes before. "Then we torment each other no more. This ends here. No more taunting, no more teasing or flirtation." A helpless resignation weighted the words.

It was too much to bear, and Cirelle fled.

Thirty-Five

WHEN THE DAY CAME for Lydia to return to Ellian's, her eagerness to be at Cirelle's side warred with her reluctance to part from the strange peace she'd found at Shai's. There had been a simplicity to routine, to days spent without tiptoeing around Ellian.

"Come on," Shai urged her as she helped shove things back into Lydia's pack without any care for folding or rolling them. "Gotta get you back to your princess, right?"

Lydia was surprised by the warmth of her own smile. "Yes. And th—" she bit her tongue. "I appreciate the sparring sessions."

"Any time," Shai grinned. "Just say the word."

"I might take you up on that," Lydia said, rubbing a bruised rib. "I have to repay you for that last match."

"Game on, human."

And then Lydia was packed, taking Shai's hand to return to Ellian's home of darkness and secrets.

To Cirelle.

The world misted and solidified. They stood on Ellian's doorstep. Shai rang the bell, and Cirelle answered in a heartbeat.

Was she waiting for me?

Lydia barely made it through the doorway before Cirelle wrapped her in an embrace. "You're back. Are you all right?"

"I'm fine." Lydia's voice was unsteady while she tried to still her heartbeat and banish the flush that crept into her cheeks. "You?"

Cirelle let Lydia go and gave a shrug, but a faint flicker of something in her face betrayed her. Sorrow, grief.

"What's wrong?"

"Nothing," Cirelle shook her head, but her breath caught. She grasped Lydia's hand. "Come on, let's catch up."

Lydia tossed a single glance over her shoulder to see Shai give a cheerful wave and blink away as the door closed to shut them in this mansion of shadows.

In Cirelle's parlor, Lydia made tea and settled on the sofa. "What's really wrong?"

"Nothing."

"Your Highness…"

For a moment, she thought Cirelle would continue to shut her out, but the princess blinked, her lip trembled, and a loud, hiccupping sob burst from her.

Before she knew she would move, Lydia's hands wrapped one of Cirelle's. "What is it?"

A bitter laugh. "You'll dance with joy. I've done a poor job keeping it secret, haven't I? I mean… Ellian. And me." She shook her head. "But you don't need to worry anymore. It's finished. For real this time."

Lydia was ashamed of the relief that flooded her. She couldn't have heard this right. "What?"

"He ended it. We're done. This thing… whatever it was… it's over."

With a gentle squeeze of Cirelle's hand, Lydia said, "That might be for the best."

The princess yanked her hand free. "You think I don't know that? Do you think that makes it hurt less?" Anger flashed in her eyes, the vitriol that sometimes overtook her, made her violent and cruel.

"I don't—"

"You don't know anything," the princess spat.

"Maybe I don't. But I can still be glad you're safe. Safer."

Cirelle remained silent, and Lydia left.

Thirty-Six

SHAI TOOK THE GOLDEN serpent brooch from Ellian and pinned it to her chest. It rested against the lace, its enameled blue wings outspread. So fancy. A bold bit of color amidst the brown leather of her pauldrons and gauntlets, the soft dove-gray of the short dress. They stood in Ellian's foyer, the princess and her guard both fastening similar pins to their own clothing before they ventured to visit the duergar and ask about the origin of that feather necklace.

Cirelle had taken her role as diplomat seriously, dolling herself up in a golden gown with a poofy skirt. Lydia dressed far more practically, her hands nervously fidgeting with the hilt of her borrowed daggers, fae metal rather than poisonous iron.

The guard scowled, a cute little wrinkle forming between her brows as she asked Cirelle, "Are you sure that's the best choice for traveling through underground tunnels?"

"I don't want to look sloppy if I'm to bargain on Ellian's behalf." The princess tugged her own serpent pin from her scooped neckline and repositioned it.

Ellian fastened a nervous look on their brooches, and Shai rolled her eyes. "It's fine, they're not going anywhere." He'd told them all a dozen times how important it was, this symbol of his heraldry. The sign that they acted on his behalf.

Shai had to admit she was a bit surprised that Ellian let the princess's bodyguard come along with them, so soon after the woman had tried to bind him. But Lydia only did it to protect Cirelle, and that was the name of the game today. That woman wouldn't let anything harm a hair on Cirelle's head.

Ellian didn't seem satisfied with Shai's reassurance. "You know the way out, right?"

"Yessss," Shai dragged the word out, shifting the heavy pack she carried. Bribes, offerings, trades. Gemstones the Duergar couldn't get from their own mountain, mostly. "We've got this. We go in and offer the shinies in exchange for info about who commissioned the necklace. If they say yes, we make the swap and go on our merry way. If they say nope, we accept their hospitality, then sneak into their library later, swipe the info anyway, and creep out the back door. Easy peasy."

"This would be so much simpler if I could go," Ellian murmured.

Cirelle stopped fiddling with her brooch and smoothed her skirts. "What *did* you do to get exiled from the mountain, exactly?"

Ellian frowned. "I ran afoul of the duergar prince in their caves when I was young and reckless, stealing an object from him. He pursued with his soldiers. I survived by leading them into Yratla's lair, the beast that dwells in the deep tunnels, when it isn't soaring the skies. The vain creature spared me on the condition that I honor her image for the rest of my life. So I made the winged serpent my heraldry, patterned my home's decor after her, to keep that oath." He shook his head. "The prince wasn't so lucky. If I set foot in that kingdom myself, the king will claim a blood debt."

Shai barked a laugh. "You killed his son? Harsh."

"I didn't. Yratla did. All I did was escape. But as long as you wear those pins marking you as my allies, Yratla will spare you if you have to take the back way out."

"Let's hope we don't," Cirelle said, smoothing her skirts one more time. "But let's go get this over with."

☙

Within minutes, they stood at the entrance to a cave. A bit of movement caught Cirelle's attention, and she watched the duergar guide emerge, holding a single torch.

He was approximately Cirelle's height, all drawn of askew angles. A pointed nose and chin matched ears easily twice as long as a sidhe's delicate ones. Pale hair surrounded his head in a tuft like a lion's mane while large, dark eyes peered at the group distrustfully.

"Skirsh?" Cirelle asked.

The duergar nodded, his gaze lingering on the pin at her collar. "Come on, then." He walked back into the cave without another word.

With a single wary glance shared between them, Cirelle and her two guards followed deeper and deeper into the mountain.

After what seemed an eternity of walking over rough-hewn rock, they emerged into a vast cavern, the ceiling so high above that it was lost to darkness. The buildings were carved directly from the stone, the streets smooth. The architecture favored rounded arches and cylindrical shapes, artfully crafted windows in perfect circles dotting the buildings.

Torches burned without smoke, dotting the walls of the buildings at eye level. The entire city seemed to be lit by fire, and the cavern was far warmer than even the tunnel had indicated, stifling in its heat.

The reason became apparent as they ventured deeper into the city. An entire quarter of the duergar's cavern was given over to forges, smiths all plying their trades. Goldsmiths and silversmiths pouring precious molten metals into tiny molds, bladesmiths hammering away at anvils.

So this was where the mysterious feather necklace had been crafted, among these sweltering stones. The very air shimmered with heat, the street beneath Cirelle's feet uncomfortably warm even through the soles of her boots. A trickle of sweat dripped down her brow. Perhaps layers of skirts weren't the best decision, after all.

The group garnered a number of curious stares. Suspicious duergar eyes followed their every step. Further onward, they passed into a more palatial district. Here, brilliant gems were inset into stone walls, the homes larger.

Their guide led them up a wide stone staircase. The doors stood proudly, defiantly open, though guards flanked the entry. When they emerged from the corridors into a large throne room, Skirsh announced them. "The emissary from Ellian of the sidhe, and her escort."

On the throne sat a wizened duergar. The years visibly weighed on him, his body crumpling in on itself. He was as pale and angular as their guide. Despite his obvious signs of age, his eyes were sharp and clear. He sat alone on a single throne, four duergar soldiers in shining silver plate flanking either side. Two more soldiers stood at either side of the doorway they'd come through.

Cirelle cleared her throat and curtsied. "King Glisrat of the duergar. We come bearing gifts, seeking information."

The king peered at her with those cold, canny eyes. "I received Ellian's missive. Too cowardly to set foot on my stone himself, eh?"

"It was my understanding that he is exiled from your kingdom, Your Highness."

"Indeed. So he sends a mortal to do his work for him. Feeble."

Cirelle bit back a retort. Beside her, Lydia's hand tightened around the blade of her dagger. On the other side, Shai managed to keep a casual pose, though her face was contorted in a scowl.

"Ellian, however," the king said, "is not the only one with allies." As if they'd been waiting for their cue, two figures emerged from a doorway in the side of the room. Two winter-pale wraiths bearing ebony and opal crowns.

Queen Ayre and Prince Adaleth entered with chilling, smug smiles, followed by a half dozen sidhe guards wearing armor marked with the crown-and-snowdrop heraldry of the Unseelie Court. The guards fanned out, circling and flanking Cirelle and her companions.

Shai and Lydia moved closer, their backs to Cirelle, though they still hesitated to draw their weapons. To do so would be an unmistakable threat, a challenge.

"King Glisrat!" Cirelle called, proud that her voice didn't shake despite Prince Adaleth's baleful eyes locked on her. "What is the meaning of this?"

"The Unseelie Court is a fellow enemy of Ellian. When I informed them of his message, they asked for a boon, and I have granted it. By entering my demesne, you place yourself at my mercy. And I have bestowed that mercy to them on my behalf."

"No," Cirelle said. "You can't do anything to us."

And yet she knew it was a lie. Adaleth stepped forward. *Anything to me that Ellian does.* That had been her promise to him. Foolish words, said by her ignorant past self.

The prince said nothing, but moved within reach. Lydia growled and Shai bared her teeth. Cirelle froze. *We can't offend.* If they struck first, Adaleth could retaliate even worse.

Adaleth's hand lifted to stroke her cheek, his fingertip trailing along her jaw, her throat, then along the top of her bodice. Cirelle closed her eyes and bit her lip. *He's just posturing. Trying to scare you.*

It was working.

But Cirelle wasn't the one that broke first. Lydia made a strangled sound and her blade rang free of its sheath.

On the opposite side, Shai swore. "Well, shit." She, too, drew her sword, which immediately burst into flame. Once, long ago, Issen warned Cirelle that Shai had promised never to use one of her magical sidhe abilities in Ellian's home. Now Cirelle knew why. Fire, Ellian's greatest fear.

She didn't have time to think on it long. A ring of flying blades surrounded Cirelle and Adaleth both. The prince stood without flinching, smiling, but Cirelle ducked, hunching in on herself.

Shai and Lydia's steel clanged against the faerie blades. But even they wouldn't be able to defeat three sidhe warriors apiece. It was a clamor of cries and grunts and clanking metal and all Cirelle could do was crouch and cover her head, helpless.

If only I'd brought the claimhte, she thought. *I could have ended this in seconds.*

Instead, it ended with a warm sidhe hand grabbing her arm and hauling her up roughly. Adaleth's ice and soil scent surrounded her, his arm around her waist.

"Stop!" he called, his other hand knotted in her hair. The fighting ceased, Shai and Lydia turning. The sidhe guards lowered their weapons. The prince sneered. "Drop your blades, or I'll take advantage of that promise your dear princess made to me."

The hand at her waist tightened, and Cirelle resisted the urge to stomp on his foot. It would only give him permission to give her actual physical injury. Right now, all he could do was grope her.

"Don't listen to him," Cirelle hissed. Though she didn't know what she expected her friends to do. They wouldn't fight their way free and leave her here. And they couldn't kill the sidhe prince, not when he could bat them aside with the wave of a hand.

Lydia's face was stricken, her chest heaving, but she dropped her daggers.

"Damn it," Shai muttered, but sheathed her sword as well.

"Good." Ayre stepped forward as Adaleth let Cirelle go and a guard moved toward her. "Now both mortals are going to let us bind you and lead you away, or my son will make good on his threat." She turned to Shai. "You will return to Ellian and make him this offer. If he comes, we will exchange the mortals for him and they will be freed."

Shai snarled. "You bitch."

The queen merely smiled. "Be that as it may, this is our offer. Or you too can stay here and rot until Ellian grows worried enough to come anyway. Perhaps you will draw that blade again and my guards will dispatch you. Your choice."

Shai swore again under her breath before giving Lydia and Cirelle a long look. "Be careful," she said with a pained sigh, then disappeared.

Thirty-Seven

CIRELLE GAVE ONE MORE useless tug on the rope that tied her arms to the chair. It was coarse, the cord, with rough bristles that chafed her skin. Prince Adaleth had been the one to bind her, all the while giving her a smug, knowing look that seethed with hatred underneath as he tied the knots. Testing the bounds of what he could do to her, finding out what Ellian had done.

Except when Ellian had bound her wrists, it had been to the headboard of one of his many guest beds, with a length of butter-soft silk. Not this painful, itchy rope.

However, the prince had left after tying her here, replaced by his mother. The woman sat in an opposite chair, back straight, ankles delicately crossed as she twirled a small knife in nimble fingers. The feather necklace rested on a table beside her.

Cirelle had to wonder... why the queen? Why wouldn't Adaleth himself remain, the one who posed a real, legitimate threat to her? He could not bring her physical violence, not without provocation, but her foolish words months ago gave him an access to her body that made her skin crawl. She didn't believe for one second that he wouldn't love tormenting her, even if only to cause Ellian distress later.

So why leave her here with Ayre instead?

Because Adaleth had somewhere else to be. It was the only answer. But where? To Lydia? The Duergar King had ordered the soldier to the dungeons, but then Adaleth had walked Cirelle up to this small room, confining her to this heavy chair. Separated.

The thought of that heartless prince interrogating her friend left Cirelle queasy.

Ayre flipped the small blade around and over her fingertips, while her other hand idly caressed the necklace that rested beside her on the table. Before Cirelle could bite back the words, she snapped, "stop that."

The queen's yellow eyes locked onto hers. "You do not command me, mortal."

Cirelle's hands itched for the claimhte, for her blades. With them, she could command the shadows themselves and be free. But they were locked safely in Ellian's Archive. All she could do was hold her tongue. The queen couldn't harm her without provocation.

Ayre flicked the blade back and forth, back and forth. "Remain silent and wait," she said coolly. "Until Ellian comes." Poison laced his name, spat like a foul word.

"Why do you hate him so?" Cirelle asked. She understood what passed between Adaleth and Ellian, their power games, the dark mirror of one another that they reflected. But the queen loathed Ellian with something deeper. Why?

Ayre focused on the bit of silver flashing between her fingers. "Imagine for a moment, a child in an apple orchard. He falls from a tree and shatters his ankle. He calls for help, but no one is near. For hours he lies in agony, surrounded by the scent of ripe apples. After he's rescued and heals, he cannot stand the fruit. Not in tarts, nor cider, nor fresh slices." The knife's motion halted abruptly, the blade pointed at Cirelle. "It is not the food the child truly hates, but the memory it stirs within him."

"So Ellian's an apple tart in this analogy?"

The queen grimaced. "Just so." She lifted the necklace in her free hand. "Where did you get this?"

"I traded it, fair and square."

The queen's next words were low, threatening. "That wasn't my question. Where?"

Cirelle bit her tongue.

Anger roughened Ayre's voice. "Tell me, human."

And suddenly, it clicked into place. "You recognize it. You know who owned this necklace once."

"I gave it to her." The queen's unsettling stare held Cirelle's. "I also killed her. So I have to know how this came into your possession."

Stars. This necklace belonged to an enemy of the queen. A dead one. Perhaps an ally once, if she was gifted with it. And did that woman steal the Lock before her demise, or had someone else come to possess the necklace after her death?

A shake of the head was Cirelle's only reply. Too many possibilities, and too many to think through now. Ellian would know the intricacies of the sidhe court and Ayre's enemies.

Ayre sighed. "Well if you won't tell, we can certainly… *persuade* Ellian when he comes to rescue you. Which I'm quite certain he will."

Cirelle closed her eyes. *He won't. He can't.* But even she knew her thoughts were lies.

In the end, Cirelle didn't spend long in the tower. She was fed once by one of the duergar, some sort of mushroom soup spooned into her mouth like a babe. Humiliating, but by that point she was so hungry she didn't care. The duergar dripped broth all over her lovely gown though, one more indignity heaped upon her.

Ayre had left after an hour or so, bored of Cirelle's silence. Adaleth visited after her meal, grimacing as he uttered vague threats and twirled her hair around one of his fingertips. It made Cirelle's skin crawl.

"You're lucky, you know," Adaleth murmured as his hand moved to trace the edge of her empty knuckle, the scarred skin where a finger should be.

Cirelle bared her teeth at him, but remained quiet.

Cold hatred filled the prince's features. He leaned in close. "If I damage Ellian's property without just cause, I'll owe him recompense. As much as I'd love to see you suffer, then witness the hurt on his face when he found out… well, I refuse to owe that man a debt."

"I'm not property."

The prince slipped the serpent brooch from her dress, holding it up. "This marks you as his, sure as a tag on a dog's collar." He turned it back and forth, admiring the blue enameling of the wings. "You *are* his, whether you admit it or not. And he'll come to collect you." He tucked the pin back into place.

Eventually, even Adaleth grew bored of tormenting her and left. She couldn't say how long she waited. There was no window, and even if there had been, no sun shone underground. Songs sung under her breath did little to ease her panic or the dark mood that washed over her. If Ellian exchanged himself for their sake, he'd be in Adaleth's power once more. But if he didn't, how long would the duergar or the sidhe royals keep her around? Or Lydia?

Cirelle's mind concocted a dozen horrible fates for her friend, each worse than the last. Tortured like Ellian had been, or maimed. Humiliated at the hands of the prince. Despair clung to Cirelle, a sooty, sticky film she could not scrape off.

Tears came, and long gasping sobs. With her hands bound,

her tears were left to dry on her face, a salty reminder of her bout of sorrow.

Then both royals came to see her, trailing a hobbled Lydia. The soldier's hands were bound behind her, while three duergar guards flanked her. The rope between her feet was barely long enough to walk with mincing steps. Lydia's glare would have been enough to light fires. Her lip was split, cracked and bleeding.

"Now," said Ayre to Cirelle, "we're going to free you from the chair, then bind your hands behind you and tie your feet. If you struggle and fight back, we will be permitted to use force in return." The queen cast a meaningful look at Lydia's injured lip. "Do you understand?"

Cirelle glared, but nodded.

"Good." The queen made a gesture and Adaleth stepped forward. With a short, sharp blade, he sawed through the knot on the ropes binding Cirelle to the chair. When she stood, he pulled her arms behind her and tied them.

Cirelle wondered how they'd managed to tie Lydia; no one here had permission to so much as touch her, unless Lydia gave it. She had a dark suspicion they'd gained the guard's cooperation by threatening to harm Cirelle.

It didn't matter now. Adaleth tied her hands behind her, then her ankles, with a scant bit of rope between them. Walking was difficult. She worried she'd lose her balance and topple over without her arms free to break the fall.

They were led to the throne room once more, the massive space echoing with their shuffling footsteps. Utter silence greeted them, King Glisrat sitting on his throne, that sour look still upon his face. His guards flanked him on either side.

But they weren't the only souls in this room. Two other figures stood before the throne, their backs to the entering group. A familiar drape of sunshine yellow hair gave Issen away. His hands were clasped behind his back, the left one gloved to the elbow, and his feet were bare as usual. Ellian had dressed impeccably, in a jacket of blue embroidered with the golden scales of his heraldry. Across his shoulders, a pattern of azure beads mimicked wings.

Defiant even in his surrender, to remind the duergar king of his bond with the serpent. And the death of the king's son.

No wonder Glisrat scowled so fiercely.

Ellian turned when they entered. At the sight of Cirelle and Lydia marching behind the royals, his eyes flashed an orange so fiercely bright it made even Cirelle flinch. His hands clenched into fists, but he sucked in a steadying breath and his impassive mask washed over his face again. He knelt as Adaleth and Ayre approached the dais to stand at its base.

"Your Highness. Your Majesty." Words uttered through bared teeth, though his head was lowered.

"Stand," the queen said, and Ellian obeyed.

"I've come as requested, to negotiate the return of these two mortals."

"And to do so," Glisrat's voice croaked. "You have set foot here, where you are forbidden to tread. Conduct your business with the sidhe, but after, we will settle our score as well."

Cirelle swallowed. Ellian had led this man's son to slaughter. She suspected what sort of punishment faerie law would demand in return.

Ayre cleared her throat. "And do you offer yourself in exchange for these mortals?"

He glanced over at Cirelle, apology in his eyes. "Yes, provided I am able to bequeath these mortals to Issen for the remainder of their time in Faerie. They will be allowed to leave here with Issen and walk free."

Adaleth smiled, a feline grin. "And we may take from you anything we wish? Including your very life?"

"No!" Glisrat's voice was a sudden burst. "Ellian's death belongs to me."

The prince did not take his hungry, vicious gaze from Ellian. "A single day, then. Give him to us for one day, Your Highness, and we relinquish care of him to you after that. As long as he promises himself to us."

Ellian cleared his throat. "For one day. Anything you desire from me."

No no no. This wasn't happening. Cirelle felt dizzy, sick. Her tongue was stone in her mouth.

The king shifted in his throne. "And what will you exchange for such a boon, Your Highness?"

Ayre waved a hand dismissively. "Use of the private cave tunnels in Pleraie, on sidhe land, for a decade."

Glisrat chewed his lip with crooked teeth, then nodded. "One further condition. However you wish to punish him, you will do it on these premises. I will not risk his escape. One—and only one—of your people may be summoned here to assist you in whatever you plan. You've use of my dungeons for the day, if you need them."

Adaleth's expression was insouciant. "We won't. I'll... entertain him."

The king merely nodded, as if this were a typical request. "At dawn, you leave my kingdom, and he remains."

Ayre and Adaleth shared a glance, then the queen nodded. "Done."

Speech finally returned to Cirelle, though the word was barely a gasp. "No." They would take him. Adaleth would force him into bed or torture him once more.

And tomorrow, Glisrat would see him executed.

"Issen," Ellian said, ignoring Cirelle's outcry, refusing to look at her. "Will you care for these two in my absence? And will you accept the remainder of their servitude in Faerie upon my death?" So cold, so flat, how he spoke of his own demise.

"No." Cirelle said again, louder.

Adaleth pinned her with his furious gaze. "No one asked you to speak. Show such disrespect in Glisrat's throne room again, and he will be permitted to punish you for it."

Cirelle didn't care. A numb, tingling sensation spread through her body. This had to be a nightmare. She opened her mouth to speak again, but Issen, standing behind Ellian, gave her the tiniest shake of his head. There was an uncharacteristic intensity in his eyes that made her pause. A signal of some sort.

So Cirelle bit her lip and took a long, shuddering breath. There, a tiny tendril of hope. Issen had a plan. All she had to do was avoid mucking it up.

Issen spoke. "Upon your death, I will accept responsibility for Cirelle and Lydia, and any remainder of their service left in Faerie."

The guards untied Lydia's hands and feet while Ayre smirked at Cirelle.

Cirelle rubbed uselessly at her chafed wrists. Beside her, Lydia did the same. The soldier seemed oddly calm, until Cirelle realized she was probably *relieved* at Ellian's impending death, not horrified.

The ropes were transferred to Ellian, binding him as firmly as they had both humans. Adaleth smiled the whole while. "Come along, then," the prince purred as he led Ellian from the room, and Cirelle thought she might vomit.

"Let's go," Issen said softly, holding his hands out to them both. They couldn't worldwalk in, but Shai had slipped out easily before. It must be another of those one-way doors. Exit only.

With one last look at Ellian's retreating back, Cirelle took Issen's hand.

Thirty-Eight

THEY RETURNED TO ELLIAN'S manor, not Issen and Shai's cottage. As Ellian's most trusted allies, he walked through the front door with ease.

Cirelle didn't waste words. "What are we going to do?"

Issen glanced wordlessly between her and Lydia, who stood with arms crossed.

Lydia replied, "We're not going to do anything," she said. "Ellian chose his path."

"They're going to kill him!"

Lydia squared her shoulders. "Maybe…" she hesitated. "I know it hurts, but in the long run… Maybe it's better off that way."

Rage flared. *Kill her.* The thought startled her. Not her own voice, but another, sibilant one. The claimhte were in the Archive, though. Never before had they spoken to her when she wasn't holding them or dreaming. She blinked, but still her fists shook at her sides. "We're going to save him." A glance at Issen. "Aren't we?"

The faerie sighed. "Ellian left a letter, with instructions that it was for your eyes only." He led the way to the antechamber.

Shai sat on one of the chairs, her foot tapping restlessly. When the door creaked open, she leapt up. "Is he—"

"As planned," Issen muttered before plucking a folded letter from the desktop, sealed with blue wax and Yratla's emblem.

"I really don't think you should read it," Lydia warned. "Whatever foolish notion he has, I fear it's going to hurl you back into danger. Again. Like all of his schemes." Anger darkened her voice. "You can't keep doing this. The dice will only fall in your favor so many times."

Cirelle's voice cracked as she took the letter and broke the seal. "I can't leave him. Not when he turned himself in to save us. You included."

"It was his mission that got us captured in the first place!"

"To save our world." Cirelle unfolded the note. The handwriting was spiky, rushed, uncertain.

Cirelle,

If you're reading this, I've successfully managed to exchange myself for your freedom. Given Adaleth's temperament, I fear I may not return. Issen and Shai will shelter you until your time in Faerie is spent. I've told Issen where the Key is hidden in the Archive, and he will continue the mission. Your world is not lost.

I—

~~Cirelle~~

If

There is more I wish to write, but perhaps it is best left unsaid.

Goodbye.
Ellian

Cirelle crumpled the note, furious tears stinging her eyes.

"That bastard," she hissed. Ellian didn't have a plan. Nor did Issen. They'd tricked her into letting him go, to leaving the duergar kingdom peacefully.

"You gave me a nod!" She spat at Issen, throwing the wad of paper at his face. He blinked, but did not flinch. She stepped forward. "You knew that look said *I have a plan.* And you let me leave thinking we'd get him back."

His eyes were full of pity. "Cirelle—"

"No!" She paced. Lydia placed a calming hand on Cirelle's shoulder. She shrugged it off and batted it away. "I'm going to save him, even if none of you help me."

Lydia frowned. "I can lock you in your room. They can't touch you, but I can."

"Would you defy a royal decree?"

The guard chewed her lip. "If it saved your life? Yes."

"Try it, then." Cirelle's eyes darted to the Archive door. Her blades rested just within it. Foolish. Even if she got to them before Lydia tackled her, the guard would disarm her easily.

But not if Cirelle could call the ilthys first. It would come down to who was fastest.

Shai stepped between them. "Both of you, calm the fuck down. Lydia, we don't need to lock Cirelle up. She can't leave without a faerie to worldwalk her."

No. Surely Cirelle's ears deceived her. If anyone would have been willing to help her mount a rescue mission, she'd have thought Shai would be itching for a rematch with the duergar. "You're going to let him die, too?"

At least Shai looked pained when she replied. "We can't just storm the duergar palace. And I can't plan things… that was Ellian's specialty."

"Issen can. He plotted the Lisovyk mission before Ellian was taken, didn't he?"

The yellow-haired faerie shook his head. "Ellian was very clear on his instructions in this. I was not to put you in further danger."

"Then go without me! You can't do this!"

"The—" he glanced at Lydia. "The mission is more important," Issen said, pacing on his bare feet. "As much a friend as I am to Ellian, if I am caught or I perish, then there's no one left to continue the quest."

"Then send in the coterie!"

"Can't risk them being taken by Adaleth and Ayre, either."

"Damn you all!" Cirelle's hands cramped, and she realized her nails bit into her palms. Lydia stepped toward her, holding a hand out as one would to a skittish horse. But Cirelle's righteous anger couldn't be placated. Ellian's impending sentence couldn't just be talked away.

"You're all a bunch of cowards," she snarled, then fled.

She went to the one place she could find a tiny measure of calm, the place that felt like home in this hollow mansion. The music room.

And froze when she walked in.

There. On her stack of papers at a small table, the mask she'd worn to the Unseelie Court's masquerade, what felt like ages ago. Golden scales lay etched on its surface, a fan of cobalt feathers on either side.

She'd worn this during her very first dance with Ellian.

For a moment, the pain was too much to bear. She couldn't suck in a breath, jagged shards of metal trapped in her chest.

Beneath the mask was a simple note.

The first game.

Cirelle didn't have to think twice. She knew what he meant.

A clue. The first game they'd ever played together. Fox-and-hounds, her favorite. She crept to the game room, eyes and ears open for the others. But their hushed voices still spilled from the crack in the partly-open door to the antechamber.

In the game room, she opened the drawer that held the pieces for fox-and-hounds. Another letter. This one was folded carefully beneath a jumble of tokens.

I promised you would always have a hand in my plans, and I will keep that oath. If you so choose, I give you permission to conduct any bargains on my behalf, at your discretion. You may use or trade anything in my Archive, for whatever purpose you deem fit while you remain in Faerie.

- Ellian

Cirelle sat down.

The Archive. Hers.

Ellian had opened his hoard to her. And she would use it to save him.

❧

After a time, Lydia found her. Cirelle had tucked the note in the pages of a library book and placed it back on the shelf. Proof if needed, but well hidden. Then she'd changed out of her heavy skirts into something more comfortable, one of her day-to-day outfits of a loose shirt and trousers.

She needed to wait until dawn, until Lydia and the others were asleep. Then she would make her move.

So Cirelle pretended. She found her way back to the music room, where she furiously and clumsily played the pianoforte again until Lydia entered.

"I'm sorry," the guard said before she could speak. "We need to go back to Issen and Shai's now."

"No." Cirelle shook her head. "Give me one more day here." It wasn't faked, the crack in her voice. "I'll be safe behind Ellian's wards, if you three want to go. But I will not leave, not yet. Let me stay here… walk the halls… say goodbye."

Lydia took a long, steadying breath. "Fine. For one day we'll remain here. But tomorrow at dusk when we awaken, we all go to Issen's."

Cirelle nodded. "All right." A lie.

Either she was getting better at deceit, or Lydia was too distracted to notice. With one last, forlorn look, she left.

For another hour, Cirelle played. Her heart raced, her nerves alight.

I can do this.

The others had been right about one thing. She couldn't leave without transportation from a faerie. Unless. She ventured into her parlor to quickly eat a small meal from her sidebar and gulp down a glass of water. She fetched her camouflage cloak, then slipped soundlessly into the Archive and pored through Ellian's massive tome listing its treasures.

You may use or trade anything in my Archive, for whatever purpose you deem fit.

Had he intended the vagueness of those words? Was it a subtle invitation to do exactly this?

Regardless, Cirelle was going to save him. She strapped the claimhte to her waist and flipped through the ledger's pages.

There. *The Longstep Shoes. A pair of enchanted slippers, which will transport the wearer to any destination.* She grimaced. Slippers weren't ideal for this rescue, but they would have to do. Once she got to Ellian, he could worldwalk himself out, and her with him. She just had to find him.

And for that… An amulet that functioned much like the one she'd used to locate the fairy ring. Like the ones at the Unseelie Hunt. She searched the antechamber and found a single sapphire strand of hair on a cushion, then tucked it inside the locket. Immediately, it veered softly to one side.

Two final items made their way into the small backpack. A spyglass that could see through walls, and a key that would open any lock. Hopefully those would be enough to find Ellian and break him free.

Her blades also came along.

In the antechamber, she took a long, deep breath. She had a handful of hours until Lydia and the others awoke to find her missing. They would surely guess where she had gone, but would they pursue?

No.

But Stars, timing was tight. If Ellian had taught her one thing in Faerie, it was to pay close attention to the wording of faerie bargains. Ellian had offered himself specifically to the queen and prince. Adaleth had promised to relinquish Ellian after a day had passed. Ellian had not agreed to any of Glisrat's punishments. If she could take Ellian after Adaleth's day was up, he wouldn't be beholden to Glisrat's judgment.

She closed her eyes, imagined the cave entrance to the duergar kingdom, and tapped the shoes on the floor in the pattern the ledger had said. Right heel, left heel, right toe, left toe.

When she opened her eyes, the mouth of the tunnel yawned before her.

It worked.

She draped the amulet over her head. It pulled her forward, and she followed the path to the sweltering underground kingdom. Cirelle crept through the duergar kingdom in those soft slippers, camouflage cloak pulled firmly about her. Still she kept just to the side of the main street, in the shadows, until she found the palace. Once more, the doors were thrown open, like a challenge. Slowly, she slipped around one guard, pressed against the wall behind him, then made her way into the palace that held Ellian captive.

Thirty-Nine

ELLIAN HAD LOST TRACK of himself. He'd tried to choose the dungeons once more, but no. He'd promised his body and mind to the royals. *Anything you desire from me.*

He knew what Adaleth would ask, but the prince had at least offered him the balm of wintersweet. Ellian had gulped it down greedily, savoring the sugary spice of it, how it made his tongue tingle and warmed his bones.

The prince only gave it to him because he knew it would make Ellian more cruel, less inhibited. Less human. And oh, how it did. Here, in this sumptuous chamber the duergar had loaned to Adaleth, Ellian made the prince his plaything.

If he were to have one last day to make Adaleth suffer, he would squeeze every drop of misery he could from it.

The prince had a peculiar habit of letting Ellian go past the point of pleasure into true pain. Never once had he said the word that would end the game. Whether this was out of self-flagellation or mere pride, Ellian was unsure. What he did know was exactly how to cross that line.

They'd passed it hours ago.

The prince knelt on the floor, his hair matted with his own

dark green blood, his wintry-blue skin smeared with it. The room was not as properly appointed as the prince's hidden chamber, but he'd brought a case of Ellian's favorite tools and toys. One of those lashed out with the flick of a wrist, its knotted tails scraping the prince's already-raw skin.

Still Adaleth begged for more, though agony made his voice brittle, breaths rasping and shallow.

Did the queen hear, in her chamber next door? Did she seethe, knowing just what her son was doing? Doubtless she only let this happen without protest because Ellian's death lingered within mere hours.

Eventually, the prince lost consciousness. But Ellian bared his teeth, sitting on the bed. He wasn't done yet. Almost idly, he flicked the bell on the bedside table.

One—and only one—of your people may be summoned to assist you.

Adaleth had not chosen his torturer.

A knock at the door, then it cracked open to reveal a scowling lavender face. Dirilai stepped into the room with a large bag, locking the door behind her. She crossed to the prince and nudged him with a boot. "You do realize there isn't any moonlight down here, don't you?"

Ellian replied, "Do what you can."

"I really don't like this version of you," she mumbled as she rummaged in her bag to retrieve a bottle of purple healing potion.

A pang of guilt pricked him. But he was locked in this room until his death. It little mattered who he was tonight. How cruelly, fully sidhe he became.

It was not how he'd have spent his last day, were he to choose. A happier vision of Cirelle swam in his mind, laughing as she sprawled beside him in bed, hair soaked with sweat. Her eyes flashing as her feet carried her in a lively reel. The rapture on her face as she sat at her harp, playing that song she'd been composing since she first set foot in his manor. *His* song. The earnest, soft gasp when he caressed her in just the right spot. And the sheer, brutal openness in her eyes as she told him she loved him.

No, this wasn't what he'd have chosen at all for his final moments. He cleared his throat. "All I have left are a few hours and my hatred."

"You have a choice. Do what he wants, or not." The woman dumped the liquid on Adaleth's back like it was water. None of the care she showed most of her patients, despite her surly demeanor.

"I gave my word. Whatever he chose."

"So break it. You're going to die anyway." So cold, those words. "At least you could perish with your precious human principles intact. If she saw you like this—" Dirilai bit the words off and turned away.

Ellian's breath hitched. "If who saw me? Cirelle?"

But before she could answer, the prince groaned. It was impossible to tell beneath the mass of half-dried blood, but his wounds must be closing.

Dirilai stepped around him. "I'll take my leave now."

Stretching, Ellian stood. "Yes, I think you should." As the door closed, he stole a glance at the hourglass next to the bell. Three hours left. And then he would die without ever giving Cirelle a proper goodbye. A letter was a feeble way to say farewell. Did she weep for him? Would she mourn?

He'd never know. Because of the man at his feet. Ellian leaned down to the prince, yanking Adaleth's chin up to meet those pained firefly eyes. "More?"

The prince swallowed. "More."

❧

Cirelle followed the amulet down dimly-lit halls. Whatever time the duergar slept, this was it. Impossible to tell with a mountain of stone above. It had been dark in this part of Faerie when she arrived at the mouth of that cave, despite daylight dawning when she left Ellian's.

Up, the locket led her, up a tower of narrow, small steps, and down another hall.

To a heavy, ornate door.

She swallowed.

Inside lay the prince. And Ellian.

Cirelle knew what she would find when she pressed the spyglass to the wall near the door, but it still made her hastily-eaten supper threaten to make its way back up. A version of Ellian she didn't recognize, straddling a bloodstained Adaleth in bed, hands wrapped around the prince's throat with pure, seething crimson hatred in his eyes.

The prince's body arched in ecstasy, head thrown back as Ellian's hands tightened. The prince's corpse-pale face darkened, his mouth gasping for air.

And then he went still. Ellian leaned back with a sigh, hands loosening. He flexed his fingers, then leaned to the side and rang a tiny bell.

Cirelle couldn't breathe. Was the prince dead? Had Ellian just killed him? Stars spun through her vision and a strange buzzing filled her ears. The hand with the spyglass faltered, dropping to her side as she pressed her forehead to the blessedly cool stone.

She didn't hear the footsteps behind her until the door opened. Startled, Cirelle's head jerked up to see Dirilai stepping into the room.

One chance. She was barely able to sneak through the door as it closed, Dirilai throwing the lock.

"Again?" The sidhe woman hissed. "Stone and sea and sky, Ellian."

Ellian now sat on the edge of the bed, bare skin damp with sweat. He shrugged, eyes still burning a fierce crimson.

Cirelle must have made a sound, because both Dirilai and Ellian's heads whirled to stare at her.

"What—" Ellian stood, that scarlet red seeping into the burning orange of anger.

No choice. Cirelle dropped the hood of the cloak. Dirilai spat a curse, but Cirelle couldn't look away from Ellian.

The shock on his face gave way to horror, then shame. "Cirelle?" His voice was suddenly soft, cracking on the name. He stepped forward. "No. I'm hallucinating." A broken laugh fell from his lips as he stepped toward her.

Cirelle shook her head and found her voice. "I came to rescue you."

Dirilai swore again, but Cirelle ignored her. "When is your day done? I lost track of the time while I searched."

Ellian glanced at a nearby hourglass. "Half an hour left. Then Glisrat will claim me."

"Only if you let him. You made him no promises." Cirelle stared at the limp form of the prince on the bed. "Is he… is he dead?"

"No. I… I know what I'm doing." Ellian wouldn't even look at her.

I could fix it. Kill him for certain. The thought was a cold one. She had her blades. One thrust in the heart, a slash across the throat, and the prince would hurt no one ever again.

She didn't even realize she'd started to draw the blade until Ellian murmured, "stop."

"Why?"

"Because if we kill the prince, the queen certainly won't rest until I'm dead. If we escape, they have nothing to hold against us. I kept my bargain. One day. Let the time run out and I'm free of the oath I swore."

"Then let's go. Worldwalk us out."

A hoarse laugh. "You can only worldwalk out of this mountain if Glisrat lets you. Right now, those gates are entirely shut."

"Stars go black," Cirelle muttered. "Can these take you, too?" She pointed at the shoes.

A shake of his head. Dirilai examined the prince while Cirelle and Ellian hissed their conversation.

"We'll have to sneak out," Ellian said. "I can glamour us into invisibility, but we need to hurry. He won't be unconscious forever."

Biting her lip, Cirelle cast a cautious glance at Dirilai.

"You two go," the woman said. "I can give him something to keep him unconscious until the hourglass runs out, and will pretend Ellian never summoned me this final time. They won't even think to ask, assuming he used the opportunity to slip free." She poured a clear liquid into the prince's slack mouth, then gathered up her bag and left.

Cirelle turned back to Ellian. "Well—"

He cut her off with a kiss, tasting of sickly-sweet clove. And something else, something she suspected came from the prince. She pushed him away. "What—"

They weren't supposed to do this anymore. And she certainly didn't want to when Ellian was covered in Adaleth's sweat.

Ellian blinked, then shook his head. "Sorry, I... it's the wintersweet. Faerie spirits. They... do that. I—"

"It doesn't matter right now," she cut him off. "You can apologize properly when we're back."

Stiffly, he nodded, taking her hand. "Come. I know a way out, but you're not going to like it."

Forty

Ellian was right. Cirelle didn't like it.

They crept through silent halls, hand-in-hand, invisible, sliding into side corridors or pressing themselves against walls, narrowly dodging the occasional passerby.

When Ellian approached a narrow hole in the wall, a whiff of fetid air wafted up from it.

Cirelle wrinkled her nose. "Is this…"

"A garbage chute," Ellian confirmed. She could picture the grimace on his face.

"Why can't we just walk out the front door?"

"Because we'd have to go past the throne room, which is the most heavily-guarded spot in this place. This is safer."

"Fine, but you go first and break my fall," she muttered.

That garnered a small laugh. "Very well." His hand slipped free of hers. Fabric rustled, then the hiss of something sliding along the stone of the chute.

Savoring one last breath of fresh air, Cirelle followed.

It wasn't a terribly long fall. She'd expected to land in a pile of trash, but fell into Ellian's arms instead. He caught her easily, swung her around, and planted her feet farther out from the top of the pile. Her boots still squished into rotten, discarded food, but only up to her ankles. She turned to see Ellian had thrown off the glamour, grinning at her with cerulean eyes even as he stood knee-deep in garbage. He picked his way out and Cirelle tried not to gag on the thick smell.

It was hard to smile back. Cirelle could never forget what she'd just seen of Ellian. Living it in a dream on Thieves' Night was one thing. It was entirely more awful finding him here in person, smelling of sex and the coppery smell of sidhe blood on top of his honey-and-smoke aroma.

She shrugged her cloak back and frowned. "I thought nothing could be more disgusting than a swamp. I was wrong."

He shrugged. "Could be worse. It could be in your hair."

Cirelle's stomach turned as she surveyed their surroundings. They were in a small cave with a single narrow exit. Ellian was already halfway to it, his boots and trousers stained dark with the muck from the midden heap. He cast one long-suffering glance down at the mess and shuddered. A moment later it all vanished. Even the smell disappeared. Cirelle looked down at her own feet to find it gone from her boots as well.

"Just glamour," he noted when she looked back up. "I can keep it up for a while, at least." He turned and kept walking.

Cirelle said nothing, following him wordlessly down the tunnel.

They should have known better than to think it would be easy. They emerged from the narrow tunnel into a larger one lit by faerie lights… right into two duergar guards. They cried out and drew their weapons, circling Cirelle and Ellian.

Kill them. She didn't even pause. Cirelle drew the blades. "Ilthys, protect us!"

Their forms emerged from the shadows, spiky legs and night-mare faces. The monsters made short work of the duergar. Once, the sight would have turned her stomach, but with the chill of the claimhte in her hands, all she felt was cold satisfaction.

Ellian stared in horror. "Put those away."

Cirelle clenched them tighter, a spiderlike ilthys circling her protectively while one of its companions crunched duergar bone.

Then another shape formed from the shadows. A familiar one.

"Scath," Cirelle breathed, lifting the knives before her. Ellian tried to step between her and the figure, but it slipped around him easily.

"No," the shape said, a humanoid form of smoke and shadow. Not the Scath's voice of hissing sand, but the whistle of wind through dead trees. "You may call me Oiche."

"Who are you?"

"I am the Scath's sister. You bared these blades and they call to me. I must admit my brother was uncouth, Your Majesty. Ambitious but foolish. I ask calmly for the blades he tried to steal by force. In exchange, I offer a bargain."

"What bargain?"

"Peace. In exchange for the claimhte, the entire kingdom of the Shadowed will vow never to take any action that may harm you or your allies ever again, either directly or indirectly. We leave you in peace, forever."

"I give you a kingdom and you merely agree not to kill me?" Cirelle shook her head. Madness, not to take such a bargain and rid herself of this deadly crown. But the knives were *hers*. Her protection in this perilous world. She needed them. If she were to give them up… "I demand more. Your brother tried to have me killed."

The creature sighed. "Point taken. We will also offer you three boons. Call my name three times with the blades unsheathed. If I hear, I will answer and you may request my aid in whatever way I am capable of giving it, but only thrice. Then my debt will be paid."

"Take the offer, Cirelle." Ellian said beside her, his voice soft. "Those knives poison you, and you know it."

Fear lanced through her. "What do you know?"

"That these aren't just daggers. They bear the souls of the first King and Queen of the Shadowed. And they corrupt their wielder."

"If they're so dangerous, then why let me use them at all?"

"Because they are yours by right. I cannot stop you, but I can ask. Please, Cirelle. Give them up." There, swirling among the emerald of his eyes, that terrible, painful rose.

"No," Cirelle's hand tightened around the hilts, and she turned to Oiche. "You are commanded never to harm me or those I deem allies, directly or indirectly, in any way. You are not to come to me unless I summon you."

Oiche's form swirled and shimmered, agitated. "Very well. When you change your mind, call me and we will bargain."

Almost against her will, Cirelle took the stone and tucked it in her pocket. "Fine. Now go."

The shadowy creature dissipated with a whistling shriek like a distant, howling wind.

Ellian's disappointment was palpable, but he didn't say anything more on the knives. "Let's go," he said instead. "We're not in the clear yet."

Forty-One

THE TUNNEL LED OUT to a larger garbage heap, one that assaulted her nose so strongly Cirelle thought she could feel it coating her nostrils, her tongue. It was a conscious effort not to vomit her hasty meal.

Ellian picked a cautious route around the edges of the midden pile, then into the outskirts of the city near the palace. "They'll have blocked the main city exit by now," he said. "So we go the back way. Here." He held out a hand, and Cirelle took it cautiously. Ellian cast his invisible glamour once more.

They skirted the city, out in the dim alleyways at the edges of the cavern, even as soldiers ran past crying an alarm.

"You know," Cirelle asked, "When you make enemies, you don't go halfway, do you?"

That earned her a small chuckle. "Well, it's only a challenge if you're enraging kings and queens. You seem to have a knack for it yourself. Ah, here we are."

'Here' was a natural crevice in the rock barely wide enough to fit Ellian's shoulders and height.

Cirelle hesitated. What if it narrowed until they were stuck, trapped under a mountain of stone?

"Trust me," Ellian said.

Cirelle gathered her courage and followed.

The fissure did indeed widen shortly after, crossing paths with a circular tunnel immense enough for half a dozen carriages to ride abreast with space between them. The walls were rough stone, lit with luminescent faerie lights in the ceiling high above. Ellian released her hand and shifted the cloak to be more visible.

The ground trembled, a low vibration that grew slowly stronger.

Ellian's eyes searched her. "Where's your pin?" he asked Cirelle.

Her heart sank. Oh no. She knew exactly where her pin was. In the torn and hastily-discarded dress lying on her closet floor.

"I… er… may have left it in your mansion."

"Avesh!" Ellian swore in Kishi. "Get behind me, Cirelle. And put those knives away."

Cirelle only clutched the claimhte harder.

"Now!" Ellian hissed. "She is allied with the Shadowed. They'll only make the situation worse."

The earthquake intensified, the floor shaking so violently that Cirelle felt it in her bones. Something glinted under the faerie lights at the end of the tunnel. She slid the claimhte back into their scabbards, but her hands gripped the hilts until the cold froze her palms.

As it drew closer, the gleam became scales of liquid gold, a serpent's face cast in shining metal coming ever closer. Glossy indigo feathers sleeked back from its head.

Yratla.

Suddenly, Cirelle was little more than a mouse, a bird with a broken wing before a viper.

The creature was titanic in scale. Its skull alone was the size of a cottage. Stopping before them, it lifted its head in the unmistakable pose of a snake about to strike. Its mouth opened wide, a brilliant scarlet inside, fangs unfolding that were as long as Cirelle was tall. The feathers fanned out around its head. Two giant wings lay folded tightly along its back, in every shade of blue imaginable.

"Yratla," Ellian said, voice smooth and only a tiny bit shaky, "you are as magnificent as I remember."

The creature's mouth shut, those fangs tucking back up inside. It tilted its head, and one brilliant copper eye focused on Ellian.

"I remember you." The voice was a woman's, husky and resonant, and echoed in Cirelle's head rather than her ears. "The sidhe." She dipped closer. "I like your jacket." A vain note in the comment, preening.

"I made an oath, and I keep it," Ellian replied.

"Indeed." Yratla's long tongue flickered out, testing the air. "But you are not alone." She slithered forward, her head whipping around to stare at Cirelle. "You have my permission to use these tunnels, sidhe. But this..." the forked tongue flicked out and in again, "human does not. I thought we agreed that anyone you brought into my tunnels would wear my token?"

Faster than Cirelle would have thought possible for such a large beast, Yratla circled them with those gleaming coils. She came to a stop with her nose barely an arm's length from Cirelle. Those scales were like polished armor, so glossy that Cirelle could see her own terrified eyes in their reflection.

Ellian had turned as Yratla circled them, and now stood with Cirelle's back to his chest. Cirelle pressed into him, heart fluttering in her throat. His arm slipped around her waist as if he could shield her.

"Sadly, it seems you've merely brought me my dinner," the serpent's voice purred, those jaws opening wide.

Cirelle's heart stopped beating. A buzzing sound filled her ears, and she couldn't breathe.

"I place her under my protection!" Ellian blurted. The way he said it, voice strained, only tightened her fear. Cirelle didn't dare tear her gaze from Yratla, but wondered what color Ellian's eyes were. Black? Emerald green?

The serpent's mouth closed again, abruptly. She turned her head sideways and the slit of her pupil narrowed. "There is only one way my bargain with you would extend to her, sidhe."

He inhaled, long and slow. "I know."

"Truly? You would claim this creature as your tilare to protect her?" She gave it the weight of a title. *Tilare.* Cirelle blinked, uncertain why her earring would provide no translation. Unless it was a word that had none, in her tongue.

Ellian's reply was tight, his voice thick. "I would."

"And you, human? Would you claim such a binding until the end of your days?"

Cirelle didn't like the sound of that, not at all. Her pulse roared in her ears so loudly it nearly drowned out her own thoughts. But if her other option was death, could she say no?

Ellian's arm tightened about her waist, and she could feel his shuddering breaths. He was afraid, too. But he'd also told her how he escaped last time, and it gave her the key. Yratla's vanity.

"I'll write you a song," Cirelle declared instead, staring at that enormous eye.

Ellian's hand tightened, clutching a fistful of her shirt.

"I'm listening," Yratla said, her tongue tasting the air once again.

"I'll compose a song of your glory, your beauty. Eyes like burning copper, gleaming scales of liquid gold. A feathered crown befitting a queen."

The smile was obvious in Yratla's voice as her head dipped.

"Of course. But who will listen? What makes your song so note-worthy? How will it spread word of my greatness?"

Cirelle lifted her chin, trying not to let her voice quaver. "In the mortal world, I am royalty. All will listen when I play. And I will compose you a song of such awe and magnificence that none can ignore it."

The serpent laughed, a rolling sound like thunder.

"Sidhe, you must speak truth. Is the human's music as wondrous as she claims?"

Cirelle's heart sank. Ellian had listened to all her fumbling and plucking at idle tunes, all of the failed and frustrated attempts before she found the melody she sought. He knew all her worst musical flaws, and he could not lie.

"Yes." His reply was certain, without hesitation.

Oblivious to Cirelle's suddenly stilted breathing, the serpent continued. "And she really is a human royal?"

"She is."

"Your oath, then, human. For safe passage from here to the surface, you will compose a song of my wonder and see it performed within three months of your return to the human world."

"Yes," Cirelle said.

"Agreed," Ellian echoed.

The world shuddered, acknowledging the bargain.

"Well," Yratla said, and Cirelle could have sworn she heard a sigh in the word, "I suppose I must seek my supper elsewhere." Without another word, she slithered away.

As soon as the serpent left, Ellian released Cirelle, almost pushing her away in his haste to untangle his arms from her. "This way," he said, his unreadable, gray-eyed mask firmly in place.

As she fell into step behind him, Cirelle couldn't help but ask. "Ellian, what does—"

"No." His voice was tight. "Please don't ask me that."

Silence held, and Cirelle's guts twisted into knots.

"Come," he said eventually, his words crisp. "It's a long walk, and we'd best move quickly. It's only a matter of time before the duergar figure out where we've gone."

And that, it seemed, was that.

Forty-Two

For days after the Yratla incident, Ellian avoided Cirelle once more. She yearned to ask him about tilare. A question that, if asked, he would be oathbound to answer. And yet, part of her was afraid of the answer, and she avoided him as studiously.

As she did so often, Cirelle sought peace in music. Despite the weather's chill, she took her lap harp up to the rooftop and played her Faerie Nocturne for the small, butterfly-like florafae while Lydia and Shai drilled. The warrior sidhe stayed here often now, sparring with Lydia, both of them caught in a constant game of one-upmanship. It made Cirelle smile to see her friend laugh once again.

Tonight, one of the florafae perched on Cirelle's shoulder, tiny legs kicking in time to the music. She now had a small company of listeners whenever she serenaded them. If she played a lively song, they would flutter about her and dance, their shiny bodies reflecting the moonlight as their iridescent wings buzzed through the air. Now, they drifted lazily in weaving patterns as she toyed with melodies for Yratla's song.

Issen found them mid-recital, carrying a new instrument. The florafae scattered, finding refuge among the leaves and blossoms of the garden. Issen settled himself on the ground beside her, cross-legged, and began to pick out a tune. The new instrument was a bit like a lap harp, but played with a small hammer. The melody was a simple one, able to play with one hand.

The sight of his motionless, gloved hand was like a rebuke, but his eyes held only kindness as he opened with a few simple chords, a familiar song. Swallowing back her guilt, Cirelle picked up the tune. They played without words for a time, and the florafae cautiously returned.

Lost in the music, she barely noticed when Shai and Lydia waved their goodbyes and left the garden.

The music drained away Cirelle's remorse and sorrow until only an empty calm remained. It was a pleasant evening, surrounded by music and tiny faeries that danced on the breeze. She didn't know how long they spent like that, both of them lost in the melody and counterpoint.

But even that could not last.

After a time, Issen set his instrument aside and stretched, standing. The florafae darted away the moment the music ended. "I think it's about time to retire for the evening." Issen's soft, bare footsteps were silent on the grass and stone.

When he was almost out of earshot, Cirelle blurted out the terrified question that had been haunting her thoughts. "What is a tilare?"

Issen stopped mid-step, but spoke without turning back. "I think that may be a question for Ellian."

"Well, he'd rather avoid me entirely than give me the chance to ask," Cirelle huffed, standing and tucking the lap harp under one arm.

Though he didn't turn to look at her, Issen did speak over his shoulder, his words thoughtful. "Perhaps you should think on why that might be, Cirelle."

"You once told me knowledge should be shared."

"Yes, but this is something you should hear from him. Try harder." And then he was gone.

Furious, Cirelle dropped off her harp in the music room and sought out Shai. She found the woman in the gaming parlor, but she wasn't alone. Ellian sat opposite Shai, each of them holding the cards for Nightswheel in their hands. Lydia was nowhere to be seen.

Cirelle's heartbeat stuttered when her eyes met Ellian's, his gray walls firmly in place.

Stars damn it all, Cirelle thought. "What is a tilare?" she asked Shai, voice sweet and a venomous smile on her face.

Ellian looked pained, but Shai burst into her braying laughter as she dropped her cards. "Oh, Ell," she shook her head between laughs. "Is *that* what put a stick up your ass lately?"

Ellian sat stiffly, laying his cards down on the table. He turned to stare with flinty eyes while he rose from his chair. "Yratla was going to kill you. I chose the only option I could." He walked out with stilted steps, slamming the door behind him.

"Oh, Ciri." Shai was still chuckling, wiping her watering eyes.

"Is *anyone* going to tell me what a tilare is?" Cirelle muttered, falling into a chair.

"It's a binding. Whatever goes for a sidhe goes for their tilare, too. Oaths and stuff."

"Like the bargains they've made."

"Yep. One of them agrees to something, the other's stuck with it. But it goes both ways."

It made sense now. If she'd agreed to be Ellian's tilare in that cave, Yratla's previous offer of protection for Ellian would have extended to Cirelle as well.

And every bargain she'd made would bind him. Would that make him partial King of Asheir, when she was married?

"Is that all? Just a sharing of oaths and agreements?"

Shai burst into a new bout of laughter at that. "Not usually. It's a whole thing. There's this balance that happens, like you'd each give a tiny bit of your powers and abilities to each other."

Stars, Cirelle thought. He'd offered Cirelle a measure of his own strength to save her. "Like his sidhe abilities?"

"Yeah. To a point. You'd get a bit of glamour, maybe a sharper memory, while his weakened. He'd get, I don't know, probably musical talent." Shai set her cards down. "But it's serious stuff. Forever."

It was a good thing Cirelle was sitting, because the world grew dim for a moment and the room felt suddenly stifling. "I'd have to stay here?" Had Ellian hoped he could trick Cirelle into remaining at his side?

"No, that's not it." Shai shook her head. "You don't have to be in the same place. Tilare are… it's hard to explain. Like bosses, yeah? Except you're both each other's boss." She snorted another chuckle, then sobered. "But there's just… a *thing*, like a sort of, I don't know, a *peace*. Like you're halves of a scale and balance each other out."

"That doesn't make any sense, Shai."

The warrior shrugged. "It does when you're part of it."

"Wait." Cirelle sat up straighter. "Have you had one?"

That killed Shai's humor. "Yes, once." She stared down at the table. "She died."

Shame washed over Cirelle for asking. *Until the end of your days,* Yratla had said. A bond broken only by death. "I'm sorry."

Shai blinked and shrugged again. Her face broke into a forced grin and her voice caught when she said, "Let's just play a game, huh? Since you drove my partner out of the room."

An hour later, Cirelle found Ellian in the library, pulling a scattering of books from the shelves and stacking them on a desk. She stood in the doorway, a hand on the doorjamb to steady her.

He cast her a single brief glance, then went back to his work.

"Shai explained it," Cirelle said quietly, staring at the floor. "I know how large a sacrifice you almost made, what it would have cost you. Your power. Even after I left. And… I appreciate that." Not a thank-you, not quite.

A loud thump made Cirelle startle and her gaze darted back up. Ellian had dropped a tome heavily onto the desk and stared at her with haunted, miserable eyes. He opened his mouth as if to speak, took a breath, then closed it. With a shake of his head, he returned to a shelf to pull more books, never saying a word even as she left.

Forty-Three

"Shouldn't the others be here as well?" Cirelle looked around at their meager group, scattered around the Archive's antechamber. Ellian had summoned Issen and Shai to discuss their next plan of action. Lydia was stuck entertaining herself elsewhere in the house, forbidden from this conversation. Ellian had only let her join the duergar mission to keep Cirelle safe. Here in the manor, she was barred from any plans or meetings. He'd even wrung a promise from Cirelle not to tell her anything about their quest for the Lock or their possession of the Key.

At first, Cirelle had only given her word on that matter grudgingly, but she no longer knew how to feel about her old friend. Faerie seemed to be souring Lydia, twisting her honorable nature into something dark, deceptive. Perhaps it was for the best that she be kept as far from these machinations as possible.

Ellian answered Cirelle's question. "This is a sidhe problem." He stood leaning against the desk, palms flat on its surface. "Right now, we have to find out where the necklace ended up after Ayre. Which means we need a new spy in the Unseelie Court."

"What about Dirilai?"

"No." Ellian pushed away from the desk. "She can get close to the prince, but not the queen. And even Adaleth doesn't trust her, he only wants her abilities."

"We could send in someone among the servants again," Issen suggested.

Ellian shook his head. "Same problem. Leilarie worked for a one-night mission, but I don't think any servant could get close enough to the queen to find out something like that. She only trusts a few longtime servants in her chambers."

Cirelle coughed. Fear coated her like slime but still she asked, "What about me? Can you glamour me again?"

The response was firm. "I'm not sending you into that viper's den again without backup. The duergar were dangerous enough, but the Unseelie Court is another thing entirely."

Despite her relief, Cirelle came within a hair's breadth of pushing the issue, but Shai interrupted her.

"We could send Issen." Shai rested her feet on the opposite arm of the sofa. "He's the only one who won't get the door slammed in his face day one."

"I'm still not close enough to the queen," Issen shook his head. "They may not quite despise me enough to forbid me from attending, but they know I associate with Ellian. The royals certainly don't trust me."

Then a thought struck. "Kith," Cirelle whispered. Then louder. "What about Kith?"

Ellian's eyes widened, and he swore softly.

"He's never been to Court," Issen said thoughtfully. "He'd be a stranger there."

"Kith is certainly clever enough, and ruthless enough," Ellian replied wearily. "I'll ask him."

"No." Kith stared with baleful blue eyes, sitting calmly in the middle of the antechamber. He hadn't shed his cat form for this visit, his tail curled tightly about his paws.

"You're the only one that can do this," Cirelle told him.

"Why should I?"

"Because I've bought your debt and indenture from Vilitte," Ellian remarked coolly, leaning back against the desk.

Cirelle sucked in a breath. He hadn't told her that.

Kith's ears flicked backward and he bared his teeth in a snarl. "You did what?"

"You heard me." Ellian's expression gave away nothing, superior and impassive. "Your rather considerable debt to Vilitte now belongs to me." He moved away from the desk to stare down at the feline. "And if you do this task for us, I'll consider it paid. In full. Your freedom earned."

Kith glared at Ellian. "And what, exactly, would I need to do to accomplish this?"

"Join the Unseelie Court." Ellian turned to pick up the feather necklace from the desk. "This once belonged to the Queen. She gave it to someone, and much later it was left behind when the Lock was stolen. We need to know who had this necklace last." He glanced up and met Kith's scowl. "Any additional information you acquire will be compensated as well."

"And if I get this information for you, you will clear my debt? All of it? Your oath."

"Yes."

Kith stood and stretched, back arching and paws extended in front of him. "It'll take time." He began pacing. "To enter the court, to find this information. It may take months. Years."

"It might."

The cat padded back and forth across the rug, silent for a

long time. He sighed and stopped moving, glancing back and forth between Ellian and Cirelle.

"For my debt to be wiped clean, I'll do it."

Ellian nodded. "If you stay here for a few days, I will teach you about the court and the sidhe that populate it."

After a moment's hesitation, Kith nodded.

The next day, Kith's lessons began. Cirelle had never expected to see such a clear demonstration of Ellian's perfect memory. *Cuimhnesidhe*, Issen had called him. Precise recall of everything he'd ever seen or heard.

"The twins," Ellian jotted notes in chalk on a large slate board in a spare parlor, carefully locked to keep Lydia out. "Identical, with light green hair." A glamour settled over him, revealing the appearance of one of the sidhe Cirelle had seen at the palace. Shorter than Ellian, with broad shoulders, skin of a pale, shimmery gold, and short hair the color of green grapes. His hand sketched the words in the sidhe language, unreadable to Cirelle's eyes.

Kith cast a sidelong glance at her. He'd taken sidhe form for this, jotting down his own notes in a slim journal. He leaned indolently back in a chair, the journal propped on one knee. His eyes still held the vertical slit of a pupil even in this shape. "Does she really need to be here?" he asked Ellian.

"She asked to join, so she's here. I gave her my oath to share information if she requested it."

Cirelle gave Kith a small, smug smile. His lip curled in a grimace, but he returned to his notes.

"As I was saying," Ellian's eyes glinted azure for a moment before he turned back to the board. "The twins are close to the queen. Rhael and Sholle. Rhael is the sourpuss, Sholle is the friendly one. But their only loyalties are to the queen and each other. They both have a weak head for spirits and a love of overindulgence."

"Next, Meivre. Petite, light pink skin, purple hair." He frowned, eyes flickering pale green and black before the glamour washed over him again. Cirelle knew this one, the sidhe who'd taunted her on the same night she and Ellian had gone to the Singing Mountain. The same woman who had once flirted with a disguised Cirelle in the Unseelie Palace, just to get under Ellian's skin.

Ellian continued. "She's on civil terms with the prince, if you can call it that. Clever and self-serving, she's best avoided."

And so it went, a litany of names and backstories and traits. There were perhaps two dozen in total, the sidhe that most often stayed at the palace for an extended time. Kith quizzed Ellian on them all. It was astounding, the small details Ellian could remember. Who was left-handed, who had siblings or parents or children away from the palace and their names, what their favorite foods were.

All from his time living there, a time Cirelle didn't want to think about. She shuddered to picture Ellian among that heartless crowd, derided and mocked, only to take out all of his anger on the prince in those twisted games.

She shuddered and looked up to find Ellian watching her. His gaze locked on hers, swirling sapphire and peridot before he glanced away.

Kith retired shortly afterward, retreating to his guest room for a nap. The sidhe kept the hours appropriate to his feline form, sleeping and waking in alternating, short bursts.

But the evening was young yet.

Early winter had settled on Faerie. Still, Cirelle donned a cloak and headed up to the garden for a brief visit to the prayer stone. It had been some time since her last talk with her gods.

They felt further away every day.

While she traced the lines of their constellations carved on the stone and murmured her prayers, the first fluttering snow-flake landed on her nose.

As she made her way back toward the warmth and comfort of the manor, she passed Ellian, leaning against the wall near the door. Arms crossed, eyes downcast. Waiting.

"I don't like you thinking about that," he stated softly, staring down at the dry grass at his feet. "About the Court, about who I was then, what happened there." His words were barely audible when he added, "When you saw me that night at the duergar palace…"

Cirelle shook her head. The sight of Ellian filled with such hatred would always burn in her memory. But how would she feel, if Ellian knew her deepest, darkest regrets? A thread of something cold snaked through her veins. Words said in anger, mistakes that had gotten others hurt. No one goes through life without remorse.

She cleared her throat. "We all have regrets." Silence fell while a light dusting of snow accumulated on the ground, like a smattering of sugar on a dessert.

"Do you regret it?" Ellian asked. "Coming here?" An echo of the question she'd asked him once.

"No."

He looked so haunted, so sad. "You can't possibly mean that. After…" he hesitated.

After she'd been maimed by Ayre, and poisoned by that creature in the Mosul's swamp.

After she'd used the ilthys to kill.

After he'd bared his heart to her. When she'd done the same, and still chosen to walk away.

Part of her would never leave Faerie. And yet… "I mean it."

His lips parted as if he were going to speak, but he closed

them again. That multicolored gaze flickered down to her mouth, and he bit his lower lip softly.

Cirelle's heart skipped a beat. No. They'd promised. *We torment each other no more.*

His smile, when he turned his head away, was sad. "I wish we could all live so free of remorse." He shook his head and stared up at the moons. For a moment, she thought he would say more, but all that hung between them was a heavy silence.

Forty-Four

Lydia turned the coin over and over in her fingers. A polished bit of silver, imprinted with the symbol of a snowdrop emerging from a crown. She paced the antechamber, chewing her lip. It was well past dawn, with Cirelle and Ellian long asleep for the day.

If I do this, there's no going back, Lydia thought, picking at the edges of the engraved flower.

The prince had tossed this into her dungeon cell at the duergar palace, the metal clinking merrily against the stone floor. The duergar weren't cruel; she was not chained to a wall nor bound in any way, and the dungeon was clean, if sparse. The door held a window with heavy metal bars too close together to reach through.

But there was enough space for Adaleth to throw his coin between them. It rolled to a stop before Lydia's feet as she sat on her cot, her head jerking up to meet those eerie, glowing green eyes. She leapt up and crossed to the door in two strides. "What have you done with her?"

The prince took a step back, though she couldn't shove her hand through farther than her wrist. "Human," he said in that voice like a winter frost. "She lives. Entirely unharmed, in fact. If Ellian comes to save you, she will remain so."

Lydia bared her teeth, but forced herself to breathe. Fae couldn't lie; Cirelle was unhurt.

"Take the coin," the prince urged.

Prodding it with a boot, Lydia snorted. "Fae don't give gifts. I won't take anything from you."

"Ah, but you will. And this is not a gift. It's a fair exchange. It's my calling coin, which can be used with Ellian's mirror. Use it to call me once a fortnight and tell me what you observe at the manor. Who arrives, who leaves, anything you overhear."

"Why would I do that?"

"You want her free, don't you? I seek artifacts to close those door between our worlds. You and your princess can remain in your human realm, free of Faerie."

Lydia almost barked a laugh. She knew exactly where those artifacts were. At least, if the Key in Ellian's Archive truly was *that* Key. She and this vicious prince both wanted the same result. Their realms separated, forever.

A faerie would not break an oath made, if carefully worded. But if she told him now where to find both pieces, she didn't trust him not to twist that promise and lock Cirelle in the fae realm forever.

But if she played her cards right… "What if…" she nudged the coin with her toe again, "what if I might have information on the location of what you seek?" She ignored the prince's hiss of indrawn breath and continued. "I might be convinced to share this information with you. But only after Cirelle and I end our sentences here and return to the human realm, after she returns hale and whole. And you will never do anything to her against her will ever again."

He frowned, but nodded. "I would agree to those terms."

"After we are both safe in the mortal world, I will tell you what I know, provided you only use this knowledge to close the gates behind us. Princess Cirelle and I will remain unharmed and undisturbed in the mortal world, and you'd have the sealed door you crave."

Adaleth's eyes flashed. "I could pry the information from you."

"Perhaps. And perhaps I'd die to keep it. Are you willing to take the risk, knowing that all you need to do is wait a matter of months? What are mere months to a faerie?"

Adaleth grimaced, but nodded. "Take the coin. In exchange for it, you will contact me every fortnight to tell me what you observe while you reside in his home. Upon your return to the human realm, I will come to you and you will give me your information on the Lock. I will leave you unharmed, nor will I ever touch your princess against her wishes again."

Lydia chewed on the words for a time, seeking the trick. But she could see none.

He must know Ellian has the Key, or at least suspect it. Which put Cirelle in even further peril, and was all the more reason to strike this bargain. After the door between realms was closed, neither Adaleth nor Ellian could reach the princess.

Cirelle would despise Lydia for it, but this realm of Faerie had wormed its way too deeply into the princess's heart. Fae-touched, they called it. Only a full break might save her.

The prince gestured toward the coin. "That is my offer. Take the coin, think it over. And when you are ready, call me."

Lydia bent and picked up the coin.

Now, in Ellian's antechamber, she turned the coin in her hand, warming the metal. The full risk of what she was doing settled upon her. If Ellian discovered her betrayal, he'd not go easy on her again, no matter how Cirelle protested.

But this was her one chance to save her princess.

Lydia swallowed and slipped the coin into the mirror.

Forty-Five

IN ELLIAN'S MANOR, days settled into a dreary routine. Cirelle practiced her forlorn Faerie Nocturne and composed her ode to Yratla, while Lydia grew even more quiet and withdrawn. Shai visited frequently, and she and the soldier spent hours practicing their swordplay. Cirelle didn't even bother to join them with her knives, though she knew she should. But a fog had settled over her mood and her thoughts.

Ellian kept his own peace, and though they shared meals sometimes, their occasional card games had stopped. His gaze remained carefully gray, always polite but nothing more.

Cirelle ached to remember those eyes full of rose, whispering her name. But no, those days were gone. Months remained of this, of walls and stilted silence and indifference.

Two more miserable weeks passed before Cirelle snapped.

∾

The doorbell rang and Cirelle ran to answer it. She'd donned a dress today, though it was a simple cotton day dress instead of a shimmery, luxurious gown.

Shai and Issen stood on the other side of the door.

"What's up?" Shai greeted her with a wide grin. Issen stood behind her, his usual enigmatic smile on his lips.

At the commotion, Lydia poked her head from the hallway. When she saw Shai, Lydia's eyes brightened and the guardswoman came into the foyer to greet their guests. A moment later, doubt flickered over her face. "Is something wrong?"

Cirelle grinned at her. "They're here for your nameday party. Well, it's not *much* of a party, but I did what I could."

Lydia tossed Cirelle a doubtful look. "Can you do that without Ellian's permission? Because I don't believe for a second you asked him first."

"Nah," Shai laughed. "She does what she wants, right?"

"As a member of the household," Issen clarified, "Cirelle is allowed to invite us to the house. Whether we get to stay, well that's up to Ellian."

"Speaking of…" Lydia nodded at the upper floor, where Ellian emerged from his wing.

"Issen? Shai?" He blinked, and Cirelle was vindictively pleased to see a flash of canary-yellow surprise in those eyes.

Issen gave a little bow, and Shai just stood, hands on hips, and beamed up at him. "Hey."

His eyes narrowed. "What's wrong?"

Cirelle rolled her eyes. "Stars, can't we have guests without it being a crisis?"

Ellian gave Cirelle a flat stare as he walked down the stairs. "Usually, I'm the one asking them to visit. I assume this time you invited them?"

"I did. It's Lydia's nameday tonight, and I want to enjoy it. We celebrated yours."

"So what's the deal, Ellian?" Shai asked, taking one loping stride to the bottom of the stairs to meet him. "Do we get to party or what?"

Ellian's glanced around the group, his face devoid of all emotion. After a long pause, he nodded. "If you must."

"Yes!" Shai's energy was infectious, and even Lydia's face broke out in a soft smile.

Right on time, the doorbell rang again, and Cirelle let in Vilitte, greeting the crystalline woman with a smile.

Ellian seemed less pleased. "Just how many people did you invite, princess?"

It stung, to hear him return to calling her 'princess'. "I invited everyone," she replied, a challenge in her eyes.

"Even Kith?" Vilitte arched one silvery eyebrow, the same color as her translucent hair, like strands of spun glass.

"Even Kith," Cirelle admitted reluctantly. "He laughed at me, but I invited him anyway." She shrugged. "The rest were more polite in their refusals. So this is all we've got. But it's enough for a party, and Stars help me, you are all going to enjoy it." Cirelle left no room for rebuttal as she led the way to the dining hall.

Earlier that morning, while Lydia drilled in the garden and Ellian hid away as usual, Cirelle had spent her time in one of the mid-sized dining rooms. All sorts of intriguing things lay buried in dusty chambers of this home, and she'd managed to scrounge up strings of beads and garlands of ribbon flowers boxed away in a cedar chest. What they'd originally been for, she had no idea. But now they adorned the walls, a tablecloth draped over the table in a deep navy blue, Lydia's favorite color.

Cirelle had even worked with the brownies, asking them to make roasted duck and the tiny decadent spice cakes Lydia's had always loved. There were other dishes as well: smoked and shredded pork in a sweet, tangy sauce, sausages fried with onions and mushrooms, stewed vegetables in a thick gravy, toasted bread covered in slabs of melted cheese.

"You did all this?" Lydia blurted, staring around at the decor with something approaching horror.

Her expression made Cirelle laugh. "Yep. Well, and the brownies, of course."

The guardswoman turned aside to brush a hand along one of the artfully-crafted ribbon daisies as they took their seats and began serving themselves. Ellian sat silent at the head of the table and cast confusing glances in Cirelle's direction. Whether it was merely bafflement or condescension, Cirelle couldn't tell. Tonight, she didn't care. Shai and Issen sat opposite Cirelle, Lydia at the foot of the table across from Ellian, and Vilitte at Cirelle's elbow.

"So, Lydia," Shai asked with her mouth full of half-chewed vegetables, "What's the first thing you're gonna do when you get home?"

"Report to Prince Aidan, of course," the guardswoman replied simply.

Shai rolled her eyes, resting her chin on one hand and grimacing. "No, *after* all the stuff you gotta do. What do you *want* to do?"

Lydia stared down at her plate. "I don't know."

Something in the way she said the words made Cirelle's stomach twist, a forlorn note. Issen caught Cirelle's gaze from across the table, those canny eyes asking a question Cirelle didn't know the answer to. She shrugged nervously and toyed with her own food.

Shai seemed disappointed by the pensive mood. "If this is a party, where's the booze?" She cast an expectant gaze at Ellian, who sighed. One by one, he removed several bottles from his pouch and passed them around the table.

"I'd recommend avoiding the blue bottles," he said pointedly to Cirelle. Her cheeks burned. "However," he added. "The green bottles are Nycenine sparkling wine. No enchantment." His eyes bored into hers, and Cirelle felt an uneasy lurch in her chest.

It was a stupid reaction. Ellian still held his distance, as he'd promised.

We torment each other no more.

Cirelle poured herself a generous glass of the wine and took a long sip. Sweet and bitter and fruity, the bubbles danced on her tongue.

Shai tossed back her first cup of faerie spirits with little ceremony, the golden liquor gone in one swallow. She belched, and Cirelle couldn't help but give a startled laugh, jostled briefly out of her gloom.

While Shai poured another glass, Issen sipped his own, casting Cirelle an amused glance at Shai's enthusiasm. Throughout all of this, Vilitte remained quiet, leaning back in her chair as she politely refused a plate. Her kind did not eat human food, she informed Cirelle.

Lydia still seemed pensive, pouring herself a mug of tea instead of wine.

"Come on." Shai pushed a wine bottle at Lydia. "Live a little!" The guardswoman shook her head, and Shai sighed. Her eyes flickered toward Lydia and away, the gold darkening to a burnt orange. "Whatever floats your boat, I guess."

And so dinner went. While Lydia remained quiet and withdrawn, Vilitte and Issen observed the rest of the table with watchful eyes. Shai did her best to fill the silence, while Ellian kept casting Cirelle warning glances as her wine bottle emptied.

She ignored him. Ellian had given up any right he may once have had to comment on such behavior. Not after that night. The way his voice had cracked on his farewell echoed in her memory, clear as crystal.

She downed another glass.

Shai, in her own attempt to cheer Lydia up, told a story about the time she glamoured herself as human and won the duelist's competition at the Midsummer Festival in Arraven.

Still, the air about the table remained heavy, and Cirelle found her own mood sinking despite Shai's best efforts. She'd wanted to do something nice, to cheer everyone up, but all it had done was illuminate the lines that had been drawn between Cirelle and Ellian, between Lydia and herself.

While Cirelle drowned her melancholy, Issen watched them all with those watchful, salmon-colored eyes.

The pressure built until someone had to break. Cirelle was just surprised it was Lydia.

The guardswoman pushed back her chair suddenly. Her breath hitched, her voice thick. "Thank you, Your Highness, but I need to retire." She fled.

"Lydia!" Cirelle called after her. But as she scooted her chair away from the table and stood to follow, Issen halted her.

"Cirelle," he said, and the word was a warning.

"What? I'm going after her."

Issen's eyes met hers, a heavy weight behind them. "She needs to talk to someone other than you right now." He turned his head. "Shai?"

Shai gulped down the last of her drink. "I'm on it." She stood and walked out, leaving Cirelle gaping.

"Sit," Vilitte urged from beside her. "She'll be fine."

"It's her party!" Cirelle snapped, angry that she'd been shoved aside here as well. "I'm her friend!"

"Exactly," Issen said calmly. "She needs to talk to someone who isn't so tangled up in everything that's bothering her."

It stung like a rebuke.

Ellian was silent, idly spinning his fork and staring down at his glass of half-finished faerie liquor.

Cirelle wanted to storm out, Issen be damned. She knew Lydia better than these faeries.

Or did she, anymore?

Once, she'd known Lydia better than just about anyone. They'd spent summer evenings catching fireflies alongside her brother, pretending the insects were tiny pixies. She and Aidan and Lydia had formed their own small coterie. Together, they playacted classic tales like the Rose Maiden, Cirelle taking the part of the cursed damsel, Aidan the vengeful sorcerer, and Lydia the brave knight-errant.

Even after the other palace children had gone their own ways, the three had clung to each other, chasing one another in games of tag or venturing down to the kennels to play with the latest litter of hounds, laughing as the pups nipped their fingers.

But Cirelle and Lydia were no longer children, no longer even the women they had once been. Since arriving in Faerie, all Cirelle had done was make Lydia miserable. And Lydia had only reminded Cirelle of the person Arraven wanted her to be. Her silent rebukes stung and irritated like burrs.

The thought was a sobering one, and Cirelle sat, finishing her glass of wine. Beside her, Vilitte reached out a comforting hand but halted an inch away. Faerie rules. Cirelle bridged the distance, shifting to let Vilitte's fingertips rest on her forearm. The faerie's touch was cool and hard as the stone she appeared to be, but it was still reassuring.

Across from her, Issen cocked his head thoughtfully, his eyes dipping to that point of contact.

Cirelle flushed. There was nothing behind Vilitte's gesture other than simple comfort, but his canny gaze made her feel judged. She poured more wine.

Vilitte's hand didn't move away, curling over Cirelle's arm. It was still a chaste touch, but more than the brush of her fingers had been.

"I'm glad you invited me," Vilitte said to Cirelle, her rich voice warm with affection. Not quite a thank you, but the closest a faerie could come to one.

Cirelle's gaze darted to Ellian. His face was expressionless as his eyes met Cirelle's. Still angry about the party? Or just bored? It was impossible to tell.

Still, Cirelle replied to Vilitte's comment. The wine left her spirits bleak, the heavy weight of tears pressing against the back of her eyes. "Glad? For this? Planning parties is one of the few things I was trained to do, but apparently I'm no good at that anymore either." Despondently, Cirelle took another bite of her roasted vegetables. If nothing else, she would be damned if she'd let the brownies' hard work go to waste.

"I enjoy the chance to get to know you better, my dear," Vilitte shrugged, finally lifting her hand from Cirelle's skin. "We spoke so briefly at the last party. And Thieves' Night left little opportunity for socializing, what with all the fighting and stabbing and blood." She grinned, making the comment a gruesome joke.

At the head of the table, Ellian's fist closed about his fork.

"Can I confess something?" Vilitte murmured, gesturing Cirelle closer.

Perplexed, Cirelle leaned in to hear Vilitte's whisper. It was faint, barely enough for Cirelle to hear and certainly not loud enough for either of the men to eavesdrop.

"I think it was very brave, how you helped on Thieves' Night. A mortal human, commanding the ilthys and helping that shrew Dirilai, all for Ellian's sake. So romantic."

Cirelle's cheeks burned as invisible, heavy vines twined about her, tightening until they strangled.

The sound of Ellian's chair scraping on stone made Cirelle startle, whirling to look at him. "As the guest of honor has seen fit to abandon the party," he said, "I believe I'll follow suit." With stiff steps and an inscrutable expression, he walked out the door.

As soon as he was gone, Vilitte laughed, a sound like glass chimes.

Issen's stare was one of quiet disdain. "That was unwise, Vilitte."

"What?" The woman grinned indolently at him.

"You shouldn't go poking into things that aren't your business."

"Pssh," Vilitte waved away his admonition. "Seems like *someone* around here could use some poking." She placed a sly emphasis on the last word, then shrugged. "Just trying to help."

Realization crept up on Cirelle. "You just did that to get a rise out of Ellian?"

"Ooh, interesting choice of words," Vilitte smiled, the expression downright puckish even on her strangely inhuman face.

"What?"

Vilitte laughed again. "Oh don't be dense, princess."

Cirelle blinked, then barked out a harsh laugh as unbidden tears sprang to her eyes. "You're a fool, Vilitte. There's nothing between the two of us." *Not anymore.* "I don't appreciate you flirting with me just to irritate him." Slamming back the rest of her wine, she closed her eyes as the surge of warmth flooded her, then shoved her chair away from the table and stood shakily.

Vilitte called out with a smile as Cirelle reached the door. "If there's nothing there, why did it work?"

❧

As so often happened when a bleakness of spirit seized Cirelle, her unsteady feet led her toward the garden and the prayer stone. A brief conversation with the gods, that's all she wanted.

She wobbled her way through the statuary and bushes, taking a path she now knew by heart, until she turned a corner and stopped short. Shai and Lydia sat on a wooden bench not ten paces away. Lydia's eyes were closed in sleep, the tracks of tears still glittering against her cheeks. She curled against Shai, who stroked Lydia's long blonde hair, now free of its warrior's tail.

Shai's eyes met Cirelle's as she halted. It felt like an intrusion, a violation, to witness this. That golden-orange gaze held a depth Cirelle hadn't expected of the brash warrior.

Wordlessly, Cirelle turned and walked away to talk to her gods. Conversation with the Iska didn't help her racing thoughts, and Cirelle abandoned the chilly garden to return to the dining hall.

It didn't take long before Ellian found her. The plates and tableware had long since been cleared, but the bottles of alcohol had been left behind. Cirelle's decorations still hung on the walls, now a forlorn monument to the party that had never been.

"I wasn't a drunkard until I met you, faerie," Cirelle greeted Ellian, taking another swig of wine directly from the bottle. There were no more glasses, taken away to be cleaned. She hadn't been quite angry or stupid enough to break into the faerie spirits, but she was already starting her second bottle of Nycenine wine. It had dulled her fury, but dragged her down into a more violent despair as well.

Ellian sat without words and unstoppered one of the blue bottles, taking a gulp.

"Can't even let me drink in peace, can you?" she snapped.

Ellian let the bottle thunk down on the table. He refused to look at her. "We can't do this. *I* can't do this."

Cirelle's stomach roiled with anger. "I don't care."

"That's a lie." Ellian held up his hand and wiggled his fingers, that lie-detecting ring gleaming.

"Well, I *shouldn't* care. You were the one who decided it was all or nothing." A painful stab lanced through her ribcage.

Ellian maintained his glamour as he took another drink, those eyes giving away nothing in their emotionless gray.

Cirelle's temper snapped, a string pulled too tightly for too long. "Say something, faerie!" She wanted to throw the bottle at him, to slap him, but her arms felt too heavy.

"Something." It was a feeble attempt at a joke, accompanied by a lifeless mimicry of his old smirk.

This time she did hurl something at him. The cork from her wine bottle, the only thing she had at hand. It struck between his eyebrows, a pitiful weapon. Still, it carried with it the weight of Cirelle's anger and frustration. Her chest heaved with furious, labored breaths. "Don't you dare," she seethed. "Don't mock me."

His reply was strained. "Isn't that what you miss? The games, the teasing?"

"Not like this."

"Then what do you want?"

"The truth." The words spilled from her without pause. "Why? Why end it early, before we had to? Why do this to both of us?"

Ellian stared down at the table as he spoke. His reply was measured and careful. "I chose to put a stop to things so you could heal before you left."

"Heal?" Her laugh was sharp, jagged. "This isn't healing."

"Then if not for you, for me. I can't bear it, going back to the teasing, the flirting, the games, knowing you already have one foot out the door. I won't do it." And this time, his eyes lifted to hers, a mingling of pale green and deepest blue. "But I miss you."

Cirelle hated how her breath hitched, how those frightened sparrows fluttered in her stomach. She wanted to scream, to break something. But like shifting sand beneath her feet, the anger slid out from underneath her. Sorrow bubbled to the surface in its place. And a brutal truth, a fact she didn't want to admit even to herself. "I miss you, too." Glass shards shredded her insides. Cirelle buried her face in her hands and loathed herself for her weakness.

How could she have let things become this mess? Hadn't she resolved not to become like Ellian's other besotted pets?

Yet she still longed for the azure glint of humor in his eyes, even that arrogant half-smile. She ached for their bickering banter again, their matching of wits.

She missed *Ellian*, the man she'd come to find under that indifferent mask, beneath all his mockery and wit and charm. The one with the insecurities he tried to hide even from himself. She wanted him back, the man who'd dyed his fingertips in penance when Orwe died, who'd had the courage to crawl into a viper's pit of shame and disgust and old, hated memories just to save the link between their worlds. The one she'd seen on that temple's rooftop as the sun rose, playfully tossing berries at her.

"So where does that leave us?" she muttered into her hands, afraid to look up, to let him see her tear-stained face.

"I don't know. Maybe we could start over again."

Starting over. None of their flirting, no dance of teasing and seduction. As if they'd only just met, no masks, no games. Allies. Maybe even friends.

Cirelle took a long, shaky breath, and looked up to find eyes mingling rose petals and sapphires and copper. Her voice cracked. "Starting again. I think I could do that."

Forty-Six

Starting over. Cirelle plucked a few idle notes on the harp and grimaced. It had seemed like a good idea at the time. A respite, a relief from her sorrow and grief. But her pain could not be wished away so easily.

Oh, she and Ellian were friendly enough with one another now. He smiled at her, made jests, played games. And she returned in kind. But it was hollow, and each of his grins felt like a burr in her shoe, a piece of string wrapped around her throat, tightening, strangling.

The longer they pretended, the worse it became.

She didn't know if he felt the same. They'd agreed not to talk of such things any more, after all.

Lydia did her best, cajoling Cirelle into their own private games of fox-and-hounds, or one memorable night Cirelle had managed to talk a brownie into leaving some wine at her sideboard to celebrate Marya's Day. After supper, she and Lydia had retired to her parlor and whiled away the hours reminiscing about past holidays while polishing off not one, but two bottles of rich Gilbran wine. They'd ended the night piled on Cirelle's too-large bed, laughing at the memory of a past Marya's Day when Aidan's new trousers had split right down the middle during a dance with a young visiting duchess.

But even that levity couldn't banish the dark splotch on Cirelle's heart, not entirely. Oh, she tried to hide it. To bury it. To pretend she was fine. But the heartache was a stabbing pain that sank into her bones. A gut-wrenching hollowness took up space in Cirelle's chest where once there had been fire.

Despite his smiles, his friendly demeanor, it still gutted Cirelle to look into a gaze now held gray as slate, as storm clouds. Those eyes would not dance with colors for Cirelle's sake ever again.

She wept as much as she once had for Briere, and loathed herself for it.

It was worse when Shai visited, but it would be wrong to begrudge Lydia a bit of happiness in this place that had done something dark and twisted to Lydia's soul. The woman who'd once been honorable to a fault had stolen that cord from Ellian, tried using his own artifact to bind him. Something dark haunted Lydia's eyes now, bleak circles forming beneath her eyes, her cheeks hollowing out.

It ate at her, being here in Faerie. And Lydia was stuck in this house as long as Cirelle remained here with Ellian.

At least Shai brought the smiles back to Lydia's face, the spark in her gaze. They sparred in the garden, sometimes with Cirelle reading on a bench nearby and offering a few taunts of her own. She brought out her own wooden practice blades once or twice, but it was humiliating to lose to them both. Other times, they'd all lounge in a parlor as Lydia practiced her letters and Shai knitted a scarf while Cirelle composed her song for Yratla or played familiar melodies. One song was conspicuously absent, though. She'd not touch Ellian's song again.

More often than not, though, Cirelle let the warriors have

their privacy. It was bittersweet to see her friend finding the joy that was denied her, like a slow-burning poison that ate Cirelle from inside.

Issen came to see them sometimes, though not as frequently as Shai. He did his best to pretend all was fine, but could not hide the injury that had devoured most of his left hand and arm. Most of the time, a long glove covered the blackened, skeletal husk, but it still felt like a rebuke when he chose easier instruments to play one-handed. He could move the hand slightly, but not enough to strum strings or hold a flute.

And yet, their plans must continue. Lydia was still forbidden from Ellian's plotting for the rest of her stay, but Cirelle was included. Unfortunately, their plans at the moment mostly relied on Kith's detective work while they tracked down any other stray mention of the Lock or of a feathered necklace.

Tonight, Cirelle let Kith into the manor, padding into the antechamber on his silent paws.

"I have one more possible name," he said as he settled on the sofa, licking a spot between his toes, claws outstretched.

"One?" Cirelle seethed. "That's it? All you've brought us are the three names of murdered sidhe, with no other clues."

Kith lifted his lip in a snarl. "I can't very well waltz into the Queen's chambers and demand details about a piece of very specific jewelry I'm not even supposed to know exists. One that she *knows* is in Ellian's possession. All I can do is dredge up the names of sidhe that landed on Ayre's bad side after her coup. I warned you this could take years. And you expect an answer in weeks."

"I knew—"

"Enough." Ellian's interruption was quiet, but firm. "It'll do. What's the name?"

"Syleris," the cat said, settling back on the couch. "She was an attendant of the previous queen. Refused to swear to Ayre and was executed for it."

Jotting the name on a piece of paper, Ellian tucked it in the drawer of the desk. Cirelle didn't know why he bothered; it wasn't like he could forget it.

Ellian's next question was remarkably steady. "And the prince?"

"Suspects nothing. He thinks I'm just a stray come to lick boots and gain a little clout. Doesn't care for me much, but he's oblivious enough."

"Make sure he stays that way."

Kith nodded, stretching and hopping onto the floor. "I'll see if I can learn more, but you might want to teach your human some patience. Push too far, too fast, and this could all fall apart. And mine is the throat that will be cut for it."

Cirelle seethed. "*His* human?"

"You are," Kith pointed out calmly.

"No," Ellian growled, "she is of my household at the moment, but belongs to herself."

"You can both pretend all you want," Kith said with a feline shrug as he made his way out the door, "but in all the ways that matter to Faerie law, she is your responsibility. And her impatience could be your downfall."

Gritting her teeth, Cirelle followed him out and ushered him out the door. Returning to the antechamber, she fell onto the sofa and ran her hands through her hair in frustration. "We can't run down rabbit trails hunting down information on every dissenter the Queen has ever killed," she grumbled. "There has to be a faster way to get this information."

"Faster, maybe," Ellian said as he sat in a nearby chair. "But riskier, too. We can't overplay our hand. Not now. Not when Adaleth thinks he still has the Key."

"There's no one else who might identify the necklace?"

"None we trust. Issen and Shai don't recognize it."

"What about Dirilai?"

"I showed her. She says she can't help us, either. We'll find another way. We have to."

Forty-Seven

IN THE NEW ORDER at the manor, Ellian didn't always take Cirelle on his summons. Though he forbade Lydia from his true plans, he still took her on his usual bargains in the human world occasionally, especially when Cirelle was working. And so it was that she paid little mind when Lydia left for a summons. Cirelle was still in the Archive rearranging a shelf when the front door opened and she heard Ellian call her name.

When she slipped through the doors to the entry hall, she froze. Standing beside Ellian and a grumpy-looking Lydia was a man. Wait, no, a *familiar* man. He'd summoned Ellian before. The one who asked for riches and fortune. She could not recall his name, but his colorful garb was hard to forget.

He was still handsome, his dark skin perfectly complementing the polished wood and cream-colored stones of Ellian's manor. An aquamarine sleeveless robe draped his form, as well as loose trousers of a yellow hue that put sunflowers to shame. The fabric was finer than last time, the beads on his long braids now gemstones rather than carved wood. Gold studs traced a line around the edge of one ear.

His stance was confident, feet apart and planted, his broad

shoulders back so that he seemed to take up more space than Ellian despite being almost a full head shorter.

"Cirelle," Ellian greeted her, his face a careful mask. "It seems you and Lydia will have company for a time." He gestured at the man. "Jhavet will be serving here for a year."

Jhavet glanced about the foyer in appreciation as Ellian gave Cirelle the usual speech about finding a room and getting the new arrival settled. He turned to Jhavet. "Ah, one thing." He dipped a hand into his pouch, pulling out one of the translation earrings and tossing it to Jhavet. "You'll want to wear this," he said to the man in Jhavet's strange tongue. "I will dine with you alone this evening. Three days hence, you will start sharing duties with Cirelle and Lydia."

And tonight, Ellian would test Jhavet with his enchanted wine. What would happen then? Jealousy bolted like a bitter spike through Cirelle's chest.

"Lydia," Ellian said, "If you'll process his offerings, Cirelle can get him settled."

Tight-lipped, Lydia nodded, but not before giving Cirelle a worried look and Ellian a piercing, vicious glare. Wordlessly she left, the Archive doors thudding shut behind her. Ellian headed up the stairs and returned to his own wing.

Cirelle turned to Jhavet. "You just accepted a gift from a faeric without question?"

The man had slipped the earring into his pierced earlobe without question, now holding a gold hoop between his fingers. "You're wearing one," he pointed at her own ear, where the teardrop stone dangled, then gestured toward the Archive doors where Lydia had disappeared. "And so was she."

"That means nothing," she hissed. "Don't you know anything about the fae?"

Jhavet laughed, motioning to her with the same sort of bow

he'd used with Ellian before, hand held out palm upwards. When he moved his head, the gemstone beads strung onto his many braids clacked together softly.

Cirelle sighed. "Just follow me."

She led him down the first floor west wing, past her own room and around a corner. One of the parlors featured a wardrobe similar to the strange and colorful clothing Jhavet wore. It would do.

As they walked, she remarked, "I thought you got what you wanted last time you summoned Ellian."

Jhavet shrugged. "Didn't really work out the way I'd hoped. My luck changed, but I learned that wealth has its own share of problems. Friends all wanted a piece of my fortune, and there wasn't enough to give them all what they felt they deserved. I didn't know who to trust anymore, who liked me and who liked the money. I tried to sell the charm, but no one believed it was enchanted. I threw it into a lake, only to have it reappear around my neck when I walked away. I dropped it into a fire with the same result, except it scorched my skin when it came back."

"You summoned him again to ask that he take back the thing he gave you? And you gave up both a year of your lifespan and another year in servitude, all to end up exactly where you started?"

She led him into a parlor decorated with joyful crimson and brilliant violet. It matched the riotous color she'd seen in both Jhavet's garb and the city he called home. Pillows were richly embroidered in gold and vibrant orange hues. The furniture was painted rather than polished natural wood, in patterns just as colorful, with gilded corners and edges. Jhavet's grin widened as he ran his fingers lightly along a countertop.

"I didn't *exactly* end up where I started," he answered her earlier question as he browsed the room, his hand brushing the back of a chair, the edge of the sideboard. "I still have some of wealth I earned from the charm. It's good enough. And now I get to spend a year in this fine manor home, with a beautiful sidhe lord and equally lovely lady." He smiled at her, no mischief or teasing in the expression, as if he stated a plain and simple fact.

Cirelle ignored his flattery, walking past Jhavet to point out both the wardrobe and washroom. "You may bathe if you wish and change your clothes. If you place your old clothes on that shelf, the brownies will see that they are washed and returned," she said simply. "There is plenty of time before dinner."

He was gleeful when she showed him the water spout. The guileless grin on his face made his youth all the more obvious.

"How old are you?" she blurted.

"Twenty-two," he responded easily, while he plucked jars of soap and scents from the shelf to sniff their contents.

She blinked. Older than she. And yet he seemed so naive. Had she looked so foolish when she first arrived here? She gritted her teeth and told him. "The dinner bell will ring in about an hour. I will be directly across the hall making sure your room is ready. Just come knock when you're done."

"Mmm," he gave a small sound of assent as he filled the tub with hot water. Cirelle slipped out to arrange his bedchamber, as colorful as the parlor.

Did this Jhavet even realize what he had gotten himself into? He seemed to treat all of this as merely a lark, as if his time in Faerie was a vacation rather than a sacrifice. Then again, for him, perhaps it was. He'd mentioned poverty before. If her rooms seemed comfortable enough to her, what luxury did Ellian's home offer to Jhavet?

And why had Ellian asked for service from Jhavet, rather than some human trinket? Her thoughts wouldn't stop drifting to Jhavet's beauty, his charming smile. Was that why?

Cirelle knew all too well what it was like to bury your heartbreak in another. When Briere had been stolen from her, Cirelle had sought the mind-numbing pleasures of a meaningless night spent with a soldier boy. Her heart twisted in her chest.

No, surely Ellian would never be so callous. Not mere weeks after the night they'd spent together.

When Jhavet knocked on the door, he wore a short coat in a vivid shade of scarlet, two rows of gold buttons down his chest. A wide sash of turquoise silk showed off his slim waist, while the cut of the coat highlighted his broad shoulders. The shirt beneath was a buttery yellow, accented at the throat with a pin of polished, clear amber.

Jhavet grinned at her surprise. "This sidhe has a fine wardrobe for guests. You like it?"

"I'm not sure," she said honestly. "Now you look like some mix of an Arravene duke and a Gilbran merchant."

"Ah," he said with a shrug. "Well, it was worth a try, something new. There were clothes from Ysaan in that wardrobe as well, so perhaps I will return to those if you think them more flattering."

She ignored his baiting, stepping back so that he could enter the room. "Ysaan." She'd been correct in her assumption then, so many months ago.

He nodded. "And still I know nothing of you, pretty servant of a sidhe lord."

"I come from Arraven, far to the south of your home."

"Mmm," he gave a small sound of assent as he strode about the chambers. He seemed to feel the urge to touch everything. A brush of fingertips across intricate molding, sitting in a comfortable chair for a moment to test it out, lifting knick-knacks to take a closer look.

Handing him the key, she said, "Keep your room locked." She could remove the earring for a moment to warn him about the summerwine and Ellian's ploy, but she couldn't fully trust this man either. Maybe it was best to let Ellian's test run its course.

Jhavet seemed to take little notice as he left his room and locked the door, slipping the key into a pocket of the jacket. "This house is lovely. Is there time for a tour?"

She nodded. A few moments later, she cleared her throat and began explaining all the areas of the house to him. Halfway through, she bumped into Shai and Lydia, returning to their rooms coated in sweat from a sparring match. It wouldn't have taken Lydia long to process Jhavet's offerings, after all.

The greetings were brief, and Lydia's look heavily weighted. Cirelle returned it with her own worried expression before the soldiers retreated to their parlors to wash up. They would join Cirelle in a secondary dining hall for supper later.

Jhavet looked upon everything with the same appreciative, wide-eyed wonder, skimming a hand along the walls or flipping through books in the library. Once or twice, he glanced her way with that wide, disarming grin, and she could only imagine him turning that same smile on Ellian later.

They were in the rooftop gardens when the dinner bell rang, Jhavet pulling a rose blossom close to breathe in its scent. Cirelle's stomach clenched at the dinner bell, but she dutifully led Jhavet to the small, private dining chamber to await Ellian.

As she walked further along the hall, the tinkling song of Ellian's boots echoed to her. Despite her better judgment, Cirelle couldn't resist a glance back at him.

He looked resplendent in one of his usual ostentatious ensembles, chest bared in one of those fae shirts. He'd donned more jewelry tonight too, including a single silver necklace with a medallion in brightest orange carnelian, glimmering with yellow flecks as if lit with a flame.

Before he could say anything, she turned and kept walking.

Forty-Eight

I KNOW NOW THAT I should never have brought him. It was a foolish, impulsive decision. Weak of me, perhaps. But I had considered that maybe Jhavet would bring some much-needed lightness and humor to all of us in this place.

I was wrong.

Ellian closed the journal and pinched the bridge of his nose. He had to admit that despite his misgivings there was a refreshing charm to Jhavet's good cheer, after so much tension and misery. It was a delicate dance every time he spoke to Cirelle, to stay on safe topics, to avoid showing the pain they both felt. Not so, with the newcomer. No fraught past to tiptoe around.

Even that much camaraderie with Cirelle was enough to make Lydia sour, though. Shai's giddy energy seemed to soothe the soldier, but only deepened the rift between Lydia and her princess.

Perhaps Cirelle thought she was adept at hiding it, but he knew her too well. The tension around her eyes, the strained quality to her smiles. She'd smile and play her harp and join in games, but there was a hole in her.

One I put there.

She'd tried so hard to throw Lydia that party, as poorly as it turned out. She seemed to thrive in social settings, even when they were with the fae. Once the dust of a new arrival settled, maybe a new human friend could still do her some good to spend time with someone not embroiled in fae games.

It will help.

It has to.

❧

It was harder than Cirelle expected.

She saw the men little during their first three days. Meals were spent with Shai and Lydia, and she only crossed paths with Ellian and Jhavet in the halls once or twice. Jhavet always had a broad smile on his face, tracing the lines of scrollwork along the walls while he nodded along with whatever Ellian said.

Once, on her way back from the kitchens, she passed the gaming parlor and was startled by a sudden burst of laughter from Jhavet. It was a bray of a sound, unrestrained and joyous.

Cirelle's chest tightened as she wondered what Ellian had said to spur such a response.

What game did they play? Jealousy once more scratched at her as she thought of Jhavet handling her pieces in fox-and-hounds. Or did Ellian teach the boy Raven's Gambit, the game in which he had used flirtation as a weapon?

Feeling queasy, Cirelle hurried away down the hall.

All too soon it was time to show Jhavet the ropes of running the Archive. Cirelle took the lead, though Lydia was proficient enough at her letters to help him by now. Still, Lydia stood quietly by while Cirelle rattled off their duties to Jhavet.

He listened with a disinterested expression, nodding absently. All too often, his gaze wandered, scanning the shelves that lay before them.

"Jhavet!" She snapped when his attention had drifted too far.

"Yes?" He grinned.

"Are you even listening? What is the first weekly task in the Archive?"

He shrugged. "I'll learn as I go. I remember things better by doing them."

Cirelle gritted her teeth. The man didn't seem to care if he fared poorly. While they walked the rows, he still wanted to touch everything. She repeated a warning about the red tiles on the shelves three times to make sure it sank in.

"It'll serve you right if you touch the wrong thing and get yourself vaporized," she grumbled to herself under her breath as she filed away paperwork.

"Hmm?" he asked from across the room, where he was poking through the shelves of blank papers. He tilted his head to hear better, and his new earrings glittered in the soft light. Jhavet had immediately made free with the wardrobe in his room, replacing all of his jewelry with even more lavish pieces. The row of piercings up his ear now glittered with precious gemstones. Today, he'd returned to an Ysaan fashion in a vibrant lime green and rich cobalt blue.

That grin flashed again, and Cirelle got the impression Jhavet had skated by on the virtue of his smile all too often.

Well, he certainly won't with me.

Over the next two weeks, Cirelle learned all of Jhavet's faults in painful detail. The man was always unfailingly, irritatingly pleasant and good-natured, no matter how snappish or ill-tempered Cirelle became. Which was all too often. Her patience frayed down to a thin thread. Lydia was spending ever more time with Shai, to the point that Cirelle was beginning to wonder if her old friend avoided her.

Which left Cirelle as Jhavet's babysitter far too often. It became frustratingly obvious after only a few days that Cirelle and Lydia would still need to perform most of the work duties. Jhavet did, however, have a deep curiosity about all of the objects in the Archive. He spent his free time going through the filing cabinets and reading avidly about the assorted sundry treasures. One day, as she was tidying, she found him looking over old, outdated Archive lists.

"You don't need to know those," she said. "Ellian only keeps them in case a dispute about a past bargain comes up."

"I know," Jhavet replied, flipping over the top page in the stack and reading the next. "But you don't *need* to read the books you peruse in the library, either. Nor do you *need* to write music."

She continued tidying in irritated silence. After the papers were stacked, Cirelle began sweeping the floors and pointed him toward the supply closet for a second broom and dustpan.

That silly grin still painted Jhavet's face as he fetched the items. Even his complaints were in good humor. "I thought the brownies kept the place clean, anyway?"

"Everywhere but the Archive," Cirelle responded shortly. "That's our duty."

Jhavet shrugged and began to sweep. Or at least he went vaguely through the motions of sweeping. His efforts were useless, resulting only in stirring up more dust. Cirelle tried to show him how to do it properly, but a lack of motivation left his skills unimproved.

Cirelle was reluctant to approach Ellian about it. Would he think she was jealous of the newcomer, or making a big issue out of nothing? Why complain about that when they had much bigger problems, like Kith's continuing inability to turn up anything of true worth or a series of dead ends in their other necklace research? So she suffered in silence, redoing all of Jhavet's work after he left the Archive at the end of their chores.

It wasn't like she had much else to do. In her off hours, she composed Yratla's song. At least the music room remained her sanctuary, as Jhavet had no predilection for music. Shai and Lydia kept to themselves more and more each day, though the guilty, heavy looks Lydia cast Cirelle during their Archive duties spoke of words still left unsaid.

So many things unspoken between them all, knots that only tangled more by the day. Cirelle grew gradually, inexorably more weary and sharp-tongued. It became an effort to maintain even casual conversation. Her harp offered little solace, and she turned to the piano again, banging out her anger on the keys. She worked on Yratla's song, but it was hard to create a piece of awe and wonder when she felt little save sorrow and irritation. Prayer was equally useless. She sought the solace of her gods less and less with each passing week.

At first, Lydia attempted to help. She offered gentle condolences and suggestions while Shai's bold cheer tried to bolster them both. But Cirelle had been swallowed by one of her dark, despairing moods, and she sliced them both with bitter words until they left her alone in frustration.

Meals were an exercise in self-control as Jhavet made his intentions clear.

The first time he'd lifted a hand and placed his fingertips gently on Ellian's forearm, the sidhe sucked in a sharp breath, eyes darting to Cirelle. She'd avoided his gaze, swallowing down a bite of dinner now gone sour in her mouth as she clutched at her fork and reminded her lungs how to work.

Jhavet, for his part, seemed completely oblivious to Cirelle's suffering, smiling that infectious grin at Ellian. The faerie shifted his arm away, but Jhavet was unfazed, continuing his thread of conversation without missing a beat.

In the following days, they all shared meals, but Jhavet

dominated the conversations. Between his words, the weight of apologies and confessions hung unspoken in the air between her and Ellian. It picked at the scabs over Cirelle's heart.

Ellian stopped asking her to attend summons, taking Jhavet instead while Cirelle remained at the manor. She told herself it didn't matter, that Jhavet was useless enough here anyway, so he might as well go.

It was a cold comfort.

Sometimes, she wondered what would happen when she left. She had less than a year remaining in her stay.

Would they even wait that long before they tumbled together? It was like watching a fall in slow motion, the slide toward the inevitable. During Jhavet's free time, which was often enough when Cirelle's temper snapped and she ushered him away, the man would stroll the gardens or while away hours in the gaming parlor with Ellian.

Twice, Lydia tried to reassure her, to repair the damage Cirelle had done to their friendship with her foul temper, but Cirelle wouldn't let her. The bitter beast that lived in Cirelle's chest told her she deserved this. That this was her punishment for every failure in her life.

She sought ways to keep her hands and mind busy, but her songs only brought her scraps of peace. Occasionally, she would retreat to the garden and play for the florafac, but her hands quickly grew stiff with winter's chill and her breath puffed in the icy air.

Her thoughts were plagued with visions of Ellian's gentle hands caressing Jhavet's arms, his lips leaving a line of kisses down Jhavet's throat. How long until Ellian took Jhavet to bed to wash away the memory of her presence there? Like she had used that sweet soldier boy Gadd, so long ago.

She spoke rarely to Ellian now. Jhavet brought back the stories of new items received in bargains, and she dutifully recorded and filed everything away.

The normal trade of clients remained. That, too, was Cirelle's dominion after the first time Jhavet had shadowed her at a meeting and carelessly agreed to barter away more than Ellian had listed.

Issen remained mostly absent, save a few brief, fruitless meetings. He spent much of his time traveling the length of Faerie, seeking any clues about this mysterious necklace and turning up little. Too much of sidhe history had been shattered when Ayre took the throne, too many deaths and too much upheaval. Much information had been lost. It seemed the queen was their only key to the necklace's mystery, but Kith's progress remained frustratingly slow.

Cirelle's only real respite was organizing what little of Ellian's rebellion as it grew. The connections he'd made the night of the Midsummer Festival were starting to bear fruit, odd faeries here and there committing to his cause, or dropping off tidbits of information. She collected them all, but still had no true clues regarding the Lock.

She took Kith's reports, but they were each the same. He was slowly insinuating himself into court, but was no closer to the queen herself and rarely had any new information of note.

How long until the Lock was secure? Would she even see it safe before she was forced out of Faerie?

As time went on, the chasm between Cirelle and Lydia also widened as the soldier left Cirelle's bitter company for Shai's. Ellian's smiles at Jhavet grew a little softer each day, and Cirelle continued to wither.

And then there were the claimhte. Oiche's offer hung in the air, waiting. Could they use the aid of the Shadowed to hunt down the Lock? Would it be worth trusting such a cause to them? The knives were the one thing Jhavet did not touch, not after Cirelle had snapped at him violently when he reached for them.

It was the only time he'd quailed at her reprimands, terror flickering across his face at something in her eyes.

Forty-Nine

Ellian watched Cirelle's shoulders tense as Jhavet placed a hand on his shoulder, commenting on the softness of his shirt.

To her credit, the princess kept her voice steady, if a bit sharp, as she pointed out, "it's your turn, Jhavet."

With a small smile, Jhavet turned back to his runes. "Hm… all odd numbers… I'm going to swap my three for your six." He pointed to Cirelle's stones, laid out in front of her. Flat and smooth, the gray runestones were carved with numbers, the lines worn from age but still readable.

Shai and Lydia had quite wisely begged off this game night, instead choosing to poke around in Ellian's storage rooms for eclectic weapons to try out. They claimed it was imperative to settle a wager between them, but he didn't blame the two for avoiding the tension that made the air thick and hard to breathe every time he and Cirelle were in a room together.

No matter how hard they both tried, it seemed they could not avoid stinging one another like nettles with their very presence, his wounds reopening every time he saw her smile, or watched her tuck a stray lock of hair behind an ear.

Right now, she hid her pain well, but it was there in a faint shadow around her eyes, the stilted motions as she took the piece Jhavet pushed toward her.

For his part, Jhavet seemed completely oblivious to the invisible sparks that flickered between Ellian and Cirelle. He smiled and laughed and teased, and every time his hand reached out to touch Ellian's forearm or shoulder, Ellian tensed. A battle waged in him, this deep and intense craving for closeness competing with the guilt at seeing Cirelle's walls grow higher and thicker.

And yet, she'd been the one to close the door between them. He'd offered her everything, and she chose her home and her waiting prince. Part of him knew that was unfair, but pain twisted any logic into something darker, something tainted.

He hadn't brought Jhavet here for this. The man was supposed to bring some much needed levity to his home. A buffer between Cirelle and Ellian, since Shai and Lydia were all too often wrapped up in each other. Or Lydia would be busy giving Ellian vicious looks while stealing the princess away for private chats. But that hadn't happened at all. Instead, it had only grown worse.

"Your move," Jhavet nodded at Cirelle. She swapped one of her tiles for a draw from the bag in the center of the table and gave a vicious grin as she flipped it over.

"Three, four, five, six." She pointed to her runes. "Guess that means I win."

Jhavet just smiled. "Looks like." He leaned over to pick up the bag and return his runes, deliberately brushing Ellian's hand as he did so. "Rematch?"

Ellian caught Cirelle's stare locking on that small spot where Jhavet's thumb had brushed his knuckle. She swallowed. "Not tonight. I think I'll turn in."

"But it's early yet. I haven't even finished my glass of wine."

"I have some reading to do, and I'm tired. I'll see you to-morrow." Stiffly, Cirelle swept her runes into the bag and left.

Ellian had remained silent the whole time, tongue glued to the roof of his mouth. Everything was spiraling out of control and it seemed he could not stop it.

No. You could stop it. Just push him away.

But as Jhavet's hand came to rest over his, cool as mortal's hands always were, the tight bands of pain around his heart loosened, ever so slightly. There was a comfort in being wanted, after he'd bared his soul and been rejected for it.

"Come," Jhavet said with a smile as he returned the rune bag to the table drawer. "Let's try a round of Pelabet." He pointed to the small table in another corner and tugged Ellian up to follow him.

Ellian went without protest. He could beg off, follow Cirelle, apologize to her all over again. But it was a dog chasing its tail, that conversation. They'd both said everything that needed to be said. Multiple times.

Setting out the pegs in the small table's holes, Jhavet was silent for an unusually long time. After the game was set, un-characteristically pensive eyes met Ellian's. "I'm not completely clueless, you know."

"What?"

"Are you two… together, somehow? Did I interrupt some-thing by coming here?"

Ellian blinked. Never before had the convivial, blissfully innocent Jhavet given any indication he noticed the tension in the manor. "I… no. We're not. And we won't be." He paused, swallowing back a sharp lump in his throat at saying those words. "A lot has happened during her stay here. It's made us… prickly at each other. I'm sorry you're here for it. But we aren't together, in that sense."

This time, Jhavet's smile was soft, and once more his hand slipped under Ellian's. He turned it palm-upward to grasp Ellian's fingers gently. "I… If I can help make things easier for you, whatever it is that haunts you… I want to."

There was more in his eyes than simple friendship, a slow and gentle fire that made the brush of his fingertips dangerous. Something Jhavet had been dancing around since the day he arrived.

"I… appreciate it," Ellian murmured, the words feeling large and clunky as they left his throat.

Another grin from Jhavet, that wide and infectious smile. "I'll take that as the thank-you that you can't say." His hand gave Ellian's a small squeeze. Then his fingers loosened, but didn't retract. Giving Ellian the choice to stay or go.

He didn't pull away.

This is folly.

But there was a vast, empty hole growing inside him, and it was a small balm, this man's attention and gentle adoration. Something to fill that void, to ease the pain that lingered day in and day out.

He twined his fingers with Jhavet's, so cool and gentle.

When Jhavet leaned forward over the tiny table, their game forgotten, Ellian met him halfway. The kiss was sweet and simple, tasting like the effervescent human wine Jhavet had been drinking. In the brush of his lips, Jhavet asked a simple question, one old as time itself.

And Ellian said yes.

Fifty

Today a familiar restless energy overwhelmed Cirelle. An urge to do a thorough cleaning gripped her and would not let go. Lydia had reluctantly allowed herself to be corralled into a thorough scrubbing of the Archive, but Jhavet was nowhere to be found. Ellian had left early this evening to call on Vilitte, who'd been poking around for more information regarding the necklace and the queen. They couldn't rely entirely on Kith; Ellian always had a backup plan.

It was now than an hour past the time Jhavet should have risen, and three since Cirelle had roused from her bed, consumed by her racing thoughts. Enough. She wouldn't coddle him any longer, and he *would* help clean.

She stomped to the man's room and knocked on his door, with no answer. "Jhavet!" she called, pounding louder on the door until it rattled in the frame.

Her effort was rewarded with a fuzzy reply from within the room.

"You're late for Archive duty!"

Another indecipherable mumble, and the sound of movement within. The door clicked open.

The sight that greeted Cirelle was like a slap in the face. A sleepy-looking Jhavet blinked at her from within his chambers, wearing only a blanket from his bed draped hastily about him. But that wasn't what made her eyes sting with sudden tears or her breath catch. The waft of scent that emerged from his room was unmistakable, honey and woodsmoke and rich earthy tea. And another, mustier smell that was all too recognizable.

"Get dressed!" She snapped, her voice cracking on the words. "Be at the Archive in half an hour." If the door had opened outward, she'd have slammed it in his face. Instead, she whirled and fled to her room before she could break down in front of him. When Cirelle got to her chamber, she barely got the door shut before she collapsed against it, unable to breathe through the shattered glass that suddenly filled her lungs.

How could he?

But she knew the answer. She was the one who had told Ellian no. Still…

He couldn't even wait until I was gone. Had there been a bit of revenge in the gesture as well? The cruel sidhe nature that Ellian hated, coming to the fore?

Over long minutes, Cirelle's tears subsided as her sorrow burned away into a slow-simmering anger. Of course she didn't expect Ellian to pine for her forever, but he could at least have held off longer than two measly months. She stood, and made a resolution as she found a handkerchief to wipe her eyes and nose. No, Ellian would never see how savagely this cut her. She would return to her duties with the same cool politeness and never let her sorrow touch her face. She'd build a ball of ice around her heart. Cold and indifferent, she would become what Faerie—what Ellian—had made of her.

For the next few days, Ellian avoided her. Coward. The few guilty looks he cast her way revealed enough, especially at mealtimes when Jhavet would trace a fingertip up Ellian's forearm and compliment a piece of jewelry. But her anger could not last forever, and eventually cooled to a foggy numbness, a dull and distant ache.

Lydia and Shai were anything but ignorant of the growing tension. One night, the three women clustered in a parlor with a deck of Nightswheel cards. Earlier, Jhavet had been particularly cuddly with an increasingly uncomfortable-looking Ellian, before the two of them slunk off together.

"What an ass," Shai muttered as she played her card.

"I thought he was your friend," Lydia said.

"Yeah, that's why I can call him an ass when he's being one. Want me to go rattle some sense into him?" This last was at Cirelle.

She shook her head. "It won't help. He knows. But… I did the same thing once. After Briere and I were over. It hurt so much, seeing her when she visited court, unable to touch her. So I found someone else who wanted me, who could clear my head. Something to get me out of my own brain. That's all Ellian is doing."

Shai snorted. "You're being a lot nicer about this than I'd have expected."

"What else can I do?"

The sidhe grinned. "Want me to find you a little side piece too? I know a few people who'd be up for helping you clear your head. Not sidhe, though. There's this pretty little lotrre I know—"

"Certainly not," Lydia huffed as she played a matching card and scooped up both.

Cirelle laughed. "Thanks for the offer, Shai, but no. I think I just need to accept things as they are."

"Easier said than done."

With a sigh, Cirelle replied. "True, but it's all I have."

And it was, at least for another week. Archive duties were over for the day, and Shai and Lydia were up in the garden sparring. The worst of winter was through, but frost still rimmed the plants. The two soldiers little seemed to mind the cold, but Cirelle chose to stay indoors and work on Yratla's song. She was close to finishing it, a rousing melody to invoke beauty and awe. She'd learned to cope for the missing finger decently enough, but suspected it would always make music more difficult.

When Ellian's boots sounded out in the hallway, she thought little of it. He often walked past. But tonight, the jingling stopped outside the door, just out of sight. Her fingers stilled, the notes dying.

She actually heard Ellian's steadying breath before he entered. His eyes were carefully silver, but his expression was pained. "I need to talk to you."

"So talk." Setting the lap harp aside, Cirelle crossed her hands in her lap, lacing the fingers together. Her chest still tightened to see him hurting, and she hated it. "What is it?"

"The sidhe have a rotating revel, one that alternates hosting duties. I usually don't even attend, but I put in a bid to host the next. Adaleth couldn't resist the bait, and he's granted it to me."

It took a moment for his words to sink in. "Here? You're going to have the sidhe *here* in your home?"

"It's the best chance to ferret out information hiding among the court. Kith's reports have been ineffective. But... I need someone I trust implicitly for a very specific task."

Cirelle swallowed. Faerie intrigues had cost her a finger, and Ellian's machinations left Issen's hand blackened and stiff. What would this task take from her? "What? Do you need me to flirt with one of Adaleth's courtiers? Slip truth potion into someone's drink?"

His fingers couldn't seem to stay still, nervously twisting his rings. "I… I need someone to watch Jhavet. As host, I can't be with him all night. And he… he doesn't understand the danger these fae pose to him. I tried to explain, but he just—"

"Was Jhavet." Cirelle had finally banished the man entirely from the Archive after he'd ignored her warnings about the dangerous items one too many times. She could imagine how he'd treated Ellian's caution, with a smile and a dismissal.

A lump formed in her throat, and she had to force words around it. "You want me to babysit the man you replaced me with." She hadn't intended the words to come out an angry hiss, but there they were.

Ellian flinched. "I know it's a lot, but if I put Shai or Issen on it, the other sidhe will see them with him and know I'm guarding him. It'll be like hanging an even bigger target on his back, marking him as helpless. You… you're both humans in my household. It would only seem natural if you stick together. And you know the dangers. I trust you."

Her hands gave a sharp pang, and Cirelle realized she was clenching them so tightly they'd cramped. How could Ellian ask this of her? If Jhavet got himself into trouble it would be his own fault. He'd had every warning. Maybe it'd serve him right.

"Do you love him?" Another phrase she hadn't planned to say. But she had to know.

"I…" Ellian paused, closed his eyes, and took a long breath. "He's under my protection."

That was neither a yes or no, and Cirelle couldn't bring herself to ask a second time. Technically, he'd only agreed to answer questions relating to the quest for the Lock and Key, or ones that related to her. "And I'm just one of your minions, here to guard your innocent lover so he doesn't suffer like I did for your plans."

Another flinch, another deep breath. "I don't order you like a minion. I ask as one friend to another."

That word hurt worse than anything he'd said yet. *Friend.* That was all they were now, and the most they'd ever be.

"Why me? Why not Lydia?"

"Because she'll be too busy watching you."

She didn't deny it. He was right. Cirelle massaged her aching hands. "I'll do it. But only because no one should be left to the mercy of Adaleth's people."

Ellian closed his eyes and turned away, but not before she saw a glimmer of pink ringing his irises. "Thank you."

Her heart skipped a beat at words so anathema to the fae, an acknowledgement of a debt owed. Before she could respond, he was gone.

Fifty-One

THE EVENING OF THE PARTY arrived all too quickly. Cirelle's nerves were frayed like thin rope, while the dark spots under Lydia's eyes grew deeper every day. Cirelle could only imagine Lydia's terror at the idea of Adaleth here, or the Queen who'd taken Cirelle's finger. Neither had responded to confirm their presence at the party, but could walk in at any moment.

By contrast, Jhavet was elated at the idea of a ball, enchanted by the concept of so many glamorous sidhe in one place. But he'd only met Ellian and Shai and Issen. When Cirelle tried to warn him about the sidhe's deadly games, he would nod and claim he understood, but there was a nonchalance to his responses that worried her.

And so she fortified herself for an evening of tailing Jhavet and keeping him out of trouble, as well as praying to all her gods that Adaleth wouldn't make a scene of the event. But the fact that he had granted Ellian hosting duties did not bode well. The prince almost certainly planned *something*, but what?

She rose early that day, long before the sun had set. After she'd bathed, she dabbed a rich scent of crushed lilies and spice on her wrists and behind her ears. For headwear, she chose to acknowledge her royalty. Ellian had not told her to keep it a secret. So she wore a delicate tiara covered in a network of sapphires.

She'd spent her free time all week searching every spare wardrobe for the perfect gown, a sidhe one in layers of shimmery indigo gauze that shifted gray or lavender in the light. The most striking feature, however, was the neckline. It plunged deeply in both the front and back, baring skin only fae dared show. Not even Nycenine fashions were so brazen.

Tonight, Cirelle felt brazen.

She made sure her room was well locked before slipping the key into a skirt pocket and making her way to the ballroom.

Ellian was already there, directing the brownies as they scurried about. The room was utterly transformed, brilliantly lit. Tables rested near the door, stacked neatly with food and drink. The floor, recently polished, gleamed like glass.

But she spared only a glance at the room before Ellian turned and her breath caught in her throat.

He wore his usual filigree boots and snug breeches in shining jet-black leather, but had topped it with a long coat in a rich red silk. A loose white shirt lay casually unlaced to bare his collarbones and just a bit of his smooth gray chest. He'd eschewed his usual heavy jewelry tonight, wearing only his rings. His hair was loose, and did the sapphire gleam of those locks shine a bit brighter tonight?

Stars, he was beautiful.

Ellian froze when he saw her, pausing mid-sentence in conversation with a brownie carrying a tray of pastries. His gaze flickered up and down the length of her.

The brownie slipped away as she approached. Cirelle's tongue suddenly felt large and clumsy in her mouth. Her eyes fastened on his lips, and how badly she wished he would grin rakishly at her again instead of this wall they'd thrown up between them.

The silence lapsed into awkwardness, and Ellian turned aside. "I need to finish preparations," he said, suddenly brisk and businesslike. But after a step, he twisted to look at her, a hint of his old smile curling his lips. "You look…" he paused, as if trying to find the right word. "Perfect."

Before she could reply, he'd turned away, calling out to one of the brownies and striding across the ballroom.

She was saved from deciding what to do next by Jhavet's arrival. He walked through the doors and gave her that Ysaan bow. "You look stunning," he said, "Like the sky at dusk."

Cirelle knew it was meant in kindness. She doubted Jhavet had a deceptive bone in his body. But she was still forced to squash down her rage to give him a brittle, polite smile and nod.

"You look nice, too," she said, the words tasting like dust in her mouth. He did, and that was what hurt. For Jhavet, the colors were practically neutral. He'd chosen a knee-length robe in his usual style, high-collared and sleeveless to display his toned, muscular arms. The color was a brilliant cloth-of-gold, bringing out a rich warmth to his mahogany skin. The robe was embroidered all over in a thread of deeper gold, in a pattern of stylized lilies. It laced up the front with burgundy ribbon, crisscrossed in an intricate weave that must have taken an hour. He wore form-fitting dark breeches, just glimpsed between the hem of the robe and the rust-colored boots he'd donned instead of his usual sandals.

Her gaze froze on the boots while she realized why he'd worn them. Sandals were no good for sidhe dances, after all. Doubtless he and Ellian would dance the evening away. Cirelle would be left to watch, only to babysit Jhavet when Ellian was pulled from his side.

She gritted her teeth and tried to think of something else to say, but Jhavet's attention had already darted away. The man called Ellian's name and crossed the ballroom, greeting Ellian with an affectionate hand on his shoulder and light kiss on his cheek. Even Jhavet, taller than she, had to lift on tiptoe to do so.

It was like swallowing nettles, watching them. For a brief moment, Ellian's gaze flickered to her, but Cirelle kept her face cool and unreadable. She hoped.

She asked the brownies if she could assist, but as she expected, they declined. This left her with little to do but wait. Chairs lined dotted the walls of the ballroom for those that would want a break from the dancing. She took a seat in one of these while she tried not to watch Jhavet and Ellian making preparations together, hand in hand. Sitting here was stifling, in this room where she'd danced with Ellian.

It seemed so very long ago.

The ballroom was a completely different chamber from the enchanting one they'd danced in, or where Shai and Lydia had sometimes practiced their swordplay when the weather was too icy for the garden. Tonight the lights were bright and golden. Sconces along the walls provided illumination, though the chandelier above also glimmered with strings of clear crystal that scattered the light into brilliant rainbow flecks.

The gilded ornamentation along the walls had been polished to a gleaming sheen, and iridescent chips in the stone floor sparkled.

Along the far wall, a small dais stood a few inches above the rest of the floor. Cirelle supposed that was where the musicians would play, and wondered who it would be. That question was answered when several brownies carried in petite instruments and began to set up on the stage. These were garbed more richly than she'd ever seen them, in strangely-tailored fae clothing of coppery brown velvet and deep green silk.

Lydia showed up before the guests did, taking a seat beside

Cirelle. She, too, had dressed well, though she didn't look comfortable about the emerald silk jacket, or the tight collar of the buttoned shirt beneath it. Lydia followed Cirelle's gaze to Jhavet and Ellian laughing together as they debated the placement of a table. Her hand slid into Cirelle's. "Only nine more months," she said. "Then we'll be home and you can move on."

It was meant as a reassurance, but those nine months felt like an eternity as she watched Ellian bend down and whisper something in Jhavet's ear that made the man lower his gaze and smile softly.

Soon, the sidhe began to arrive, brownies greeting them at the door and showing them to the ballroom. The music started, in haunting melodies that fit a cold winter's night. Cirelle browsed the food and drink that had been set out, sampling small pastries and sweet fruits, small cubes of some soft white cheese, and bite-sized sandwiches of cold meats and herbed bread.

She steered well clear of alcohol, taking instead a small cup of tea. It was a spiced blend, and its warmth seemed to calm her anger as she sipped it in one corner near a pillar. Lydia stood next to her, but when Shai arrived and tugged Lydia reluctantly onto the dance floor, Cirelle waved her on. "I'm not going anywhere. If you absolutely must, you can still keep an eye on me while you dance. And I'll be fine. I know the rules and no one will dare hurt me in Ellian's home."

She wasn't sure if that applied to Adaleth and the Queen, but neither of them had arrived. Yet. Hopefully they never would.

Jhavet had little need of her guardianship at the moment either, glued to Ellian's side while they greeted newcomers.

Her eyes wandered the crowd. Issen was here, mingling. He had greeted Cirelle briefly, but spun back off into the crowd. Eavesdropping, she was certain. Cirelle also caught sight of Dirilai among the revelers, wearing a white gown that hung in asymmetrical layers on her willowy form. Kith stood among a circle of fawning admirers, looking distinctly uncomfortable at the attention, and Cirelle grinned at that.

The festivities here were so much more like an Arravene ball than that Unseelie Palace revel. And yet they were unmistakably fae, with their rainbow hues and a few outfits that would make a courtesan blush. What would her Arravene courtiers make of this, she wondered?

She'd lost sight of Jhavet, and cursed herself silently as she circled the column to find him. She need not have worried. He and Ellian had joined the ranks of the dancers, swaying slowly. Jhavet's head rested against Ellian's shoulder, and Cirelle fought back a sudden pressure behind her eyes.

"Still here, hmm?" A rich voice purred behind her. Cirelle startled, nearly spilling the last of her tea. She turned to find a petite sidhe woman standing behind her, the one who had taunted her the night of the Singing Mountain. Meivre. One of Adaleth's Inner Circle.

Her violet hair was loose now. Wine-colored cosmetics made her fuchsia eyes startlingly bright, while her lips were stained a deep black. Her dress was the color of a berry stain, baring one long pink leg in faerie fashion.

Meivre gestured with one long-nailed hand at Ellian and Jhavet's dance. "I see he's already found another pet," She tilted her head. "What did you do?"

"What?" Cirelle blurted, before she remembered that she shouldn't talk to this woman. Meivre was in Adaleth's pocket, and who knew what part she played in his games?

The woman flicked her eyes back at Ellian and Jhavet. "Oh please," she said. "Don't play stupid with me, human. He's playing the oldest game in the book by flaunting that boy in front of you, and you know it."

Cirelle didn't answer. Whatever was going on between her and Ellian, it was none of this woman's business.

Still.

There was a streak of deeply vicious faerie cruelty buried deep in Ellian. She'd seen it turned on Adaleth. What if this whole thing with Jhavet was partly a ploy to make her regret turning him down? Petty faerie vengeance?

Ellian twirled Jhavet into a turn with a laugh, and that doubt burrowed deeper.

Do you love him?

He's under my protection.

Ellian hadn't answered her question.

"There are two ways to handle this, you know," Meivre said calmly. "If you let envy eat you alive, he wins. But the game of jealousy goes both ways. He's not the only one with power here, my dear." She set aside her wine glass and held out a hand. "Dance with me." It wasn't really a question.

"I think not," Cirelle said flatly, taking another sip of her tea. "Why not?"

The princess gave her a flat look. "You told me not to act stupid. A sidhe does nothing without a selfish motive, and I've even less reason to trust you than anyone else here."

"Ah. Perhaps you speak truth. But you also know a fae cannot tell a direct lie, yes?" She peered up from beneath dark lashes. "So you can believe me when I say that in this, my motive is simple. I saw his pink-stained eyes fawning over you at the autumn revel. As much as it must pain you to see another in his arms, so it will cut him to see you in mine. That is my goal. Is that plainly-spoken enough?"

"Why?"

Meivre grimaced. "I also trade with your kind, and Ellian seeds your realm with tales of his own bargains, while destroying any mention of my name he finds in the human world."

It had worked. Cirelle had read nothing of a fae named Meivre in her research.

"So you want to make him jealous by dancing with me?"

The woman nodded once more. "Precisely."

"And only a dance?"

A sly expression seeped across Meivre's features. "A dance is all I ask for now. It's not all I may offer, but it's the only thing you will be agreeing to at this time." She cocked her head again. "Is that clear enough for you, too-clever human?"

Cirelle opened her mouth to decline. But this woman was a part of their opposition in the great game for the Key and the Lock. An enemy, offering Cirelle an open hand.

Could she use this?

At that same moment, the music slowed, the song ending. She had a clear view of Ellian and Jhavet as they smiled upon one another, Ellian's eyes glinting the bright blue of joy. Their faces drew closer, and Jhavet stood on tiptoe so their lips could meet. Cirelle's stomach twisted into a hard knot.

"A dance, and a single dance only. That's all I agree to," she said hoarsely, setting aside her teacup and holding out a hand to Meivre.

The woman took it with a small smile of triumph. Her smooth skin was warm, as warm as Ellian's. Her fingers twined into Cirelle's.

"I think you'll find me a pleasant enough partner," Meivre said, leading Cirelle out to the dance floor. "You're taller, so you lead."

Meivre settled into the embrace as Cirelle's hand came to rest on her bare hip where the dress gaped open. Something about that small touch of skin on skin sent a little thrill through Cirelle, and her breath caught for a moment.

Meivre must have heard it, for she made a small, pleased

sound in the back of her throat that set Cirelle's pulse to racing. She covered her furiously beating heart by leading them into the crowd of twirling dancers, like leaves scattered by a lazy gust of wind.

To her credit, Meivre was indeed a good partner, her steps sure and graceful, following where Cirelle led. There was something comforting in her soft femininity, an entirely different sensation from the confident power of Ellian's embrace. It was like standing near softly glowing embers instead of the blazing heat of a bonfire. Meivre's scent was a summer garden after a storm, roses and damp earth.

Only a few steps into the dance, Cirelle's eyes sought out Ellian. He and Jhavet danced nearby. His eyes blazed the brightest orange she'd ever seen them. His lips were set in a hard line, his brow lowered in a simmering fury.

For just a brief second, Cirelle felt guilty, but it quickly faded, replaced by a triumphant sort of anger. *Yes.* This was exactly what Ellian had done to her for weeks. How had she become this pitiful, sulking thing? So what if Ellian had taken another. That also meant he could not claim her affections if she chose to place them elsewhere. Even if it was just a single dance.

Cirelle was not weak. She was Queen of the Shadowed, had faced down danger, had skirted death. She'd saved Ellian's life. She was not one to be undone by mere rejection. A matching fierceness blazed in Meivre as the two women smiled at each other. Cirelle had not known that such vindictiveness dwelled in her heart, but it felt good, a simmering heat in her belly.

And Meivre was a joy to dance with in her own right, her slender body appealingly soft in Cirelle's arms. The dance was over all too soon, and the music faded away into a brief silence. For a few tense seconds Cirelle held Meivre close, staring perhaps a moment too long at those dark lips, into her brilliant pink eyes.

As the musicians started another tune, Meivre stepped out of Cirelle's embrace. "One dance. It was all you agreed to and all I'll take. However, I would not decline were you to offer another later." Then she slipped away into the crowd.

Cirelle shook her head and made her way to the edge of the room, taking a glass of cool, clear water rather than hot tea as she scanned the room for Jhavet. Despite her recent display, she'd made a promise and she intended to keep it.

She didn't have to look far. Ellian was striding toward her, Jhavet on his heels. She set her shoulders, lifting her chin and meeting his glowing-ember gaze squarely. But Ellian walked past her to the refreshment table. He selected a pastry and came to stand beside her, his stance too deliberately casual. Jhavet pored over the foodstuffs a few paces away as Ellian said in a low, dangerous voice, "You know better than to consort with one of Adaleth's Circle."

"No deals were made, no secrets revealed. It was a single dance, no more, no less. Unless there's some specific reason you wish me not to be courteous to our guests?" She lowered her voice. "Besides, if she's talking to me, we can use that."

His eyes blazed like fire when he looked at her, his pastry still untouched. "It's too dangerous."

"What, like getting poisoned or losing a finger? Also," she said quietly and coolly, "I'd cast a glamour over those eyes if I were you, unless you want everyone here to know your mind as clearly as I do."

He frowned, but silver washed over his eyes. "This is about more than just the plan."

Cirelle croaked a bitter laugh. "What, is it about us? You said that was over. You made damn sure of that with Jhavet, too." Her voice was quiet, barely more than a murmur, as her eyes flicked over to find Jhavet still out of whispered earshot, grazing the food table.

"You told me no. Not once or twice, but thrice." He sounded wounded, like a petulant child.

"What else could I do?"

He stared down at his uneaten pastry.

Cirelle said, "We both broke each other's hearts. And no matter how many pretty men you seduce, it won't erase me from your bed." In Ellian's shocked silence, a soft thump sounded behind him. Jhavet had ventured within hearing range, his dropped fruit tart broken to pieces on the floor. He looked like a puppy that had been kicked.

With a single choked sound, he turned and fled.

"Jhavet!" Ellian said. He took a step, but Cirelle held up a hand to stop him.

"I'll go," she sighed, her anger draining into weariness. "You can't leave your own party. I'll make sure he's safe." At his doubtful expression, she added, "I promise."

A quick glance at the room showed Lydia distracted as Shai awkwardly pointed at her own feet and showed the guard a fae dance.

Cirelle took her chance, and left in search of Jhavet.

Fifty-Two

CIRELLE TRIED ALL THE obvious areas first. His favorite place, the library, was dark and empty. The garden, his rooms, even the gaming parlor, all likewise unoccupied. Well, except the gaming parlor, but that amorous couple certainly didn't include Jhavet.

For a few tense minutes, she feared he'd sought refuge in Ellian's private chambers and debated whether to seek him there, in those rooms now forbidden to her. But she'd only search there if the rest of the house turned up nothing.

She found him in the Archive. Jhavet sat cross-legged on the floor in a corner, his back against the wall, a hopeless look on his face. Cirelle tried to remember if she'd ever seen Jhavet without a smile. Now he looked hollow, like a doll on a shelf. He'd somehow stolen not one but two entire bottles of faerie liquor, probably on his way out of the ballroom.

From the looks of it, he was well into the first bottle. He watched her approach with distant eyes, but didn't stand or move, other than to take another swig. Cirelle flopped down on the floor next to him, careless of her elegant gown. She'd just swept this damn floor yesterday anyway. She snatched up the other bottle, pulled the cork, and took a gulp.

It burned fiercely the whole way down. Most certainly not wine. The flavor was spicy and sweet, like cloves and sugar, with a fiery alcoholic burn. She bit her lip. What could she say? 'I'm sorry' didn't really seem adequate.

"He lied to me," Jhavet said, his voice quiet and small.

"Can't," Cirelle murmured, savoring how her second swallow of liquor seared its way down her throat.

"What?"

"He can't. Lie, that is. The fae can't. They're incapable."

"But…" Jhavet sighed, twisting one of his many small braids around a finger. "I asked him, you know. About you, if you and he are… well, lovers, or something. He said no. So I thought… well, I thought that was it." He took another drink directly from his bottle. Cirelle wondered if it were the same fiery vintage she held or something gentler.

"It wasn't a lie. Not really." She paused. The man deserved the truth. "It happened. But in the end, it didn't work. He asked for a final answer and I told him no. So when you asked, he was telling the truth, if not the whole story."

"Do you love him?" Jhavet's voice was barely more than a whisper.

Cirelle didn't answer.

"And then I showed up, and he used me." Jhavet pulled his knees up to his chest, throwing his arms around them in a tight ball. It was such a helpless, childlike gesture that Cirelle felt compelled to ask him the next question.

"Jhavet, have you figured out what his eye colors mean?"

"Yeah. They're moods. Orange is anger, bright blue is joy, purple is…" his voice drifted off awkwardly.

"I know," Cirelle said. "But has he ever looked at you with pink in his eyes?"

Another pause, then a small nod.

Oh, it hurt. How that knowledge hurt. It shouldn't have. She knew that, but it didn't make her feel it any less. She washed away the wave of sorrow with another long, fiery swig. "Pink means he cares about you. Maybe loves, even." A sob hiccupped out of her throat. "Stars, I'm a mess."

"We both are," Jhavet admitted, and held his bottle up in a mock toast. She clinked hers against his, and they both drank deeply.

"A fine tangle he's worked us into, isn't it?" Jhavet asked.

Cirelle said with all the gallows humor she could muster. "If you're getting tangled, try easier positions first."

Jhavet burst into a laugh, nearly choking on the last of his bottle and setting it down with a thump. "I doubt there will be any more of that, not after tonight."

The despair in the words smote her. She leaned her head back against the wall, staring up into the dimness of the Archive ceiling. "I saw you on the dance floor tonight, you know. He does care about you. He was worried about you and the fae, wanted me to watch and keep you safe. That wasn't easy for him to ask. And I meant what I said. I had my chance, and it's long gone."

The alcohol was making her limbs heavy, and Cirelle closed her eyes. Jhavet's head leaned into her shoulder, and she startled. But she didn't push him away.

"I'm sorry," he said softly.

"Not your fault."

"That's why you hated me so."

"Well, that and the annoying fact that you always have to *touch* everything," she said.

He giggled, and soon they were both overtaken by that helpless laughter that consumes the very drunk and the very weary. They fell into one another, laughing so hard they cried, until they both giggled themselves out.

Cirelle sighed, the room spinning pleasantly. Everything seemed strangely distant, like she was underwater. "I think we're drunk," she mumbled blearily.

"Uh huh."

"We should go back to our rooms," she said. "Ellian is going to be so mad that we drank the faerie alcohol." With an effort, she stood and held out her hand to help Jhavet up. He stumbled and nearly knocked her over before they steadied themselves.

When it became apparent neither was going to fall over immediately, Cirelle looked up into his face. She'd intended to push herself away, but the liquor had muddled her thoughts. Instead she found herself clutching his strong arms for support, admiring the inky darkness of his eyes.

She could blame it on any number of things; her fight with Ellian, that dance with Meivre that had started her heart beating, the alcohol, their shared sorrows. But whatever it was, a similar madness seemed to have taken over Jhavet as well. Hesitantly, he tilted his face closer, and she met him halfway.

She could taste the faerie wine on his lips, and wondered if her own were coated in fiery, sugary spice. Even drunk, he was good at this, tender and gentle.

I can see what Ellian likes about him now, she thought.

It was like being doused with icy water.

"No," she managed to croak. "We can't."

"Why not?" The carefree smile that crossed his face was so like the old Jhavet she knew. In any other situation before today, it would have irritated her. Now, after his hopelessness earlier, it was heartening.

She counted on her fingers. "One, we're drunk. Two, Ellian. Three, did I mention drunk? And I still don't know if I even actually like you much when I'm sober." She grinned at the last one.

He shook his head and shrugged. "Yeah. We should sleep."

They stumbled together back to the residential wing. They passed a few sidhe along the way, who had apparently started claiming free rooms for trysts or for their own overnight bedchambers. Cirelle was glad she'd locked hers.

She helped Jhavet to his room, watched him fumble to unlock the door, and warned him to lock it again on the other side. The latch clicked, and she hoped he would find the bed.

When Cirelle made her way unsteadily back to her own door and dug the key out of her pocket, it seemed an insurmountable task to get the damn thing into the keyhole. Her clumsy fingers were still fumbling at it when she heard a now-familiar voice behind her.

"Curious," Meivre said.

Cirelle whirled and dropped the key. "What are you doing here?" A wave of vertigo washed over her and she leaned against the door to steady herself. The key had clattered to the floor a few feet away. It might as well have been a mile.

Meivre ignored Cirelle's question and moved closer. "What were you doing, being oh so friendly with your rival, hmm?" She placed one hand lightly under her chin in a pantomime of deep thought. She leaned in even closer and inhaled. "And if I'm not mistaken, that's the aroma of faerie wintersweet, a strong beverage for a human like you. It does, however, get the blood *flowing*, does it not?" Her grin grew wicked. "Now… whatever were you and that handsome human man doing, sequestered all alone in that room barred to anyone else?"

Cirelle's thoughts were fuzzy, but one lurched to the front of her mind. "You were spying on us?"

"Not particularly," she murmured. "At least, I missed the most interesting bits. But yes, I watched you enter, and I watched you both leave much later, hanging on each other's arms and looking far less like rivals than I would have expected."

"He was drunk," Cirelle said defensively, pressed back against her own door as if she could sink through it by sheer force of will.

"As are you," Meivre pointed out, "which is precisely my point." She stepped even closer, and Cirelle was enveloped in the scent of flowers and thunderstorms. She remembered how soft Meivre's skin had been and found herself staring a little too hard at those full, black-painted lips. A jolt of something warm shot through her and pooled in her stomach.

"Ah," Meivre murmured. "You feel it, don't you? The wintersweet." Her smile grew wicked as she leaned in. Her breath warmed Cirelle's ear as she whispered, "Do you know what the fae use that for? I told you earlier I offered more than just a dance. Perhaps now you would consider such an offer. I would give you a night you would never forget, one that would eclipse all human lovers you may ever take."

Cirelle swallowed, her pulse pounding so hard it was difficult to hear Meivre's words. The wintersweet had taken her now, her every nerve screaming, a heat burning low in her body. Her voice, when she spoke, was hoarse. "In exchange for what? The sidhe never offer anything for free."

Meivre's chuckle was low and deep, and Cirelle felt the vibrations of it thrum through her body. "Oh, my sweet. Sex is already an equal bargain, when done correctly. I require no more than what pleasure you choose to give this evening. I offer no more than my own body, tonight. But if you let me in, I can show you such wondrous things." Her eyes closed, her lips so near Cirelle's she could almost taste them already.

"Why?" she asked, her voice barely a whisper. "Is it just because I'm Ellian's?"

"Mmm," Meivre made a small sound that was neither denial or affirmation. "Some. But you also intrigue me, human princess. Ellian is not alone in his attraction to your kind. Humans have a passion that burns fierce, and you in particular are so very fascinating. The ripples of what you've done spread far and wide, princess. I know you killed the Scath. And it's been decades since someone got so fully under Ellian's skin. You're more than his usual pets, and I want you."

It was those last three words that pushed Cirelle over the edge. So simple. *I want you.* Such a clear declaration. A fae could not lie, and the sheer knowledge that this woman desired her was more than enough while the wintersweet burned in her.

She met Meivre's lips with her own, the sidhe woman making a low sound of pleasure deep in her throat. Meivre pressed the length of her body into Cirelle's. The princess's hands tangled in Meivre's hair, holding her close for kisses until she was forced to pull away to catch her breath. Meivre took the opportunity to trail a line down Cirelle's throat with lips and tongue, along the edge of Cirelle's breasts where the dress bared the space between them, and down the exposed skin to the waist of the gown at her navel.

"Wait," Cirelle managed to gasp as Meivre knelt and pressed her lips against the lowest bit of exposed skin on her belly. The sidhe's hands gripped Cirelle's hips over the layers of her dress. "Key. Room," were the most coherent words Cirelle could form. Meivre grinned wickedly and leaned back to let Cirelle pick up the key and clumsily open the lock. She grasped Meivre's hand and pulled the woman up and into the room, closing and locking the door again.

While she was throwing the latch, the fae woman trailed the long nails of one hand lightly down Cirelle's bare back. She shuddered.

"Tell me yes," the faerie said in that voice like a soft purr. "Tell me I can have you tonight."

Cirelle didn't even hesitate. "Yes."

It took little effort for Meivre to slide the edges of Cirelle's gown over her shoulders, pressing small kisses along the edge of Cirelle's shoulder, at the nape of her neck. Her upper half now lay bare, the chill of the winter-cold room caressing her skin.

Cirelle pressed both her palms hard into the wood of her door to steady herself. Meivre gave her little time for that, pulling her around for another set of feverish kisses. The faerie tasted like rose tea, floral and sweet.

Meivre's hands trailed shivery lines along Cirelle's skin, an electric touch that shot straight to her core and left her gasping. It was like tiny jolts of heat, a pleasant prickling sensation unlike anything Cirelle had ever felt.

"That," Meivre said, "Is one of my gifts." Her fingers trailed along Cirelle's skin, a delicate tingle. Meivre flattened her palm against Cirelle's stomach and triggered a sudden rush of shivery, electric pleasure that forced Cirelle to lean back against the door with a low moan.

"Mmm," Meivre nipped at Cirelle's earlobe. "Make that sound again, princess."

Fifty-Three

CIRELLE AWOKE TO COOL sunbeams peeking around the edges of her curtains. Though she was thirsty and exhausted, she was also delighted to realize the wintersweet had not left her with a headache or queasy stomach.

Meivre's head rested on her shoulder, the sidhe's fine, violet hair tangled and draped across Cirelle's chest. Their legs were entwined beneath the blankets, Meivre's sidhe heat keeping them both warm despite the winter chill. Cirelle shivered at the memory of last night. Meivre had been true to her word; it was an experience Cirelle would not soon forget.

The small motion must have awoken Meivre, for she yawned and sat up, stretching, unfazed by her own nakedness.

The woman turned her head and caught Cirelle watching her. A satisfied grin touched her lips. Her cosmetics had mostly worn away, with smears of purple around her eyes and one smudge of her black lip stain trailing across a cheek.

Cirelle's cheeks warmed at Meivre's knowing smile. "Um," she fumbled for words as she slid out of bed. That awoke a host of aches, but none she regretted getting. She stared despairingly at her elegant gown crumpled on the floor. The nightdress she had set out yesterday was still across the hall, as she'd intended to wash and remove her cosmetics before going to sleep. It seemed silly to don the pretty dress again just to walk across the hall, but she didn't want to leave her room nude. Not when a host of sidhe could be wandering the halls.

So instead, she rummaged in the chest she hadn't opened in months, the one that held the clothing she'd worn when she first came here. As she settled the knee-length tunic over her head, the linen triggered lines of fire on her back, and she hissed in pain before she recalled Meivre's long nails scoring her skin. It had seemed like a good idea at the time, but now she was paying for it. She lifted the snug leather trousers and sighed at the thought of wrangling them on and lacing them up just for a quick jaunt across the hallway.

Meivre hadn't said a word, sitting cross-legged on the bed, still with that sleepy, satisfied expression on her face. She seemed in little rush to get up.

Cirelle was still staring at her trousers, trying to muster the energy to don them, when a sudden knock shook her door.

"Cirelle!" The voice on the other side was unmistakably Ellian's, and he sounded worried.

Cirelle glanced back at Meivre with a panicked expression, but the fae woman raised an eyebrow and grinned wider.

"Well, this should get interesting," Meivre purred.

"Hide!" Cirelle whispered, but Meivre shook her head.

"It would do little good, my human princess. He knows my scent, and the room must reek of it."

The knocking grew louder. When Ellian called her name again, a hint of urgent fear had crept into his voice.

Cirelle set her trousers aside. It would take too long to put them on, and Meivre was right. He'd know immediately what she'd gotten up to last night anyway. *Fine.* Still, she opened the door only enough to peek out. "What is it?"

"What did you do with Jhavet?" Ellian asked her angrily, eyes flickering between the emerald-green of worry and the orange of anger.

One brief, guilty flash of memory, of that unfortunate kiss in the Archive. When she spoke, her words were cautious. "What do you mean?"

"I can't find him. He's not answering my knock, and even though I have a skeleton key, I can't enter his room when he locked it. Permissions and damnable fae rules."

"Oh," Cirelle said. "He's probably still sleeping. He, um. Well, he may have stolen some faerie wine and drank it."

"What?"

"I walked him back to his room. He went in and locked it behind him."

Ellian blinked. "Oh." Then his eyes widened. His chin lifted as he took a sniff of the air. His gaze scanned her face and Cirelle realized her own cosmetics probably looked as smeared as Meivre's. His voice was low. "You reek of wintersweet. And…" he peered over her head through the crack in the door.

"Hi," Meivre chirped cheerfully from behind Cirelle. She was now holding up her own gown, looking worse for its night spent balled up on the floor. She shrugged and slipped it over her head anyway.

Ellian stood silently in the doorway, hands clenched into tight fists, eyes blazing. "Meivre," he hissed. He lifted one hand as if to push the door open wider, but Cirelle smacked it away.

"Tsk, tsk," Meivre clucked her tongue and pouted at him with her lipstick-smeared mouth. "Seems you aren't welcome here. Too bad."

"Stop it," Cirelle hissed at the woman. "Don't make this worse."

"You," Ellian said, seething. "You come into my home, accept my hospitality, and then this?"

Meivre was busy staring into a small mirror, fastening the hooks of her dress. She didn't even look at Ellian as she replied. "I took only what was willingly offered."

"You used her," he growled.

"Enough!" Cirelle shouted, throwing the door open so she could stab Ellian in the chest with an accusing finger. "I don't belong to you, and I gave nothing that wasn't my own to give! You have Jhavet, and I can give myself to someone else." Her voice had risen, and she felt a new sort of heat enflame her cheeks as the simmering anger filled her.

"You know this isn't about that. It's about the fact that you chose *her*, of all people." The rest of the sentence remained un-spoken. *One of Adaleth's people*, he meant.

"I daresay she has no complaints," Meivre said.

"Meivre, please leave," Cirelle sighed, suddenly tired of it all. She looked to Ellian. "You can follow her or you can come with me while I open Jhavet's door for you with that skeleton key."

Meivre said her farewell by slipping an arm around Cirelle's waist and planting a kiss on her cheek. "See you soon then, my pet," she murmured, and left.

Ellian's hand shot out and grasped Meivre's wrist as she slipped by. He gave her a look that could melt stone. "This isn't over," he told her, voice so quiet that Cirelle could barely hear.

"Oh," she smiled wickedly and darted a glance back at Cire-lle, "I'm counting on it." She tugged her hand free, and he let her go. She sauntered slowly down the hallway with little care for how Ellian's orange eyes shot daggers at her back.

Ellian turned back to Cirelle, and his eyes flicked down to her bare legs and back up to her face. She scowled. "I'm going to get dressed," she told him, pointing across the hall. "Then we can go to Jhavet's room and I'll wake him to prove he's there." Picking up her key from the table where she'd left it last night, she locked her room, walked across the hall, and shut the parlor door in Ellian's face.

She still rushed dressing, dampening a washcloth and scrubbing off as much of Meivre's floral scent as she could, along with the smeared cosmetics. A brush quickly and painfully yanked out the tangles in her hair, and she chose a quick, simple day dress to throw on.

Ellian's rage had cooled into sulky indifference when she opened the door. When she stepped out into the hall, he trapped her between his arms by placing them against the door. He did not touch her, and she could easily have slipped under them, but Cirelle was so startled that she froze in place. His eyes were a deep indigo blue as he asked her in a very small voice, "Why? How could you?"

For some reason, Cirelle's anger surged. Perhaps she should have felt pity, or guilt, but that's not what bubbled up within her. "Perhaps I gave it as much thought as you did when you bedded Jhavet. I saw a thing I wanted, and I took it."

His eyes flashed bright yellow and he dropped his arms, turning away from her. "Let's go find him, then." He sounded almost as weary as she felt.

Outside Jhavet's room, Ellian tried knocking, but there was no answer. He gave Cirelle his skeleton key, which she used to open the door and slip inside. She left the door open as she stepped in and let her eyes adjust.

Jhavet hadn't even made it to the bed. He was sitting up in a well-padded armchair, head thrown back and snoring softly, still wearing his clothes from the evening before. Cirelle pointed at him while she raised an eyebrow at Ellian.

Her victory might have held a little more savor if Ellian hadn't looked quite so relieved. He waved at her to leave the room, and she did, locking the door again behind her. "I promised you I would watch over him and ensure no fae tricked him, and I did," she said softly. "But I never promised you that I would withhold my affections from others."

He took a long, shaking breath. "She's one of *his*." The prince's, a member of his Inner Court.

"Dirilai is deep in the Unseelie Court, too. But you use her when you need to. What if I can use this?"

"It's too dangerous. Meivre is old, and cunning."

"Too late now, either way. What's done is done."

Ellian shook his head, ending the conversation as he handed her the skeleton key once more. "Make sure Jhavet is awake and presentable at breakfast, for we still have guests, and I will not see either of you embarrass me further." He turned away, muttering, "Maybe Lydia can keep you both in order."

She watched his back retreating down the hall, and only now found guilt. It struck her so deeply she leaned against Jhavet's door for support. Stars. She knew what it had done to her that day she found Jhavet looking tousled and covered in Ellian's scent. Now she'd done the same, with someone he loathed.

How had they all gotten so tangled in this mess? Her old life seemed so far away, caught up in these games and intrigues.

She sighed, rubbing her eyes and unlocking Jhavet's door yet again. She had the feeling he would need ample time to be made presentable. Not to mention, she still needed a proper bath. If she didn't scrub off all of Meivre's rosy scent, everyone at the table would know how she had spent her evening.

"Jhavet," Cirelle said softly as she shook his shoulder, but he still slumbered on. More vigorous attempts to wake him also failed, until she ventured across the hall to find that the reliable brownies had left a magically-chilled pitcher of water in his parlor as usual.

When a glass of this water was flung in his face, Jhavet

spluttered awake. He groaned and let his face sink into his hands, moaning miserably. "My head feels like it's been trampled by a thousand horses. Please just let me die."

It seemed the aftermath of whatever liquor he'd had last night was not as kind as the wintersweet she drank.

"Well, that's not an option," Cirelle told him, tugging on his arm to haul him to his feet. If he'd truly resisted, Cirelle could not have budged him. But Jhavet groaned again and stood shakily. His face had a greenish tinge to it as she helped him across the hall to his vibrantly-hued parlor.

She got him settled in a sofa and made him slowly drink a full glass of the cool, clear water while she started brewing peppermint tea. A scone came next. Maybe the dry, bready texture would settle his stomach.

"Um," Jhavet said awkwardly after a few tense seconds when the scone threatened to come back up. "How much do you remember of last night?"

Cirelle hesitated. "How much do you?" she responded.

He met her eyes miserably. "Everything. Until I entered my room."

"Oh."

"I have to tell him, Cirelle. About the kiss."

Panic flooded her. That would only make things so much worse. "No," she said. "You can't."

He looked at her miserably. Stars, he looked so young right now, when he was vulnerable like this. It was the complete opposite of the confident, cocky man he usually appeared. He started to say something else, then hesitated, curling up on the sofa and tucking his feet beneath him. "Cirelle?" he asked hesitantly.

"What?"

"You really think he cares for me, too?"

With a sigh, she poured the magically-heated water from the

enchanted teapot into a cup with a sachet of mint. It also gave her a moment to form a reply. "Yes," she admitted, though the word left a bitter taste on her tongue. "You said his eyes had been pink around you... he can't lie with those. If you saw it, it's real."

Oh, how that hurt, that Jhavet had the thing she wanted most and could never have. She bit her lip. "But you really can't tell him about the kiss. Please."

"Why not?"

She sighed, closing her eyes for a moment and stirring the tea while it steeped. After a deep breath, she poured the water over the peppermint leaves and spoke. "I had a... liaison, with one of our guests last night, after leaving you in your room."

Jhavet's eyes widened, and a bit of his old self peeked through as he gave her a friendly grin. "Ah, so that's the glow," he teased.

"It's not a joke," Cirelle snapped, then softened her tone when she continued. "Ellian found out this morning." She handed him the mug of tea, admonishing him, "Drink this. It'll settle your stomach. When you didn't answer your door, he came to mine. She was still there. He was... less than pleased."

Without warning, she had a sudden memory of those deep, deep blue eyes. The color of pain. It hit her so quickly that it forced the air from her lungs. She looked at Jhavet and remembered how it had felt when she first saw Ellian hold his hand so protectively, or the knives that pierced her when Jhavet would press a light kiss on Ellian's cheek.

How cruel they'd all been, stabbing each other in a futile attempt to patch up their own wounds.

Cirelle didn't realize she was crying until she felt Jhavet's callused fingertip brush a tear from her cheek. Suddenly, that kindness meant so much. Just a hand extended in friendship. She fell beside him on the sofa and let him enclose her in one arm as she wept against his shoulder. Strange, how he had irritated her so. But they were both caught in this ugly, tangled web together.

When she'd cried herself out, Cirelle wiped her face with one hand. "I'm sorry. I don't even know how this all got to be such a mess." She stood. Jhavet looked steadier now, his face a less green as he took a sip of the tea. Cirelle realized she wanted nothing more right now than to escape this room, to be alone with her thoughts. "You can get yourself ready now, can't you? I need to wash as well."

When her hand was on the doorknob, Jhavet spoke softly. "I won't tell him about the kiss."

"Thank you."

"If I were you, though," Jhavet grinned, "I'd be more worried about what happens when Lydia finds out."

Fifty-Four

By the time breakfast was served, Cirelle had washed and dressed again.

She'd tried not to think of what her liaison meant as she soaked her injuries in the tub, cataloging her bruises and sore muscles. Meivre had not been a gentle lover, and last night had contained pleasure and pain both. But Cirelle had embraced all the sidhe woman had to offer on both sides of that coin.

It was a new sensation, to know that pain could be as intoxicating as its opposite.

Something Ellian already knew well. And Adaleth.

It turned Cirelle's stomach to realize she might have something in common with the vicious prince. And yet, the memory of last night made her breathing quicken, as if the wintersweet still coursed through her, a burning under her skin, an itch she needed to scratch.

Still, she forced those thoughts aside as she finished her morning routine. Breakfast would be served soon, and she had no idea how many guests remained in the manor. Doubtless Ellian had evicted Meivre already, leaving Cirelle left to untangle the knot she'd made of herself, Ellian, and Jhavet.

Worse, Jhavet had been right. How would she tell Lydia about this? The woman had been protective of Cirelle when it was Ellian, let alone this unknown faerie. Well, hopefully Shai could talk her down. It was the best Cirelle could hope for at this point.

The bell for the meal rang. Straightening her shoulders, Cirelle stepped out into the hallway.

"Hello, my pet," a familiar voice murmured, and Cirelle whirled to find Meivre leaning against the wall beside the door.

"You're still here?" She blurted before she could help herself.

Meivre grinned wickedly. "Of course." She'd also bathed and donned a new dress in deep violet lace, lacking any sort of lining. It somehow concealed just enough to tease, while also leaving nothing to the imagination. A bold choice, one meant to flaunt herself before Cirelle and Ellian. Cirelle found herself staring, her heartbeat quickening, a small and slow shiver trickling through her body.

Maybe the wintersweet did still linger, after all.

"Ellian can't force me to leave. Not yet," Meivre said, looking insufferably smug with herself. She began walking down the hall, and Cirelle fell into step beside her.

"Guest rights," Cirelle realized.

Meivre nodded. "Most of last night's revelers would rather return home, but I think I'd like to stay here." She glanced sideways at Cirelle with a knowing smile. "Two more nights and days can be a long time."

Cirelle shivered. Would she repeat last night if Meivre asked? She hadn't lied to Ellian. There could be a way to use this in their efforts to find the necklace's owner and the Lock. It was possible Cirelle could ferret out something meaningful from this.

Or at least that's what she told herself.

Still… "This isn't wise," Cirelle said.

"Wisdom is not always one of my stronger suits," Meivre said teasingly.

"*You* don't have to live here," Cirelle said, perhaps a trifle sharply. "Two days hence, you will leave, and I will still be here. I'd rather not make Ellian angrier before you go."

"He'd forgive you. And for two days, I could help you forget about him. I assure you, it would be a pleasant enough experience for you. You *did* enjoy last night, did you not?"

Cheeks burning hot, Cirelle glanced aside. But Meivre held her position, staring at her with those teasing eyes. She cleared her throat and told the sidhe, "Meanwhile, you get the enjoyment of getting under Ellian's skin. Much as he did to you, when he took that man into his bed."

Thoughts churning, Cirelle remained silent the rest of the walk, until they entered the dining room. Every eye turned to the pair. Perhaps half a dozen guests remained, plus Ellian at the head of the table and Jhavet to his right. Lydia sat a few spaces away, next to Shai.

Still, there was nothing untoward about arriving at the same time as Meivre, not in the eyes of the guests. It was all too possible they'd merely crossed paths on the way here.

Ellian knew, though. His eyes narrowed, cautiously silver.

Cirelle met hsi gaze squarely and tried to ignore how violently her cheeks flamed as she took her seat and elegantly placed her hands before her, fingers laced together. Meivre took a seat next to her.

A moment later, conversation resumed. One guest turned to Ellian. "As I was saying, I must get the recipe for those honey cakes your brownies served last evening. They were quite delicious."

It was idle talk, and it eased the tension. Ellian turned to nod at the guest who had just spoken with a small smile. Did everyone else see the brittleness of that grin, or note how tightly his hand gripped Jhavet's?

Lydia's gaze flickered toward Meivre and back to Cirelle, her concern plain. Cirelle tried to give her a reassuring smile and shake of the head as chatter began again around the table.

Other than Lydia's questioning gaze, only one guest continued to stare at Cirelle. She recognized them, this faerie across from her who watched her so keenly. This same sidhe had once given her a cryptic warning at the Unseelie Palace, words that had led Cirelle to the kitchens, to the poison meant for Ellian.

Destroying that poison had lost Cirelle a finger. Her knuckle ached, and she resisted the urge to run a thumb over it.

The sidhe still had the most unusual eyes Cirelle had ever seen, pure black like a crow's, without even a hint of white anywhere. Skin the color of scorched soot stretched over sharp features. "Meivre." The greeting was cheerful.

"Ren," Meivre sighed.

The sidhe stared at Cirelle and gave an unnerving grin. Slim shoulders gave them a waifish look. Long black hair, a single streak of brilliant cobalt blue framing their face on one side. Their jacket seemed cobbled together from assorted scraps of black fabric of every conceivable type. Velvet-flocked satin brocade, rough cotton, brushed silk, all stitched together in haphazard shapes as if Ren had raided the floor of a tailor's shop and assembled the jacket from whatever they found. The collar was a proliferation of glossy black feathers that fanned out over their shoulders like a mantle.

The faerie regarded her with a small smile, head cocked slightly.

"Ren, do try not to be rude," Meivre said tartly.

Cirelle couldn't have said how she knew those unreadable orbs flicked sideways to regard Meivre, but they did. Ren returned Meivre's comment with an impish grin, teeth startlingly white. "Why start now?" they replied cheerfully with a small shrug. "I do have a reputation to uphold, you know."

"As an unwelcome irritation," Meivre replied coolly.

"Indeed," Ren plucked a small pastry from their plate and took a quick bite. There was a sharp and deliberate quality to their movements that reminded her of something, but she couldn't recall what. "And no one is quite as enjoyable to irritate as you are, my dear." Ren cocked their head in the other direction to regard Cirelle again. "But I confess, I'm more fascinated by your dining companion this evening."

"Well," Cirelle spoke before Meivre could interject. "I suspect you'll find I'm not so easily annoyed," she said with a small smile.

A little snort from the other end of the table caused her to glance up sharply, only to find Jhavet covering his mouth and turning away. The separation of the party into two groups had given the illusion of privacy, but the table was small enough that he'd obviously overheard.

Ren either chose to ignore Jhavet or didn't notice.

"Why are you even still here?" Meivre asked Ren, her voice disdainful. "You never stay after the drama is over."

"Is it over?" They tilted their head again, glancing meaningfully at the head of the table. "I do believe the true drama is just beginning, Meivre. There are heavy portents hanging over this house right now. What occurs here will have… repercussions."

Something in the words and tone sent a shiver down Cirelle's back and made her pause in lifting a pastry to her lips. But Meivre just waved a dismissive hand. "I can handle Ellian," she said confidently. "Any blowback from him is easily dealt with."

"Not just you," Ren said with their mouth full, having taken a large bite of a ripe strawberry. "For everyone."

"What do you mean?" Cirelle asked.

"Exactly what I say," they replied with a toothy grin.

When Cirelle looked to Meivre for clarification, the woman only raised an eyebrow. "I told you they were irritating." She pointed at Ren with one long-nailed finger. "Ren claims to have the gift of foresight, but all they do is spout vague warnings. Then later, any time something goes wrong, they can say 'I told you so'."

Ren merely smiled at her derision. "But I'm never wrong, am I?"

"Only because you never say anything specific."

"My dear Meivre, merely refusing to believe something does not keep it from being true."

Cirelle's gut tightened. She'd seen mention of such abilities in her reading on the fae. Prescience seemed to be highly uncommon, but there were still some records of it.

What if Ren truly did have a gift. What if they were correct?

Cirelle asked, "What do you mean, repercussions?"

Without a hint of a grin, Ren turned to her in a small, sharp movement. Those dark, unknowable eyes bored into her, their voice low and ominous. "The choices you make while you remain in Faerie will begin a chain of events that affects both our worlds."

Cirelle had a crawling suspicion they were talking about the Key and the Lock, the gates between the realms. She swallowed her bite of pastry, which had turned tasteless and dry in her mouth. "How? Which choices?"

"If I tell you, I run the risk of disrupting it all. My curse is to observe, not to change."

"Don't listen to them," Meivre repeated. "Like I said, vague warnings."

"All I can say is this. Think carefully on what you do between now and your return to your world," Ren said, turning aside. "Or we'll all pay for it."

❦

After breakfast, Cirelle did a quick sweep of the Archive and returned to her private parlor. There were still too many strangers about for her comfort, and she had a book she could read to pass the time.

Predictably, Lydia came to see her.

"Your Highness. We should talk."

Cirelle set her book down and tucked her feet under her, as if curling into a ball would armor her like a hedgehog. "We should."

Lydia sat down opposite her. "What did you do? With that woman?" Blunt.

"It's none of your business."

"I think it is. Your brother sent me here to keep you safe, and yet you seem determined to fling yourself headlong into danger."

"It's not dangerous."

Lydia shook her head, her lip curling. "She's a *faerie*, Cirelle."

Cirelle's temper snapped. "So's Shai."

For once, she'd managed to shock the guardswoman, those hazel eyes growing wide before narrowing in defiance. "That's different."

"Different how?" Cirelle's lips curled into a snarl. "A faerie in your bed is all the same thing, isn't it?"

Lydia's lips thinned, her gaze growing dark. Her hands balled into fists at her sides. "I haven't bedded Shai."

"Yet," Cirelle bit off the word, angry at Lydia's hypocrisy. "But you chide and judge me. You're just like the rest back home, shoving me into the box you want me to fit in. Maybe I'm tired of being a princess. Of rules and propriety and burying my true self."

"And how often did you even follow the rules? When you lied and slipped away from your lessons? When you tumbled Countess Briere?"

Cirelle's voice came out a low growl, and she uncurled from the sofa to stand. "You leave her out of this."

"I would, if you had." A strangled note caught Lydia's words. "You played with fire, both of you acting like besotted tavern girls. You're better than that. And you're better than falling into bed with a faerie."

"With anyone, you mean, if you had a say. My choices are mine to make, Lydia."

Lydia's jaw clenched, a burning light in her eyes that Cirelle had never seen. "Your mistakes, you mean."

The impertinence was astounding. Cirelle gaped, then closed her mouth with an audible clack. Fury consumed her. "Briere was not a mistake."

Something dark passed over Lydia's features, a scowl that twisted her narrow face into something ugly. "Wasn't she? Was it worth it, to risk it all? Was she so good between the sheets that you'd risk everything?"

Cirelle's temper snapped, flaring into white-hot heat that left her dizzy. "I loved her!" The words were a shout, tears spilling free.

Lydia jerked back as if struck.

Hot, furious tears brimmed in Cirelle's eyes, and her fists gripped her skirt tightly. "Is that all you think we were? Is that all you care about? Will Shai just be a bedwarmer for you?"

"No." Lydia lifted her chin, the most disrespectful she'd been with her princess in her entire life. "It might be hard for someone like you to imagine, but not everyone is ruled by what's between their legs." The guardswoman's cheeks were brilliant scarlet, but her eyes glared with a steady fire.

For a few long moments, words failed Cirelle. Angry red sparks obscured her vision. "What did you say?"

They stared at one another, the weight of the air between them heavy and thick.

The guard's words were contrite, but her tone was still sharp and her shoulders were rigid. "I apologize for speaking out of turn, Your Highness." There was nothing of supplication in her voice, though, and she didn't take back the words. The insult still echoed in the air, in Cirelle's ears. Lydia had as much as called Cirelle a harlot. Had insinuated the same of Briere, of Ellian, of Meivre.

A cold rage burned in Cirelle's belly. "Lydia, you are dismissed." The statement was firm, final and icy.

The guardswoman met Cirelle's gaze, an unsettling muddle of emotions lurking in her eyes. "Understood, Your Highness." She whirled on a heel, her movements wooden, and left.

Cirelle retreated across the hall to her bedroom, still exhausted. Perhaps she could nap the day away. But that was not meant to be. Meivre came to her next, and Cirelle's willpower crumbled at the sidhe's sultry smile when she answered the door. The day passed in a dreamlike blur. Once she'd had a taste of Meivre's gifts and skills, Cirelle seemed utterly consumed by the need for them over and over again. It was a new hunger, one that she could not sate.

Meivre was true to her word. For blissful hours, Cirelle did not think of Ellian at all. Only Meivre's kisses and slender hands and that teasing, tingling shock of her fingertips.

They barely even paused for a meal, Cirelle slipping into her parlor and retrieving the small snacks left there by the brownies. But eventually, even they were spent, and Meivre left with a lingering kiss. "I'll be back tomorrow," she promised.

Cirelle probably should have taken that nap, but guilt gnawed at her like rats. She couldn't leave things with Lydia like this.

Lydia answered her door warily.

Cirelle spoke first. "I don't want to fight with you."

The soldier was quiet for a moment, opening the door and

gesturing Cirelle in with a weary sigh. "Neither do I." They sat on the edge of Lydia's bed. Silence held, an awkwardness grown up between them like weeds. Neither could unsay the things they'd barked at each other hours ago.

Cirelle asked softly, "So where do things go from here?"

"I don't know, Your Highness." Lydia scrubbed her face with one hand, a weight in her eyes. "Too many months stretch between here and home."

"Just nine more."

Anguish painted Lydia's features. "And who will you be then? How deeply will Faerie have sunk its claws into you?" The guardswoman shook her head. "We already aren't the children we once were. If we met now for the first time, we'd share little more than a polite word or two. Even were we both soldiers, or both nobility, do we have anything in common?" Lydia's hands rested in her lap, and she spoke down toward them. "The only thing that links us, Your Highness, is our childhood. Is who we *used* to be."

Cirelle's breath halted in her chest. "Doesn't that count for something?"

Lydia shook her head. "Not enough."

Tears burned. "If it's nothing, why did you even come to Faerie?"

The laugh that burst from Lydia's lips was a harsh sound. "Void take me, Your Highness, are you seriously that dense?" When she looked up, her eyes had grown dark, thick honey and pine needles mingled. For the first time in Cirelle's memory, tears lingered there.

The stare held for a few moments.

Cirelle's stomach lurched, a falling sensation with nothing to grasp for support.

"Oh, Stars."

Lydia broke the stare, glancing once again at the back of her hands. "Don't worry. I never harbored any foolish thoughts. I saw how you were with Briere." She shook her head. "Even if I were a duchess, I would never have been what you wanted."

Cirelle couldn't speak.

"So that's your answer, Your Highness," Lydia's voice was uncharacteristically soft. "But now we are barely even friends, aren't we?"

"We are."

"No," Lydia shook her head. "We're people bound together here in Faerie by the home we both left behind. I remind you of the things you want to forget, and you grow farther from me every day. Maybe it's best if… if when we return, I will be a guardswoman and nothing more."

The tears stung, spilling suddenly and freely down Cirelle's cheeks.

Lydia closed her eyes. "I think I need to be alone for a while." Her voice was thick.

All Cirelle could manage was a forlorn nod.

When she reached the door, Lydia spoke again. "Your Highness, there's a small part of you that will always love your Countess, isn't there? No matter what comes in the future?"

The word came out a choked rasp. "Yes."

It was a painful, cutting farewell, but there was no mistaking it for anything other than a goodbye.

Fifty-Five

CIRELLE DIDN'T DINE WITH Ellian or his other guests that day, or the next. Instead, she spent more time in Meivre's arms. According to standard guest etiquette, Meivre was given food and drink during her stay, including wine she shared with Cirelle.

"I'm sorry you have to go," Cirelle murmured dreamily as Meivre lay curled against her side. "Soon I'll be stuck here with two moon-eyed couples and I don't know if I can bear it."

"Ah," Meivre's voice held a note of seriousness as she said, "And what if that weren't the case?"

"What?" Everything seemed slow and syrupy, drenched in faerie wine. She wasn't sure she'd heard Meivre correctly.

"What if you didn't have to stay here?"

The thought stirred a conflicting slurry of emotions. What if she had the option to leave? The first thing she felt wasn't relief, or joy. Instead, she remembered those small moments here. The times she'd sipped her favorite earthy, aged tea in the parlor and played Sailor's Runes with Toben. The florafae in the garden dancing playfully as she played a lilting tune. The library full of unread books. Lydia showing her how to anchor her fighting stance during their lessons.

And so many memories of Ellian, laughs and teasing smiles and games of strategy, hours spent lying in bed and spilling bits of their lives' stories to one another.

A pang of sorrow plucked at her. Those days would never come again. Now Cirelle was stuck here as the eternal fifth wheel on a cart that did not need her.

"If you want," Meivre said, "I may be able to buy the remainder of your servitude from Ellian."

Everything froze. Cirelle swallowed. "You can do that?"

Meivre nodded. "Yes, but we'd need both your permission and his."

What about Lydia? But Cirelle knew. Lydia's bargain was to remain in Faerie as long as Cirelle resided in Ellian's home. If Cirelle left to stay with Meivre, Lydia could go back to Arraven, far away from faerie games and machinations. Shai could visit her there. Lydia would be free.

Could she really abandon Ellian and Jhavet? Her heart raced, the room spinning and her chest tight. Her thoughts bounced rapidly. She knew this sensation. This rush of energy, this giddy high. In this jittery, bold state, she often made decisions too quickly, too impulsively.

But right now, that didn't stop her. She *had* to do this. To free everyone of the misery she'd wrought. Ellian could be free of her, Lydia could go home to heal.

But. "Ellian will never agree."

"You can convince him. Only Ellian or one granted permission to bargain on his behalf can seal such a bargain."

Oh, Stars.

Cirelle sat up suddenly, bracing herself when her head spun at the motion. "Wait. *I* have it. Permission."

A few minutes later, she tugged the book off the shelf, the one where she'd carefully hidden Ellian's letter giving her permission to make any deals on his behalf, for the remainder of her time in Faerie. She handed it to Meivre, who gave it a quick read, then stared at Cirelle with wide eyes. "Stone and sea and sky."

A mad grin crossed Cirelle's face, and she laughed. "Yes." It felt like bubbles all through her body. The fae wine, or just a normal bout of manic energy? "Just let me grab my things. I'll be back here in a moment."

A few minutes later, Cirelle returned to the library with the claimhte in their sheaths, belted to her waist. She'd taken only one other thing from Ellian's Archive; she still wore her translation earring. Not technically theft. *You may use or trade anything in my Archive, for whatever purpose you deem fit while you remain in Faerie.*

Still, it felt like a crime, but she would return it after she left Meivre's. Cirelle also held the pack she'd brought to Faerie, containing just her old human clothes and the magical pendant that led her to the faerie ring where she'd summoned Ellian.

Ellian.

Her breathing stopped.

Could she do this? Leave him behind?

But until they were parted, neither of them would be able to heal.

The silvery, shining light that coursed through her and left the world pleasantly hazy around the edges said yes. This would be a clean break. Easier for the wound to knit back together without them picking it open every day.

And in less than a year, she'd be back in the human realm. In the meantime, Meivre could be a tantalizing distraction.

Yes. This would work.

Cirelle penned a quick goodbye letter to Ellian and Lydia and Jhavet, addressing it and placing it on a table where one of the brownies would see it. "I'm ready."

The faerie linked hands with her, their fingers twining together. "Princess Cirelle telArraven, do you agree to transfer the remainder of your servitude in Faerie to me, Meivre of the sidhe?"

Last chance now.

Meivre licked her lips and smiled wickedly, and Cirelle's heart skipped a beat. She blinked slowly, her eyes suddenly heavy. "Yes."

"And do you make the same agreement on behalf of Ellian of the sidhe, to bestow the remainder of your service to me, Meivre of the sidhe?"

A deep, shaky breath. Cirelle nodded. "Yes."

Fifty-Six

MEIVRE'S HOME WAS A warren of stone, its pale gray walls polished to a smooth shine and lit by steady faerie lights. Art of all kinds littered the place. Sculptures rested in niches along the corridors, made of every imaginable material — marble, clay, copper. Where other homes had windows, her walls were dotted with paintings, the subjects eclectic, save a single one. Portraits of Meivre lay scattered throughout her tunneled home, some ancient and faded with time, others looking as if they were painted yesterday, all in a myriad of styles.

Cirelle followed the sidhe wordlessly through corridors as wide as Ellian's manor halls.

"We all used to live underground, once, the daoine sidhe," Meivre said, taking in Cirelle's wonder. "In barrows and hollowed-out hills. The old ways have been forgotten by so many, tossed aside." One pale pink hand trailed along the wall as they walked. "But not me."

Cirelle nodded. Her footsteps felt light, her head spinning. She was free, free of Ellian's secrets, liberated from that home that was far too stifling while Jhavet filled it. And Lydia was free, too, back to Arraven. Safe.

This rabbit's warren was her new home, and Cirelle smiled softly, giddy from the wine or the rush of this new adventure.

In the middle of the hallway, Meivre tugged the princess closer, showering her skin with small kisses. A brush at the corner of her smile, her cheek, the place where her neck met her shoulder.

"Perhaps it is time to show you your room," the faerie murmured.

A shiver ran down Cirelle's spine. "Oh, yes."

❧

Cirelle's room was adjacent to Meivre's, connecting directly to the faerie's bedchamber through an open archway. Two other adjoining rooms lay empty, everything dark and tucked away. There was little privacy, but Cirelle didn't mind. What was a closed door worth, after they'd come to know each other so intimately?

The claimhte were placed in a chest in Meivre's room. Cirelle could still feel their voice in her mind, but they were drowned out by Meivre's presence.

They dined in Meivre's chamber that first night, her servants bringing the food on trays directly to the faerie's large canopied bed. Succulent fruits that dripped juice down chins and made their skin all the sweeter, soft bread warm from the oven, and dark, rich wine that left Cirelle flushed and shivery, magnifying every touch tenfold.

And Meivre showed Cirelle another of her little gifts. Some nights, Meivre's bed was replaced with a field of soft wildflowers and grass under an endless night sky, or a gilded Arravene palace room. Illusions, faerie glamour that exceeded even Ellian's.

"I will admit," Meivre told her as imaginary waves surrounded them on a false beach, "that Ellian is better at glamouring himself, specifically. But when it comes to concealing other people or places, none can top my skill. Not even him."

The days were spent with little thought for time's passage or other duties. Their whole focus narrowed to this chamber, this bed, and whatever tiny, private worlds Meivre crafted for them. Cirelle indulged herself, diving fully into what Meivre offered. The faerie showed Cirelle how to dance along the knife's edge of pleasure and pain, making both all the sharper and all the sweeter. They left only for necessities—sleep, food, baths that only led back to the bed.

And there was always faerie wine, burning a fire through Cirelle's veins that could only be quenched by touch, by sweat and blood and small sounds made in the dark.

Cirelle lost count of the days. Two, three, a week? Then one day, Meivre stirred Cirelle from her slumber with teasing hands, kisses, and little love bites that stung. A faint tingling remained where she'd touched, sometimes a sharp jolt of pain, sometimes a pleasant warmth. Meivre's gift, her sidhe magic, the ability to set nerves aflame with her fingertips.

Afterward, while they lay tangled together, Meivre murmured in Cirelle's ear. "I must leave today, my pet. My usual business has waited long enough, I fear."

Cirelle made a small sound of protest, burrowing her face into Meivre's neck, her hand tangling in the faerie's hair.

"I'll return on the morrow. And make it up to you."

"You'd better."

❧

Left to her own devices, Cirelle bathed and dressed, then emerged from their linked bedchambers for the first time since arriving here As if in a dream, she drifted through the hallways, admiring the art tucked into every corner. She found the music room and wept, a sudden pressure filling her chest, so tight it pushed out the tears. It was even more beautiful than Ellian's, the instruments exquisite, the resonance of the chamber perfect. She lost herself for hours in a trance, the notes spilling from her fingertips like raindrops in a summer storm. They were wild songs, like ripe berries bursting with dark juices, or shadowy silhouettes entwined in darkened corners.

She wrote them all down on nearby paper, and when one of Meivre's servants found her to deliver supper, she left the sheets stacked on the side table and followed the small faerie to the dining hall. Meivre did not have brownies, but some willow-thin type of fae with features sharp enough to cut and skin the color of the moon.

The wine tasted less sweet without Meivre's company, and the fire it stoked within her left Cirelle enervated and restless. So she returned to the music, playing until her fingers cramped and sleep nearly overtook her.

Somehow, Cirelle found her room again. She gave a longing glance at Meivre's bed, now neatly made by the servants. But it wouldn't be the same without the faerie's small, warm body to lie against, and Cirelle slid into her own cold sheets instead.

When Meivre returned, she was not alone. Behind her trailed another human, a man older than Cirelle, broad of shoulder and barrel-chested, with a round, ruddy face and inky black eyes.

He stood sullen, those eyes sharp as a crow's, his mouth a perfect pout. His name was Piotr, and he barely spoke the Trade tongue. But he watched Meivre with a frightening intensity, tilting his head as if memorizing every plane of the faerie's face while they ate supper.

After dinner, while the wine thrummed in Cirelle's veins,

Piotr's canny eyes softened when Meivre touched him. The faerie kept one hand in Cirelle's, the other tracing Piotr's jaw with a feather-light finger until he closed those raven's eyes and shivered.

That night, there was ample room in the large canopy bed for all three of them.

Piotr had been a sculptor in the mortal realm, with roughened hands from chisel and hammer. Those callused, worn fingertips scraped across skin, but his touch remained surprisingly gentle.

Cirelle smiled as she lay atop Meivre's sheets, the world a pleasant fog, her head spinning and her skin hot and slick with sweat. Perhaps it all felt like a dream because it was. Maybe soon she would awaken in her bed at Ellian's manor and return to that old life.

But until then, this world was hers and she dove headlong into it.

Fifty-Seven

"She's gone," Jhavet reminded Ellian for the dozenth time. The tone was gentle, but the words still sliced and burned.

"I know," Ellian snapped as he turned the carved game piece over and over between his fingers. The red stone was polished by the wear of decades, the edges of the fox's snout gone soft. No longer just a mere token, it had become a talisman. A reminder. He set it back down on the table with a clack, their current game forgotten. "I shouldn't have let her go."

"It wasn't your choice to make. She chose to leave." A soft frown replaced Jhavet's usual easy grin. He lifted a hand and set it atop Ellian's, his work-worn hands compassionate as he coaxed Ellian's fist open and twined their fingers together.

Jhavet tried his best, but the man didn't understand. He didn't know what Cirelle had leapt into. Ellian did, and he'd slept miserably since the princess left.

Too proud. He'd driven her away with his mistakes. And now she was gone.

Lydia had shattered at the news, and Shai had carried her back to Arraven, her bargain complete.

The ache in his chest should be familiar by now. Should be

fading. But even with the balm of Jhavet's company, it grew. It ate away at him like a wasting disease. "I'm sorry." Ellian tugged his hand free, but not before giving a small squeeze.

Jhavet's dark eyes watched in empathetic silence as Ellian pushed back his chair and left.

In his room, Ellian paced. He paused, leaning over his desk. Crumpled notes still lay upon it, the brownies forbidden from clearing them away. The same message, penned a dozen different ways, sent so many times. Each and every one ignored, returned without a response.

Meivre had won the game. She'd stolen his favored playing piece, and would never relinquish such a victory. Not for any price he could offer, not for a dozen fortunes.

Ellian snarled and swept the wadded papers onto the floor. Scribbled words, those Meivre could ignore, but she would not pass up the opportunity to gloat if he arrived at her doorstep to beg.

Jisanti knew, he'd suffered plenty of humiliations in his life, some of them at Meivre's hands. And Cirelle was worth it. He straightened, tugged his clothing into place, and headed for the library, Jhavet's favorite refuge.

The man's expression was easy to decipher, as always. Jhavet glanced up from his book with concern plastered on his features.

Ellian spoke first. "I'm leaving. I'll be back before supper, one way or another."

Though the question was a needless one, Jhavet asked anyway. "What are you going to do?"

"I'm going to get her back, whatever it takes."

Fifty-Eight

Cirelle's days were now spent in an aimless cycle. Sometimes, Piotr would spend hours on end in Meivre's sculpting studio, chipping away at a large block of marble while Cirelle whiled away the time in Meivre's arms. Other days, they switched places, Cirelle feverishly translating musical notes onto paper or recording her songs onto an enchanted harp while Piotr enjoyed their host's attention.

The burning jealousy she'd felt for Ellian and Jhavet did not rear its head on the days Piotr spent in Meivre's bedchamber, even when his moans of ecstasy or cries of pain echoed through the halls and punctuated Cirelle's songs. This was not the matter of a heart denied her, then given to another. It was merely pleasure, and there was plenty enough to share.

From time to time, Meivre would leave for a day or two, and Piotr and Cirelle would be left to entertain themselves. Without the faerie there to lead the dance, they worked at their crafts with a single-minded intensity until their fingers bled.

Almost in a trance, Cirelle filled books with her music, tucking them away onto shelves in the music room amidst thousands of other compositions. Poitr's sculpture took shape, a slender form Cirelle knew all too intimately, veiled in sheer silk and lost in a dance.

As it neared completion, Cirelle stood beside the life-size sculpture one day and ran a hand along the smooth stone arm, down to the slim hands she knew so well.

"You've a gift," she murmured dreamily as she caressed the silken folds that wreathed the form. How had he managed to render translucent fabric from solid stone?

Piotr dipped his head, a thanks, as he chipped away at the sculpture's feet.

Then, a new sound in this maze of tunnels. A man's voice, raised in anger but the words lost to the echoing stone.

Curious, Cirelle slipped through the doorway and made her way through the halls. The argument became clearer as she drew near, coming from the front entrance to the barrow.

"Sir, you've no permission to enter this home," one of the servants said. Her voice was like mist, ephemeral, ghostly.

"I just need to speak with her," the man replied, a plea.

Cirelle went very still. She knew that voice, a tone like sand and honey, like velvet.

She turned the corner, and her mouth went dry. Ellian was here, and her dreamlike bubble of a world shattered.

"Cirelle!" He stood on the other side of the threshold, the arched door wide open. He lurched forward, but was stopped by an invisible force in the doorway. Wards.

His boots jangled as he pressed his hand flat against the invisible wall.

Before she knew it, Cirelle was standing beside the servant, a single step from crossing that threshold. Her head felt thick, stuffed with cotton, and still her pulse raced.

"What are you doing here?" Her voice, meant to be imperious, came out a quaver. No, this wasn't happening. She'd built this new world around herself, a world of art and music and Meivre's sharp little pleasures. He shouldn't be here.

Ellian stopped pushing against the barrier and dropped his hands to his sides, clenching them into fists. His gaze raked up and down her form, taking in Cirelle's filmy fae gown and all the skin it left bare. His eyes narrowed on the marks at her neck, on her thigh, bruises and the red reminder of teeth buried in flesh.

His gaze flashed orange as a sunset, blue as sapphires. A hand lifted, as if to reach for her, then fell back to his side when she shrank away despite the barrier that kept him out.

"My messages have all been turned away," he said with a glare at the servant. "So I came myself.".

"And I've given you an answer," the servant said in her voice like morning fog. "You're disturbing the mistress's pet." With no more ado, she shut the door in his face.

Cirelle's heart fluttered in her chest. "Wait." She yanked the door back open, staring up into Ellian's startled eyes. Her head spun, and she blinked owlishly in an attempt to settle it. "You shouldn't be here."

He answered her statement with a question, softly spoken. "What has she done to you, Cirelle?"

"Go away," Cirelle said, with more force now. She blinked again, but her eyes couldn't seem to focus, Ellian's form swaying in her vision. Footsteps echoed behind her, Piotr leaving his studio to investigate the commotion.

"Cirelle." When Ellian spoke her name, he said it like a caress, gentle, mournful. He stared at her for a few long, hard seconds. "She's given you something. Your pupils are so wide they smother the gray."

She closed her eyes, tears stinging behind them. She could smell him now, smoke and honey, and it stirred things inside her she'd so nearly forgotten.

"Go," she said again, and this time it was a plea. "I left."

"I'll find a way to get you out of here. You don't know what Meivre can do."

Cirelle barked a laugh, bitter and cruel. "Oh I know quite well what she can do, and she does it so very, very skillfully." She hurled the words up at his face, the world bucking beneath her feet and her belly churning.

He flinched, and she pressed on despite the way her stomach lurched.

"I left, Ellian, and I like it here."

"You can't—"

"I do. Now go." She shut the door.

"Who was that?" Piotr asked behind her in his accented Trade.

She stared at the floor. "An old memory."

ॐ

In her mirror, Cirelle noted the changes in her appearance, but found little room to care. If this was the cost of a dream, it was worth a few dark circles and a little lost weight. It seemed she needed less food daily, sustained only by Meivre's attention and the faerie wine that filled her veins with fizzy, giddy light.

Piotr waned much the same, the area beneath his eyes the color of bruises, his cheeks sallow as he single-mindedly worked to finish his sculpture.

Then one day, Piotr was gone. The statue was finished, a perfect likeness of Meivre, his legacy left behind in Faerie.

He was followed soon after by Dez, a dancer with hair like cornsilk and golden skin. She was lithe and limber, and Meivre spent hours watching her dip and turn and twirl. Her body was covered in twining patterns of scarlet ink, birds in flight among swirls of abstract clouds.

She was an artist too, a painter of skin with needles and pigment. At Meivre's urging, Cirelle became her canvas, her left leg and thigh turning into its own work of art in vivid purple patterns of roses mingled with leaves drawn in thin white scars. Tiny black spiders hid among their thorns and leaves. Meivre's heraldry, the lavender rose and the spider lurking within.

Then Dez, too, was gone, leaving Cirelle alone and once more the sole recipient of Meivre's affections. Her life was wrapped in Meivre's scent of spring flowers and summer storms, the sharp tang of roses and rain. Cirelle had learned much about the thrill of pain and the tantalizing satisfaction of pleasure denied, then at long last, finally granted.

But there was always more to learn.

Fifty-Nine

"Do you miss him?" Meivre asked one day as they lay in bed, her fingertip tracing lazy patterns on the skin of Cirelle's belly. Tonight's illusory landscape was an enchanted grotto, a soft blanket laid upon the stone with water lapping nearby, illuminated by the glow of faerie mushrooms along the walls.

Cirelle, half-asleep, murmured back, "Who?"

"Ellian."

The name was a jolt in the fog, a twist in her stomach despite the pleasant lassitude that had settled into her limbs. *Ellian.* She hadn't thought about him in days. Weeks? Since his visit, at any rate.

What was he doing now? Happy with Jhavet? How long had Cirelle been here with Meivre? Had she faded in Ellian's memory yet, another of his human lovers that had moved on, to be disregarded and forgotten?

Despite the many days that lay between them, her chest still ached to think of him. She rolled over, ignoring the way it made her head spin. "No," she lied.

Meivre was silent for several seconds, her hand going still.

"It must have been lonely there, though, just the two of you for so long, no real visitors."

There was a leading quality to the statement. Not a question, but a tone that begged Cirelle to contradict her, to declare that no, there had been visitors.

Even through her haze, a warning bell rang in the back of Cirelle's mind.

"Ellian is a sad case," Meivre murmured, planting a small kiss on Cirelle's shoulder from behind. "Rather than spending time with his own people, he's left to cavort with other species. They must all have seemed so strange to you."

Again, the question took the conversation by the hand and led where Meivre wanted to go.

Cirelle blinked away the mist that clouded her thoughts, focusing with all her willpower. "All of Faerie is strange to me, my lady."

Meivre propped herself up on one arm, her other hand turning Cirelle's face until their lips met. "And me? Am I exceeding strange to you?"

Her kisses tasted like her scent, like rose hip tea and candied flower blossoms. Vertigo crashed over Cirelle and she rode the wave of it. "Strange and wondrous," she replied with a soft laugh, turning into Meivre's arms as her worries vanished like mist in the morning sun.

That night, Meivre opened a bottle of a new vintage, a faerie spirit that tingled in Cirelle's throat like nettle tea. The rest of the evening was a haze of tangled limbs and the scent of a spring garden, the taste of sweat on her tongue.

Her dreams were fitful, strange things, blurring the line between sleep and reality. Cirelle walked a forest trail in the dark, shivering from an icy chill that danced along her bare arms. The way was lined with tiny, razor-sharp pebbles that cut her bare feet and left bloody footprints behind her. She wore a gauzy faerie garment, and the path was lined with bright, glowing eyes in the shadows. They whispered and giggled, but never came out onto the walkway.

And in the distance, a harp strummed a forlorn melody.

A shift. A new dream. Cirelle knelt on Meivre's floor, the stone hard against her bare knees and shins.

"Tell me about him, about Ellian," Meivre murmured, her hand caressing Cirelle's hair as she circled.

"Why?"

"You belong to me now, don't you, my pet?" She knelt in front of Cirelle.

It was hard to concentrate on the words while the heady aroma of roses and lightning filled Cirelle's nostrils. "Of course."

"You are no longer his, then?" A bite of warning, of displeasure in that voice, and Meivre drew back a little.

"No," Cirelle was quick to reply.

"Then prove it. Tell me his secrets." One long-nailed fingertip brushed Cirelle's collarbone, traced a line down between her breasts, across her stomach, to her navel. Cirelle shuddered, and her head spun dizzily.

Something deep down inside her cried a warning, but it was smothered, drowned out with the need that burned along her skin. "What do you want to know?"

Meivre smiled, a cat's grin, and kissed her. "Everything."

The vision faded, the world lurching beneath her.

Another slip sideways, into yet another dream.

Cirelle dreamt of Ellian for the first time in weeks, of dancing with him in a wintry landscape, a dusting of snow dragging at their feet. It was unbearably cold, her skin like frozen marble.

Ellian held her close, his warmth a balm as he planted gentle kisses against her cheek, her neck, her shoulder. "It's all right," he murmured. "I forgive you."

☙❧

Cirelle awoke hours later, groggy and languid, sheets twined about her legs. Her knees ached, along with several other parts. Her head felt wreathed in clouds, like she still half-slept.

But that wasn't unusual, and Meivre was already awake, breakfast on a tray beside the bed. So Cirelle sat up and ate the delicate pastries, drank the sweet faerie brandy that tasted like oranges and sunlight in dappled meadows, and gave in to another day of Meivre's charms.

Meivre, like Ellian, had occasional visitors. Unlike Cirelle's former master, Meivre's were entirely sidhe. She hosted small dinner parties, Cirelle sitting on the floor beside her chair as Meivre stroked her hair like a loyal hound. It was another of her games, and Cirelle was always amply rewarded for her compliance later.

The other faeries, for the most part, ignored her. She recognized few of them. Shai and Issen never made an appearance, and certainly not Ellian. Once, Dirilai came, but she never dropped a sour expression, like she smelled something faintly rotten.

Ren showed up a few times, always sitting to the side, always silent. They stared at Cirelle with those canny, solid-black eyes in that soot-colored face, showing not even the faintest hint of expression.

Kith was the worst. He began to appear more frequently at Meivre's dinners as the weeks wore on, watching Cirelle with smug amusement. All part of the act? Or his faerie cruelty showing through? She had no way of knowing, and no way of telling Ellian even if Kith did something awful.

Meivre often provided some form of recreation after supper. Occasionally, Cirelle was the entertainment. Often, she would play her harp for the gathered sidhe. Sometimes, there were other amusements she would later try very hard to forget.

The worst night, the one she'd gladly have purged from her memory, happened unexpectedly.

It started with a voice in the hallway. Cirelle was playing on the enchanted harp, recording an old Arravene serenade into the instrument, when she heard the patter of conversation echoing down the hall.

Meivre's voice said something, musical and low. The response was a man's cool tenor.

Cirelle shivered, but couldn't have said why. Her fingers stilled on the instrument. Did she know this man? Something tugged at her memory, a faint thread of fear that told her to run, to hide.

But a curious part of her needed to know, needed to see. She set aside the instrument and made her way to the door, peering out into the hall.

Her eyes met his, a sickly green with a faint glow, and Cirelle's mouth went dry.

He looked exactly as she remembered, skin pale blue, lighter than forget-me-nots, and that pearlescent white hair like moonlight. He wore a black diadem and frock coat, looking every bit the cold-hearted prince.

Adaleth.

Her heart beat like a rabbit's, and she froze in place.

The prince's lips drew into a frown of distaste and his gaze skittered past her, dismissing Cirelle like one would a stray dog passed on the street.

"So you still have Ellian's old pet," he remarked to Meivre, completely ignoring Cirelle.

"Yes." She smiled at Cirelle as they approached. "And it devours him alive to know she belongs to me now, heart and soul. And body. Come," she beckoned Cirelle to follow.

Despite her fear of the prince, Cirelle could not resist Meivre's command. She fell into step behind them, but Prince Adaleth halted suddenly. "No."

Meivre chuckled. "Yes."

"I am your prince," he said in a voice like glaciers shifting. "And I forbid it."

"You come to me for one thing, Your Highness," Meivre said. "And you let me make the rules here. I say she plays." She tilted her head, her reply dripping venom. "What is more deliciously degrading than a human?"

Adaleth looked as if he would vomit.

"Unless you wish to leave, my prince." Meivre shrugged and walked down the hall.

He shuddered and cast Cirelle a gaze that could have frozen her solid. But he followed, Cirelle trailing behind them both.

❧

"Play well," Meivre murmured to Adaleth, "and you'll be rewarded."

The prince knelt on the floor. His head hung low, that snow-white hair covering him like a curtain. He didn't respond, merely gasping in ragged pants as his back dripped black blood onto the stone floor.

"Again," Meivre said to Cirelle. The small crop cracked, and another dark line appeared on the prince's skin. He cried out with something that wasn't entirely pain. Meivre rewarded Cirelle with a kiss and the tingling caress of a hand. "You're a quick learner, my pet."

Cirelle had never wielded a lash before, but Meivre had shown her how the perfect flick of the wrist could make it dance. Her head spun, the thrill dizzying.

I'd take great pleasure putting stripes on that back. Adaleth's words to her, in a time that seemed so long ago. Inwardly, Cirelle laughed at the irony.

Meivre was the conductor of this symphony, Cirelle and Adaleth players and instruments both. After a time, Cirelle was banished to the bed to watch, half in a dream. The world was fuzzy and the air thick. Her blood boiled, leaving her itchy and restless and needy.

Meivre had shown Cirelle the basics, but the sidhe was an artist. Adaleth was putty in her hands. He whimpered, he gasped, he screamed, all at her whims. Cirelle wondered if Ellian knew who had replaced him in the prince's games. Or perhaps Ellian was the one who'd supplanted Meivre in the first place. She shuddered, and the thought was gone like sand through her fingers.

Still, she savored the prince's whimpers of pain. The claimhte whispered their pleasure at such violence from their shelf in the corner.

When it was over, Meivre murmured something in Adaleth's ear, too quiet for Cirelle to hear. After a few long moments and several shuddering breaths, he stood on shaky legs.

"You did admirably, Your Highness," Meivre said as she led the prince toward the bed. She cocked her head at Cirelle, lying on the sheets watching her mistress with greedy eyes. Meivre smiled wickedly as she pointed to the princess. "And as promised, your reward."

Adaleth turned aside in disgust. "That's no reward," he hissed.

"Is it? You won't enjoy telling Ellian you made his beloved moan your name? Or that you made her scream it in anguish? Whichever you prefer."

Though his mouth still snarled his disdain, Adaleth's sickly green eyes glowed brighter and he stared at Cirelle where she lay, her breath held.

This sidhe had wanted to hurt her since the first moment he laid eyes on her, in that sylvan disguise. Even if it was only to wound Ellian.

"I doubt she'd bear my touch, anyway," the prince growled, though Cirelle could see him considering it, a cruel and greedy gleam in those cat's eyes. "I have promised not to touch her against her will," he admitted reluctantly.

"Cirelle," Meivre stared down at her. "Will you allow Prince Adaleth to do whatever he wants tonight, short of permanent harm?"

It wasn't truly what Cirelle wanted, not at all. "What about you?"

The sidhe woman shook her head. "I'm leaving. If you won't have the prince, you'll have no one tonight."

The thought left Cirelle with an unbearable knot of frustration coiled in her belly, and she made a small pleading sound as she clutched at the sheets. Her skin was on fire from the wintersweet she'd had earlier, a single-minded torment.

Meivre purred, "I ask again. Will you let him do anything short of permanent harm?"

Cirelle stared into the prince's lambent gaze. Nothing but cold cruelty there. He would hurt her. That much she knew without a doubt. The idea filled Cirelle with a dark thrill, along with a thread of fear that spiced it. "Yes."

"Good girl," Meivre murmured, and left them alone.

Sixty

SITTING ON A HARD cot in a dungeon cell, Lydia tilted her chin upward and tried to keep her voice steady. "No."

"You agreed to tell me the location of the Lock when you returned," Adaleth told her coolly, his presence seeming to fill the tiny space of Lydia's cell. Though Aidan had given her some small comforts, the king and queen had sentenced her to remain imprisoned until Cirelle returned.

Most worrying was the fact that she'd returned late. Prince Rhine and his retinue were here in Arraven, expecting his future bride to return within the week, despite Lydia's insistence that it had still been winter when she left Faerie.

Shai had given her the answer. Someone must have disturbed the Lhyrria; when that happened, time flowed oddly between the worlds for days, months. Sometimes years.

Meaning here in the mortal realm, it was already autumn.

What Rhine would do in five days, when Cirelle didn't return, Lydia didn't know.

And now, this creature had come to find her. Between one breath and the next, he was standing in her cell, wrapped in his colorless finery. The scent of snow and soil filled the small stone chamber.

"No," she refused the prince of the sidhe. "I agreed to tell you when both Cirelle and I were safely in Arraven. When she returns hale and whole. While she remains in Faerie, I take my secrets to the grave. If you want them sooner, return her to me."

Adaleth's fists clenched at his sides, but he could not strike her. Not while she posed him no threat.

"Her bargain holds. She must spend six more months of her life in Faerie."

"And in her six months, how much time will pass here, in the human realm?" She grinned bitterly and barked a humorless laugh. "I certainly hope they don't put me to death before then. That would be unfortunate for you."

"Don't taunt me, human." Low, that voice, and full of daggers.

"I'm merely stating fact," Lydia said. "If you want your information, you'd best see my princess safely home, and keep me alive until then."

The prince stared at her for several long moments, then he was gone.

Sixty-One

"You look good enough to eat," Meivre purred, nipping lightly at the base of Cirelle's neck. She'd garbed Cirelle in Unseelie fashion again tonight, a filmy dress of blood red that left her shoulders and the entire length of her left leg bare, the better to display Dez's handiwork. The tattoo twined about Cirelle's thigh, a pattern of roses in violet ink and pale scars. Dez had long since vanished from Meivre's home, but her artwork remained on Cirelle's body for eternity.

It marked Cirelle as Meivre's, irrevocably and forever.

She shuddered as Meivre's teeth turned to kisses and a caress of tongue against her throat.

Wasn't there something we were supposed to be doing? The thought tugged on Cirelle's memory. With great effort, it came to her. "The party."

"Yes," Meivre murmured, her hand stroking a line of fire and ice down Cirelle's spine. "But they can wait."

Half an hour later, the wide doors to Meivre's ballroom swung open and all eyes turned to watch them enter.

It had been a long time since Cirelle had been surrounded by such light and sound. She squinted against the brilliance of the immense chandelier, made of a hundred dangling stalactites crafted into a tinkling masterpiece, each with a glimmering white light at its tip. As if that weren't enough, sconces held additional lights along the glossy stone of the walls, sparkling with flecks of quartz and arching high above into a graceful dome.

Food had been set out, the scents so rich that Cirelle's stomach turned. The revelers seemed to have no trouble with the music, but it pounded against her sensitive skin.

Meivre guided her into that confusion and brilliance with one slim arm encircling her waist. It was like trying to focus one's eyes on a bright winter day, with the sun glinting painfully on snow. The faces of the guests were a blur to her watering eyes, everything blending into a solid wall of chaos. They took up a position near one of the refreshment tables, greeting guests.

Cirelle understood the words, but they instantly faded, like a dream after one wakes. She felt like a spool of thread unraveling, and only Meivre's slender strength anchored her. So she drifted, closing her eyes and leaning into Meivre's warmth. The sidhe woman rewarded her by loosening her hold to trace a single finger down Cirelle's exposed spine, leaving a line of pleasant tingles in its wake.

Until one voice pierced through the fog.

"What have you done to her?" A low growl, barely above a whisper.

"Hm?" the sound that left Cirelle's lips wasn't quite a word. There was something familiar about that voice, something that stirred an uncomfortable bubble of emotions within her like a hand reaching into a streambed and stirring up the silt at the bottom.

Cirelle lifted her head, blinking against the light. She squinted up at the speaker, a tall man with skin the color of damp ashes.

"Ellian?" she said softly, not even sure where the name had

come from. The man's eyes were so strange, unable to settle on a color, shifting from a brilliant orange to the deep blue of ocean pools. Fire and water. The thought made her smile softly.

"Cirelle," he breathed, his voice heavy with something she couldn't interpret. Sorrow? She cringed away from it, turning to hide her face against Meivre's shoulder.

"What did you do?" he asked again. But the question wasn't directed at Cirelle.

"It's none of your concern," Meivre told him, voice thick with satisfaction. "She doesn't belong to you anymore, Ellian."

"She doesn't belong to you either."

"Ah," Meivre purred, "there I beg to differ. I could do absolutely anything I wanted to her, right here and now, and she'd only beg for more." She stroked Cirelle's hair softly, her voice gentle as she asked, "Isn't that right, pet?"

Cirelle knew the correct response when Meivre asked her a question like that. "Yes."

Another voice whimpered her name. A human man stood beside Ellian. His dark arms were bare, his long black hair braided.

She scowled, racking her brain for his name. It danced about the edges of her mind like a butterfly just out of reach. Suddenly, she had it.

"Jhavet," she said softly, pleased that she had remembered. The next words out of her mouth surprised even her. "Why are your clothes so drab?" A flash of memory came to her. Jhavet, in a coat so brilliantly orange it hurt to look at, embroidered all over in turquoise, and trousers the color of mint leaves. The image conflicted sharply with his grey and white ensemble tonight.

Jhavet's dark eyes widened. He gasped and placed a hand lightly on her arm. She flinched. It felt like tiny ants were crawling all over her, and only Meivre's touch soothed them away. But

Jhavet seemed undaunted, his worried expression softening into a small smile. "You're still in there, Cirelle, aren't you?"

Ellian's fists had clenched into fists at his sides, eyes blazing like a sunrise, and he took one aggressive step forward before Jhavet pulled him back, muttering, "No, don't."

"Your other pet has grown wise," Meivre said. "Any action you take against me might make me annoyed enough to take it out on her later."

A low growl emerged from Ellian's throat, a sound barely human.

"Oh, don't worry," Meivre laughed. "She'd enjoy every moment of it."

"Ellian," Jhavet's voice was quiet, heavy.

Meivre added, "I could, perhaps, be persuaded to bargain some of her time away. A single dance, perhaps? A slow one," she warned, voice bright with amusement. "I fear she may not be up to much twirling."

Cirelle winced at even the thought of spinning. The world felt unsteady beneath her feet, the lights dancing at the edges of her vision.

Ellian took one long, slow breath. Through clenched teeth, he asked, "And what would you ask for such a bargain?"

"An even trade of dance partners. For the duration of the dance, you may have my partner if I can have yours."

The answer didn't come from the sidhe, but from the human at his side. "Yes." Lower, he said, "I can handle one dance, Ellian."

"I'd listen to the man," Meivre said. "I'm feeling particularly magnanimous at the moment. I will not offer this chance again. Or do you have as weak a grasp on this pet as you did on your princess, that you fear he will defect to me as well?"

After another sound of frustration, Ellian turned to Jhavet. "One dance. Agree to nothing. Take nothing from her, not even something she hands you in passing. And certainly don't eat or drink anything she gives you."

"I know," Jhavet's voice was steady. "I can do this. Please. Just… for Cirelle."

Ellian took another long breath before his shoulders slumped. "You may dance with Jhavet for the length of a single song or ten minutes, whichever ends first. Dancing only, and neither of you can leave this room for the duration. I will accept the same terms with Cirelle."

It was an odd sensation, these words drifting in and through Cirelle's mind, knowing they were talking about her but unable to care. At least, not until Meivre said, "agreed," and separated herself from Cirelle. She placed the princess's hand in Ellian's. "My pet, it would please me if you danced with him." Her voice dropped to a sultry whisper as she added, "I will reward you for it later, I promise."

That was all the encouragement Cirelle needed. The thought of how Meivre would uphold that promise sent heat from her toes to her fingertips. Ellian's scent surrounded her, honey and woodsmoke and warmth, and a sharp pain pierced her chest. It tugged at her, this feeling, the sense that she should know this man. But specific memories eluded her.

She tried to look more closely at him, but her eyes were having trouble holding their focus. Had the light grown more piercingly bright? Blinking and squinting only made her eyes water, leaving her unable to see at all.

When the man spoke, his voice was gentle, all traces of his angry growl absent. "You can close your eyes," he said. "I won't harm you. I suspect I know what she's given you, and the only solution is to let it run its course." A trace of fury crept into his tone. He gave her hand a light squeeze, probably meant to be reassuring, but it sent stinging tingles running up her arm. She almost pulled it away again, but remembered Meivre's words and willed her arm to stillness.

Cirelle wasn't certain she trusted this man, but the room was starting to spin and she had little choice but to steady herself against him. When she closed her eyes, she realized she had forgotten his name again. The floor felt spongy beneath her feet. "I don't think I can dance," she whimpered, worried that her mistress would chastise her if she didn't fulfill the request.

"It's all right," he said, sliding an arm around her, his skin prickling against hers everywhere he touched. "I will accept ten minutes of sitting beside you instead."

"But Meivre said I needed to dance," Cirelle protested weakly. She risked opening her eyes for a moment, and the way the walls spun made her stomach clench. Even with her eyes closed, she felt as if her arms and legs weren't connected to her body.

After a few moments, he stopped moving. "Sit," he said. "It will help. Meivre didn't say we were required to dance, only that we may."

By cracking her eyes open a fraction, Cirelle was able to find the stone bench carved into the wall and sit.

"I'll be right back," he told her before sliding his hand from hers. Cirelle barely noticed his absence, relieved by the cool touch of the stone against her exposed back. It cleared her head a little, and made her realize just how hot her skin burned. It was a blessed relief to press a hand to the cold stone for a few moments, then hold it to her cheek. She turned to rest one side of her face against the gently curved rock wall, smooth as glass. The world still spun and twirled, but anchored to the wall like this, the sensation was more pleasant than sickening.

Cirelle startled when the man's voice spoke nearby. "Here." He sat beside her, so that when she opened her eyes he sat directly before her, an arms-length away. He held out a cool silver goblet.

Cirelle blinked. "I can't take food or drink from anyone except Meivre."

His jaw clenched tightly for a few moments. "It's a bit late for those precautions, considering what she's fed you," he said bitterly. "But I swear to you, this is cold water, no more and no less. It bears no enchantment other than the one that keeps the goblet full. It is not poisoned in any way."

She asked him to repeat the words three times. They kept fluttering out of her head as soon as they were spoken, hard for her to grasp and hold onto. But she knew a sidhe could not lie, and her fuzzy mind could not puzzle out the trick in his words. She was so hot, and the contents of the goblet were crystal-clear, condensation forming on the sides of the cold metal.

After a few moments' hesitation, she took it and sipped carefully. Just as he'd said, she tasted only water, so cold it nearly numbed her tongue. Cirelle soon found she could not get enough of it, and drank deeply of the goblet three full times before she felt sated.

It was like a bubble popped. The world righted itself, and the lights grew dimmer, less painful. Her skin still burned as with a fever, but she remembered his name. Ellian.

"Better?" Ellian asked her. Now his eyes sparked the deep green of emeralds.

Cirelle tried to nod, but a wave of vertigo washed over her. Still, it was milder than before. "Yes."

"Cirelle." He lifted one hand as if to touch her cheek. But before his fingertips touched her skin, he curled his fingers and pulled away.

Some craving in her chest had wanted him to touch her. A softer, deeper hunger than the ones Meivre stirred. She clutched the goblet in both hands, but searched his face. "Ellian. I… we know each other, don't we?"

His eyes changed color again, cobalt bleeding out from the pupils like a drop of ink spreading through water. "Yes," the word was so quiet she almost didn't hear it over the music. "We did."

"I can't remember. Everything is fuzzy. But…" She hesitated to ask the next question. "I get the feeling… were we… lovers?"

Ellian still wouldn't look at her, but his small laugh was dry and bitter. His hand tightened on the edge of the bench's seat, those knuckles turning white. "Once."

"Oh," Cirelle murmured. She set aside the cool goblet and placed a hand over his. "I'm sorry I don't remember." She tucked her feet beneath her and leaned into his shoulder. Her skin still tingled where it touched his, but now the sensation was pleasant, much as the room's swaying had become enjoyable.

For a moment, he remained stiff and unyielding, every muscle so taut that she could feel the tremble in them. But then he wrapped one arm around her, holding her tightly and burying his face in her hair.

"Stone and sky, you reek of her," he mumbled, but his words held only sorrow, not jealousy.

Cirelle lifted a lock of hair in front of her nose to breathe in Meivre's scent, spicy and heady like fresh-cut roses, with the earthy aroma of a rainstorm. She remembered Meivre's small hands tangling in that hair, pulling her head back to bare her neck for tongue and teeth. A shiver ran through her.

Meivre's scent may have lingered, but right now Cirelle breathed in deeply of Ellian's sweet and smoky aroma, and it stirred something similar in her belly. Testing, she pressed her lips lightly against Ellian's throat, feeling his pulse beating fiercely.

"No," he said softly, though the word seemed torn from him.

Ellian squirmed out of her embrace and moved away. "It's the vieda she fed you that's doing this, not you."

Cirelle reached for him again, but he batted her hand away.

A flash of anger. "Vieda? I don't even know what that is."

Meivre's familiar purr came from behind her. "Getting cozy, were we?"

Cirelle's cheeks burned, and she lowered her head. Though her mistress sounded more amused than angry, Meivre's temper could change in a heartbeat. She risked a quick peek. Jhavet stood nearby.

Meivre sat, lifting Cirelle's head with one slender finger under her chin. "Feeling a bit… hungry, are we?"

Cirelle could only nod, still trembling.

"Well." Meivre kissed Cirelle fiercely, deeply, leaving her breathless. "I suppose it may be time to retire for the evening, hm? I've made my appearance, and the servants will see to the guests. I still owe you a reward for being such an obedient pet, after all."

"Yes," Cirelle breathed, her voice catching.

"No." The deep, quiet anger in that tone jolted Cirelle from her dreamy desire. Ellian still stood beside them, fists held at this sides, Jhavet's hand on his shoulder.

"You have no say in this, Ellian," Meivre said, triumph oozing through her words. "Your time is up, and she is mine once again."

"No," he repeated, though a note of despair clung to his voice.

Meivre smiled. "Perhaps I might be willing to conduct one more bargain, for this night only." Her eyes raked up and down Jhavet's frame. "You have excellent taste in pets, my dear. That one is perhaps not quite so clever as the girl, but he is pleasing to the eye."

"Hey!" Jhavet said, but Meivre ignored him.

"I would bargain once more," Meivre said, reclining on

the stone bench like a queen passing judgment on her throne. "Tonight only. Cirelle for Jhavet."

Jhavet's eyes met Cirelle's, his dark gaze heavy with something she couldn't decipher. "Yes," he said quietly.

Ellian shook his head. "No. You don't know what you're offering."

"I see her bruises and scars. I know exactly what I'm volunteering for." His next words were so quiet that Cirelle had to strain to hear. "If we can spare her just this one night, shouldn't we? Our mess helped put her here in the first place." He pulled Ellian into a fierce embrace, his next words lost in a whisper. Ellian clung to him for a few moments, then kissed him tenderly.

For her part, Meivre watched with casually alert interest, like a cat waiting for a bird to land before pouncing. She traced small, aimless patterns against the skin of Cirelle's arm with her fingertips, tuning Cirelle's rising passion to a fever pitch.

"These are the terms," Ellian said. "Eight hours, ending at sunrise. You will select one room in your home and remain there for the duration. No additional bargains or agreements made by Jhavet during those eight hours will be valid. You do nothing that leaves a mark of any kind, and no permanent damage whatsoever. Nothing that threatens his life or maims."

"No," Meivre shook her head. "Those terms leave no room for any fun. I would agree to everything except the lack of marks of any kind. I will promise not to threaten his life or leave any injury that takes longer than two weeks to heal. Agree to that, and she's yours for the next eight hours, as long as you remain in the chamber I select for you. I won't even place any stipulations on what you can do with her." Meivre's hand trailed up to Cirelle's shoulder, then her long, sharp fingernails dug deeply into Cirelle's skin, hard enough to puncture. Small beads of blood welled up. The pain brought Cirelle's desire to a flash point, and she cried out softly.

Ellian took a step forward despite Jhavet trying to hold him back. For his part, Jhavet looked a bit green, staring at the small spots of blood.

"Choose quickly," Meivre said. "I grow bored. If you decline, the princess and I will retire for the evening and seek our own amusements."

"I can do this," Jhavet said.

Ellian gave him a stricken look, but nodded and replied to Meivre. "You win. Yes. We agree to your terms." The sorrow and defeat in his voice was so profound that Cirelle felt a wave of pity for him.

Meivre smiled. "Very good. "She stood briskly and stretched, fingers laced together over her head and arching like a cat. "I shall show you to your room." She took Cirelle's hand and helped her stand.

"Wait," Ellian said. "The bargain isn't binding unless all parties involved agree."

"We have," Meivre said. "You, he, and I have all said yes." She cast a glance at Cirelle. "Her words hardly matter at this point," she said dismissively. "She'll agree to anything I ask of her."

Ellian winced. "Nonetheless, I won't have you slipping out of this with a loophole."

Meivre sighed. "Cirelle, my pet, will you spend the evening with Ellian? Just for tonight, you have my permission to be with him. To do whatever you both please, without punishment from me." Her lips quirked upward into a wicked smile. "Tomorrow, you will be mine again. But for tonight, it would very much please me for you to stay with Ellian instead. Will you do that for me?"

Cirelle nodded. "Yes."

"Good," Meivre kissed her., taking her hand and leading the entire party out of the room. If Cirelle could have focused on anything save her own desires, she would have noted how eyes followed their departure, and the whispers that sprung up in their wake.

Walking was easier now, the dizziness fading. But something new had overtaken Cirelle, a gnawing hunger that made it difficult to focus on anything save Meivre's hand entwined in her own. Her skin was aflame where they touched, and she craved more with a fierceness that consumed her.

She barely noticed the walk until Meivre stopped them before a guest chamber next to her own. "This one shall be yours for the evening," she said to Ellian, opening the door. "There is an hourglass on the table. When the door closes, your eight hours begin."

With a passionate parting kiss, Meivre left Cirelle standing in the hallway and led a reluctant-looking Jhavet to her chamber. Jhavet cast one sorrowful glance backward at Ellian, straightened his shoulders, and stepped through the doorway. It closed behind him with a soft, ominous click.

Sixty-Two

STILL GIDDY FROM MEIVRE's parting kiss, Cirelle wandered dreamily into the guest room. She only gave a cursory glance around the room, lavishly appointed for Meivre's best guests. Apart from an adjoining bathing room, it was all one spacious chamber. A large bed covered in plush pillows and a thick comforter rested against the far wall, while an area near the door was set up as a parlor area with armchairs and side tables, a small hearth burning opposite.

Two glasses and a pitcher of cool water sat on the low table between the chairs, frosted with condensation. On one corner of the same table, a simple hourglass sat, full at the top as if it had just been turned over. Black grains of sand spilled through the opening, their time slipping away.

No sooner had Ellian closed the door behind him than she reached for him. The need that burned in her was fiercer than hunger, more painful than thirst. If she didn't slake it, she felt like she would die. And if Meivre were not here, Ellian would do.

He resisted, pushing her gently away. "No."

"Please. You can do anything you want," she stated breathlessly.

"No," he repeated, shaking his head.

Anger sparked. "Is that all you can say?"

"At the moment, it seems so," he said, keeping her at arm's length. He dipped a hand into a pouch at his waist and pulled out a small object. "I hate to do this, but I fear you won't let me treat those puncture wounds on your shoulder otherwise. Since you just gave me permission to do anything..." He held up a small, curling vine of ivy, then threw it at Cirelle.

She flinched away, but the ivy struck her on the wrist, where it curled and writhed like a living thing, growing and tightening around her. It pinned her arms to her sides and tangled around her legs until she lost her balance. As she started to fall, Ellian caught her. Everywhere his skin touched hers, she was aflame. But he did not carry her to the pillow-covered bed in the center of the chamber. Instead, he set her in the armchair farthest from the fire, kneeling on the floor beside it. She wriggled around to face him, but he just frowned and prodded at her shoulder. A small spike of pain throbbed, and Cirelle remembered Meivre's fingernails piercing her skin earlier.

He set a few items from his pouch on the small table next to the chair, unstoppering a vial and dribbling a few drops onto the puncture wounds. It was cold, unbelievably cold, and a tingling numbness spread where it touched. He pressed a small bit of cloth to her skin, where it stuck as if glued.

Cirelle shivered at the press of his warm palm. "This isn't what I had in mind when I said you could do anything to me."

"Of that, I am well aware," Ellian said softly. "And if you weren't riding the wave of a heavy dose of viedalan, you'd be thinking more clearly." He sighed, dabbing some of the chill liquid onto his fingers and gently rubbing it into the redness at her wrists, left over from last night with Meivre. It was such a gentle motion, working the serum into the half-healed wounds

with light circular motions. She couldn't help but picture those sure, gentle hands caressing other parts of her body, and a small moan of pleasure slipped past her lips.

Ellian froze, and the sorrowful indigo in his eyes washed away with a sudden flood of violet. But his jaw tightened and he finished his ministrations, wrapping her wrists in the same cloth that adhered to her skin.

Then the first noises drifted from next door. Sound echoed oddly in these stone caverns, but the voice was unmistakably male, the cry an indeterminate one of either pleasure or pain. With Meivre's ability to stir either at a touch, it was anyone's guess which.

Ellian stiffened, his eyes closed as he remained very carefully still for a few moments. When he moved again, his motions were very carefully controlled. He picked up the last item he'd retrieved from his bag, a smooth round stone of milky opalescent white, just big enough to nestle comfortably in his palm, strung on a silver chain.

With his other hand, Ellian tugged on one end of the vine that held her. It loosened, shrinking away until it was once again a small curl of green. It went back into the bag as he took quick steps away from Cirelle and draped the pendant about his neck. The stone rested on his collarbone, pale as the moon against his charcoal skin. Then he took a seat in the other armchair, the low table between them.

Cirelle couldn't focus on anything except his bare chest and the way those trousers clung to him so tightly. In a moment, she'd stood, moving toward him to sit in his lap and wrap her arms around his neck.

Or at least, that had been her intent. Instead, an arm's length from the chair, she ran into an invisible, impassable force. "What?"

For answer, Ellian touched the pendant. "Shielding stone," he said. "While it touches my skin, you will not reach me."

"Why?"

"If you were in your own mind, I would grant your every desire. But right now, you're not yourself." A flicker of orange flashed through his irises. "Meivre has seen to that."

"I don't know what you mean."

"Viedalan is a powerful faerie intoxicant. Worse than wintersweet. Sidhe use it recreationally, but it's also used to make their thralls more compliant. It fogs the memory, leaves the user in a dreamlike state, then as it runs its course, becomes a very powerful aphrodisiac before it leaves the user exhausted and sick." He shook his head. "Speaking of which, you should drink some water." He withdrew another small item from his bag, a slender silver spike twice the length of a human hand. Something tugged at her memory, but she couldn't grasp it. He dipped the spike briefly into the water, then shook it off and returned it to the bag.

He poured the water into both glasses, one of which he placed before her. Apparently the shield did not prevent inanimate objects from touching him. Only her.

Cirelle stood beside the table and his chair, trembling. "I won't eat or drink anything you give me," she snapped. "I don't even know what that was."

"That was a piece of a unicorn's horn," he said gently. "You've seen it before, you just don't remember. I used it to purify the water, in case Meivre had dosed it with anything or placed a spell upon it. It's nothing more than water now. Something that you need to drink to combat the crash when the viedalan fades." To reinforce his words, Ellian picked up his glass and took a long drink. "If there were a cure for the drug, I'd dose you with it. But there isn't. Drinking enough water will help with the aftermath tomorrow, though."

"I don't care." She shoved the glass away.

He sighed, leaning forward in the chair and dropping his head into his hands. The silence was punctuated with another low moan from next door. Ellian flinched, but didn't look up. "If you drink two glasses of water, I will consider taking you over to that bed with me," he said softly.

A soft thrum of heat crept through Cirelle, and she reached for the glass. At first she sipped slowly, but then thirst consumed her. It seemed to soften the cutting edge of her desire as well, though not completely.

"Well?" she asked after her second glass.

He looked upon her with a gaze full of pity. "I've considered. But the answer is still no."

The rage that flooded through her was like a snarling beast. Cirelle threw her glass at the wall, where it shattered. "You tricked me," she hissed, pressing her hand against the barrier as hard as she could. It remained immovable.

"I am still a sidhe. You're smarter than this, Cirelle," he said gently. "You would never have agreed to a bargain with such vague wording if you were in your right mind."

In a mindless fury, Cirelle paced the room, hurling anything she could get her hands on. Ellian winced at every shattering piece of pottery, every heavy book that landed haphazardly on the floor, pages crumpled. But he did not move, and he did not let down the shield.

She tried to peel off the bandages he'd applied, but they resisted all her attempts. Ellian told her they would not come off until the wounds beneath them healed, and she gave it up after several failed tries.

Much later, Cirelle would feign no memory of that evening. But she recalled every moment of that long, awful night in excruciating detail, all the humiliating ways in which she tried to coax Ellian out of that shield. Pleading miserably, stalking the room in nothing more than her bare skin, whispering detailed depravities at him, shouting in anger, throwing things, even threatening to harm herself. The last was the only one that got his attention, and he only responded by standing up, walking about the room, and collecting everything that could be used to injure herself before tucking it all beneath his chair, inside his invisible shield.

After a few hours, Cirelle stood before him, her skin misted with a sheen of sweat. "I know you want me," she said flatly. "You made a bargain for this. Why? Why did you give your pet to Meivre in exchange for me, if you didn't intend to make use of me?"

"To spare you what happens next door," he said bitterly.

"Why? He takes what belongs to me. You 'spare' me nothing, but only deny me the pleasure that is rightfully mine. *I* belong to Meivre, not him!"

Ellian shook his head. "No. Neither of you belong to her. Or anyone. That's something you know, deep down somewhere. Tonight, I hope that you will remember that after the drug burns itself out. *That* is why Jhavet made this sacrifice, why I agreed to it. In the hope that a night's respite may help you remember who you are."

"And who am I?"

"Someone I love."

She blinked, a fierce twist of pain making her heart skip a beat. Dizziness overwhelmed her. The floor lurched under her feet, and her knees collapsed. She managed to fall into the other chair, her limbs trembling. Her stomach turned. The rush of heat abandoned her, leaving her skin clammy. She shivered. Briefly, she considered getting a blanket, but the distance to the bed now seemed insurmountable. Instead, she pulled her knees up to her chest and wrapped her arms about them. Her dinner threatened to come up. She closed her eyes and took a few short, sharp breaths through her nose.

"Cirelle," Ellian's voice was unbearably gentle. He knelt before her, the remaining glass in his hands, filled with cool water. The pendant no longer rested against his skin, the gem draped over one shoulder where the fabric of his shirt provided a barrier.

The victory seemed to matter little now, with her stomach twisting itself into uncomfortable knots and ice coursing through her. The last thing she wanted was something cold. She pushed feebly away at the glass of water. "Too cold," she said, her teeth chattering.

"It will help," he insisted. "I'll make you tea, but until it's ready, you need to drink this."

She closed her eyes and turned her head away.

"Please." The word was so quiet she almost didn't hear it. Her eyes flew open again. She accepted the glass and took a careful sip. It was cold, so unbearably cold. But it seemed to push aside some of the nausea, and she took another, longer drink.

Ellian stood and crossed the room in quick, long strides to pluck a blanket from the bed. He draped it over her chair, tucking it around her.

There is a specific moment when one awakens from sleep, a single sparkling instant after a time of drifting in dreams. At one moment, everything was vague and Cirelle's memories fogged. Then within a blink, she was herself again. Her head spun painfully and her stomach still threatened to eject its contents. But Cirelle recalled herself. Her memories returned as if they'd never left, and her thoughts cleared.

Ellian once again knelt beside her, one hand on the arm of the chair beside her elbow. Shame flooded through her, a wash of humiliation so deep that every ounce of her wished she could worldwalk away as the sidhe could do. She squeezed her eyes shut as tightly as she could and huddled deeper into the blanket. "Oh, Ellian," she breathed, feeling the hot tears squeeze through her eyelids. "I'm so sorry."

"Cirelle." It wasn't a question. It was a statement, a naming, acknowledgment that she had returned to herself.

"I'm so, so sorry. Stars." How could mere words ever make up for this night?

As if to remind her that she was not the only one who had tormented Ellian this evening, a violent cry of pain echoed from next door. Cirelle winced, burying her face in the blanket. "Why? Why would both of you do this for me, after I abandoned you?"

"You know why," he said quietly. Something in his tone made her look up at him. Ellian had dropped the glamour, his eyes a deep rose color.

Suddenly, Cirelle couldn't bear the stickiness of her damp skin, the sour smell of her own sweat. Underneath that, Meivre's heady aroma still lingered in her hair and on her skin, and it choked her. How long had it been since she'd been herself? How long had Meivre kept her drugged like that? Weeks? Months?

Beside her, Ellian's cozy scent battled with the odors that made her stomach churn.

"I need to bathe," she declared abruptly, and uncurled herself under the blanket. She kept it wrapped tightly about her as she stood and hurried to the adjoining bathing chamber. Ellian didn't follow.

Cirelle filled the tub with water so hot it scalded, but that was what she needed. When she sank into the water, everything she'd been holding back in the other room spilled free. Horrible, racking sobs burst from her, again and again, as she huddled into a small ball in the water. Meivre had been drugging and manipulating her even before she left Ellian's manor. And the woman would continue to do so for months yet. Cirelle didn't even know how much time had passed.

Her skin crawled upon remembering all the things she had let Meivre do to her. No, that she had practically begged Meivre to do to her. Jhavet now suffered the same treatment, and for what? Tomorrow, her world would again be reduced to a haze of subservience, pleasure and pain mingled as Meivre did with Cirelle whatever she wished.

Even the worst sorrow and grief comes and goes in waves, and eventually the sobs began to subside, replaced with an aching hollow in her chest. The nausea and dizziness fled, leaving her with bone-weary exhaustion.

Anger filled her, a rage she had never known. She scrubbed at her skin until it was red and nearly raw, but she couldn't seem to wash away the shame. Her hair was lathered with soaps and doused in scented oils a full five times before she could no longer smell Meivre's aroma tangled in it.

Eventually, the water grew cold. Soon she'd have to face Ellian and everything she had done this evening. She left the tub and donned one of Meivre's soft robes. It was a simple thing, made of fine brushed cotton in a shade of sky blue, loose and tied with a belted ribbon around the waist.

When she opened the door, Ellian once again sat in his chair. True to his word, he'd retrieved the items for tea from his pouch and had a steaming cup ready for her. Even though it had meant placing a kettle in the flames of the hearth, facing his phobia of fire.

He'd come for her. Even after all the horrible things she'd done tonight, he'd still looked upon her with rosy pink eyes. Cirelle smiled and approached the sitting area. He'd forgive her. It would be all right. Maybe he would find a way to buy her servitude back from Meivre.

Two steps later, her legs gave way completely. She was aware enough to feel her knees and palms smack painfully against the stone floor, then everything went dark.

Sixty-Three

CIRELLE RESTED FITFULLY, waking up twitchy and hot to push aside the blankets that had been piled on her, then stirring minutes later in a cold sweat and pulling them on again. Her dreams were sharp and fever-edged things. When she awoke in truth, the hourglass rested on the small table next to the bed, perhaps two-thirds spent. She sat up, wincing at the deep ache in her bones and wondering if there was still hot water for tea.

Ellian had moved one of the chairs to the bedside, within arms reach. Her chest tightened at that. A glass of water stood ready on the nightstand. He held it out to her, but the thought of icy water only made her teeth chatter. "Tea?" she asked hopefully, her voice rough.

"I'll make some more." He went through the motions briskly, pouring water into the kettle and setting it on the hook in the fireplace to heat. He leaned as far away from the flames as he could, a tightness in his jaw and around the eyes.

The silence stretched between them. Cirelle cleared her throat. "It's quiet." She didn't need to explain further.

Ellian nodded solemnly. "For over half an hour now," he said quietly.

Silence could only mean one thing, that Meivre had over-played her hand and Jhavet had lost consciousness. If fate was merciful, he'd stay that way until the time was up, but Cirelle doubted fate would be so kind.

"What do we do now?" she asked.

"I don't know." Ellian sounded more lost than Cirelle had ever heard. "You still have over six months left in Faerie. I can invoke the rule of hospitality and stay here for two more days, but I fear it would just make Meivre even more cruel to you while I remain."

Cirelle shivered, and it turned into a violent bout of shuddering that left her teeth clacking together. "Can you buy my service back from her?"

"I will try, but I suspect I could offer Meivre everything I own and still she would refuse. This isn't about material wealth for her. It's vengeance and cruelty."

Panic crept up on her, a sense of overwhelming dread. How could she go back to that mindless, puppet-like state, for months on end? How many more scars would she bear by the time she returned home? "Then it's hopeless."

"It's never truly hopeless," Ellian said grimly as he produced the unicorn horn again and dipped it briefly in the steeping tea. He poured her a cup and brought it to her.

Cirelle wrapped her fingers about it gratefully. The warmth sank into her skin, but only seemed to make the rest of her body even colder. She sipped the tea, though it was not done steeping yet. Weak, but also hot. For a brief moment, it was the finest comfort she had ever known, but the heat vanished within a heartbeat, leaving her as cold as ever. She scalded her tongue, but still shook. The cold, or terror? "I can't do anything to stop her. I have to eat. She'll drug me again."

"What about the claimhte?"

Cirelle swore. She'd forgotten entirely about the knives that now rested in Meivre's bedchamber. Now that she thought about them, she could feel their soft, greedy pulse within her.

"Oiche offered you a boon, did she not? You can call her and trade."

"But Meivre's wards—"

"Nothing can fully keep out shadows. The only thing that truly kept us safe from the Scath at my manor was your decree as his queen."

"I have to touch them to call her," Cirelle said. "And Meivre will never let me. She keeps them in a chest in her room."

"Then get to them. You can do this."

"You want me to kill again. To ask Oiche to murder."

"Are you pleading mercy for Meivre?"

"Never. I'd stab her myself. But I suspect she'll hide the knives after tonight. She'll know I'm thinking clearly again, and she's not that stupid." Cirelle tossed back the last of her tea like an unwelcome draught of medicine. Her skin felt just as cold and clammy as before, beneath the blankets and her robe. Why couldn't she stop shivering? She held the cup out to Ellian. As his fingertips brushed the back of her own, they were so pleasantly warm that she held on for another moment before letting it slip away. Her teeth chattered. "I can't seem to warm up."

"Here," he said, sliding into the bed. Gratefully, Cirelle lifted one edge of the heavy blankets, then eagerly slipped between his arms and pressed her shivering body along the length of his. He felt like a furnace. Cirelle rested her cheek against his bare collarbone.

"You're freezing," he said quietly.

"I told you that," she murmured against his chest, tugging the blanket all the way up to her ears. It was the first time in months that she felt safe, wrapped in his arms, breathing in his old, familiar aroma. This time, the sleep she drifted into was the deep, dreamless sleep of exhaustion.

When she awoke again, her back was pressed against his chest, his arm curled around her stomach. How long had she been asleep? Cirelle sat up a little to crane her neck at the table behind Ellian. The hourglass looked more than three-quarters spent now. Still maybe two hours left.

"Awake?" Ellian whispered sleepily into her ear. "You seem warmer."

"Yes."

They remained like that for a while. She could feel his heartbeat against her back, his warm breath against the nape of her neck. Mercifully, there were still no sounds from next door. Cirelle dared hope that perhaps Meivre had grown bored of Jhavet and let him sleep. But then she remembered a game Meivre liked to play, one that rewarded a plaything for silence and punished them for making a sound, all while she teased them mercilessly.

Cirelle shuddered. Ellian's arms tightened about her and he whispered, "Don't. Whatever makes you shiver like that, you don't need to confront it yet."

"But Jhavet—"

"Jhavet is strong. He'll be okay when this is all over, and there's nothing we can do for him right now. I… he's asleep. Or unconscious."

"How do you know?"

Ellian's gaze darted away. "It's hard to explain. But I do. He's all right for now." Sapphire eyes met hers. "But I only have two more hours with you, and I want them to be pleasant ones. Or as best as we can make them, here."

Cirelle didn't know what to say to that, and let the conversation lapse into silence. After a long time, she whispered, "I should have said yes. I know that now. I knew it before I came here."

Ellian was very still for several heartbeats. Then she heard her name breathed softly, so low that she felt it rumble through him. She turned to face him and tried to blink away the tears that had brimmed in her eyes. With one gentle hand, Ellian brushed them away, then cradled cheek against his palm.

He'd dropped his glamour, and she looked into eyes of the deepest rose, the color of the sky at sunrise.

When he kissed her, he was unbearably gentle, as if she were a delicate bauble that might shatter if treated too roughly. His lips were warm, brushing with soft caresses and small kisses at the corner of her mouth.

After a few moments, Cirelle pulled away from him and buried her head in his chest again. His arms curled around her, a wall against the nightmare world she'd built.

She'd have thought it impossible, but in the safety of that embrace, Cirelle found restful sleep once again.

Sixty-Four

WHEN CIRELLE AWOKE, she stretched and yawned. Ellian's hand trailed down her side, over the robe, and came to rest at her thigh where the garment had ridden up in her sleep. On her tattoos.

"She did this to you."

The words stuck in her throat, and Cirelle coughed to clear it. "Yes. A brand, to tell the whole world that I'm hers, forever."

"Not forever. Find the claimhte, use them. Then call me, and I will come for you."

Cirelle felt his faith was sorely misplaced, but this faint thread of hope was all she had. This thin hope that she'd someday return to his home.

And yet.

"What about Jhavet?" she asked. "If I came back to you?"

"What about him?" Ellian asked, but his voice was cautious. His fingers went still.

She sighed, rolling over onto her back and staring at the ceiling. "You love both of us, right?"

"Yes."

"Would he… share?" She turned to face him again, propping her head on one arm. "Jhavet infuriates me sometimes, but he's important to you, and he made a sacrifice for me tonight. I won't forget that. I wouldn't take him from you, even if I could. Even if he gets under my skin."

Ellian's voice held a note of amusement and his eyes flickered bright sky blue for a moment. "If you care for him so little, what about that kiss?"

"So he told you." Her cheeks warmed. "That was two drunk, heartbroken souls seeking comfort. It was a mistake, and one I wouldn't really care to repeat." She glanced at the hourglass. Their time was nearly up. Ellian pressed a hand lightly on her upper arm, against a long scar that lay there. Another souvenir of Meivre's.

Cirelle waited for him to speak, but he didn't. He caressed her scar as if he could wash away her pain with gentleness. She could have had this, for the past months. Forever. But her own impulsive foolishness had left her here instead.

"I'll find a way," she whispered.

He took her hand in both of his, kissing her fingertips lightly. "If anyone can wriggle out of a bargain or tangle Meivre in a new one, it's you. You will escape and come back to me."

The black grains flowed through the hourglass, and Cirelle wished she could reach out and stop them. That she could have just a few more minutes.

Cirelle sighed and untangled herself from his arms. "At the very least, I have little desire to greet her in a robe." Her dress lay crumpled on the floor where it had been discarded the night before. She stepped over to it and poked it with a foot, but even that small motion wafted Meivre's rose-and-thunderstorm scent upward, making her stomach clench.

Instead, she checked the armoire and found it stocked with a small selection of clothes. There were dresses in a few sizes, including a long blue dress that looked like it would fit her well enough, along with the needed undergarments.

As she removed the robe, she caught Ellian staring, his eyes skating over her. But not taking in her nudity. No, his gaze lingered on the worst of her scars and the line of bruises along her ribs. Guilt and shame washed over her, and she turned away.

In one graceful movement and two swift strides, he'd left the bed and wrapped his arms around her.

"I'm all right," she lied, feeling hollow.

"You know I can tell when you lie."

"But I need to believe it."

He kissed her softly. "You will be."

"Someday."

As Cirelle dressed, the hourglass neared emptiness. Meivre would be here soon, and she would know what had happened after one whiff in Cirelle's presence. Ellian's smoky scent clung to her, over the less-pleasant smell of Cirelle's drug-induced sour sweat.

Well, that was what Meivre had intended, wasn't it? Let her think she had won, that she'd broken Ellian's will, that Cirelle had seduced him while under the sway of the viedalan. For there was no doubt that had been her intent, aside from tormenting Ellian with Jhavet's cries. If Ellian had taken advantage of a drugged Cirelle, Meivre knew the guilt would gnaw at him forever.

Sound finally stirred from the chamber next door. Voices, muffled.

The last grain of sand fell, and Cirelle felt her heart drop with it, watching the tiny fleck slip through the narrow opening and tumble as if in slow motion. Her small bubble of safety was gone. She was on her own again, left to whatever torments Meivre could concoct. She forced herself to breathe as a slow trickle of fear seeped through her veins. Ellian's hand reached for hers as they approached the door, but she shook her head. She needed to gather her own strength now, not borrow his.

When the knock came, terror flashed so intense she could think of nothing save her impulse to run, to flee as far as she could, to hide. And yet, that same fear turned her legs to stone.

Ellian opened the door and Cirelle's eyes met Meivre's smug, satiated ones. A small, wicked grin touched the woman's lips as she took in their disheveled state and Cirelle's change of garments.

Behind her, Jhavet stood, his shoulders hunched, wearing the same clothing he'd had the night before. Except now, faint splotches of dark red seeped into the fabric of his shirt. Cirelle winced. And yet, when their eyes met, Jhavet offered her a faint, exhausted smile. "Hi again," he said, his voice hoarse. "You look like… you."

Cirelle couldn't help but give him a small, sad smile in return. She coughed, clearing her throat, and managed to croak out a small, "Thank you."

"Well," Meivre said, "Time is up. It's been fun, but I think I'll take my property back now." She held out a hand.

Cirelle hesitated, but refusing would only bring her more pain later. Playing meek and cowed was her only chance for Meivre to let her guard down, so Cirelle could retrieve the claimhte. So Cirelle placed her hand in Meivre's slender pink fingers. Meivre pulled her forward, out of the room, guiding Cirelle to stand at her left side.

Jhavet moved beside Ellian, holding himself with the careful, hunched stance of someone whose body aches, but he met Meivre's eyes with a fierce scowl.

"Still so fierce," Meivre purred. "It was such a pleasure to break you," she murmured. "Now, we've all had our fun, and I'd appreciate it if you left."

"I could invoke the rights of hospitality," Ellian warned. But the next words out of Meivre's lips confirmed what he'd told Cirelle the night before.

"You could," Meivre said. "But then I might try all the harder to make her scream tonight. For your benefit, of course."

Ellian's eyes blazed brilliant orange, his glamour faltering.

Cirelle couldn't stand it anymore. All these games, all Meivre's wickedness, it was a sickness. And that sickness was spreading to Ellian and Jhavet both, because of her.

"Just leave," Cirelle snapped at Ellian, her voice cracking. She met Ellian's eyes, watching as his glamour fell over them. "Please."

Jhavet reached for Ellian's hand, twining their fingers together. "Let's go," he said softly, giving Cirelle one last apologetic glance.

Still, Ellian hesitated, asking Meivre, "What do you want? Name your price."

A cruel expression spread across Meivre's face. "I suppose there is one thing I would take from you, Etishen."

It took a moment for Cirelle to realize what Meivre had just called him. A bleak, utter silence fell as Cirelle's heart stopped beating, the world going dark and fuzzy around the edges.

If one were to know a faerie's true name, what could be done with it?

Any number of things. The worst? Crawling into that faerie's head and turning them into a puppet.

"Oh, yes," Meivre said casually, as if she'd merely forgotten a minor fact. "You don't remember telling me his name, my pet?"

"No," Cirelle gasped, but it wasn't an answer to Meivre's question. It was a protest. As if saying that could make it untrue. When had she told Meivre his name? Her recollections of the past weeks were vague things, like fever dreams. And if she'd told Meivre that much…

"The Key," Meivre purred, staring up at Ellian with triumph in her eyes. "Give me the Key, and she's yours."

No. No no no. If Meivre knew about the Key, did Adaleth?

Obviously not, or he'd have already taken it back.

Ellian's voice was cold, but there was the tiniest quaver in it. "You don't have enough power to use it."

"No," Meivre admitted. "But our prince does, and I wonder what he might be willing to give to get it back, if he knew it was gone. A future king could certainly use a queen. The princess for the Key."

Ellian's struggle played out on his face while Jhavet gripped his hand tightly. He'd nearly given up the Key to save her once. He would do it again.

But it didn't matter. Meivre only hesitated to torment him. Her brilliant pink eyes bored into Ellian's terrified black ones. "The Key for the girl. Agree with me, Etishen Ral Ves."

At the utterance of his name, Ellian's face went slack. His shoulders bunched with tension, but his now-gray eyes showed no expression. "Yes."

Meivre laughed, and Cirelle felt sick. This couldn't be happening.

"You get your wish then, princess," Meivre purred. "You do want to go back to him, do you not?"

Cirelle felt as if she stood outside her body, watching the scene unfold with horrified eyes. The Key they'd worked so hard for, gone in a flash.

Meivre's fuchsia gaze pierced Cirelle expectantly.

Waiting for her agreement. The realization settled over Cirelle, and she barked a sudden, triumphant laugh. "No."

"What?"

"No," Cirelle repeated more firmly. "You can't exchange my servitude unless I agree, and I don't."

Meivre glowered. "You will." The threat that hung on those words was enough to turn Cirelle's blood to ice, but she lifted her chin.

"Cirelle," Jhavet pleaded, stepping forward and taking Cirelle's hand in both of his own. "You have to say yes." But Cirelle barely noticed his words. Instead, she forced herself not to look down at their clasped hands, where Jhavet had just pressed something small and hard and smooth into her palm.

She swallowed. "I won't."

Jhavet just nodded sadly and stepped back.

It seemed Meivre was done with games, however. "Etishen Ral Ves," she said, "take your pet and leave us."

As if in a trance, Ellian's hand fell on Jhavet's shoulder and they were gone.

Meivre reached for Cirelle, but she flinched away. "No," she said flatly. "I give you no consent to touch me."

"Oh, my pet," Meivre said smugly, her hand darting out to grasp Cirelle's shoulder in a grip as hard as stone. Her fingers pressed painfully into Cirelle's skin, even through her dress. "But you have. You've given me permission to do every possible thing I could imagine to you, at least a dozen times over. You've even begged me." Her hand moved to Cirelle's tangled hair, yanking her head backward.

"But—"

"You thought it had to be renewed?" Meivre purred. "One of Ellian's foolish notions, I'm afraid. A part of his silly infatuation with humanity, this concept of repeated consent. That is not the true way of the sidhe. Once a faerie has your permission, it lasts forever, my pet." She nibbled Cirelle's earlobe with her sharp little teeth. "I think I may avoid the wintersweet for a few days, so you can truly experience all I have to offer."

Meivre chuckled softly as Cirelle's breathing quickened in fear. She pulled away and shoved Cirelle back through the door into the guest chambers. "Bathe," she commanded. "You stink of him." She yawned prettily. "And then I suppose you're probably hungry. I'll need you fed and awake for what I have planned this evening. I will have food brought to your room. I expect you to come and eat it after you bathe. If you're quick about it, I may even allow you to get some sleep before tonight."

Sixty-Five

CIRELLE RE-ENTERED THE GUEST room, shut the door, and breathed a small sigh of relief that Meivre had not noticed the thing clenched in her fist. She uncurled her fingers to reveal a lump of red wax, the small corner of parchment barely exposed. The wax was hard, crumbling when she picked at it. When the paper was free, something fell out of the remaining wax, and Cirelle barely caught it before it clattered to the floor.

A tiny oval of glass sat in her palm, filled with a pale russet liquid. The note that had been wrapped around it was carefully scrawled in Trade, the handwriting tiny, scratchy.

Poison. Deadly to fae, not humans. Stole it.

Cirelle read the words again. Stolen. Probably from Ellian's Archive. There would be a price for such theft, and yet Jhavet had done this for her. A lump formed in Cirelle's throat.

Poison. Such a small amount, but the note said it was deadly. Surely Jhavet would only give her an effective dose.

She may not even need the claimhte and Oiche after all. Even though it had been weeks—months—since she'd held them, the bloodlust of the knives still sang in her every limb. A craving, dark and dangerous, anticipating Meivre's murder.

It was a tug on her chest, a plucking. Not from the direction of Meivre's room, though, not anymore. True to Cirelle's suspicions, they were hidden elsewhere now.

When she'd bathed and dressed again, she combed and braided her hair. She took a long look around the room before leaving. Various items lay scattered about the floor where she had hurled them the night before. Shards of the broken glass she'd flung against the wall lay in a small pile beneath Ellian's chair, where he had collected anything sharp or dangerous and kept it safely within his bubble.

She didn't know why Meivre had pushed her back into this guest room to bathe, unless it was to remind her of this shame. Or to keep Cirelle out of the way while the sidhe finished hiding the claimhte.

The blankets were still rumpled where she and Ellian had lain together. Cirelle sat on the corner of the bed, her hand fisted around the rich comforter that still held his scent. She took a deep, shaky breath and held it before she stood, letting the heavy fabric slip from her fingers. Then Cirelle tucked the smooth pellet of poison between her back teeth and her cheek and walked next door. For a brief moment, Cirelle wondered what would happen if she fled. If, instead of walking next door, she escaped down the halls. But these hallways weren't empty. Meivre's allies filled them, guests left over from the party. Any one of them could grab her and bring her back for punishment.

When Cirelle entered, Meivre gave her a wicked smile. "Now," she murmured, a hand lifting and reaching out to caress Cirelle's cheek. "Will you do this the easy way, or the hard way?"

Cirelle kept her eyes focused on the floor, hoping she appeared meek enough. If she tried to talk, she worried the poison vial would make her words sound odd, thick.

But she knew that look in Meivre's eyes, the hunger there as the faerie's stare lingered on Cirelle's lips.

Yes. Now or never.

As Meivre grasped her hair and yanked Cirelle's head up to kiss her, Cirelle maneuvered the vial between her teeth and bit down. It crunched, the 'glass' dissolving like sugar and just as sweet. The liquid it held was metallic and bitter on her tongue, and she nearly coughed.

Meivre's lips met Cirelle's, the faerie's tongue pushing her lips apart. Cirelle spat the poison into Meivre's mouth, holding the back of Meivre's head tightly, and breathing out to push the venom further in.

The sidhe pushed Cirelle away violently, so much stronger than her petite frame should ever be. But she gagged, falling to her hands and knees as she retched.

Cirelle's heart fluttered, a crushing weight settling on her chest. What if Meivre hadn't swallowed enough of the poison? The punishment for attempting to kill a sidhe could only be one thing: death. And Cirelle suspected that Meivre would make it last a long, long time.

Meivre gasped in great breaths of air and glared, her teeth bared. "You dare…" she rasped between coughs. "You *dare* poison a sidhe?" Her breathing grew labored, her pupils large and dark.

Cirelle backed away, hands clutched to her chest.

Meivre's eyes almost glowed, the heat of her anger enough to burn Cirelle alive. But her voice was strangled, shallow. "I curse you, Cirelle telArraven." Another hoarse gasp of air. "Every time you look in the mirror, you will remember and regret this moment. Your beloved will look upon you and despise you." A series of coughs shook her then, each coming quicker and harder than the last. She forced out the final words, a harsh croak. "You will never be able to forget me." She snarled up at Cirelle for one final moment, her skin losing its rosy luster as she collapsed. Her fingers twitched once, then grew still.

Cirelle didn't wait to see if it was a trick. She rushed to the chest in the adjoining room, grabbed her bag of personal items, and fled.

The claimhte sang to her. *Here, over here.* Down the hall, drawn to a storage room of clutter. On a shelf behind another box, lay her knives. She drew them and didn't hesitate.

"Oiche," she called. "Oiche, Oiche. I'm ready to bargain."

In a breath, the shadows shimmered and coalesced, four eyes glowing. "You accept my offer?"

"Three favors in exchange for the claimhte and your oath never to harm me or those I claim as allies ever again, directly or indirectly."

"Agreed."

"What are the words I need to say to exchange them without violence? Your brother mentioned a ritual."

"Yes. Say the following. These blades I forsake, and the throne with them, never to seek it again."

Cirelle repeated the words and held out the knives. Oiche's shadowy hand grasped them, plucking them both from Cirelle's grasp.

The new Shadowed Queen held out a ring of blackened metal. "Wear this, and if you say my name three times, I will come to you and fill a boon, but only thrice."

"I claim my first and second favors now," Cirelle said before Oiche could leave. "The first... Meivre the sidhe lies down the hall. Make sure she is dead, and that her body is disposed of without witnesses." At least if Meivre disappeared, the murder could never be fully proven.

"Done. The second boon?"

"Can you hide me in shadow until I leave Meivre's home, so I can escape unseen?"

"Also done."

The air around Cirelle fogged into a smoky haze. Through it, she could just see the shadows flitting out of the room.

Cirelle didn't linger. She ran out of the palace, slipping right past some of Meivre's guests, out into blackest night and a thunderous downpour. Lightning arced overhead and raindrops fell hot as bathwater. It soaked her through in moments, her gown hanging limply about her and tangling in her feet.

Still, she ran. While she hurtled down the hillside, across rocky ground slick with rain, she had enough presence of mind to take the pendant from her pack and drape it about her neck. It tugged at her throat, and she followed, scrambling over the rocks. They cut her feet and her palms, but she didn't care.

Free.

She was free.

No matter what came next, if she died out here, Meivre would never touch her or another human again.

And she laughed, tilting her head upward as the storm washed the final lingering scent of roses from her skin forever. Flickers of blue lightning lit her way. The wind blew the rain sideways, the storm wild and untamed.

Cirelle felt like a force of nature herself right now. A murderer, a huntress, a fox that had outwitted the hound.

She laughed, and she ran.

The pendant took her past the rocks, down the hill, and into a circle of firs the color of crushed grapes. The ground was sodden, covered in purple pine needles. It seemed a miracle that mushrooms could grow in this. But this was Faerie, and there stood a ring of toadstools, half-soaked and sagging into rot.

But the pendant had led her here. It had to work. She had no gifts to give, but still, Ellian would come. He'd promised.

"Ellian, I summon thee. Ellian, I summon thee. Ellian, I summon thee."

As if it heard her call, a loud crack of thunder tore open the sky, flashing purest white and blinding Cirelle.

And Ellian stood before her, illuminated only by the pure white glow from one of his many rings.

But his eyes were not adoring, nor welcoming. No bright blue, no sunrise pink. They were red, the color of the deepest rose, of blood.

Your beloved will look upon you and despise you.

"What did you do to her?" he asked, his voice trembling with barely constrained anger. His arms were crossed before him, and she got the impression they somehow held him back. He'd never looked so livid.

A tremor of fear snaked through Cirelle. She took a step backward, slowly, hands clenched to her chest. "I... she's dead."

Ellian snapped. There was no other word for it. Something broke loose inside him. Those eyes flashed a burning orange, a bonfire of rage. He moved, faster than she could see, and then he was towering over her, one hand clutching her hair to prevent her escape. "You killed her?"

"Ellian," she gasped, tears flowing as she looked into the face of the man she loved and saw only fury, only hatred.

Had she escaped her captor only to die at the hand of her beloved?

Meivre's cruelty lasted even unto her dying breath. Her curse had turned Ellian against her somehow. Something collapsed in her chest, her breaths great sobs. She looked deep into those angry orange eyes and whispered her apology, and a small prayer. "I'm sorry, Ellian. I love you." She closed her eyes, muttering the death prayer quickly. "Divine Iska, please guide my way and lead me to my home among your stars." If she died here, if her body were not burned so her ashes floated up to the heavens, would she ever find her place in the night sky?

Ellian let her go, yanking his hand away as if he'd been burned. Cirelle stumbled backward.

"What trickery is this?" Ellian hissed.

"I don't understand. There's no trick. Meivre… she cursed me, and—"

"Cirelle?" The question was shocked, confused, and… gentle. That gaze no longer glowed like embers. It flickered a dozen colors within a heartbeat.

She nodded.

He spoke her name again, but it wasn't a question. It was an affirmation. Again, he moved quickly, pulling her into his arms. He buried his head in her hair. "It *is* you." His voice was incredulous, awestruck.

Relief flooded Cirelle, vast and drowning. He didn't hate her, not at all. No, he touched her gently, his fingertips warm on her rain-chilled skin. "Who else would I be?"

He pulled away. "You don't know."

"What? You're not making sense."

"Cirelle…" He lifted a hand and took a lock of her hair, holding it before her eyes.

It was purple, the color of amethysts.

The color of Meivre's hair.

By the light of his ring, Cirelle looked down at her hands. But they weren't her hands, not at all. She knew them, knew them well, but they weren't her own. Pale carnation pink, slim and long-fingered, with long, dark nails like claws.

"No." *Every time you look in the mirror, you will remember and regret this moment.* "No," she said again, as if she could make it a lie, as if it would put her back into her own body.

But it was real, and immutable. She was stuck in Meivre's skin, forever.

You will never forget me.

She fell to her hands and knees, keening screams racking her. She sobbed so hard she thought she would vomit. Even her limb failed her, and she would have collapsed entirely if Ellian hadn't scooped her up into his arms.

Ellian misted the world around them and took her home.

Sixty-Six

Cirelle awoke slowly, in fits and spurts. The first time, voices spoke beside the bed.

"Are you sure?" Jhavet's low bass rumble, quiet and whispered.

"Yes. She spoke to Cirelle's gods. How would Meivre know that?" Ellian's reply, hissed quietly.

"Maybe she got the information from Cirelle. I'm not sure. But it could be a trick."

"It's not." Ellian's voice was certain, firm and unbreachable.

She could *hear* Jhavet's silence, heavy in the air.

But she couldn't find the energy to protest. Tears found her, and she sank into sleep once again.

cx/cy

Cirelle wasn't sure how much time she spent in a state of half-sleep. Every time she awoke, she found herself exhausted, and fell back into slumber again.

Ellian was often in the room when she awoke, but never too close. Perhaps he knew. Maybe Ellian understood that upon awakening, Cirelle was still trapped in that nightmare. That it took a few moments for her to come to her senses and realize she was home, she was safe.

That Meivre was dead.

Cirelle felt no remorse, no guilt. *Fae-touched.* Perhaps her time in Faerie had indeed left her hollow and cruel. Not one of the dreaming, but one of the hunters. Turned half-faerie herself, as Lydia had warned.

And now she looked the part. Every time she awoke, Cirelle held up a hand to check, but it was not a horrible dream. She lived in Meivre's skin now.

Once, after she'd banished the terror, she'd curled on her side and held out a hand. Ellian sat upon the bed and took it, her carnation-colored fingers twined into his gray ones. She shuddered at the sight.

"I look like her," she rasped. For the briefest moment, Ellian's eyes met hers, but he couldn't hold them. Couldn't stare into the eyes of the woman he'd hated, the woman who had stolen Cirelle away.

This was her fate now, forever. The old Cirelle was gone, murdered as surely as if Meivre had killed her in truth.

Ellian glanced away, his eyes deepening to midnight blue, ringed with emerald. "Yes."

"Undo it," she asked, hating the note of hysteria in her voice.

"I can't." He shook his head. "I tried, while you were asleep. I've glamoured you before, but I can't cast a glamour over this. Her curse is fueled by the power and rage of her death. She put all of her life force into it."

Cirelle shut her eyes again. "You can't even look at me."

"I will," he said. "Eventually. But... it's disconcerting." His hand tightened in hers.

Something broke inside Cirelle, shattered like a glass hurled to the floor. She barked out a laugh, a mad sound, not one a human should ever make. "Disconcerting? You know what she said? She told me that my beloved would look upon me with hate. And she was right. You think I don't see the bit of red around your pupil? That I can't feel it in your shaking fingertips?"

Her breath hitched even as she clutched his hand tighter. She was drowning in her misery, and Ellian was her only lifeline. "You can't look at me without thinking of her. And you never will." She yanked her fingers away and rolled over in the bed. In Ellian's lavish, comfortable bed. "I want to sleep," she said softly.

He didn't answer, but she felt his weight leave the mattress and heard his footsteps padding over to an armchair on the other side of the room. Cirelle lay in silence, certain he knew she was still awake. Her thoughts chased each other about her head, spiraling down in despair.

Amongst her self-loathing and hatred of her new appearance, Cirelle had other worries. What happened to a human that killed a faerie? Had she escaped her captor only to be executed for the crime? She was consumed by the dread that her new, hated state was only a temporary step before the gallows. When she couldn't bear the worry any longer, Cirelle asked Ellian, "What will happen to me, for killing her?"

Ellian was silent a long time, and she almost rolled over to see if he had fallen asleep in the chair. "Nothing. No one knows."

"What?"

"I brought you here, then went to Meivre's home. Oiche took care of the body, and I bribed Meivre's servants into oaths of silence about her absence. She was fickle, known for going to the human world at long stretches without warning. It will be a while before anyone truly knows she's gone."

Cirelle shivered. "What happens when people do find out?"

"We'll deal with that when the time comes."

She still faced the wall, but Cirelle could picture his expression, tight-lipped, tension framing his eyes. And despite all that had happened, something about that level of familiarity was comforting. Her world had fallen apart, but Ellian was here. Would always be here. And someday he'd learn to look upon her without hatred.

Right now, that thin thread was enough.

So she slept. Ellian or Jhavet brought her food. She would leave the comfort of the bed to use the privy closet, but most of the time she spent unconscious.

Meivre still haunted her dreams, sometimes. She'd awaken with cry and Ellian or Jhavet would comfort her. After Jhavet had helped free her from Meivre's clutches, it was hard to find her old irritation with him again. Even now, his easy smile remained unchanged, though it had a brittle quality that saddened her. Faerie had left its mark on him, too.

Once, when both men were in the room, she asked, "How long has it been? Since she took me?"

"Three months."

"Three months," she repeated, then glanced up at Jhavet. "You've not got long left, do you?"

He grinned. "As it turns out, you're not the only recipient of a faerie curse in this room."

The words still made Cirelle flinch. "What?"

"For stealing the poison and aiding in the murder of a sidhe," Ellian said, the hint of a smile dancing around the edges of his mouth. "I cursed Jhavet never to set foot in the mortal world again."

Cirelle sat up. "What?"

"Yep," Jhavet said. "Stuck here. So sad."

Cirelle flopped back down on the bed. "So after I'm gone, you'll stay."

"I'm sorry."

"No, I'm not angry," she told him. "But I am tired." With that, she rolled over and ended the conversation there.

Then one day, when her eyes fluttered open, Jhavet stood beside the bed with arms crossed.

"You smell," he told her simply.

Irritation blossomed. "Stars, Jhavet, you do know how to make a girl feel special."

"It's true. You want to feel special, maybe you should try a bath."

Just thinking about a bath made her weary. "Later."

"Now."

"Before Ellian takes watch and lets me stay under the blankets?" Her voice held some of her old fire once again, though even she could hear something hollow in her snappishness.

"Maybe," Jhavet's smile turned mischievous, and he threw back the blankets to scoop Cirelle up in his arms.

Cirelle yelped and pushed at his grip. "Put me down!"

"I'd stop fidgeting if I were you," Jhavet said flatly as he made his way over to the bathing chamber. "Just delaying the inevitable."

The bathtub steamed, and the scent of vanilla and apples hung in the humid air. The water did actually look inviting. And she did feel disgusting. She even itched all over, now that she took the time to think about it.

But she couldn't bear to admit to Jhavet that he'd been right.

"Put me down this instant," she demanded, mustering up her old regal tone.

"Whatever you say," he shrugged, and set her down into the water, nightdress and all.

Cirelle shrieked, scrambling to stand up and reaching out to smack him. He just danced away, laughing.

"There. That's the Cirelle I know." His dark eyes twinkled with merriment. "Now bathe and get dressed. It's time for you to spend some time out of that bed."

Sixty-Seven

It was a difficult recovery. In truth, Cirelle suspected she'd never fully recover. The ghosts of what Meivre had done, of the guilt Cirelle felt for willingly participating, would linger for the rest of her life.

But all she could do was carry on.

Much too early, Cirelle ventured into the garden. She desperately needed to visit the prayer stone, to speak with her gods.

As soon as she emerged onto the roof, the scent assaulted her. The cloying aroma of flowers and earth, the green spice and sweetness of roses.

Panic struck sudden as a blow. Her pulse raced, and a roaring sound filled her ears. The world darkened around the edges. She was back in that underground burrow, the burn of lashes stinging her skin. Meivre's laughter echoed in her head.

Surrounded by that noxious, too-sweet smell of roses, Cirelle couldn't breathe.

I'll never get away from her.

She sank to her knees as great racking sobs tore through her. The hair that curtained her face was a hateful swath of amethyst, the hands that clutched the earth the color of pale pink blossoms. The world dimmed around her, and the ground tilted beneath her palms.

Cirelle awoke with Ellian kneeling beside her, his voice tight with panic as he called her name.

She mumbled a reply, but the sickening scent hit her again. She curled up on her side on the damp grass. "Inside," she gasped.

He carried her. Any other time she'd have complained about that, but that scent still filled her nostrils, the aroma of pain and torment. And a reminder of what she'd become.

So she let Ellian carry her to her room and lay her on her bed, then sank back into fitful sleep.

ℰᴈ

When Cirelle awoke again, a burning fury filled her.

How dare she let Meivre make her a weak, quivering thing? She knew what she needed to do.

With angry, confident steps, she stalked out to the garden again, the stone floors cool beneath her bare feet. At some point, she'd been dressed in a night gown and her shoes removed, but she didn't take the time to change. She had to do this while the strength of her rage washed through her.

This time she was prepared for the scent, for the smell of flowers and damp soil. She steeled herself against it and strode over to the nearest rose bush.

The petals came away in her hand so easily, such a fragile thing for all its thorns. She crushed the rose blossom beneath a bare foot, then tore at the rest of the bush, unleashing her desperate wrath along with angry sobs. She would destroy everything Meivre had ever made of her, everything that reminded her of the woman.

She was not a weakling. She was a princess made of fire, unbreakable and resilient.

Except she wondered if the fire had turned to ice. Everything she'd done in Meivre's lair was still there, still lurking beneath her skin, a frozen wasteland in her heart. A cruelty she'd learned, and a determination never to be a victim again, no matter what the cost. She stomped on another rose as tears spilled down her face.

Cirelle only realized how badly she'd scratched her hands and feet when Ellian burst through the door, Jhavet on his heels. Ellian cast one distraught look at her and froze. Cirelle's hands and forearms dripped blood, her feet burning with the itchy sting of the thorns.

She pulled herself up to her full height and met eyes blue as the darkest oceans. No words needed to be said. Understanding filled that gaze, a deep and vast well of patience.

He sighed softly. "Come. There is healing elixir in the Archive."

With one last, spiteful look at the roses, Cirelle followed.

The next day, every rose bush in Ellian's garden vanished, leaving gaping holes in his beautiful garden. Eventually, they were replaced with other shrubbery, green and flowerless.

The scent of roses would never grace his garden again.

༄

After her wounds were tended, Cirelle stood in front of her mirror for the first time since Meivre's curse befell her. Her curves and weight were gone, replaced by Meivre's slim frame. The regal nose that had once been the source of vain pride was now the faerie woman's lifeless upturned one.

Even her tattoos were covered. All that work to mark her, covered up by an even larger curse.

Not a trace of the original Cirelle remained. She'd never see her own face again. How long until she forgot what she had once looked like?

Moreover, her once-innocent soul was dead too. No longer the ignorant, willful princess that had arrived in Faerie, a dark thing had taken up residence within her. She'd become a temptress and a murderer. A spy, a warrior, a queen of shadows.

And a victim.

But not anymore.

Cirelle wiped her face on a damp towel and stood on legs that did not tremble. She was what Faerie had made of her. Something harder, something stronger.

Fae-touched.

Meivre was dead, but Ellian's mission remained. She would help him find the Lock, and together they would destroy the artifacts. No matter how many scars Faerie gave her.

And she was not alone. That reminder was clear when a knock sounded on her door. She opened it to see Jhavet and Ellian standing in the hallway, Jhavet's familiar grin a welcome sight.

"So," he said casually, "We never got that re-match on that game of Sailor's Runes."

Cirelle sucked in a deep breath and returned his smile. Shaky, but there nonetheless. "You're on."

THE END

To be concluded in:

BOOK THREE OF THE FAERIE CONCERTO

Coming Spring 2024

Acknowledgments

First and foremost, the biggest thanks go to my husband, Nathan, for infinite patience, understanding, and support. It's not always the easiest thing to live with a writer, but you take it all in stride and never complain. None of my books would exist without you.

And D.C., I have so many things to thank you for that I don't know if I could list them all. My podcast co-conspirator, an amazing critique partner, creator of the most beautiful cover art, and a brilliant writer. But more than all of that, an awesome friend, and I couldn't ask for a better one.

I also appreciate my writing groups so much: Abi, Alicia, Audely, Elina, Emily, Lesia, Naomi, Renee, and Sifa. You're more than just critique or writing help. You're there for the whole journey and I am so thankful for all the encouragement you provide, the venting sessions you've listened to, and the communities we've built that make my life brighter every day.

To all the beta readers, this book wouldn't be what it is without your help. And all those who've read Cambiare, each and every review and comment has made me smile, and keeps me going when this whole writing thing gets rough.

There are moments when being an author feels like a lonely business, but I'm so, so lucky to have a whole brilliant and beautiful web of people who've made Serenade happen.

I am so grateful for you all, and all the words in the world wouldn't be enough.

Thank you.

About the Author

Avery Ames is a graphic designer currently residing in Wichita, Kansas. A lifelong lover of lush fantasy, she writes novels that toe the line between glittery and dark, for lovers of fairy tales and everything gothic. When not writing, she can be found playing video games with her husband, crafting cocktails, or catering to the whims of a very demanding tuxedo cat.

She also publishes traditionally under the name Amy Avery.

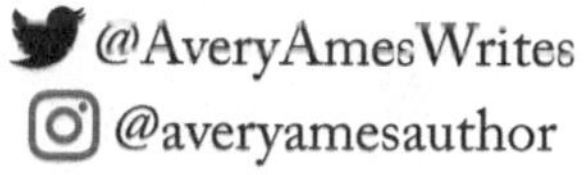

averyames.com

www.ingramcontent.com/pod-product-compliance
Lightning Source LLC
Chambersburg PA
CBHW051308190726
48290CB00001B/55